Pizza Parties and Poltergeists

Curated by

NICOLE PETIT

Pizza Parties & Poltergeists
An 18thWall Productions book published by
arrangement with Nicole Petit
verba mea in minibus
desiderium meum
Cover by Johannes Chazot
Jacket Design and Book Design by Adventure on Earth Productions
Illustration by Sophie Iles

ISBN-13: 978-1-946033-16-1

Table of Contents

Don't You Forget About Me

SUZANNE GRIECO MATTABONI

If you live for music, we want to capture you on video.

It was an interesting audition headline. The call in *Backstage* said they wanted someone *hungry*. And to dress for a new wave video. So I put on my best drop waist mini, a kick-ass pair of Billy Idol-looking leather ankle boots and fishnet stockings to give it a punk edge. That way I'd feel *authentic*, and give off a cool vibe. None of that Katrina and the Waves, *Walking on Sunshine* shit for me. I refused to do the Madonna black rubber bracelets, either. Too derivative.

The directions in the ad led me to a Glamour Shots studio in the Sunrise Mall. Things were already taking a turn toward bubblegum. But when I peered through the glass storefront, I saw a moody-looking guy in black leaning against the desk who had a certain coolness factor to him. He wore unlaced combat boots and smudged guyliner, and had one of those smolder-stares going on. Behind him, a wall was swathed with black-and-white graffiti, with an oval, stand-up mirror in the middle of it, the kind with a hinge so you can tilt it.

I still clutched the copy of *Backstage* in my hands when I pushed open the door. A song by The Cure was playing on the stereo speakers. Always a sign of good musical taste.

The guy pushed himself off the counter, eyes flashing like some animal that caught the beam of a flashlight in the night.

"Are you Linda Molley?" he said as I stepped through the threshold.

"Yeah, that's me." I let the hydraulics of the glass door hiss shut behind me. Bells on the back of the glass tinkled as

5

it slowed into its frame and fell into place. I felt a chill as it clicked loudly…like a lock.

"We spoke on the phone. I'm Joel." He reached out a hand clad with open-fingered, black leather gloves.

I shook his palm. It was hot, like he was sweating right through the leather. The only illumination in the place was a spotlight over the desk, and a couple of photography lamps in front of the mirror.

"You closing up?" I asked. "The ad said to come at six." I shoved my hand into the pocket of my oversized black blazer and wrapped my fist around the heavy metal scissor I always brought along with me to auditions. Because you never know. This city can be pretty ruddy.

"Sit," he said, opening his arm toward a chrome-armed chair that was upholstered in sickly-looking pink velour. He pulled a second chair around to face me and leaned in, resting his elbows against his knees. Dyed black hair fell over his eyes.

"Mind telling me a little more about what kind of video this will be?"

"It's for a new band. They just did a demo. Kind of, Aha meets The Alarm." He shrugged his hair out of his vision.

"That doesn't tell me much," I said, squeezing the chilly metal arms of the chair.

"It'll be kind of like what you see back here." Joel pointed to a video screen in the corner, the only bit of flagrant color in the room. It ran a loop of repeating images, women running as if to escape, curtains flying against high windows, guitar players riffing on the brink of ecstasy, boats kicking against a midnight dock, people screaming. Everyone lost, forlorn, posing, images dissolving from scene to scene.

"Can I listen to the band?" I asked.

"Oh, you will. But not yet. I need to screen you first. To make sure you've got the right look."

"Well, you're looking at me," I said. "How about I sing?"

"First, I want to find out how much you want to be in a music video."

I stood up from my chair. "If this is some kind of casting

6

couch come-on, I'm *outta here,* buddy."

"Oh, no, no!" he said, popping up from the seat and backing away. He waved his arms like a scarecrow in the wind. "It's nothing like that." He stepped toward the mirror. "It's just that, we want this opportunity to go to someone who really *lives* this scene. Someone who could listen to this music *forever.*"

"Are you kidding? That's me. I *eat and breathe* this stuff. Although I lean toward more experimental music. Kate Bush. Laurie Anderson."

Robert Smith of The Cure droned on in the background, loopy guitar riffs and sticky, sad vocals reverberating through the room. The swirls of graffiti along the walls almost vibrated like tuning forks, all around the mirror. I started to sing along to "Why Can't I Be You?" as it poured out of the speakers. You could almost see the air moving through the room in animated lines.

"Right...right. Love the attitude," he said to me. "We'll do some test shots for the band to take a look at." He reached for a clunky SLR camera that was hanging from a strap, slung on a coat rack.

"All right," I said. "But I'm telling you, I'm not so much as taking off my blazer."

"I like the blazer, especially the metal buttons on the lapel. Keep it on," Joel said. A smile curled his lip and he lifted the camera to his eye. He twisted the fat lens with one hand, held the body of the camera with his other.

I stepped toward the mirror, which glinted silver at me like a flash of heat lightning. "You planning to completely rip-off the 'Take On Me' video, or what?" I tilted my head at Joel. For a second, I thought I saw a shadow in the mirror, an imposing frame of a tall, thin man. The soundtrack around us juddered for a second.

"The mirror's only for the test shots. Reflections make things interesting." Joel clicked photos of me peering into the glass. The repeating snaps sounded like the intro to "Girls on Film."

"How *derivative.*" I frowned, turning around to check

whether some towering person had snuck up behind me, passing a shadow over the surface of the mirror. I squinted into the glass, blinking at clouds of green and blue in the mirror that seemed to play behind me.

I whirled around once more, but the blue and green clouds weren't there.

"*Weird*," I said.

"Now come on," said Joel, his kohl-lined eyes peering over his Olympus. His voice deepened. "You said you were hungry for this."

"Oh, believe me—I am," I said. "I just want to make sure what I'm involved in is totally creative. I'm a music major. And I'm an *artist*. This is my *life*."

Joel froze, then let the camera drop around his neck.

"*That's what I've been waiting to hear*."

Joel's arm suddenly shot past my chin, grabbing the edge of the mirror and shoving it violently on its hinges so it spun like a dime dropped on the sidewalk, whacking me so hard I went numb....

The silver of the glass became the whole world, strewn with deafening guitar licks, flashing lights and animated squiggles, flickering like the first movie frames that ever clicked over a projector. I fell backward, end over end, into a wafting void of smoke and stage gels, amplifiers squealing all around me.

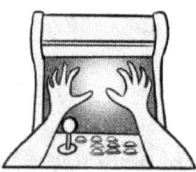

I've been infinitely in that moment, in a world where curtains always blow with blue lights streaming through them, paneled glass doors flying open perpetually in the wind. Sheets of graffitied paper backdrops fall constantly from the ceiling and roll under my ankle boots like a Keith Haring table runner gone mad. Wet, relentless synth riffs morph their way through a never-ending new wave chorus.

Flash bulbs continuously pop here in my analog world,

where men wear shantung suits in shining sapphire and ruby and turquoise, chasing feral women with painted faces through the underbrush of the jungle. I can feel the spray of a tropical ocean on my face as their yacht speeds past me in slow motion, sticking like Aqua Net.

But I can never quite touch those men, running through overgrowth, singing but never sweating. They fly past me in a sick blur, echoing lyrics, drowning in plush bass notes that never quite organize themselves into a song.

And when I run past the foliage, past the neon and teal streaks and the mishmash of cobalt Steven Spielberg lighting, past the staring automaton women with vampire makeup and tight pencil skirts, I glimpse the outline of an oval stand-up mirror through the brush. The music still blares in my ears and strobe lights pierce every moment, but I can just barely see the rim of the glass.

When I squint my eyes, there beyond the silver chloride of the mirror is the studio with the graffitied walls. Hanging from the ceiling is a video screen, playing the scenes that I'm living. My torment, on an infinite loop in neon colors.

My copy of *Backstage* is still on the pink velour chair.

When I scream, no one hears me over the synthesizers.

The Gap

TINA MARIE DELUCIA

"The future isn't dull yet, boys?" an older dude with poindexter glasses asked as they climbed aboard Future Port.

No, sir. Never, sir. Not in a million years, sir.

The two boys happily accepted high fives from the older dude attendant as their ride's doors automatically closed. Everyone knew them. After all, they were frequent fliers. Whit winked and Skipper gave him a sharp salute, nearly knocking his hat clean off his head as they disappeared into the void, never to be seen again until they'd pop back to the past once more.

"Did ya catch the number?" Skipper asked, peering into the darkness of the corridor.

Whit scoffed, holding up his video camera up to his eye. "Of course. 56."

His friend grinned wickedly. "Not bad, not bad."

"Not good either," Whit muttered. "When do you wanna get off?"

Skipper tapped his chin, face crunching up in thought. Where *did* they want to hitchhike to?

"Future Living?" Skipper suggested. "After we ride through it once?"

Whit nodded in agreement. "Future Living it is! And that way that bird-looking chick won't be suspicious if we don't make an appearance at the exit."

Speakers crackled to life, as a techno-orchestral score filled the box-like ride vehicle. A voice, all at once maternal and sweet and familiar said, "Hello! And welcome to Future

11

Port. Where if we can think it—it's within our grasp."

There was a creak in the speaker to their right, and a male voice joined the female one, happily spouting, "Yes indeed! The future is not so far away, not at all. And we should know, we live here!"

Whit primed his handheld, making sure it was actually on and that the lens cap was now dangling from a string. He'd left it on before and it was a whole waste of tape.

"It's amazing to see what the future might hold, isn't it? And it's amazing to see how different it is compared to what we thought it might be."

"Yes, we sure did get it wrong!"

Skipper crinkled his nose. *"Boy, did we ever!"* He mimicked the man's tone.

Whit snickered.

The man continued "Why don't we take a look back on how we thought the future would be—"

The void pulsed and swirled with lights. Music swelled to match the changing of colors.

"Come along with us, and we'll show you!"

A flash of purple. Jules Verne floated in the void beside them, surrounded by aliens, frogs and all sorts of 'cool' looking creatures with the mobility of fishing wire.

The woman chuckled. "Ole Jules Verne had some funny ideas, didn't he?"

The scene moved and suddenly it was filled with more accordion music than even France allowed. Diagrams of old newspaper art and art deco structures were pattered here and there. But then the deco décor devolved into bright neon lights. They look the shape of asteroids and astronauts. Skipper began to jive a bit in his seat, bopping along to the swinging tempo, and Whit sputtered into laughter.

"The future was far-fetched in the past, wasn't it?" the man declared over their speakers.

"You can say that again, my man," Whit replied. But the scene was soon left in the dust as they chugged on, until finally they had reached their future. Their real future. With a blast of refreshing cold air, everything turned dark. Little twinkles of lights appeared this way and that, dotting the darkness. They might have appeared to be stars at first, but as more and more light appeared closer together a beautiful and sleek skyline appeared. The twinkling dots turned into lights turned into windows, the blinking lights of a moving maglev train, and vehicles hustling on a distant street.

But it was one window in particular that was of the most importance and they moved swiftly over towards it.

Through it, the people narrating their journey finally appeared.

An older couple, clad in too-many-shades-of-blue futuristic tunics sat comfortably in their living room.

"Welcome to our home!" The voice now obviously belonged to the elder gent to the left. Outside his window, blinking buildings and monorail lights cut out of an otherworldly purple haze.

The couple engaged each other in conversation, rather than their guests, as though Skipper and Whit's little blue car had interrupted their routine.

"Everything alright, dear?" the woman asked. She tilted her greyish-brown updo this way and that, as she spoke to her husband. "Oh, don't worry about me. I'm just chipper. Tonight's going to be wonderful."

"Sure is. I almost forgot! You'll have to excuse us, we're helping our daughter with setting up for our grandson's birthday party! Telecommunication still takes some planning you know! Why don't we check in on the preparations, and we'll catch up with you folks later!"

The woman giggled. "We'll see you soon!"

Skipper and Whit left their living room, puttering on through and beyond it and into a desert. Amid the dust, a lady in a yellow jumpsuit was hard at work making the desert-bots move up and down. Across the way from her, a bearded man and a small boy held strange fruit. The boy impatiently demanded to know when the cake would be done, but Skipper and Whit ignored him.

The sky held thunder and rain and Whit took in a deep inhale. "God, I will never get sick of that smell."

"Do you think they pump in real orange scent? Or do they have trees in the future?" Skipper asked, teasingly.

"I dunno, but whatever it is, they need to bottle it."

Past the desert, they found another bedroom. A red-haired girl in a pink jumpsuit talked to a large screen with a young man on it. They had caught them mid-conversation.

"Who cares?" the screen boy said.

"I care! Well, it is a party!" the girl exclaimed, her head barely moving.

The boy on the screen sighed. "Fine, I'll be there. I won't be late."

"Thank you," the stiff girl said, her grateful tone not matching her lips quite right.

"You're lucky I love you," the blonde boy said, just as the bedroom vanished from sight and in its place was the boy himself over a large hatch, scrubbing at what might have been a diving-container-boat-thing if you squinted. Now the red-headed girl was upon a screen and her face was much more animated. It was the same conversation, though. Skipper and Whit quickly moved along and plunged in the deep blue. As five children, a teacher, and a sea lion...seal...ocean dog thing dived in their scuba gear. As their silhouettes swam deeper and deeper, the ocean became the inky blackness of space, twinkling with lights. A family of three were at all angles, on a space walk through a circular space station, trying to grab a lost floating teddy bear lost in zero gravity.

Then Skipper and Whit's favorite part arrived. Which was stupid. Because it wasn't as cool as everything else. It was the aforementioned birthday party for a two year old boy who probably wouldn't even remember it (and no one was even taking polaroids to capture it for prosperity). But it was still pretty sweet. The grandparents they met earlier, the red-haired girl, the blondie boyfriend—everybody was there, singing happy birthday.

Can't end on sentimentality though, we gotta have action. Three buttons lit up on their car's dashboard. These were labeled: *Space. Sea. Desert.*

"Pick your poison, Skip," Whit said, gesturing to the

buttons.

Skipper grinned and slammed his palm down on SEA. "Wet and wild, my dude!"

"You. Are. Gross."

But a giant screen now stood before them, spanning up and over what must be a huge cavern of a room as their car moved on its final landing. Into the ocean the screen dived, narrowly escaping sharks, and coral and dolphins and angel fish and whatever the hell else was in the ocean and was probably scary. But there was another dark hallway, a flickering logo of a national electric company formed in stars—the sponsor of their excursion into the future—before the harsh white light of the unloading dock appeared. Both boys practically clambered out of the car as soon as the door opened, onto the moving walkway straight out of the Orlando Airport and into a rainbow tinted corridor before being thrust into the Florida heat.

Again.

Through the past, into the minds of the Victorian science fiction dudes before finally getting to that place again. Today's promised land: Future Living

Their vehicle slowed, as it always did, to allow the passengers to absorb their destination. Both boys exchanged an excited look before none too elegantly clambering over the closed doors of their cars and into the world of the future itself.

Skipper peered at the car farthest to the right, still half in the darkness of transition. "Nobody at all!"

Whit gave him a thumbs up and slowly panned his camera around the room as Skipper cheerfully tossed his cap with a flourish, moving away from his friend to closely examine the world beyond the window.

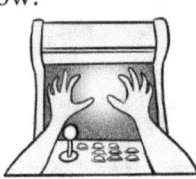

Time must have gotten away from them, because when Whit

turned to look at the endless procession of vehicles, the numbers in bold black paint on their tops had risen dramatically.

"Car 126!"

"126? Ah crap, that's not a lot of time."

"Dude, your hat!"

Skipper looked at the animatronic robot butler, sporting a very ill-fitting baseball cap with a big E on it. "Shit! Thanks Whit!" He reached up onto his toes and snatched it off the robot, placing it firmly back onto his own head of messy blonde hair. "Did ya get that on camera?"

His friend rolled his eyes, "No dude, I'm holding this shit up for my health!"

"You know what I meant!"

Whit moved his JVC handheld off his shoulder and let it dangle at his side. "I'm not gonna waste more battery on your face. I didn't bring any spares."

"Yeah, I got it." Whit peered back at the slow moving bright blue box-shaped cars, devoid of passengers. "We've still got half a decent gap, if we run over to Mesa Green—"

ATTENTION FUTURE PORT PASSENGERS

The friendly female voice of the announcer crackled through the speaker system, sounding far too cheerful and way too professional for its own good.

**OUR JOURNEY IS GOING TO BE DELAYED
PLEASE REMAIN SEATED
YOUR TRAVELS WILL RESUME MOMENTARILY**

Music to their ears.

"I guess they've got wheelchairs coming on," Skipper said with a shrug. "Better for us,"

Whit nodded. "Yeah but once they start moving again, we should try and get ahead."

"Good idea," Skipper agreed. "I'm gonna take pictures of the window guy, so why don't you try and get video of the kitchen?"

Whit's eyes lit up. "Oh sick, I could check out the counters!"

"Then go do it! It doesn't take too long to load a couple of old broads into the car." Skipper picked up the battered Panasonic video camera at his feet. He then dashed over to where a man was standing in a fine silken smoking jacket, staring off at a city blinking with lights. The man didn't move as the boy approached. Even if he saw Skipper coming, there wasn't much he could do about the intruders in his home.

Because he was made out of gears, plastic and sculpting clay. In fact, the kitchen that Whit was so eager to take snapshots of was made of painted wood and fake food.

The two very human boys were the only non-synthetic life in the whole room; a room made by talented artists, painters, construction workers and engineers to entertain the tourist masses of central Florida. They were on a ride called Future Port, which was situated on the west side of a theme park empire's miniature World's Fair.

And they really should have remained seated.

Future Port was actually how they met. It was 1983 and they'd both just graduated high school. They went to a special event called Grad's Evening, a fancy term for the night graduates got drunk and were allowed to stay special late hours at various theme parks in Florida. Now, normally the fancy fantasy themed castle land would play host to the budding adults, but now that the world had expanded, this new land was their oyster.

Whit and Skipper had both been drawn to the new park, and theme parks in general. As Orlando natives whose parents could afford Annual Passes meant that they could go as often as they liked. When something was this shiny and this new how could any kid resist? Sure it had a stupid acronym of a name—something along the lines of Unconventional Template Region for Horizons or some shit—but they were drawn to it never the less.

Specifically, they were drawn to Future Port. Sure, there were cooler rides with dinosaurs or dragons or whatever, but there was something about this big ole hexagon of a building that was special.

They were both in line, both showing off to their friends about stupid facts they had learned about it from asking ride attendants or custodians or the poor sucker stamping hands at the exit. Whit had overheard Skipper. At first he thought he was some goofy looking kid—paler than glue, thinner than a string bean, and lost in the dark green baseball cap hanging lopsided on his head.

Whit was just gonna ignore him, when he heard the goofy kid say the magic words, 'The last scene uses Pepper's Ghost.'

How could he not strike up a conversation?

Skipper thought Whit was going to slug him or something when he walked over, pushing past other waiting high schoolers to get to him. He was about the same height as him, but much more built. His button up Hawaiian shirt dangled open—which was a sign he meant business, dark floofy hair notwithstanding. But all that anxiety melted away when the other guy opened his mouth.

At some point their school friends abandoned them but they did not notice or care. They talked all along the queue, all along the moving platform to get on the ride, and even shouting to each other from their different ride vehicles.

They rode the ride thirteen times more that night, and the rest was history. Six years later, they had finished college, and not much had changed. Well, Skipper got a master's degree in Art History and gotten stitches from falling up some stairs, while Whit got into computer and let his dark hair get curlier. But, they still were best friends. And they still loved Future Port.

Plus…

They didn't exactly have steady jobs yet—at least, not outside of taking a shift or two delivering pizzas to the greater Orlando area—so when they weren't doing odd jobs for their folks, or babysitting their neighbors, they'd be hitting the theme parks.

By this point, Whit and Skipper could recite the damn ride

in their sleep, right down to musical cues. It was almost drilled into their skulls. Introduction with grandparents chilling in their apartment, to the look back on the future through the eyes of someone from 18-whenever the hell, the neon 1950s with all its joy and hope, to all the funky science stuff they were doing now in 1988. Then it was into the 'TRUE' future! With the desert irrigation of Mesa Green, where a family was busy with plants and stuff while their daughter video-chatted a Luke Skywalker lookalike boyfriend. Said boyfriend could be found in the next scene above the ocean floor before you dove down to its depths. There, there was exploration, and the Aqua Base complete with a school room populated with diving suit wearing kids and one clunky looking sea lion. Then it was up into space to walk in and interrupt a family trying to deal with zero gravity along with some NASA-esque stuff closing it off with a giant screen taking you back to 'Earth.' The cool part about that was that you and a dozen or so other riders could choose what film you saw based off space, the desert, or the ocean through pressing a button on the doors of the ride car.

Of course they'd seen each option more than twenty times each, probably.

They knew the ride better than they knew themselves. Some of the rotating ride operators would give them a little wave or a nod as they entered.

It's not like they were going to get caught. With all the flash and money and guys walking around with walkie talkies, Future Port didn't boast the security and infrared like certain other movie and intellectual property based theme parks in Orlando. How they'd figure that one out? Well, the runaway train in another park slowed to an emergency stop when Skipper stood to save his hat from flying into the cowboy-themed ether.

But standing up in the ride vehicle on Future Port did no such thing.

In fact, the thing didn't even have seatbelts or (apparently) ride attendants watching. Many a time they had turning the corner caused them to witness a neighboring car go full on

Rated NC-17 in the dark of space-esque tunnels. And never once had anyone stopped it. Plus, they stuck their feet up all the time and had them dangle over the edge of the cars without a pause in the ride-filled action.

So if there was anything there like a camera or a pressure pad, surely security would have gone off long ago. One dull Tuesday when the whole Radical Example District-of-the-Future or whatever the acronym stood for was a ghost town, on a dare, Whit stood and climbed over and out the ride vehicle. Of course, Whit being Whit, he got his foot stuck and practically fell into the Grandparents' living room.

And...

Nothing.

No lights. No sirens. No security.

Nada.

He hustled back into the car before it rounded the corner but what a thrill it was.

One night after one too many sodas and nachos, they started to plan. A way to explore their favorite ride without getting caught. They couldn't just be popping off the moving ride vehicles when there were other riders in the neighboring cars. They would have to wait for there to be a lull in people getting on, then get on the ride themselves, keeping in mind their vehicle's number.

The ride was something called an Omnimover dark ride, according to one know-it-all ride attendant. It meant the ride never really stopped to load people on or off, just slowed down. While that was a little daunting in terms of escaping the ride and then getting back in, they weren't deterred. Once they were sure they had a healthy gap, they'd jump off, keeping in mind the passing numbers as the ride moved. Then it was a simple matter of keeping far enough ahead of any other rider.

All the show scenes were elevated, so there were plenty of places to hide underneath without being seen. They even had discovered a series of tunnels that lead to the secret areas behind the ride and passages that traveled over two or three show scenes.

At first, it was just for fun and games: looking around where no one was meant to look

But over time, they'd gotten it down to a science. Endure some flashy effects, Jules Verne and H.G. Wells and crafty cut outs before getting to the aptly named 'Future Living' scene. That's when the fun would begin. Out they'd pop, and then the ride was their playground. They could go downstairs and under some wood to come back up into Mesa Green. Or into the depths of the ocean blue. However, getting to space and the space station Delta Centuari would require diving back onto a car, but that was fine by them.

When that grew dull, they took to hiding in between flats. Under the stairs in Future Living was a hole with a flap over it. Either it was for an oversized dog, or just in case some electrician needed to tamper with some AC/DC bullshit. They'd stay for hours on end, even taking to smuggling in some overpriced pizza from the nearby *Orbito's Intergalactic Pizzaria.*

At last, they went balls to the wall. Some doors led backstage, where they found hallways behind the ride vehicles, projector screens and film reel rooms full of treasure and abandoned operating manuals. But that was like Mecca. They went once in a while, but they knew they risked their asses if they made a habit of visiting. Besides there was nothing REALLY interesting to film there. The really cool parts came from the feature presentation...

Future Port! As the park maps boasted, A Look Back and Forward on the Future Today! However people might've imagined the future in the past, but it was going to be better and brighter than they could guess: from crazy ideas like plant growth in the desert, to underwater cities, to people just chilling out and living in space like it was no big deal.

Such creativity meant creative show scenes to dazzle the public. And every trip they were discovering new shit on the ride.

Screens that were half-hidden behind props had full-color scientific displays; the future living scene had a lady bathing, and even though you only saw half of her from the ride, she had a full naked body; the buttons glowing on consoles and space station panels could actually be pressed and flicked into different positions. Little touches like that made the ride—well, the theme park itself—so special and so different from the roller coaster or fish-focused parks that littered Orlando.

Maybe that's why they loved it so much.

Maybe that's why they kept risking a lifetime ban to keep finding new things.

Maybe that's why looked jailtime in the face to keep saying, "Yes, sir. Always, sir." to visiting the future.

Whit aimed the camera down at the kitchen counter, where food was splattered all about. Bacon, eggs, what could've been sausage but looked more like an unfortunate phallic incident, and broken china. "I'm getting hungry looking at this, Skip. Why don't we get a churro or something when we get off?"

"You're paying," Skipper replied, and stuck his tongue out at the unmoving future-man-robot. "You still owe me for that burger,"

Whit didn't even bother looking up. "Hey! I'm not the one who lost a whole cheeseburger in outer space. That was all you."

"You hit my arm!"

"I fell!"

ATTENTION FUTURE PORT PASSENGERS

This time it was a male voice. Never a good sign.

WE REGRET TO INFORM YOU
THAT OUR JOURNEY TODAY CAN NOT CONTINUE

"Come on!" Skipper whined. "This happened yesterday too! What gives?"

"I don't know, man, probably some dumbass threw up or something," Whit guessed.

PLEASE REMAIN SEATED

**AND WAIT FOR AN ATTENDANT TO GUIDE YOU
BACK TO EARTH
THANK YOU FOR JOINING US TODAY
AT FUTURE PORT**

"Aw, shit." Whit clicked a button, and his camera shut off. "Forget about Mesa Green man, there's barely anyone here today, they'll be over here any second."

Skipper groaned, and angrily shut down his camera, letting the heavy machinery thump against his chest, dangling from a shoulder strap. "So much for a decent gap."

The boys, as quick as they could, stepped around the show scene, which still was happily playing without a care in the world, unaware of their turmoil. Whit climbed over first. It was much easier getting out then in, they had to drop their cameras onto the ride's benches before practically swan diving over the doors. Skip's scrawny ass always needed help getting back in unless he got a running start before the jump.

They settled into the ride vehicle and sighed.

"What do you wanna do tomorrow?" Whit asked, leaned up against the wall.

Skipper shrugged. "I kinda wanna go under again. We haven't done that in awhile."

There was a pause of silence, before Skipper spoke again. "The news said that the pavilion lost its sponsor. What if that's why there's all this breaking down?"

Whit scoffed. "That doesn't mean anything. The park's loaded. They don't need any stupid electric company shelling them a few thousand bucks to keep this stuff running. Don't stress."

"Too late, dude." Skipper kicked the bottom of the door, lightly. "What if they do to this place what they did to that mine train ride? Nature's whateverland or something? Replace it with a thrill ride?"

"If they do that, I'll eat your hat."

From the side appeared a ride attendant, in a blue and white uniform that was probably missing from George Jetson's closet.

23

"One moment, guys," she said, very chipper. The ride's doors opened, and both of the boys stood up. "Please step out carefully and then move behind your ride vehicle to the walkway and then follow me!"

Whit stepped out first, then Skipper, but Skip cupped his hands around his mouth and bellowed: "GOODBYE FUTURE PORT, WE'LL MISS YOU!"

Whit cackled, but the girl seemed less than amused. As they were guided behind the hanging ride vehicles, both of them let their jaws drop in faux shock. "Wow, bud, there's a whole path back here! Can you believe it?" gasped Skipper.

"Sure can't!" Whit agreed, and the girl's smiled grew brighter with obvious annoyance. The boys followed, two steps behind, but oh that poor girl was going to give her coworkers an earful later. Every time they passed a door or fuse box, they made some sort of shocked comment. "Golly gee! What will they think of next?!" and the like until they reached the loading area.

There was a familiar face at least, the glasses-wearing ride attendant. "See ya soon boys, sorry the future got put on hold." He was also talking in a chipper tone, but he was leagues more sincere than the girl.

Whit smirked and gave him a thumbs up. "Aww, we'll be back tomorrow. The future isn't so far away."

The attendant winked. "That's the spirit!" And he waved as they went through the queue and out until the mild March air.

Skipper started to walk towards the exit, but Whit whipped his friend's hat off his head and smacked him with it. "OW! Dude?"

Whit thumbed towards a food cart. "My churro?"

"Oh my God."

Tomorrow was a brighter day. In more ways the one. Mostly

because Florida decided to be Florida and stick a heat wave in the middle of what was supposed to be the start of spring. It was so hot that Whit ditched his jeans for cargo shorts and Skipper opted for a tank top. It also meant that their gap was at risk.

"People are going to try and beat the heat with air conditioning." Whit sighed, watching family after family parade into Future Port. "We're not gonna get a half decent gap."

"Hey, at least we'll blend a bit more," Skipper said brightly. "Come on, I put in new batteries this morning, so we've got all the time in the world."

Skipper was very quickly proven wrong.

For forty-five minutes they stood in the winding queue, listening to the ride's theme song over and over, waiting for the people to thin out, or at least stagger in. They tried to keep themselves occupied with stupid questions.

"Do you think the desert-girl is hot?"

Whit blinked. "The one in the yellow or the red-haired daughter?"

"The red head!"

The dark-haired boy shrugged. "I guess?"

Skipper laughed. "You guess? I've got photo evidence of you sitting on her lap!!"

"So?"

"Kissing her cheek!" Skipper added, earning him a swat on the arm.

"Sure!" Whit relented, throwing up his hands. "She's hot! Christ!"

Skipper cackled. "That's hilarious."

"You think the narrator lady is hot!" Whit countered, poking his friend's chest. "That's screwed up."

"No it's not! She looks lovely in aqua blue!"

"...Dude, she's a GRANDMA!"

Skipper wriggled his nose. "...Just means she's experienced."

"DUDE!"

"Oh look, a gap!" Skipper quickly dashed away from his

companion and headed towards the loading queue.

Whit was laughing so much he almost didn't notice their ride number. 81 this time. "Does her voice sooth you?" he asked in a comically lustful way.

Their female ride attendant's eyebrows shot up, as she shut the door to their vehicle.

Skipper turned a bright shade of pink. "N-Not you miss, he's been an idiot! I'm sorry for him!"

She didn't look like she believed him, and Skipper got redder. "I-I mean it! I'm not interested!" He froze. "NOT THAT YOU AREN'T LOVELY—" Thank God, by then their vehicle had moved away from the queue and into the first corridor, and only his pained groans and Whit's loud cackles could be heard.

"You suck!"

Whit whipped a few well-earned tears from his eyes. "Oh that was too damn good, thank God I had the camera on!"

Skipper turned from red to white. "Delete that shit! I swear to God!"

"Maaaybe I will, and maaaaybe I won't," Whit teased. "I can't wait to play this at your wedding."

Hello and welcome to Future Port, where if we can think it, it's within our grasp! A soft, gentle narration said through the ride's speakers.

"There she is!" Whit whispered, "Your lady love!"

Skipper just glared, as a very old-fashioned male voice joined in. *Yes indeed! The future is not so far away, not at all. And we should know, we live here.*

It's amazing to see just all that the future holds, isn't it? The female voice continued *And it's amazing to see just how different it is to what we thought it might be!*

Whit pressed his chin into his chest and recited along with the male voice. "Yes, we sure did get it wrong! Why don't we take a look back on the future and see just what ideas we came up with?"

Skipper flipped back imaginary hair. "Come along with us, and we'll show you!" His voice squeaked, in a very bad attempt to match the sweet maternal tones of the narrator.

The friends held up their hands ready for the music drop into French accordions and bombastic French Horns. And a one, and a two and a—

MESA GREEN! A Desert paradise! Our daughter lives here, you know!

What.

Whit looked and Skipper, and Skipper looked at Whit. "…Mesa Green? They fuck up the soundtrack now?"

Whit shook his head. "They can't dude, it's all individual. Or something. It can't get messed—" Whit had turned his gaze to the now visible show scene, expecting to see H.G.Wells and old Art Deco drawings, but it wasn't. It was the irrigating desert, and woman in a yellow jumpsuit keeping close eye on it.

"…What." Skipper stood up. "Dude did we pass out? Did we miss something?"

"No," Whit trembled, his camera nearly falling from his hands. "No we both—we couldn't…something's wrong."

They watched confused, as the scene continued as normal, each detail. The girl talking to her boyfriend via a video call, the boyfriend that was supposed to appear in robotic form in the next scene, in three two—

—Centauri! It's hard to get used to zero gravity right dear?

Whit scrambled to his feet and pressed up against the walls on their ride vehicle. "Dude, what the FUCK?"

Skipper by then had turned on his own camera, capturing the madness and trying to keep his hands steady. "I-I don't know man I don't know—"

Sea Base Beta! A kingdom—

"DUDE!" Whit's breathing was heavy, his eyes wild in shock as he pushed himself further and further into the corner of the ride car. "This is bullshit, man, this is complete bullshit."

"I know, man, I know I just don't get it! The track can't— it doesn't work like this!" Skipper exclaimed. "I want off man, I want off right now!"

Ole Jules Verne sure had funny ideas!

27

The future sure was farfetched in the past!
Happy birthday to you—happy birthday to—
Welcome to our home—

They were hyperventilating now, Skip was muttering over and over and wringing his hat with his hands with Whit kept banging against the car. "We gotta get out man, walk back to the loading station, say shit went wrong—

—Ipper!

"What you say, man?" Skipper asked, still staring like a deer in proverbial headlights at the unfolding show scene.

Whit's voice cracked. "Nothing. I didn't say anything."

"...Bullshit, you said my name!" Skipper insisted, finally pulling his eyes away to look at his friend.

"I didn't!!"

W—it!

Neither of their mouths were moving. Slowly, but surely they both turned towards the animatronic show. The grandparents, the narrators, were sitting in their very upscale apartment in Nova City Center. The old gent was playing some sort of future-xylophone or whatever, while his wife lounged on the sofa, video calling on their oval shaped television set to the yellow-jumper woman from the Mesa Green scene. The man's hands were hovering over the colorful instrument, different parts glowing as his plastic digits passed over them. Usually. The whole thing was lit up brightly, cheerfully playing all the musical tones at once.

His head was tilted towards them.

—Ipper!

That part was the worst. They knew what it was from. The husband asks something to his wife and she would say, right before the scene transition:

"Oh don't worry about me dear, I'm just chipper!"

And he'd respond:

"Sure thing, dear. Now why don't we go and check in on the preparations!"

Chipper. Ipper...to make it sound like Skipper.

W—it!

That was harder, what it sounded like someone trying to

say 'With.' When the hell did the grandmother say with!? But wracking his memory, Whit could think of only one really clear example, as you made the journey into the Sea Base and the narrators left you for a while.

"I almost forgot! You'll have to excuse us, we're helping our daughter with setting up for our grandson's birthday party. Telecommunication still takes some planning you know!" says the wife, indigently.

"We'll see you soon!"

"...I-It's talking to us..." Whit whispered, grabbing Skipper by his sleeve and tugging him close. "Dude it's talking to us!!"

Skipper opened his mouth. "Hey wh—"

But the ride hadn't stopped chugging along, and the living room soon vanished behind a wall and a black corridor; the long dark journey to the unloading platform complete with the sponsor's electrified logo.

They were still standing up and clinging to each other when the low lights of the unloading station finally came into view.

"Uh...everything alright, gentlemen?" asked an older ride attendant, looking a more than a little annoyed that they weren't remaining seated at all times.

Whit and Skipper didn't answer, they just quickly bobbed their heads and practically dashed out of their car, onto the moving belt and out of the building as fast as their legs could take them.

The boy stumbled onto the main pathway and sped to the park's exit.

"Dude, we had to have been tripping out, or something! Maybe that citrus scent they pump in Mesa Green was, like, laced with something or a bad batch!" Skipper was shaking, wringing this hat between his hands. "There's no way—"

Whit smacked him, straight across the chest, harder than he meant to. "We saw, what we saw, man! It was talking at us. It knew us!"

"Yeah but, they're fake! It's all programmed!" Skipper rubbed his chest. "Ow..."

"Sorry," Whit said quickly, and then grabbed him by the collar of his t-shirt. "Explain how everything was out of order then?"

"I—I—" Skipper stammered. "...It had to have been fumes!"

"We gotta go back," Whit turned on his heel and marched back the way they came, a man on a mission.

"WHAT!" squeaked Skipper. "Dude are you nuts?"

"We have to see if it happens again!" Whit looked down at his camera. "We filmed it sure, but it probably looks like shit."

"Are you on glue? What if—what if it's some Terminator thing, what if this is the robot uprising? Maybe this *is* Skynet?" Skipper waved his arms about, drawing the ire of passing families who gave the boys dirty looks.

Gripping his friend's forearm, he grabbed him and dragged him to a nearby utility door. "Skipper, if there is something going on, we can't just ignore it. This could be the coolest, biggest discovery in the world! We can't ignore it!"

"Yes, we can!"

Whit narrowed his eyes. "Come on!"

Skipper made an attempt to dig his heels in but Whit practically lifted him up by the shirt and carried him back to the Future Port building, smiling at any passerby who gave them a weird look.

Even with Skipper's pleading, Whit got him back onto Future Port. The attendants seemed perplexed but Whit just said it was nothing but a bad taco and nerves and that was that.

Both boys had their cameras ready, Whit's eye glued to his view finder while Skipper's picture probably looked like an earthquake was taking place. And...

...Nothing changed.

Everything was in order, all the way to the halfway point of the Future Living scene. "...What."

Skipper just shrugged. "See? We were just having a moment of insanity, or it was a gas leak. Let's just enjoy it— WHIT!!"

His friend was already climbing out of the car, so he scrambled to follow. "Ya could have warned me!"

"Could've. Didn't." Whit peered around, looking at the robot butler's movements and the bathing lady's blinking. Nothing seemed wrong. Seemed like any other day at Future Port. "Why don't we try and get ahead? See if something's missing or smells funky."

Before Skipper could argue, Whit was making his way towards the wall. The path under the show scenes could only get them so deep and so far, so more often than not they'd carefully stand on the plywood under the cars and walk to different closeby scenes. They'd done it a hundred times before, and every time it worked like a charm.

Skipper hurried to follow his friend, suddenly staying with the animatronics he knew and loved didn't exactly seem comfortable anymore. But just as he stepped onto the plywood right at the edge of the wall, his foot gave way. He grabbed onto the ride car, and tried to pull himself up, only to smack his head against the side wall.

"Woah! My foot fell into outer space!" He steadied himself onto what was hopefully a less rotten piece of wood and touched his forehead. It was wet and sticky. "Shit dude, my head split open!"

But there was only silence in return. He squinted his eyes into the darkness and the low light, looking for Whit. "Dude, I said I cut my head!"

Still nothing.

He stepped out onto the now visible show scene of Sea Base's preamble. "...Whit?" He looked around, even peered down the show scene's gaping hole where the ocean was meant to be. "Whit!?" But his friend was nowhere to be found. "Shit..." he whispered. "Wait..." Sea Base didn't happen until AFTER Mesa Green anyway. And yet, here he was. "SHIT!" He fumbled with the camera, trying to get it to stop recording. He needed to get back on, and now. He couldn't be worrying about the stupid camera! Did he even have time! The nearest ride vehicle said 36. But he realized all too quickly he couldn't remember what cars he counted. His gap could be closing and he wouldn't even know it.

"SHIT!"

He was scrambling now. He could try and hop back on a car but what about Whit? Maybe he was stuck somewhere too. He hated to do it but the safest place was probably on the walk way behind the cars. He hit another button on his camera, accidentally ejecting the tape from it and it clattered to the ground by the boyfriend-matronic's tools. Screw it.

He ran to the cars and shimmied his way between two of them, clattering onto the back platform. He leaned up against the back wall, attempting to take deep, easy breaths to calm down. He had to find Whit, he had to. Whatever this was it was getting too dangerous. Too batshit. He clambered to his feet and started power walking along the platform, following the flow of the ride, and as he rounded the corner—

"HEY!"

A flashlight blinded his eyes.

"SHIIIT!!"

Skipper turned quickly and booked it like he never booked it before, the thundering sound of security guard feet pounding on the metal behind him just ringing in his ears. They were caught. They must have Whit. The cops were probably on their way. He had to hide! Thank God for long legs and being forced to do track.

There was only one place to hide, under Mesa Green and between the flats. Even if security knew about it, how could they know that the boys did too? It was a risk but he had to. He urged himself forward, flinging himself between two cars and back onto what he hoped to God was Mesa Green.

By some miracle he was greeted with cactuses and over-eager girlfriends. He dove into the hole behind the yellow jumpsuit woman and crawled his way through the passage, up into Future Living and rolled into the fabric covered hole that was the entrance to their once secret base. Only he hit something, someone.

Whit.

"DUDE!" Skipper started crying and threw his arms around his friend in a tight hug, "Oh God, I thought they got you."

Whit clung back just as tight. "No, man, I thought they got you! What happened?"

"I don't know," Skipper sobbed, "I don't know."

"You're bleeding!" Whit grabbed the hem of his Hawaiian shirt and started dabbing at Skip's head.

"Yeah well that's pretty low on the totem pole of bullshit that just happened to me, man!"

"Where'd you go?"

Skipper shook his head, gasping a little. "It was the Sea Base. I don't know why, but it was the Sea Base! And then security was there and I just—I don't know."

Whit grabbed his friends' forearms, looking at him up and down. "Are you okay, though?"

"Y-Yeah, Whit, I'm fine. Just bonked my head trying to dive into a car...nothing that hasn't happened before," Skipper pressed his palm against his temple, the bleeding was already slowing down but it still didn't look pretty. "Where did you end up?"

"With the old lady on the space station, after the family's spacewalk..." Whit ran his hands through his hair, tugging a little. "It just doesn't make sense."

Skipper gulped. "I, uh, may have more bad news, dude."

"Great, what now?"

"...I dropped the tape."

Whit blinked once, twice, face growing redder each time. "What?"

"In the ocean! I dropped the tape!" Skipper frowned. "I'm sorry, I just, I panicked! I saw the flashlights and I wasn't thinking—"

"No—No, just—" Whit sighed, "You know what? It's fine, it's not like we can't go back and get it, we've left food here before...it'll be fine."

Skipper looked unconvinced. "You sure?"

"Yeah," Whit pointed at Skipper's head. "I'm more worried about you bleeding out. Come on, let's get out of here."

"How *are* we going to get out of here? The security guy

33

saw me—they're probably looking for us," Skipper rubbed his eyes.

"…We'll just have to wait, I guess?"

Sometimes, Skipper hated when Whit was right.

It was hours before there was a decent gap. They occupied their name playing I-Spy with the various props and 'First to Spot someone wearing THIS color wins' as carefully as they could. But they were getting irritated, to the point where Whit was considering just going for it and hope no other rider said anything. But almost as if the ride heard his thoughts, there was a long gap and they ran for it.

The ride ran like normal, in order. As they approached the Sea Base scene, Skip looked carefully at the pile of tools next to the tinkering boyfriend. "…Whit, the tape's gone…"

Whit tensed but sighed. "They probably chucked it, or something…or maybe it didn't fall there."

"No, dude, it was there. I know it was," Skipper insisted. The rest of the ride was tense. Not just worry about the lights suddenly going on and there being a dozen red lasers aimed at their chests, but also there was something still off about the grandmother animatronic. "…She's looking at us."

Whit wanted to insist that she was looking at all the riders, as she should. But it was the final scene, a birthday party, and all other animatronic eyes were on the birthday boy. "We're paranoid, man. That's all."

—Ipper! W—It!

"…P-Paranoid. Sure…"

As they stepped off the ride, they still were not met with resistance, even with the girl from the boarding area giving them dirty looks as they walked away. They had made it.

Two weeks passed and neither of them had gone back to the park. Skipper had to go get three stitches for his head. Lied and said he tripped on a sidewalk. Whit was still worried about the tape but not worried enough to even bother stepping back into that place after everything. They called each other nightly; no cop had shown at the other's home. And their parents didn't say anything other than, "You're not going to that Invented Blue-Print Neighborhood Theme Park today?"

Not that Future Port was far from their minds. More breakdowns were being reported, both through their grapevine of friends or on the news. Delays, animatronic malfunctions, sound issues—but nothing about sequence breaking. Nothing about hearing the narrator call your name.

The boys felt almost bad. Future Port was almost a ritual at this point, and to leave it cold turkey, made a gnawing feeling stay inside their stomachs. The two explorers couldn't keep away forever. They couldn't.

It was a Monday night, rainy and miserable. The rush of spring breakers encroaching on their precious park time was coming soon. If they were going to dare to go back on their beloved ride, tonight was the night.

They met up at the Pizza Parlor like usual, just armed with Whit's JVC—no still cameras, no extended batteries, nothing. Just them, and ole-reliable.

"You sure about this?" Skipper asked. Somehow in the two weeks since he'd gotten even skinner and paler. "What if— what if we get there and Rod Stirling's there telling us we suck and that we've been dead for thirty years?"

Whit rolled his eyes. "If we don't do it, we're going to spend the rest of our lives wondering what the hell happened. It's now or never."

Skipper's shoulders slumped, but he nodded all the same.

"Now or never," he echoed.

Their walk over to Future Port was slow. Their sneakers shuffled through puddles and drowned futuristic paving stones. Soon the grand and tan hexagon of the future stood before them, large and stretched out and despite the clouds in the sky and the rain pouring down, it still looked as bright and as welcoming as ever. That was strangely comforting, despite everything.

Whit and Skipper entered the rainbow-lit queue, its lights

pulsing with delight.

"Welcome home boys!" The poindexter attendant stood guard almost at the doorway before the loading stations. "We missed you. Future wasn't as bright without you two."

The two boys gave him a half-hearted smile.

"We missed it too," Whit assured, looking up at the vehicle number. Number 1. "Slow day?"

"Never a slow day for progress!" The attendant responded with a grin. "Have fun!"

The friends clambered inside their ride vehicle, wondering what to do. "We've got a gap a mile wide," Skipper pointed out. But he didn't make any move to prepare a leap of faith onto Future Living.

"People came in after us. Let's just watch one time through," Whit suggested, biting on his lip. "See what happens."

"Sure thing, dude...sounds good," Skipper said, sounding neither sure nor good.

And it was...

Normal.

More than normal. Dulled lights flickered with full force; clear music blasting through the speakers. Even the animatronics, whose skins were due for a face lift seemed to be fresh off the assembly line, motion and expressions clear. It was like watching a whole new ride, watching the ride like they did when it first opened to the high school grads, watching it as two budding friends again.

It almost relaxed them.

Before they knew it, they were at the final scene before the grand finale; the birthday party. It's supposed to be cute; the grandparents, desert teenager, and her aqua-living boyfriend all on "holographic teleconferencing" singing to the little boy and his parents from the space scene. But it didn't look right. The lighting was a fierce blue, almost blinding, and the animatronics were stiff and still. The cheerful music and singing were painfully absent. The ride then stopped, leaving the boys smack dab in the middle with what seemed to be three empty cars on either side of them. A small, but decent, gap.

The speakers crackled. *–Ipper. W—it.* It said, sending a chill down the two boys' spines. And the battery of their camera suddenly died.

"Should we bolt?" Skipper whispered.

"Bolt where? The next scene is the movie and there's no floor for us to stand on," Whit hissed.

Well it is a party! A party! A party—for—Ipper! And W-it!

It should have been creepy, hearing the dialog so choppy and out of order, but it wasn't. It was the normal grandmother dialog just slightly changed around.

"Party? For us?" Skipper gulped.

Both boys glanced at each other. "Uh, do you want us to get out?" Whit asked, rubbing the back of his neck. The grandmother animatronic suddenly jerked its head up and down. They jumped in their seats. But it was a nod. A yes.

Skipper slowly swung his leg over the closed vehicle doors. "Uh sure thing, um…ma'am?"

Whit smacked him upside the head. "Don't call it ma'am!"

"I'm just being polite dude!" Skipper countered.

" *–ipper!* " it said, in that same oddly choppy way. *"W— it!"* Her body movements resumed, in that very uncanny animatronic way, but it was better than the rigor mortis the other robots were still stuck in. Her head moved slowly, arms moving up and down every few seconds but smoothly. *"You—FORGOT—something!"*

"Uh…yeah, our tape," Whit said, grabbing onto Skipper's belt loop. "How'd you—"

"Saw it—HAPPEN!" Almost in agreement, the other animatronic heads moved to nod, before going back to stiff stillness.

"Do um…do you have it?" Skipper asked.

"Yes indeed!" She recited. *"DON'T worry! BeHIND–you"*

Whit turned, behind them was the space scene parents, stiff as well, and their kid on the mother's lap. Usually you only saw the back of their hair, but they did have faces and even slightly moving heads. They were even more uncanny than the other audio-animatronics because their faces were static—

never built for eye or mouth movements or any movement aside from slight head turns. But on the mother's thigh, next to the child, was their missing tape's label.

"T-Thanks," said Whit with uncertainty and quickly snatched it off the animatronics clothes. "Can we have it back too? Like physically?"

"*Soon!*"

Well, that wasn't vague.

"You're not...mad at us for breaking in all the time?" Skipper dared to ask, stepping a little closer to the grandmother.

"*No!*" The voice was still happy, not that there was ever a point where the narration got evil or scary—sarcastic maybe, but not angry. But still it was strange to hear the inflections out of context, and phrases out of order. "*We—don't Care!*"

"Oh," Whit rubbed the back of his neck. "Sorry for, uh...touching you guys?"

"*We—don't care!!*"

"Right," Whit nodded. "Um why—"

"*Thank you for riding with us, here at Future Port!*" The grandmother's body swiveled at the waist, to look at both boys in turn. "*Thank you—Thank you—Thank you!*"

Skipper grinned, still a little uneasy. "Well, you've got a good ride here ma'am—uh—sir—yeah. We love it."

"*We know IT! We know—We—GAVE YOU, a guh-AH-p!*" The last bit was **very** mashed together, the two friends stood confused for a moment.

The animatronics' eyes narrowed. "*A guh-AAAH-P!*" It's arms went wide, stretching to show space between them.

"We're shit at charades, lady," Skipper said, only for Whit to tug on his belt loop, making his friend stumble.

"I think she means gap," Whit explained, and the animatronic grinned. Well, tried to grin. It only had so many mouth movements, but it meant well.

"*FOR—You To explore, to play, to LOOK and record!*" Her hand moved towards the video camera in Whit's hands. "*No one else. It's amazing to see—YOU two! It's amazing to see—YOU two—care and give—US love. Love—love—love—*

like no one ELSE!"

"Aww, shucks," Skipper smiled, genuinely this time. "Well, lots of people love this ride ma'am. It's so popular for a reason. We don't know what we'd do without Future Port. We just wanted to remember it in a cool way."

The grandmother shook her head this time. *"No one else."*

"Thanks but just so we're like, clear," Whit interjected. "The changing up of the order, the name calling, that was all you?"

The grandmother nodded.

"The...the gap of riders? The delays or slow downs? That was you too? Because you like us?"

Again, the grandmother nodded.

"...So I did all that math counting passengers for nothing?

This time all the animatronics nodded.

Whit nodded, "Cool, cool just, making sure—HOLY SHIT DUDE THE RIDE LIKES US!" He cackled and spun Skipper around in a bear hug. "THIS IS INSANE! THIS IS INSANE! I'm so happy!"

"Dude! My spine!"

Skipper was once again placed on the ground, "Sorry, sorry just, I'm excited. This is heavy," Whit said still practically vibrating with excitement. "I'm never counting shit for as long as I live, but shit, I'm excited."

"Hey! Can we just—talk to you now?" Skipper asked, eyes wide.

"Yes—please do!"

"Oh, sweet," Skipper's skin suddenly flushed soft pink. "Sorry about uh—saying you were hot, uh, the other day. I mean, you're married. And you have kids, and I'm not ready for that type of commitment."

Whit groaned. "She isn't alive, jackass."

"DON'T—Worry!" The grandmother's eye winked. *"I am—Future Port! You—can't—DATE me!"*

"Right, no, that's—fine—good—I mean not good I—I'm jumping off the platform now." Skipper buried his head in his hands, and Whit gave him a comforting pat.

"'Man marries dark ride.' Only in Florida."

"Shut UP, Whit."

"Don't GO—too far away!" The grandmother's head tilted to the side. *"We got you—BOTH—a present."* Her hands pointed back towards the ride vehicle, now slowly moving again. *"Come back real soon—Thank you—LOVE—Future Port!"*

"Hey wai—"

But it was too late, the animatronics were back on their programmed movements, the soft twinkling sounds of the birthday song now echoing and filling the heavy silence and their camera's battery suddenly blinked back to life. And the two boys quickly darted back into the ride just before the doors shut.

Happy Birthday to you! Happy birthday to you!

Soon the animatronics and the birthday party fell away and a dark, wide room took its place. Now was the time to choose their own ending.

"I can't believe it," Skipper said softly. "Did we really just…talk to the ride?"

"Either that or the brownies mom made me were special." Whit grinned. "We'll have to come back tomorrow. Seemed like it's lonely."

"Man, what about the tape? We only got back the sticker!" Skipper slapped the label onto the back of Whit's shirt.

"Forget it man, Future Port has it now. What are you feeling? Space? Desert? Or Ocean?" Whit asked, staring done hungrily at the flashing buttons displaying correlating cartoons. But Skipper didn't respond. "Skip? Come on man, I can't ever make decisions. Pick one." Still nothing. "Earth to Skipper?"

"…Dude, look." Skipper's voice was wavering. Somehow even a higher pitch than his usual warble. "Look."

Whit glanced upward, and his jaw dropped open. On the giant screen wasn't a space trek, or the deep blue, or the raging canyons of the desert. It was them. Their dumb adventures through the whole ride. There was Skipper ruffling the kid's hair in Mesa Green, and Whit climbing into the little space speeder. Now there was the time they propped the camera up against a rock and an octopus and recorded the passengers undetected. Then they were doing relay races through the ocean floor and into outer space. Everything that had ever been on that stupid little tape, every stupid close up of eye sockets to figure out their color or documentation of button flashes in order, or their juvenile antics pretending to dance with or kiss or be slapped by an animatronic. In glorious full screen, there they were. Soon the screen faded away.

Thank you for riding with us, here at Future Port!

We hope we'll see you soon!

The normal farewell from their favorite narrators.

Bye-bye—Whit and Skipper!

Okay maybe not completely normal.

The boys buzzed with excitement as they exited the ride, giggling like crazy. Right before they left the unloading station, the girl attendant, the always-annoyed one, stood there with her arms folded. "If you're going to keep lugging that thing around, you need to take better care of your stuff, gentlemen."

They exchanged a look. "Huh?"

She held out the tape, labelless, but it was for sure their tape. "I thought it was yours, no one else bothers to record this ride."

Skipper quickly snatched it out of her hands. "Oh, thanks."

"Mhh-hmm."

Whit grinned. "See ya real soon. Gotta see how the future is looking tomorrow you know."

"Oh yes," Skipper agreed. And both boys linked arms and practically skipped out of the ride. The sun had finally decided to show its face.

Whit turned and bellowed into the open air. "GOODBYE, FUTURE PORT! WE'LL MISS YOU!"

Although the boys couldn't be sure, they thought that Future Port's glowing blue entry sign pulsed just a bit brighter.

Betamax

NATALIE POTTS

I'd been blinking dramatically from the moment Cass arrived, but she still hadn't noticed my blue mascara. She was too busy fluffing up her new perm. It was a redundant move really, given the perm made her blonde hair poof out perfectly anyway. In her coral lip gloss and pastel blue ruffle skirt she looked like a movie extra. Her waist was cinched in, impossibly small, by her white elastic belt. It made me regret my decision to wear my high-waisted acid-wash jeans. Even if they did look cool with the matching jacket.

"So, are we going to the Miss Shop?" I asked, keen to get out of the food hall. The last weekend of school holidays had turned the eatery into a child-minding center, complete with the offensive noises and odors that little kids usually gave off.

"Daniel called just before I left," Cass said. At first, I thought it was just another opportunity for her to rub in the fact that she had a boyfriend and I didn't, but her sheepish expression told me there was more to it than that. "His parents are away, so he thought we could borrow a movie or something?"

"You're ditching me for Daniel?"

"No, dummy, I said 'we' could watch a movie. He said you could come too."

"Ugh, that means Steve will be there as well doesn't it? He's such a mouth-breather."

"Steve's alright," Cass said. "And I think he likes you."

"Steve likes anything with a muff."

"Anne! Don't be gross. Just give him a chance."

"You'd love that wouldn't you? Then we could double-date."

"Well, that would be cool, don't you think?"

"Not if I had to date Steve." I nearly added that I'd be alright if we swapped boys, but caution censored me before I made that mistake. "Look, I really need to get a new skirt before school starts. And the Miss Shop sale ends this week."

It was as if I hadn't spoken. Cass was looking into the distance with a glazed expression, with which I was becoming all too familiar. Daniel was walking toward us with practiced calm. His tight black jeans and flannelette shirt made him look like a rockstar. His black hair was sprayed, not gelled, into position like a helmet. Behind him ambled Steve. Steve was Daniel's antithesis, his lank mullet clung to his skull, at least two days past when it should have been washed. His eyes were downcast, his hands shoved into the pockets of his jeans, pulling them below his waist. He wore a Hypercolour t-shirt that was all salmon, his mother having accidentally put it through a hot-wash at some point.

"Dan!" Cass called. "Over here!" Her enthusiasm was sickening. I looked away as they came together and pashed. I briefly caught eyes with an equally awkward Steve. His cheeks blushed the same color of his t-shirt before he looked away.

Daniel finally came up for air and Cass tittered as she wiped away the smear of coral she'd left on his lips. Daniel dragged his eyes from Cass to me.

"Duran," he said to me. "Like the blue mascara, it brings out the blue in your eyes."

The night before Daniel and Cass had gotten together, he and I had spent hours talking in a backyard of a party. I'd confessed that I wanted to be an actress and that *Anne Duran* was going to be my stage name. Soon after my confession he'd gone inside to sleep and by chance had curled up next to Cass. The rest was history. I liked to think the moniker he gave me was a secret code that he hadn't forgotten our night together.

"What movie did you get?" I asked, pointedly ignoring his

complement.

"Nothing yet. Thought we'd all go to the video shop and pick something out."

"I've got some movies at home if you want me to pick one up," I offered.

"Can't," Cass said, while hanging onto Daniel as if her legs had stopped working. "Dan's got a Betamax, so it won't play VHS."

"Better quality picture," Daniel boasted. His father liked to be on the cutting edge of technology. There was even a rumor he was getting a phone installed in his car. Why anyone would want a phone in their car was beyond me. What was so important that it couldn't wait for you to finish driving?

"The beta section is really small," I complained, gaining a grunt of what I assumed was support from Steve.

"We'll find something. Come on," Cass said, before she and Daniel walked off without waiting for agreement. Steve and I fell into an uncomfortable silence behind them. At least I wasn't the only one who didn't want to be there.

The video shop was pretty quiet. Just after lunch was not peak time because tapes weren't due back until 4 P.M., so there was every chance that what you wanted to borrow was still out. From habit I walked over to the new release stand before I remembered that we were limited to the beta tapes.

Cass was in the corner of the store, reapplying her lip gloss in the reflection of a mirror on one of the pylons. I couldn't see Steve, but with the height of the racks he could have been in the next row along for all I knew. Not that I cared. I spotted Daniel in the Betamax section chatting to a guy who looked just like Simon Le Bon. He was gorgeous. I made straight for Cass.

"Who's the hot guy with Daniel?" I asked as quietly as I could.

"Where?" Cass pulled her eyes away from her reflection to glance across the store. "The only hot guy I see *is* Dan," Cass said with a giggle.

I turned around. Daniel was standing alone at the video rack. "Maybe he works here?" I speculated, noticing there was a door to a back room near the beta section. "I might have to come back more often," I joked, but Cass was already ignoring me. Daniel was walking toward us with a tape held high.

"Got one!" He declared as he got closer.

"*Wither*," I read from the cover. "From the bleeding pentagrams, I'm guessing it's a horror film?"

"Oh, I hope it's not too scary!" Cass said, grabbing onto Daniel in what I was sure was going to be the first of many such moves she would find any excuse to make.

"Who was the person who gave it to you?" I asked, fishing for the name of the Simon Le Bon lookalike.

"You saw," Daniel said. "Don't know, but she was a dead ringer for Daryl Hannah, eh?"

"Daryl Hannah?" I said confused.

"Cool," Steve said, diving in from who knows where. "What's this?" He grabbed the tape and turned it over as if he might find something intelligent written on the back. "I haven't seen this one."

"Then it's settled," Daniel declared. Before I could voice my opposition, he took off for the counter to pay.

"Cass, I hate horror films," I said.

"Come on Anne, it'll be fun."

"No, it won't. A comedy, that's fun. Horror films, they are the opposite of fun."

"Please," Cass begged. "Holidays are nearly over, and this might be the only chance I get to spend some time at Dan's place without his parents around."

His house was just a street over from the mall, so if we watched the film straight away, we'd be able to come back in time to buy me a new skirt from the Miss Shop before it closed.

"Okay," I agreed. "But if I don't like it, then promise you'll come straight back to the mall with me."

"Of course!"

I had a feeling Cass would agree to anything if she thought it would make me go alone with it. We walked up to the counter to join the boys.

46

"Can't find it on the system," the pock-faced attendant said as he looked at the screen. "Looks like the boss hasn't entered it yet."

"I can pay for it as a new release," Daniel offered, getting out a ten-dollar note.

"Nah, it's beta. Take it as a weekly," the boy said, keying something into the computer before he scanned Daniel's membership card. He handed both the card and the cassette back to him. "Just remember to rewind it before you return it, or we'll charge you another dollar."

Daniel shrugged off the warning. "Come on, let's go," he said. Daniel lifted his arm and Cass moved into place below it. They fitted together like the edge-pieces of a jigsaw puzzle. Steve and I, however, were the awkwardly shaped background tiles, pushed to the side and left until there were no other pieces that matched.

As soon as we were outside, Steve moved around beside Daniel and I took up position next to Cass so we walked four-across, blocking the entire footpath. I'd been to Daniel's once before, and remembered that there were two two-seater sofas in the TV room. I was already dreading the seating arrangements. I should have thought to negotiate with Cass to sit with me before I'd agreed to come. Before I could quietly bring it up, we were at Daniel's house.

"You girls get some snacks," Daniel said as we walked into his house. "We'll run through the previews."

Horror was not my style at the best of times, so I didn't mind missing out on whatever b-grade flicks made it onto the promo reel at the beginning of the film. Cass and I walked into the kitchen while the boys loaded the tape.

"Oh! They've got a microwave!" Cass said, clapping her hands together before running up to the TV-like box on the counter. "Let's cook something in it."

"What can we cook?"

"Anything. It's a microwave."

I walked over to the fridge and opened the door. A box of last night's pizza and garlic bread was sitting on the main shelf. The oddly alluring arm-pit smell of it made my stomach grumble.

"How about this?"

"Sure," Cass agreed. She got out a plate to fit the remaining pieces of pizza, because the box was too big to put in the little oven. I scrunched the aluminum foil of the garlic bread closed and popped it on top of the pizza before we put the whole lot in the microwave.

We stood looking at the little machine, flummoxed. There were a bunch of numbers and pictures and none of it made any sense. A big button beside the door opening paddle said 'start' so I pressed it.

For a second the machine hummed into life, lighting up the inside so we could see the plate start to revolve. Almost immediately sparks burst from the garlic bread and arced from the plate to the walls of the oven. Cass screamed and jumped back while I lunged forward to hit the stop button. The little machine fell silent, as if it was dead.

"What are you doing?!" Daniel yelled as he ran in to see what the fuss was.

"Cass wanted to use the microwave," I said, aware how guilty I looked standing right next to it. Daniel shouldered me out of the way and opened the door. A strange metallic odor wafted out along with a garlic-cheese smell that now made my stomach turn. From where I was standing, I could see the brown scars across the back wall of the microwave. They hadn't been there before.

"What were you thinking?" Daniel said, pulling the plate out so he could better inspect the damage. "You never nuke metal! It's a microwave."

"I didn't know…" I burst into tears. Cass didn't step in to comfort me. Instead Daniel turned and pulled me in for a hug.

"Oh, don't cry, Duran. It's not broken. You stopped it before it did anything serious." He let go so he could look me in the eye. Cass was sending me daggers over his shoulder. "The marks will wipe out," Daniel said. "They built these things for the astronauts, do you think it'd be that easy to break?" He turned to the sink and came back with a cloth. True to his word, the stains wiped off. "See, no harm." He turned and smiled at Cass. "How about chips?" He grabbed a bag of salt and vinegar crisps from the pantry.

We walked out into the lounge and the TV screen was flicking between two frames as the tape waited to be released from pause. The back and forth revealed the beginnings of a bloody knife.

"Did you fast forward the previews already?" Cass asked.

"Weren't any," Steve said from one of the sofas. Cass and Daniel sat down on the other two-seater. "There wasn't any warning about copying or public performances either. It just starts at the beginning of the movie."

"Maybe it's European?" Cass said, snuggling into Daniel.

I looked from the dagger on the screen to the empty seat next to Steve.

"Guys, I'm really sorry, but I don't want to watch it," I said. "I think I'll just go back to the mall."

Cass raised her eyebrows and slightly shook her head in a silent threat. Clearly her promise was forgotten and I'd be returning alone.

"Duran," Daniel said, leaning forward and displacing Cass, much to her annoyance. "Don't worry about the microwave thing, it's no big deal."

"No, it's not that," I lied. "I've just got some things I need to get before school starts." I looked at Cass, but she just snuggled back into place.

"Might see you tomorrow?" I said to Cass.

"Yeah, maybe." She pointedly glanced at Daniel before looking back at me. "Or at school on Monday."

"Fine." I nodded. "Enjoy the film." I let myself out of the house and made the trek back to the mall on my own.

The Miss Shop no longer had my size in stock, so I briefly considered going back to join the others, but I was too embarrassed. I couldn't believe I had cried in front of Daniel and Steve. Instead I went home and waited until after dinner to call Cass so I could find out what happened after I left. Her mother answered.

"Hi, Mrs. Brown, can I talk to Cass?"

"Is that you Anne?" She seemed surprised. I hoped I

hadn't blown Cass's cover. Had she said she was at my place?

"Um...yeah. There were a few of us from the mall over at Daniel Kalinowski's house, but I left because I wasn't feeling well. I guess Cass must still be there." I tried to make it sound less exclusive than it was.

"Kalinowski," Mrs. Brown repeated, disappointment heavy in her words. "I guess I'll have to go around and pick her up now it's dark." None of the adults liked going to the Kalinowski's. Mr. Kalinowski was heavily into Amway and almost no-one got away without hearing about the great business opportunity it offered.

"Well, when you see her, could you let her know I'm feeling much better now if she wants a chat?" I wasn't sure Mrs. Brown was even listening to me anymore. I said goodbye and hung up.

By 9:30 I still hadn't heard back from Cass, and wondered if I should have been more explicit with my request for Cass to call me back? I'd have to wait until tomorrow to find out what went on.

Only Mrs. Brown didn't let me speak to Cass on Sunday. She said Cass was unwell. How sick could she be not to come to the phone? Cass must have been angry with me and didn't want to talk, but over what, I had no idea. Surely, I hadn't embarrassed her that much. I could almost imagine her, Steve and Daniel laughing about it as soon as I left. I'd have to wait until school to find out what I'd done that she thought was so terribly wrong.

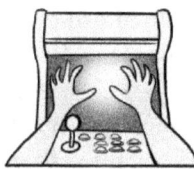

The final bell for the start of class went before Cass walked in. She looked like death. She was in the same clothes she'd worn on Saturday, but now they were crinkled as if she'd slept in them. Her hair was greasy, the perm split down her center part making her look like a blonde clown. She sat heavily in the seat beside me. I wasn't sure if she was even aware that I was next to her, or if she'd just gone for the last empty seat in the class.

"Cass, are you okay?" I asked.

"Erm," She grunted. I wasn't sure what she meant, but the answer was clearly 'no' regardless of what she was trying to say. "I've got some spare make-up if you want to swing by the loos between class," I offered. Again, she grunted an ambiguous reply.

"Ladies!" Mrs. Hargraves bellowed, silencing us all. For the next hour Cass stared blankly into space while the rest of us wrote notes from the overhead projector.

"Cass," Mrs. Hargraves said. "Can you tell us the trigger event for the first world war?" We'd only been hearing about it for the last hour.

Cass rolled her eyes over to Mrs. Hargraves and shrugged her shoulders.

"Cass isn't well," I volunteered, seeing the red rising in Mrs. Hargraves cheeks. "I think I should take her to the sick bay."

Mrs. Hargraves seemed to take in Cass's less than impeccable appearance for the first time, and a veil of concern fell over her.

"Yes, I think that's a good idea."

Of course, I didn't take Cass to the nurse. We went straight to the toilets. I didn't have to hold her up, but she needed me to lead her. It was like she had lead weights strapped to her feet.

"Cass, what's wrong?" I propped her up against the wall and got to work fixing her make-up. The build-up of coral gloss at the edge of her mouth came off with some difficulty, like it had been left on too long.

"Do you want some water?" I asked, looking at her dry lips.

"Ugh." Her disgusted grimace translating the meaning of her grunt.

Not wanting to look at the cracked skin on her lips any longer, I painted them with some of my cherry gloss. I even parted with some precious blue mascara to try and lift her eyes. The best I could do with her hair was scrunch some water through it, which lifted it slightly, but I had to rub her fringe in circles against her forehead to make it stand up properly. At least now she looked better, but she still hadn't said anything.

"Talk to me!" I demanded.

"I don't want to be here," she said. "I want to go back to Dan's house."

"Dan's in our next class," I said. His nickname was unfamiliar on my tongue, but I had a feeling that in this state Cass might get confused if I called him Daniel.

"I want to go to Dan's house," Cass repeated. She licked her lips and screwed up her nose as if she found the cherry flavor off-putting.

"Have a drink of water," I said, turning on the faucet. "That might wake you up a bit."

"Have some water, eat something…you sound like my mother."

"Cass," I turned the tap off. "Have you eaten since Saturday?" She'd gone anorexic once before, and her pallor was very reminiscent of then.

"I want to go to Dan's house."

The bell rang. Maybe Daniel could talk some sense into her? I ferried her along the hall to maths class. Neither of us went via our lockers to get our books, but I didn't think it was important. When we walked in both Steven and Daniel were already there, having had their previous class in the room.

They were both still in the same clothes they had worn on Saturday. Their eyes were red and their faces pale.

"Did you take drugs?" I said as I dumped Cass into a chair next to the boys. They all looked up at me as if they knew that I was talking, but couldn't understand the words. "Are you stoned?"

"I want to go home," Daniel said, then looked back to the front of the classroom. "But Dad won't let us watch it again unless we go to school. He's hidden the tape."

"Maybe we can find it?" Cass said, with the most animation I'd heard from her all morning.

"He took it to work with him," Daniel said, as if the idea had already occurred to him. Daniel suddenly leaned forward and tapped Emilio on the shoulder. "Hey, I'm having a movie night at my place after school if you're interested?" He almost sounded like normal Daniel.

Cass suddenly lit up and followed Daniel's lead. She leaned across to the girl next to her and passed the invite on. I could see how excited the girl was that Cass had even spoken to her.

"What are you doing?" I said to Daniel before leaning forward. "Emilio, it's just a stupid horror film, it's not worth it." Apparently, that was the wrong thing to say. If he'd been on the edge before, I tipped him over.

"Cool, what time?"

"7:30." Daniel stood up. "Everyone, movie night at my place, 7:30 tonight, all welcome." Daniel sat down, and after passing out a few thumbs up around the classroom, he dropped back into his well of darkness. None of them spoke for the rest of the lesson.

At lunch time I couldn't find Cass. She wasn't in the refectory. She'd never brought lunch from home in the whole time I'd known her, and I was willing to bet she hadn't started today. Daniel and Steve were missing too and I had a feeling none of them would be in my afternoon classes. I had to do something.

"Mr. Stanley," I said, knocking on the principal's door.

"Ah, Miss Dunn, come in."

I stepped in the small office and shut the door before sitting down.

"What's the problem?" I wasn't sure if it was impatience or concern emanating from him.

"I'm worried about Cass, Daniel and Steve." A bit of a lie. I wasn't worried about Steve. "They are acting weird."

"Mabel, um, Mrs. Hargraves mentioned something in the staff room." Mrs. Stanley leaned forward, slipping into his cultivated guise of concern. "Do you think it's drugs?"

"I'm not sure." Clearly that had been the speculation in the staff room. "I'm just worried is all. And...they've invited a bunch of people over tonight."

"Ah. I see." Mr. Stanley tapped his index fingers together while the cogs turned in his head. "You did the right thing, coming to me."

I was just starting to think the exact opposite. If Cass and Daniel found out what I'd done they'd kill me, or worse, never talk to me again.

"I'll give Cass's mum a call," the principal promised.

"No," I said. "No, if you are going to talk to anyone, talk to Mr. Kalinowski. Whatever is going on, it's happening at Daniel's place."

Mr. Stanley leaned back. He didn't look so keen anymore. Likely as not he'd experienced the Amway induction a few times himself. "I'll look into it," he promised. "Now, get back to class, and I don't want you worrying about anything."

English confirmed my fears. Cass had never cut school, but her desk remained empty for the rest of the day. When the bell finally went, I considered going over to Daniel's place. Maybe if I warned them of Mr. Stanley's visit, they'd stop doing whatever they were planning to do. More likely they would turn on me, knowing I was the only one who could have tipped off the principal.

Instead I went home and immediately called Cass's house. There was no answer. I tried right up until 10 P.M., but no-one picked up the phone. Maybe her Dad had pulled out the cord from the wall? He'd done that once before when she'd been grounded, and if Principal Stanley had dropped by her home because of suspected drug-use, there was no question she'd be grounded. But at least she'd be safe.

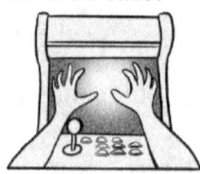

Cass, Daniel and Steve were missing the next day at school. Several of the desks around where we usually sat were also empty. I went to the principal's office at first break, but he hadn't come in yet. I felt sick. Had he called the police? Was

54

he in court right now, telling everyone how I'd dobbed them in?

I went to the pay phone near the gym and called Daniel's number. I had to know what happened.

"Hello," Daniel's father answered. Why wasn't he at work?

"Hi, Mr. Kalinowski. I was wondering if Cass is there?" I winced, waiting for his reaction.

"Yes, Anne, everyone's here. Why don't you join us?"

My blood froze.

"Catch a taxi. I'll pay for it when you get here."

"No, that's okay," I said, the chill seeping further into my body. Instinct told me to hang up, but I resisted. "Um, one more thing..." my voice cracked. "Is Mr. Stanley there?"

"Yes, Anne, everyone's here."

I hung up without saying goodbye.

My next thought was to call my mother, but I didn't trust that she could go over to Daniel's place without getting caught up in whatever was going on. I had to get the police involved. I knew they wouldn't believe me, but if I could get someone at the front office to call Daniel's house, hopefully they would see that something weird was happening. It wasn't much of a plan, but it was all I had.

I ran to the staff room, ignoring the bell signaling the start of class. When I got there a mass exodus of teachers blocked my way.

"Mrs. Hargraves!" I yelled as my history teacher walked out. "I have to speak to you. It's urgent!"

"Darling, I've got to get to class. As do you!"

"Please, Mrs. Hargraves, it's about Cass." From what Mr. Stanley had told me, I knew she was worried about Cass's strange behavior the day before. Now I just had to convince her that the problem was spreading. I could see her personal fight between her abhorrence of tardiness and concern for her pupil. She stepped out of the flow of teachers to hear me out.

"Cass is caught up in something at Daniel Kalinowski's house!" I said. "I told Principal Stanley, but now he's gone over and..."

"Principal Stanley just called," Mrs. Hargraves interrupted. "He's on his way to school now."

"What?" I asked.

"Yes, next period we're having a special assembly because he has some kind of big announcement."

Maybe he'd got to the bottom of what was happening at Daniel's place after all? Was I just imagining all this weirdness?

"Now, young lady, time to get to class," Mrs. Hargraves said, giving me a friendly tap on the bottom to get me moving as if I was six not sixteen.

I didn't hear a word of the next class. I wasn't sure if I was even sitting in the correct classroom. There were fewer empty chairs, which made me again doubt the negative portents I'd thought were so abundant before. Maybe a stomach flu accounted for the missing students?

Ten minutes before the end of class the teacher told us about the assembly. We had to go back to our homerooms before going to the hall.

Cass was at her desk, still wearing her wrinkled clothes from the weekend. Her eyes looked sunken and her face was so white I could see smears of blue mascara on her cheeks. Her cracked lips now had brown bobbles of dried blood on them.

"Cass, are you okay?" I asked, not really knowing what else to say. It was obvious she was not. She didn't speak, only nodding a little while later as if it took time for my words to filter through. "Have you eaten anything?" This time she shook her head. How long could a person go without food and water?

Suddenly everyone stood up. It was time to go to the gymnasium. As we pushed out into the corridor, it was clear the principal intended to include everyone. Out on the quadrangle a serpent of little kids, holding hands in twos, snaked up from the primary school. What on earth was he going to announce?

We squashed into the gym, with the little kids down the front. Lined up along the far wall were the teachers and some parents, including Daniel's dad. Mr. Stanley stood beside him.

My stomach dropped as I realized the principal was wearing the same clothes he'd had on when I'd seen him the day before. Even from this distance, I could see his eyes were red.

Then I saw something more terrifying; a giant TV screen set up at the front of the room. Below the TV, a mission-brown box was tethered to the screen by several cables, and I knew it had to be Daniel's Betamax video player. The school only had VHS, so they must have brought it in on purpose. That could only mean one thing.

Mr. Stanley started to walk forward, the pentagram-emblazoned cassette in his hand. Who knew if he would say something first, or just press play? Something told me we'd go straight to the film. With no previews, no warnings and no credits, I knew I didn't have much time.

I peeled away from my class, ducking low so my homeroom teacher wouldn't notice, and I skirted down the side of the gym. All eyes were on Mr. Stanley as he moved toward the screen.

I ran, at the last minute, dropping my shoulders like I'd seen the boys on the football field do. If the jarring pain that slammed through my body was normal, the guys on the field never showed it. Both Principal Stanley and I went down like a sack of potatoes.

The tape fell from the principal's hand and slid along the floor. I could see both Daniel and Mr. Kalinowski starting to move for it. I tried to get up, but Mr. Stanley grabbed my leg. I kicked at him, screaming like a banshee until he let go.

I was up, in a race with the Kalinowskis. My heel found the tape just as Daniel's fingers closed around it. I don't know if some of the crunching under my foot was from him, but he screamed like he'd just been stabbed.

All around the gym cries of pain howled out; Cass, Steve, Mr. Stanley, and below it all something much worse. The shriek of something primal filled the air. Its wailing was torturous to my ears, but I turned to face it. The awful sound came from the hot guy from the video shop, now standing at the front of the gym.

Up close, he no longer looked like Simon Le Bon. His face was distorted, as if it was melting. His eyes were threatening to fall from their sockets as his lower jaw came loose from his head. Around me, the bewitched were falling, clawing at their heads, screaming.

The man, who no longer looked like a man, scooped up the broken cassette, cradling it like a struck kitten. For just a moment he looked at me, before running out of the gym. The moment he left the screaming stopped.

"What happened?" It was Daniel. He looked at his bleeding fingers, truly unaware of what had just transpired. Behind him, Mr. Kalinowski and Principal Stanley looked confused to find themselves standing in the gym in front of every student in the school.

"Get back to your classrooms!" Principal Stanley said after picking himself up from the ground. He looked at the TV and then back out to the students, trying to make sense of the scene. "Now!"

It took weeks for what happened in the gym to stop being the main topic of conversation. Who people saw running off with the tape varied according to who was telling the tale, for those who could still remember. Daniel had seen Daryl Hannah running away, Cass saw George Michael. The lack of consistency led the police to give up on any investigation.

A few weeks later, Daniel and Cass broke up. Daniel called me just after and asked me to come around. I knew Cass would hate me if she knew what I was doing, but the night of the party still played on my mind. I'd always wondered what might have happened if it had been me Daniel had fallen asleep next to instead of Cass.

"Duran," Daniel said when he opened the door. If he was happy to see me, his body language didn't say it.

"What's up?" I said, trying to keep the hope out of my voice.

We walked into the TV room. The new VHS below the television was the only change since I'd last been in there.

"I need to tell you something," Daniel said.

"I'm here for you," I said, and sat down on the lounge. He didn't sit down next to me, instead he walked over to the book shelf.

"You know our video player was a recorder too," he said, moving some books apart. My skin went cold and my body tensed, ready to run. Daniel pulled out a cassette case so I could see it.

"You recorded it?"

"Yes." He was still holding the blank cover.

"Well, let's destroy it!"

"I can't," Daniel said.

"Then give it to me, I'll do it." I didn't fancy another encounter with the malevolent spirit, but we had to stop anyone else from seeing it.

"No, I don't mean I don't *want* to," Daniel said, turning the cover so I could see it more clearly. "I mean I *can't.*"

The case was empty.

The Heartbreaker

MARK WHEATON

"Hey! Is anyone in there? Hello?"

Brady Harrington banged on the door of the gravedigger's shack as hard as he could without waking anyone in the surrounding East LA neighborhood.

"I'm sorry about the hour, but I've got to talk to Edwin. Is he here?"

The front gates were locked, so Brady had parked on a side street and jumped the fence. It was past midnight. The security office was empty as was the mortuary and chapel. He'd approached the shack because an old truck was parked alongside it.

"Hey! Is anyone in th—"

The door was flung open so fast Brady almost fell inside. An old man in coveralls squinted out at him from under a wild mane of silver hair. He had the smallest pistol Brady had ever seen in his hand.

"You crazy, son?" the old gravedigger said, voice whistling through a gap in his front teeth.

"Maybe? I got your name from a medical student in Sylmar? Jasper Choi?"

The old man eyed Brady a second longer. "I don't know any Jasper Choi."

"He said his school gets dissection cadavers from you," Brady explained before the gravedigger could close the door. "In a pinch."

"You're looking for a cadaver?" the old man asked, incredulous.

61

"No," Brady said. "I need skeletons."

The gravedigger made a sound like a dying pipe organ. It took Brady a second to realize he was laughing.

"Skeletons?" the gravedigger asked. "You into Santería or something? Hoodoo?"

"I'm an effects technician at Reliance-Majestic Studios," Brady explained. "We've got a big shoot tomorrow. All our usual skeletons are, well…busted."

"You want to use real skeletons? For a movie?"

Brady nodded. There was a long pause.

"How many are we talking about?"

"Five."

"You've got cash?"

"Yes."

The gravedigger sighed and stepped out of the shack, indicating around the dark graveyard. "Evergreen Cemetery is a potter's field. That means we've got mostly transients, unclaimed bodies—folks like that. Also means our corpses aren't embalmed. Still, it can take a decade or so for a corpse to lose its meat, so you won't want anything from the rows closest to the front."

"Back row then?" Brady asked.

"Not there, either," the gravedigger said, leading Brady to a work shed. "The skeleton itself starts to crumble after about forty years. The back rows date back ninety. You'll get nothing but dust. No, your sweet spot are bodies between twenty-five and forty-years-old. That'll be rows 1312 through about 2900."

The old man flipped on the shed's light. Shovels and picks lined the wall. Brady reached for one. The gravedigger laughed and brushed his hand away.

"Don't I need a shovel?" Brady asked.

"Five skeletons would take you two or three days with a shovel and you'd break your back," the gravedigger said, lifting a set of keys off a hook. "These are for the excavator. Take you fifteen minutes to get to the box. Stop digging when you hear a crack or a scrape. Hop in the hole. Sling a chain around the box. Haul it out."

Brady reached for the keys. The gravedigger pulled them back.

"$150 up front."

"Jasper said it was $20 apiece."

"Newbie rate," the gravedigger said. "I don't know you and I sure don't trust you."

Brady froze. He'd spent every dime he had on the last skeletons.

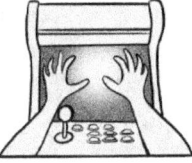

Twenty-four hours earlier...

"Roll sound!"

"Sound rolling."

"Roll cameras!"

"A camera rolling."

"B camera rolling."

"Scene 58A. Take 2. Mark."

Slates were clapped in front of each camera.

"Cue background."

The 1st AD signaled the rain-soaked extras. They stood in a mud-filled tank at the base of a polyfoam Mesoamerican temple that rose almost to the rafters of Reliance-Majestic's famed Stage 12, one of the largest soundstages in Los Angeles. As one, the extras shouted and pointed as if something was moving beneath the mud's surface.

"Cue rain."

From high above, water fired out from hundreds of tiny holes drilled into a latticework of pipes to mimic rain. Two high-velocity wind machines on the edge of the tank came on with such force the raindrops fell at an angle.

"Ready effects."

Outside of the tank, a small effects crew gathered around air compressors that would trigger the practical effects for the shots. Brady was among them, having been at the studio since four that morning rigging the gag. He'd been in Hollywood for eight months and this was his very first big screen special effect.

He'd waited his whole life for this moment.

"Action!" called the director, an old-timer named Marberg.

A stuntman in a dirigible pilot's uniform and an unfortunate wig shot out of the top of the temple. He led a stuntwoman in a white cocktail dress by the hand. They hurried down the steps to the extras.

"Cue mud," was whispered over the effect team's radio.

The "mud" was really a mixture of water, colored powders, a quarter ton of a particularly fine dirt found only in Arizona, and a hint of translucent gel to make it look like it was boiling out of the ground. It rippled out from several vents hidden around the temple's façade. The extras screamed and followed the stuntman.

Marberg watched all this from a platform above the wind machines. As the stuntman neared the edge of the tank, he signaled the 1st AD.

"Cue skeletons," the first assistant director whispered into the radio.

Whit Elcar, a longtime visual effects director whose credits dated back to the original *King Kong*, signaled Brady.

Brady triggered the compressors. Pressurized air blasted through long tubes that ran into the tank. The force launched four, spring-loaded skeletons up and out of the mud to surround and menace the stuntpeople and extras. Mud sluiced through their jaws and ribcages. Bony fingers clawed the air inches from the human actors.

Brady tapped a pedal under the hydraulics to make the skeletons twist and thrust forward. The extras shrieked and cowered.

But then a muddy jawbone fell from a skull. A bony hand went flying. Somebody laughed.

"Cut! Cut!" the 1st AD yelled over the radio.

The rain stopped and the wind machines fell quiet. Marberg called out, "Effects!"

Brady tensed. "Are we in trouble?" he asked one of the other techs.

"Nah," the tech replied. "Marberg was dragged out of retirement by the studio for this one anyway. He doesn't want anything delaying his return to his fishing boat."

Whit, a large man who favored Hawaiian shirts on set, limped toward the director's platform. When he got to the top, Marberg put a hand on Whit's shoulder and spoke a few quick words. Whit listened and nodded.

Brady glanced to the nearby makeup chairs. The film's star, Lance Caruso, was being readied to go on in place of the stuntman. But Brady's gaze fell on the makeup artist powdering the shine off his forehead, Esmeralda Pereira.

Like Brady, she was in her first year working as an assistant on the Reliance-Majestic lot. So far, they'd worked together on three commercial shoots, two music videos, a TV pilot, and now their first movie.

Esmeralda laughed mildly at something Lance said then caught Brady's gaze. She grinned and stuck her tongue out at him before returning to her work.

"I don't know what they expect," Whit said, ambling back to the effects team. "These old bones have more credits than Rin Tin Tin. We try to budget for new ones every shoot, but it's the first thing they cut. Brady, did you bring the jumble drawer?"

Brady opened one of the footlockers they'd rolled to set from the prop shop. It contained a handful of extra bones and repair wires.

"Can't fix much with that," acknowledged Whit, shrugging up at Marberg. "The mud's playing hell with the air hoses."

"We need a good close-up of Lance punching one," the 1st AD said over the radio. "Can we get that?"

Whit looked around the effects crew. No one seemed optimistic. But Brady had an idea.

"What if I went into the tank and operated one manually?" he said. "Bypassed the air pumps?"

"You mean puppeteer it?" Whit asked.

"Yeah," Brady said. "I can swivel it from below then use the wrist rods to grab at him. Should hold together until after the cut."

Whit looked skeptical.

"Might be worth a try," someone said from nearby.

The voice belonged to Reliance-Majestic's President of Production, Julia Gautrand. She wasn't the head of the studio but definitely third or fourth in the line of succession. She had a habit of arriving unannounced at film shoots from time to time.

"Could work," Whit offered.

"Great," she said, waving up at Marberg as if she'd rectified the situation herself before exiting.

Whit shot a wry grin Brady's way. "All on your shoulders now, kid."

Brady climbed into the tank to inspect the skeletons. Though none were in good shape, he salvaged three and locked them into place standing up in case they appeared in the background of the shot. He tightened the wires on the remaining one, lowered it into the mud in front of Lance's starting position, and hunched down behind it.

As cameras were placed behind and in front of the skeleton at different angles to get the closeup, Brady thought of how many movies he'd seen growing up in which skeletons looked lifeless and inert. For this shot, he wanted the bones to look so r ealistic and terrifying, kids across the country would jump out their seats when it burst into the shot.

"You ready, effects?" the 1st AD asked, eyeing Brady dubiously.

Brady gave a thumb's up.

"Places," the 1st AD called.

Lance Caruso let out an unhappy yelp as he stepped into the tank. "It's cold!" he moaned as the stunt coordinator walked him through the scene.

Once he was in place, the lead actress, Petra Ahrweiler, got in place behind him. A pair of effects assistants hurried over to add mud splatter to Petra's dress and Lance's dirigible pilot's costume. She laughed, amused. Lance snarled.

It was time to shoot.

"Roll sound!" the 1st AD called out.

"Sound rolling."

"Roll cameras!"

"A camera rolling."

"B camera rolling."

The 2nd assistant camerawoman clapped different slates in front of each lens.

"Scene 58B. Take 1. Mark."

"Cue background."

The extras prepared themselves to chase after Lance and Petra.

"Action!"

The two leads, acting out of breath, stepped in front of the camera. On cue, Brady launched his skeleton out of the mud and into frame. Its back was arched, its jaw open and teeth bared. Its fingers were splayed apart like a falcon's talons as it swooped in for the kill.

It looked terrifying.

So terrifying, a frightened Lance flinched backward, knocking Petra into the mud. She was drenched, her hair, makeup, and costume ruined.

"Cut!" the 1st AD yelled.

"Goddammit!" Lance yelled, furious.

A pair of extras helped Petra, who seemed more amused than angry, to her feet. Lance, however, stalked through the mud like an angry bull. He bumped into one of the other skeletons and grinned.

"Action!" he yelled, punching it so hard its head launched off its body.

He laughed and moved to the next skeleton. Brady waited for somebody to say something. No one spoke. Lance kicked this skeleton with such force the ribs splintered and the spine broke in half.

"Action!" he yelled again.

Brady looked to Marberg to say something. The director simply watched as if bored.

"Action!" Lance cried, delivering a roundhouse kick to the third skeleton, breaking off its left arm.

The actor looked around, seeing only one last intact skeleton. The one that had frightened him. He swaggered over, smirking at Brady as he raised his fist.

"Act—"

Brady took his foot off the skeleton's air hose hidden under the mud. There was just enough of a blast remaining inside to lurch the skeleton forward to strike Lance. The actor, already off-balance, spun around and landed in the mud as well.

Brady stared. He meant to startle the actor, not send him flying. He extended his hand to help Lance up.

"Hey, man, I'm sorry—"

"Screw you, dipshit!" Lance yelled, sending a muddy fist into Brady's face.

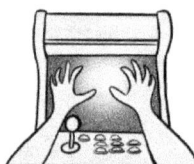

"The good news is you've still got your job," Whit said as he cleaned the cut over Brady's eye once they were back in the prop shop. "But only because that idiot punched you in front of witnesses instead of waiting for you in the parking lot like a civilized human being."

"Like you would've done?" Brady asked.

"Would've done," Whit agreed, "and *have* done."

"What's the bad news?"

"To cover up his lead actor's bad behavior and the loss of a half day of shooting, Marberg'll have to put the word out on you. No one's going to let you work production. You're confined to the prop shop. For now, at least."

Brady's eyes went wide. "But Lance ruined the shot, not me!"

"Of course! But he's the star. You know how much his last movie grossed? Thirty-three *million* dollars. Which is why you're back to go-fer duty. They need a shrub on Stage 2? You deliver it. They need a candy glass window to throw a cowboy through on Stage 9? You cut it, deliver it, and wait to see if they need a second for another take. Got it?"

"Got it," Brady said.

"But don't worry," Whit said. "Regimes change, stars fall, memories fade. Stick it out and you'll be back."

"When?"

"Ten years? Twenty?"

Brady couldn't tell if Whit was joking.

"Also, Marberg needs four replacement skeletons—let's say five to play it safe—by tomorrow morning. Seven o'clock sharp."

"Did they give us the budget for more?"

"Nope," Whit replied.

"But…that's impossible. Do they want me to quit? Or are they trying to fire me for cause?"

Whit sighed and headed out the door. "See you at seven."

Brady was furious. He hadn't worked all this time to get canned over someone else's bad behavior. He hurried to the office at the back of the prop shop, grabbed the Rolodex, and spun the cards. He plucked out the ones for the other studios' prop warehouses and pulled over the phone.

"Skeletons?" said the first person he called. "Ours are out of town on a commercial shoot. Sorry."

"Nah, we rent our bones from you guys," another replied.

"Ours are split between a witch-movie, a sci-fi actioner down in Mexico, and a Vietnam War-thing," a third said. "Can't help you."

It was the same everywhere. All in use or rented out. It made sense. It was summer after all. All of next year's movies were in production now.

"When we run low, we call up the medical supply warehouses or the nursing colleges," one helpful prop master suggested. "A lot of them will let you rent, especially since school's out. Others, you pay a couple of bucks to the right janitor and make sure they're back the next day."

Brady tried this, calling USC, UCLA, Cal State Northridge, Long Beach City College, and every other university in Los Angeles only to get turned down. It wasn't until he rang a community college in Sylmar that he found a sympathetic ear, or at least a self-interested one.

"Sure, we rent them out all the time," someone who'd

identified himself as Jasper Choi said. "How many do you need?"

"Five."

"$75 for two days."

Brady exhaled. He'd never been more relieved.

"But I'm heading home, so you'd have to pick them up right now," Jasper replied. "And you need to bring cash."

"None of that's a problem," Brady said, confirming the address before he got off the phone.

Except, it was.

Brady only had $15 in his wallet. He raided the prop shop's petty cash for another $25. He considered hitting up Whit for another $20 only to find out from another assistant he'd already gone home. Worse, the nearest grocery store had a $25 limit for cashing checks.

"Quite a stunt today," said Esmeralda from the prop shop doorway. "Meant a lot of extra work for me, though."

"I'm sorry about that," Brady replied.

"It's okay. Lance is a major dweeb. I think I know a way you could make it up to me, though."

"Anything," Brady said.

"My roommate Nadia and I won four tickets from KROQ to see Jetboy at the Whisky tonight, but we're too broke to buy drinks. If you come and buy us a round or three, all is forgiven."

Wait. Was this a date? Was Esmeralda asking me on a date?

Brady eyed her closely. Her face betrayed nothing.

"Would love to," he said.

"Excellent. Meet us out front around nine?"

Esmeralda took off leaving Brady to run the math. It was six now. He had time to get to the North Valley, pick up the skeletons, and drop them back at the prop show but not enough time to get them camera-ready before he'd have to meet Esmeralda on the Sunset Strip. He'd have to return to the lot after the show and pull an all-nighter.

No problemo.

He jumped in his car, hit two grocery stores, then raced up

to Sylmar. He arrived at the community college after dark. A kid in a lab coat two sizes too big was waiting in the parking lot with a rack of five bulky garment bags.

"Is $70 okay?" Brady asked, holding back a twenty for drinks.

The student rolled his eyes and took the bills. "These gotta be back here day after tomorrow, okay?"

"Sure," Brady said. "By the way, I called all over looking for these. Where do you get them?"

"We do a lot of cadaver dissections—bodies donated to science, you know—then melt the flesh off after using a solution of ammonia and concentrated hydrogen peroxide," Jasper said matter-of-factly. "But every so often we need an extra skull or something. That's when we use the Evergreen solution."

"What's that?"

"Evergreen Cemetery in East LA," Jasper said. "It's a Potter's Field, baby. Unclaimed bodies as far as the eye can see. Guy named Edwin's my hook-up."

"Good to know," Brady said, trying not to sound as disturbed as he felt.

Brady raced the bones back to the studio with just enough time to get to Sunset. Since he'd moved to LA from Indiana, he'd only found time to drive the notorious, neon-soaked strip. He couldn't wait to finally see a show there.

He parked on a side street in the hills over Sunset then hurried down to meet Esmeralda. To his surprise, she was alone.

"Nadia's manager made her double-shift last minute, so it's you and me," she explained. "Should we go in?"

So. It was a date.

Brady followed her inside the Whisky a Go Go, a cavernous, two-story club with a small stage at the back and a

71

second-floor balcony. He bought them both beers and they headed upstairs to watch the band from above.

"Do you like Jetboy?" Esmeralda asked.

"Never heard of them," Brady admitted.

"Oh, me neither," Esmeralda said. "But hey, free tickets!"

They chatted as the band set up. Esmeralda was a rarity, a native-born Los Angeleno who'd attended North Hollywood High before trying to break into movies.

"I'm doing hair and makeup now, but I want to get into creature effects," she said. "Like, my dream job would be to work on a new *Star Trek* show or something. Every week you're making some cool new alien. You?"

"Same," Brady agreed. "My mom was a teacher and used to watch monster movies while she graded. I grew up watching *Wolf Man, The Fly, Quatermass*—all that. I was sculpting my own monsters by eight or nine."

"My sister and I did that, too," Esmeralda said. "My dad had a Super 8 camera and we'd steal it to make little movies. Every time we took the film to get developed, the lady at Fox Photo gave us the craziest looks. My dad didn't mind, though. He loved monsters, too. Especially Rodan."

Jetboy took the stage a few minutes later. Everyone in the club went crazy for their ear-shattering blast of punk-metal. People danced, sang along, and screamed.

Except for Brady and Esmeralda.

After the third song, the two eyed each other.

"Want to take off?" Brady asked.

"Definitely," Esmeralda replied.

She'd taken the bus to the Strip, so Brady offered her a ride home. On the way to his car, they joked about how much hairspray and yellow dye Esmeralda would need to replicate the singer's stratospheric hairdo. Their conversation continued after a detour to Canter's for cherry colas and rugelach before finishing off the night.

They commiserated about the insane hours, the low pay, and the energy and excitement of working in Hollywood ("especially for one of the greats like Whit Elcar," Brady said) that made it worthwhile. At the end of the night, Brady drove

Esmeralda home where they spent another twenty minutes chatting before she finally got out.

"Tonight was great," she said.

"We'll have to do it again sometime," Brady agreed.

"Definitely," she said, leaning back in to give him a peck on the cheek. "See you in a few hours."

Brady looked at the clock. It was almost midnight. He had maybe six hours to get five gleaming white skeletons aged and temp-dyed to get ready for the day's shoot.

He waved good-bye to Esmeralda, raced back to the Reliance-Majestic lot, and pulled up to the prop shop's towering front doors. He had just hung the last of the skeleton-filled garment bags on a rack when he smelled something burning.

The warehouse was filled with volatile chemicals and gases. A fire would be deadly. He whirled around looking for smoke but saw none.

Instead, he heard laughter.

"Hello?" he asked the darkness.

Silence. Then a giggle. Then a crash.

"Hey, hey, yeah, sorry," a male voice said followed by gales of female laughter.

A thirty-something man in an expensive suit, tie wrapped around his head like a sweatband, emerged from the back of the warehouse. It took Brady a minute to recognize him. It was Paul Staggs, a VP of Production at the studio. Staggs was famous for two things—being promoted from assistant to head of his own division at a rival studio faster than anyone in Hollywood history, then getting fired as quickly for his outrageous drug use.

He'd cleaned up, cashed in a favor, and landed a job at Reliance-Majestic. Most assumed he'd squander the opportunity. Two hit movies and the launch of a successful franchise later and he was back on top.

If the bitter stench of freebased cocaine in the air was any indication, his drug habit was back, too.

"Sorry, we couldn't find a match," Paul said, holding up a pack of cigarettes as two young women dressed for a night on the town emerged from the darkness behind him. "Thought there'd be something in here."

That explained the smell. Staggs must've used an acetylene torch to cook with. *Brilliant.*

"You can't really do that here," Brady said. "You could blow this whole place up."

This made Paul and his guests laugh even harder.

"No, no, I get it," he said. "We'll get out of your hair. Sorry."

But as Paul escorted his dates to the prop shop door, he turned back to Brady. "Wait. Aren't you the guy who punched out Lance Caruso?"

Brady sighed. "That's me."

"Well done!" the exec said, extending his hand. "He deserved it. Anyway, nice to meet you."

The smell returned to Brady. Stronger now. He looked over to the acetylene torch. A shallow pool of blue flame was slowly expanding under a pair of worktables on their way to a jug of industrial solvent.

"Down!" Brady yelled.

An enormous green and yellow fireball erupted from around the jug. Brady tackled Paul and the women, throwing them to the ground as the flames passed by overhead. The women shrieked. Paul looked dazed.

Brady stayed in place for a ten count then sat up. The fireball had gone out. He saw a couple of drop cloths were still burning, but nothing el—

"What's in those?" Paul asked

He pointed to the garment bags. They were on fire, burning with such intensity the bags soon burst open, releasing burning skeletons onto the floor as if from amniotic sacs. The women screamed in horror.

"No!" Brady yelled.

The warehouse's sprinkler system finally kicked on, dousing everything.

It was too late. The skeletons were destroyed.

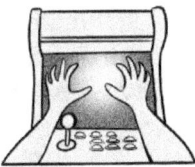

"I am *so* sorry," Paul told Brady a few minutes later as the lot's fire team put out the last remnants of the blaze. "Hope I didn't make too much work for you."

The exec tucked a hundred-dollar bill in Brady's shirt pocket and put a finger to his lips.

"I owe you," Paul said, then stepped away to rejoin his companions.

Brady went back to skeletons. There was no salvaging them. It wasn't bad enough that they had burned; the heat had melted the vinyl of the garment bags which now dripped over them like a thick coat of paint. Smoke slithered out of the eye sockets of one of the skulls as if to mock him.

It was past two in the morning.

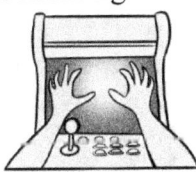

Which is how Brady came to find himself in a dark cemetery across town. It was only when the gravedigger had started walking away when Brady remembered the hundred Paul slipped him.

"I have this," he offered the gravedigger.

The gravedigger stared at the bill scornfully. "I'll regard this as a down payment. Another hundred by the end of the week."

"Agreed," Brady said.

The gravedigger tossed him the excavator key.

It took Brady twenty minutes to roll the heavy piece of equipment to one of the rows suggested by the gravedigger. He pushed the excavator past the first dozen or so graves, marked only by numbers on small tin placards, before lining it up at the next one.

Sorry about this, 2813, he thought.

He keyed the ignition and the machine roared to life with an oily belch. Brady prayed no one in the surrounding neighborhood wondered why someone was at work in the cemetery this time of night.

Raising the scoop, he dug in.

It turned out that every movie he'd ever seen that showed gravedigging as a difficult, laborious task had it wrong. With the right tools, it was easy. It took only minutes to reach the simple wooden coffin buried below. Before long, he had it fully excavated, chained to the scoop, and hauled up to the surface.

It had barely been half an hour since he'd hopped the fence.

He plucked a flashlight and crowbar from the excavator's equipment pouch and got to work opening the coffin's lid. He hesitated at the last nail, fearing what might lurk inside. He shook this off, popped the lid, and looked down not at the loose pile of bones he expected but a cloth shroud tied at the top. When the twine proved too hard to untie, he cut through the cloth with the tip of the crowbar and tore it the length of the coffin.

Inside was a human skeleton wearing the tattered remnants of a shirt, pants, and shoes. From what Brady could tell, the skeleton was complete and in good shape.

Perfect.

He set the shrouded body aside, closed the coffin, and lowered it back into the grave. Using the excavator, he poured the dirt back in and moved on to the next grave. Fifteen minutes later, he added a second shrouded skeleton to the pile.

Twenty minutes after that, a third.

The eastern sky began to purple with the coming dawn. Brady hurried to claim a fourth and fifth body. He didn't even bother opening the shrouds of the last two. He simply popped the coffin lids, yanked out the bodies, resealed the boxes, and put them back in the ground.

When he was done, he returned the excavator, dragged the bodies two at a time—skeletons were fairly heavy, who knew?—to the fence and slipped them through. Half an hour later, he was back on the Reliance-Majestic lot, offloading the shrouded remains into the prop shop. If the condition of the first skeleton was any indication, he didn't think they'd need much beyond wiring the bones together. He could do a hurry-up job that would last the day then come back and do something more permanent that night.

By 6:45, he'd wired up the first four skeletons and was feeling rather good about himself. He'd pulled off the impossible. He grabbed a pair of wire clippers, snipped off the twine at the top of the last shroud, and opened it up.

A noxious stench erupted from the shroud, billowing into Brady's nose and mouth. His eyes watered and his lungs burned. Hives boiled up from beneath the skin of his arms, face, and neck. His body shook violently as if it was trying to evacuate the poisonous fumes.

"*Gah*," he exclaimed.

He stumbled out of the warehouse, gulping in the fresh morning air to soothe his throat. It was as if he'd inhaled mustard gas. He hurried to a nearby water spigot and fired cold water into his face. He guzzled down several mouthfuls then let it pour down his skin.

What was that?

Brady staggered back into the prop shop, head throbbing, and opened all the doors and windows. The cloud dissipated. Still, he waited a few more minutes before returning to the worktable.

He took a deep breath then opened the shroud all the way. Inside was not a skeleton but a *corpse*.

One that, to use the gravedigger's words, hadn't lost its meat.

"Jesus Christ!" Brady exclaimed, heart racing.

What was a recent corpse doing in an old grave?

He gingerly moved the shroud back to look for a tag or other identifier but couldn't find one. The clothing the body wore—a white t-shirt, red shorts, men's red Nike sneakers—also suggested a much more recent demise than the 1940s or 50s.

He noticed something wedged in the body's chest. It was a short piece of metal, possibly brass, stabbed directly through the dead man's breastbone.

Was this man...murdered?

"Phew, what's that smell?" asked Whit.

Brady had barely enough time to pull the shroud over the decomposing corpse before the effects director was beside him.

"Um, I..." Brady stammered.

"Oh, yeah," Whit said, spying a singed support column. "Guard at the front gate told me about the fire. Also said, no matter what excuse you made for him, Paul Staggs started it. Is that right?"

Brady shrugged. Whit laughed.

"He's a moron," Whit declared. "Now, you got my skeletons?"

"All four, ready to go."

"Thought I said, 'five'?"

Brady sighed, trying to remember the solution Jasper said would remove flesh from bones. If he had another hour, he could somehow prep the fifth body as well.

Whit grinned. "Aw, never mind. This is enough of a rabbit to pluck out of your hat for one night. They look good, too. Pulled an all-nighter, huh?"

"Yep."

"Take the morning off and get some rest. Be back here by lunch, though."

"You got it. Thanks, Whit."

After Whit was gone, Brady returned to the half-decomposed corpse. He considered stashing it in his car but worried about driving around the City of Angels with a dead body in his trunk. He had to hide it in the prop shop until he could return to Evergreen and consign its mysteries back into the earth.

He had no idea what had happened but knew for certain he wanted no part of it.

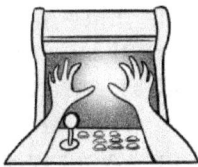

Brady lived in a tiny, second-floor apartment in the heart of the San Fernando Valley about a twenty-minute drive from the studio. He'd been up almost thirty hours straight by the time he reached his apartment door. He made it as far as his bedroom before sleep overtook him and he collapsed onto the bed.

His slumber was cruelly interrupted soon after by a ringing phone. He opened his eyes long enough to raise the handset and bring it down again, hanging up on the call. It was only when his eyes were closed again that he realized there was a young man sitting on the edge of his bed.

Brady sat up.

"Hi there," the young man said.

Brady screamed.

"Sorry," the intruder said, raising his hands defensively. "Didn't mean to startle you."

Brady jumped out of bed. "How'd you get in here?"

"I was hoping you could tell me that," the young man said. "Must've been a crazy night, huh?"

"I don't know you," Brady said.

"You sure? Maybe we had a one-night thing?"

Brady eyed the man closely. He couldn't have been more than twenty-three or twenty-four, had a deep tan, shaggy brown hair, and a mustache, and wore red shorts, a white t-shirt, and red Nike sneakers. Brady had never seen him before in his life.

"Nope."

"Oof. Sorry, friend," the man said. "Starting to think I wandered into the wrong apartment."

Brady realized he'd probably forgotten to lock his front door.

"Okay, well, maybe it's about time for you to leave," Brady suggested.

"That's the tricky part," the young man said with a light chuckle. "And why I think there might be drugs involved? I slipped out your front door earlier only to end up in your bathroom. I tried to climb out the bedroom window to the alley below only to appear in your kitchen."

"Okay. *Weird*," Brady said, worried his visitor was bonkers. "You don't have an ID on you or anything? No wallet?"

"Nada. Zilch."

Brady nodded. His gaze fell on the young man's red Nike sneakers. Then traveled to the red shorts. And white t-shirt.

Brady's eyes went wide.

No.

"Question," Brady said, reaching out to the young man. "You wouldn't happen to have some kind of injury? Maybe to your chest?"

The young man recoiled. "What're you doing?" he asked.

Brady missed his chest, but his fingers touched the young man's arm.

Or, well, *didn't*. His hand passed right through his visitor's skin, muscles, and bones as if there was nothing but empty space. Only, the space was so cold it was as if Brady had stuck his hand in a bucket of ice.

"What just happened?" the young man cried. "Why did your hand do that?"

Brady sat back down on his bed. Hard.

"I can't believe I'm saying this, but I think you're a ghost," Brady said.

The young man burst out laughing. "A *ghost?* You're crazy. There are about a hundred possible reasons for all that's happening before you get to, 'I'm a ghost.'"

Brady reached out to the young man again. This time, the intruder went to bat his hand away.

His fingers passed right through Brady.

"Why can't I touch you?" the young man asked in a panicked voice. "This *is* drugs."

Brady didn't know what to say. He looked at the young man's clothes again and realized he was holding his breath.

"I think I found your body last night," Brady said. "And I think you'd been stabbed in the chest."

"Are you saying you killed me?" the ghost asked. "Is that why I can't leave here? Am I haunting your apartment? Am I haunting *you*?"

"No!" Brady cried. "Well, no to the first thing."

"So…you randomly happened upon my murdered body?" the ghost asked skeptically.

"Um, not quite," Brady said.

"You should probably explain," the ghost suggested.

Brady hesitated. He worried that unloading his tale of graverobbing to the ghost might make it unleash some unholy, demonic revenge against him. Still, he figured he owed the ghost—or spectral invention born from his overtired imagination—an answer. He related the tale in as much detail as he could provide, the ghost listening with a thoughtful expression on his face.

"Hm," the ghost said at the end.

"What?" Brady asked.

"Two things. First, your story shook at least one of my memories loose," the ghost said. "I think I was an actor when I was alive."

Brady stared at the ghost, trying to remember if he'd seen him in anything.

"Second, you robbed five graves, right? Yet, I'm the only ghost that's appeared. If I were murdered, that'd make sense."

"How so?"

"Isn't that how these hauntings work? Ghosts are those who were wronged in life coming back to put right their unfinished business?" the ghost asked. "And since you're the one who opened my grave, you're the one who has to help me solve my own murder."

"That's a stretch," Brady said.

"Oh, yeah? Then why aren't I haunting my murderer?"

The ghost had Brady on this count. He didn't know.

"Before we go crazy are you positive it was me you dug up?" the ghost asked.

"Pretty sure," Brady said. "Pretty sure. Same shoes, shorts, same shirt. The watch is different, though."

The ghost looked at the watch as if remembering something. He took it off his wrist and flipped it over. On the back was an inscription.

Jake. Too late to turn back now. Love, Jules.

That's my name," the ghost said. "I'm...Jake."

"Jake-what?" Brady asked.

The ghost shook his head. "I can't remember. But hey, our first clue!"

The phone rang again. Brady answered before the second ring. It took him a moment to recognize the voice of one of the other effects assistants on the other end. What the young man said chilled him to the bone.

Whit was dead. He'd collapsed outside the prop shop after getting breakfast with Marberg's crew. The studio medic was by his side in under a minute. An ambulance arrived in under five. Neither could do a thing. The old effects director was dead of a massive heart attack before he hit the pavement.

Brady hung up the phone, grabbed his keys, and was out the door and on his way to the lot in under a minute. He wanted to be alone, wanted to clear his head after the double shock of Whit's death and Jake's appearance.

This didn't happen.

Everywhere Brady went, Jake was made to follow.

Though Brady left him behind in the apartment, Jake appeared outside on the landing as Brady ran down the stairs to the apartment's courtyard. When Brady reached his car, Jake materialized on the sidewalk. As Brady raced away down the street, Jake emerged from thin air into the passenger seat.

"I guess I am haunting you," Jake said.

They reached the lot in fifteen minutes flat. They were almost to the prop shop when Brady saw Harvey Marberg waiting for him.

"Hold back," Brady whispered to Jake. "I don't want him to see you."

"Okay," Jake said.

No matter how much distance they put between each other, Jake kept vanishing from one spot only to appear again at Jake's side.

"Sorry!" Jake said.

Brady turned to say something to Jake only for Marberg to approach, reaching out to shake Brady's hand.

"I knew Whit almost fifty years," Marberg said. "It's cold comfort, but he died doing what he loved. I know you really appreciated his work."

"I did," Brady said, shooting a glance Jake's way.

"And he yours," Marberg added, scrunching his brow as he followed Brady's gaze only to see nothing.

"He can't see me," Jake said. "This is a very localized haunting."

"Now, we both know I can't have you on set anymore, but Whit's absence creates a vacuum," Marberg continued.

"Blaaaaaaaah!" Jake said, sticking his tongue out at the oblivious old director. "Boooooooo!"

"Cut it out!" Brady hissed.

"What's that?" Marberg asked.

"Nothing, nothing," Brady insisted. "You were saying?"

"Um," Marberg said, as if having second thoughts. "I was hoping you might come back to Stage 12 in the morning to oversee set-up. We can't have you there officially, but I think I can arrange a production bonus."

"*Brrrrraaaaaaaapp*," Jake said directly into Marberg's ear.

"That'd be amazing," Brady said, stifling a laugh.

"Great," Marberg replied, though confused. "He had a lot of faith in you."

"Thank you," Brady said.

As soon as Marberg was gone, Jake turned to Brady. "You were close to this Whit-guy?"

"Sort of," Brady admitted. "He was my mentor. Gave me a lot of crap but was kind of the first friend I'd made in Los

Angeles."

"I'm sorry," Jake said.

"You can't...you know, see him, can you? Like, his ghost?" Brady asked.

Jake shook his head. "Sorry."

"It's okay," Brady said. "Let's find your body. I stowed it in a footlocker."

Jake stopped short. "You put my body in a footlocker?"

"Sorry, I was exhausted," Brady said. "Not like you can breathe anyway."

"True."

Brady looked from one end of the prop shop to the other but couldn't find the right footlocker. He kicked himself for being in such a hurry the night before and hiding it so well.

"What did it look like?" Jake asked, trying to help.

"One of the green footlockers with yellow latches," Brady said. "It has to be here somewhere."

"Are you looking for your monster prosthetic?" asked one of the other effects assistants as he ducked into the prop shop to grab a toolkit.

"'Monster prosthetic?'" Brady asked.

"Yeah, the gnarly body for Shelley Jensch's slasher movie on Stage 7," the assistant said. "I saw it in action. It looks amazing."

Brady blanched and turned to Jake. The ghost looked back, aghast.

"They're using my corpse in a horror movie?" Jake asked.

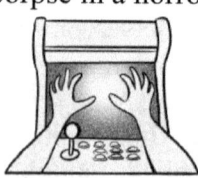

Two teenagers stumbled back from an open grave. The coffin they were after burst open, sending up a shower of splinters. As the teens shrank back in horror, a maggot-filled monstrosity pulled itself out of the ground. Live worms wove in and out of eye sockets and mouth. A dull green-gray ooze seeped down its neck. In its hand was a fire axe, edge encrusted with what was meant to look like dried blood.

Hidden behind the creature crouched two puppeteers, one manipulating the beast's arms, the other levering it up from the grave as the camera rolled.

"Is that what happened when you found me last night?" Jake asked, mortified.

"Pretty much," Brady whispered.

When the monster had risen as high as it could, the film's director, Shelley Jensch, called, "Cut! Looks great, y'all!"

The tension of the moment broke. Everyone relaxed. The actors moved away to get their makeup touched up. The effects teams carefully lowered the "prosthetic" back into the grave. An animal wrangler dropped the live worms back into their terrarium.

Jensch grinned over at Brady. "Great work on the prosthetic, Harrington," she said. "Couldn't tell this was a refurbish job at all. Looked brand new. You really went the extra mile."

"Thanks," Brady said.

"Shouldn't I get credit?" Jake asked, pretending to be miffed. "I'm the one who ran five miles every morning on an 1800-calorie-a-day meal plan."

"Mind if I take a look at it?" Brady asked. "Want to make sure it's holding together."

"Sure," Shelley said. "I was sorry to hear about Whit this morning. I grew up memorizing the names of horror movie makeup artists. Seeing his name in the credits always meant no matter how bad the movie, at least the creature would look great."

"Same for me."

Jensch turned her attention to her cinematographer. Brady led Jake to the waiting body. The clothes had been changed and the shoes removed, but the shattered breastbone remained. Brady put his hand into the ribcage, looking for the piece of metal.

"Not sure I can put into words how weird it is watching you do that," Jake said.

"You guys remove a piece of metal from the chest of this

thing?" Brady asked the effects artists.

"No, but you can check the footlocker," one replied, indicating the nearby box.

Brady looked inside. The chunk of metal wasn't there either.

"It's gone?" Jake asked.

"I probably dropped it in the prop shop," Brady said. "We'll find it."

"Doubt there'll be any fingerprints on it," Jake said. "Or some tell-tale initials that'll lead to my killer."

"No, but it's a start," Brady said. "Anything else coming back to you? Last name? Potential enemies?"

"No, but I do remember all this," Jake said, indicating around the soundstage. "Being on a movie set. You've got some cool new toys here in the future—better radios, more elaborate lenses, and effects—but a lot's the same. I miss this energy."

"Picture's up," the 1st AD called. "Places, effects."

Brady stepped away from Jake's body-turned-movie-monster. The worms were returned. Mud was smeared on the monster's hands. The teen actors got into place as everyone prepared for the next take.

"More fear this time," Jensch said. "Real 'drop your popcorn' moment, okay?"

The actors nodded. Sound and camera rolled. The slates were clapped.

"Action," the director called.

The prosthetic monster slowly lumbered out of the grave a second time, crawling toward the teenagers as they squirmed away. The effects artists moved its head, but it looked stiff and unrealistic. Jake grunted in frustration.

Then vanished.

Brady looked around for the ghost but didn't see him.

"Jake?" he whispered.

Suddenly, he felt a sharp pain in his stomach and doubled over. He gritted his teeth to not cry out and ruin the shot even as his body spasmed and twitched.

He was in agony.

In front of the camera, however, the creature emerging from the grave seemed to swell with new life. It squared its jaw and inhaled deeply as it clambered after its intended victims. The muck around its mouth fell away as it bared its teeth. It reared up and raised the fire axe.

The teen actors scrambled back, terrified for real this time.

What had been little more than a dummy moments before was now a living, breathing monster. The scene, though seconds in length, was scarier than anything Brady had ever witnessed in real life.

"Cut!" Jensch cried, delighted. "Well done, effects!"

The crew applauded. The teen actors looked relieved to have the scene over. Brady's pain slowly abated.

Jake appeared next to him, smiling at the applause.

"Was that you?" Brady asked, amazed.

"Should probably keep a checklist of all my ghostly abilities," Jake said, then noticed how sick Brady looked. "Are you okay? You look more like a corpse than I do."

"Yeah, just tired," Brady said.

"Every actor in Hollywood is going to learn to fear you," Jensch said, walking up to Brady.

"Marberg's editors were showing everyone their dailies last night. The look of terror on Lance Caruso's face when you jumped at him with that skeleton was the most realistic acting I've seen from him yet. Thanks again."

Brady nodded and looked to Jake, expecting him to lap up the praise. Instead, he looked stunned.

"What is it?" Brady asked once they were alone.

"Lance Caruso," Jake said. "I know that name. Who is he?"

"This huge actor. Did you know him when you were alive? Or remember seeing him in movies?"

"Not sure," Jake admitted.

A production assistant called over to Brady. "Julia's looking for you."

There was only one Julia on the lot, so there was no confusion as to who he meant.

"Great. Thanks."

Brady glanced back to Jake, but the ghost was still lost in thought.

Julia Gautrand's office was so large Brady wondered if it had once been a conference room. It had a seating area near the front door, an area in the center where presentations could be made, then finally Julia's desk all the way at the back wall. Her walls were devoid of the usual self-congratulatory framed certificates, photos, and movie posters found on most Hollywood exec's office walls.

Instead, she hung real art including what Brady thought was a Basquiat with a Haring alongside it. A huge, museum-quality Grace Hartigan painting dominated the room from where it hung behind Julia's desk.

"Mr. Harrington," Julia said, getting to her feet as her assistant ushered Brady in. "I'm so sorry about Whit. I've spent the morning reaching out to his entire team. Many have commented on how much he liked you."

"Thank you," Brady replied. "The feeling was mutual."

He glanced to Jake, but the ghost had wondered over to the windows and was looking somberly out over the lot.

"You certainly share his work ethic," Julia continued. "You were the first to jump in the mud yesterday and Shelley showed me the monster you fixed up for her grave scene today. You really put that together in a single night?"

Brady gulped. "Yep."

"Great work," Julia said. "If you can see to it you don't punch anymore of my stars, you'll have a great future here. Can you do that?"

"Yep," Brady repeated.

"Fantastic. Go to it."

Brady turned to leave only to see Jake staring at the studio boss.

"*Julia?*" Jake shouted. "Brady, it's Julia! Can you hear

me? Julia, it's Jake! *Jules!*"

The Jules from the watch? Brady wondered.

Jake hurried to Julia's side, throwing his arms around her. She shivered.

"Oof, did you feel that?" she asked.

"Feel what?" Brady asked.

"Never mind," Julia said.

"We went to the same small-town Minnesota high school, both dreaming of Hollywood," Jake explained. "Strange to see her in a suit now. She was crazy back then. She was in a band, like this all-girl version of the Stooges or something."

"Is there something else, Mr. Harrington?" Julia asked as she returned to her desk.

"Nope, sorry," Brady said, heading for the door.

"She might know what happened to me!" Jake exclaimed. "You really want me haunting you forever?"

Brady hadn't considered this.

"Come on, Brady!" Jake said.

"Actually, there's one more thing," Brady said, turning back.

"What's that?" Julia asked.

"Were you in a band? Back in Minnesota? Like, a girl band?"

Julia's eyes went wide. "Where did you hear that?"

"Somebody mentioned it on set."

"Impossible. Who?" She sounded more curious than annoyed.

"He didn't say his name. Only that he'd known you as 'Jules' and the two of you came out here together. 'Too late to turn back now!'"

Anger flashed across her face. "Is this some kind of sick joke?" she demanded.

"No, no," Brady protested. "He...he seemed to have known you."

"Jules," Jake said, though she couldn't hear him.

"That's not funny," Julia said. "Of all days how can you make light of something like that?"

"I'm...I'm sorry," Brady said.

89

"Jules, it's me," Jake whispered. "Come on. You have to hear me." He turned to Brady. "Tell her we used to put away a lot of pizza and beer at Bard's talking about *The Wizard of Oz* and how we wanted to make movies like that."

"I'm not going to tell her that," Brady said.

"What?" Julia asked.

"Nothing."

"No, tell me," Julia said. "Is it something else this mystery asshole said to you on set? I'd love to know the rumors you men spread."

"Please, Brady," Jake pleaded.

Brady took a deep breath. "He said you two used to put away a lot of pizza and beer at Bard's and talk about *The Wizard of Oz*."

Julia looked stricken. Tears formed in her eyes and she turned away.

"Get out of my office," she whispered. "*Now.*"

Brady hurried to the door, trying to usher Jake after him. The ghost stood in the doorway staring at his old friend until Brady was halfway down the hall and whatever force was at work between them yanked Jake to Brady's side.

"Thanks for trying," Jake muttered.

Brady nodded but said nothing.

They spent the rest of the day on Stage 7 keeping an eye on the prosthetic even as a stuntman in makeup was brought on to play the monster in wide shots. Brady was silent for much of this, the proximity of Jake making him feel oddly claustrophobic.

Jake seemed to notice and walked as far as he could from the soundstage, eyeing various people and even the new cars that passed through the lot, yet always to return if Brady so much as moved a few feet to his left or right.

"It almost feels like a prank," Jake observed at one point.

"'Welcome back to life! It's the future! You just can't talk to anyone, can't touch anyone, and you're on the short leash of a total stranger, about fifty feet at most. Other than that, enjoy!'"

Brady sympathized, realizing he had it a lot better than the ghost. "This isn't forever," he remarked, praying he was right.

When the shoot wrapped for the day, the monster no longer needed, Brady packed it into the footlocker and hurried it back to the prop shop.

"Let's look for that chunk of metal," he told Jake.

They scoured the warehouse for the second time that day. Brady opened drawers and cabinets, turned over tables, took down boxes, and climbed into the rafters. He jogged out to the other stages in case it accidentally went out with other props but still came up dry.

"I wonder if it got thrown out," Brady said as the pair stared down at Jake's body and the shattered breastbone.

"Could it have happened after I died?" Jake asked. "During the burial?"

"Dunno," Brady admitted. "Speaking of which, do you have any memory that might explain why you'd have been buried in an unmarked grave?"

"Zilch. That's why I wish we could've talked to Julia more. Was that reaction because she was remembering I was dead? Or, if my body went unidentified and unclaimed, could I have been missing? Or still be missing?"

Brady hadn't considered this. It seemed plausible. "We'll approach her again. But maybe pick our moment a bit better."

Jake nodded, holding his hand over his body's shattered ribcage. "When I took control of my body earlier, I managed to turn my head a little and move my arms, nothing more," Jake said. "But maybe if I tried to access whatever's left of my mind in there…?"

"The skull's empty, right?" Brady asked.

"Yeah, and there's no muscle mass left on the bone, either," Jake said.

"Touché," Brady said. "Give it a try."

Jake vanished from view. For a moment, Jake's body

remained still. Then, its arms slowly began to move. It grabbed the edges of the footlocker and tried to lift itself out the same as it emerged from the grave on Stage 7.

"Whoa," Brady said. "You remember anything?"

The words were barely out of Brady's mouth when the pain came. It arrived first behind his eyes, a red-hot burning behind his brow. His muscles tightened, locking him in a rigid pose as he gnashed his teeth.

Jake, or whatever was present of Jake, didn't seem to notice. The body wasn't quite standing but had managed to pull itself up onto one of the worktables. The upper half of its torso was splayed out on the tabletop, its hands gripping the edges as its legs bent and bowed, unable to balance the weight.

"*Gah*," Brady gasped, barely able to breathe. His chest squeezed in on itself, forcing out all the oxygen. "*Jake...stop...*"

The ghost still didn't hear him. As the half-skeletal corpse took its first couple of steps along the worktable, Brady fell to his knees, hands clawing at his throat.

"*Jake*," he whispered.

Brady collapsed face first onto the warehouse floor.

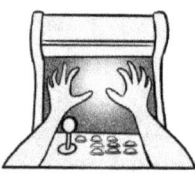

"Brady! Oh my God! Wake up!"

Brady's eyes opened slowly. It couldn't have been more than a few minutes later. Jake's corpse was in a heap on the floor. Jake, in ghost form, stood over him, a panicked look on his face. He had both hands pressed against Brady's temples; the icy touch reviving his friend.

"What happened?" Jake asked.

"Something about when you merge with your body," Brady said. "It happened on set, too. It makes me sick."

"That was more than sick," Jake said, alarmed. "You looked like you were dying."

"Felt like it, too."

"Let's not do that again," Jake said.

"Agreed. I think we could use some professional help," Brady admitted.

"Brady! What happened?" It was Esmeralda. She hurried into the prop shop and kneeled beside him. "Are you okay?"

"Yeah, was packing up for the day and slipped."

"You sure?" she asked, helping him to his feet. "You look awful."

"It's been a long day," Brady admitted.

"I can imagine," Esmeralda said. "I heard about Whit. It really sucks. I'm sure everyone's saying stuff like, 'He died doing what he loved,' but it's Hollywood. No one should have to work themselves to death for the movies."

"Your girlfriend's smart," Jake said.

Brady was about to say she wasn't his girlfriend then remembered Esmeralda couldn't hear him.

"Anyway, I know today was pretty bad," Esmeralda continued, "but I wanted to tell you again what a nice time I had last night."

"I did, too."

"Good, because I need a favor," Esmeralda said. "I've got a job on Saturday, an *After School Special* shooting at a high school down on Melrose. Only thing is, my roommate's borrowing my car and with all the transfers, the bus ride home would be almost two hours. And that's with all my makeup equipment. Think I could get a ride? Buy you a taco!"

"Could totally do that," Brady said.

"Great! Awesome. I'll be done around eight. Thanks."

Esmeralda headed out with a wave. Brady watched her go, feeling better than he had all day.

"She's good," Jake said. "Crafty."

"What do you mean?"

"She managed to ask you out on a date without you ever realizing what she was doing. Even better, she got you to say, 'yes.'"

"She asked me for a favor," Brady corrected.

"You're picking her up on Saturday night and going for

93

tacos."

"Well, okay."

Jake sighed. "What was the thing last night?"

"Her roommate won tickets to a concert but they were broke, so she invited me as long as I bought their drinks."

"But the roommate never showed, right?" Jake asked.

"How'd you know?" Brady asked.

"Being a ghost gives you psychic powers," Jake replied.

"Really?"

"I'm kidding. She's as into you as you are to her."

Brady looked down. "How do I tell her that?" he asked.

"Instead of, I don't know, being the guy who pulls up on Saturday night all, 'Uh, thought I'd wait and find out where you wanted to go, babe?' maybe come up with a solid evening that shows you have at least some insight into what she might enjoy?" Jake suggested. "I mean, given the amount of effort she's put into asking you on these stealth-dates already, you could at least try to reciprocate."

"That feels like good advice," Brady said.

"You're welcome," Jake said. "Now what were you saying about us getting some professional help?"

One of the first stores Brady had seen when he'd moved to Los Angeles was an intriguingly named bookstore called The Psychic Eye. It was open late as it not only catered to night owls but also offered fortune tellers available to read late into the evening.

Brady and Jake debated what to do with Jake's body, eventually deciding to stash it in the props warehouse, though this time locked up in a cabinet.

"I swear to God, if we come back tomorrow and I've already booked my second lead in a horror movie..." Jake said.

"Eh, you loved it," Brady countered.

Jake grunted in grudging agreement.

They arrived at the Psychic Eye at dusk, finding a parking space directly out front. The store was a colorful menagerie of not only books but candles, religious icons from around the world, and several statues. It was a wonderland at the intersection of religion and the occult.

"Whoa," Jake said as they entered. "Your apartment could really use all of this."

A chipper young man with Clint on his nametag nodded to them from behind the counter. "Evening. Help you find anything?"

"Books on ghosts?" Brady said.

"We've got a whole section on the paranormal," Clint said, coming around to lead Brady through the shelves. "Interested in a specific haunting? Spectral phenomena in general?"

"Different types of ghosts," Brady said.

"*Hm*," Clint said, looking across the titles. "We have some reference books that might work…"

"Clint? I'll take this one."

A young woman in maybe her late teens emerged from a curtained-off room. She smiled first at Clint.

Then Brady.

Then *Jake*.

"Sure thing, Yvette," Clint said as if this wasn't an entirely uncommon occurrence. "Holler if you need anything."

The young woman, Yvette, gestured for Brady and Jake to follow her into an alcove in back. "Welcome to the Psychic Eye. There is no judgment. Everyone is welcome here."

"Can she see me?" Jake asked.

"Did your friend ask something?" Yvette said, indicating for Brady to take a seat opposite her at a small table.

Brady and Jake exchanged a surprised look.

"He asked if you could see him," Brady replied.

"Not really?" Yvette admitted. "I detect his presence, but that's all. You can see him, though? And talk to him?"

"As if he's right beside me."

"That's rare," Yvette said, smiling. "My grandmother had encounters like that but not me. Not yet anyway. So, what

95

brings you here tonight?"

As much as Brady wanted to hold certain things back, he didn't think that'd get them anywhere. So, he laid out the whole story from start to finish. She'd said no judgment, right?

Yvette nodded along like a doctor who'd always seen worse.

Until the end.

When she shook her head like Brady was a madman.

"I *think* I understand what you want," she said. "You did this unholy thing—removing a dead body from its rest and using it as a *movie prop*—and now you want to put the proverbial genie back in the body now that it's grown inconvenient?"

"Um. Yes," Brady confirmed.

"Unfortunately, it won't be that easy," she said. "There are consequences to an act such as this."

"Oops," Jake said.

"The problem is also you believe it is only your actions that precipitated this," Yvette continued. "It is not a one-way street. Why did you choose that one grave out of thousands? You think that was a coincidence? He called to you and you answered the call whether you knew it or not. You offered yourself to him as host."

"As a host?" Brady asked, incredulous. "A host of what?"

"Your ghost's need for resolution in our plane of existence is so strong that he needed to return here," Yvette said, speaking slowly as if explaining the phenomenon to a toddler. "In order to do that, he needed to latch onto someone still living in order to borrow their lifeforce, their life's energy, to stay in our world long enough to accomplish this task."

My life's...what?

"You've been getting sick?" Yvette asked.

"Um, a little actually."

"The longer the ghost remains in our world, the more of your lifeforce he drains away until..."

"Until what?" Brady asked.

"Until there's no more."

Brady shot a look at Jake. The ghost looked horrified.

"It is not a voluntary process," Yvette said. "What creates a ghost is trauma. What results is need. Hunger. Unless it is sated, you, too, will die."

Brady blanched. "How soon?" Brady asked.

"I don't know how much time you have," she said. "But I'd hurry if I were you."

"Come back and see us!" Clint chirped as Brady and Jake headed to the door.

Brady nodded absently only to notice Jake had stopped in his tracks.

"That's me," Jake said.

Brady followed Jake's gaze to a stack of old movie fanzines on the bookstore counter. Clint was perusing one called *Heartbreaker*.

"I was on one of the pages," Jake insisted. "He flipped past me."

Brady nodded to the clerk. "What're you reading?"

"Oh, we buy, sell, trade," Clint explained. "Some old lady was in here earlier with two crates of fan mags and all she wanted in return were a couple of charms to help her dog sleep. I couldn't say no."

"Can I see the one in your hand?" Brady asked.

"Um, sure?"

Brady put the magazine on the counter. It was from the mid-seventies and filled with photos of Donny Osmond, Shaun Cassidy, bands like the Cowsills and the Jackson 5, and plenty of people he'd never heard of.

"Anything familiar?" he asked Jake.

"All of it," Jake said, amazed. "I'd see these guys in acting classes, at parties, at auditions. This was my world."

Brady came to a full-page, black and white image of a preening Lance Caruso.

"He was supposed to have been such a jerk back then," Clint said. "Stabbed all his friends in the back trying to get to number one."

Brady raised an eyebrow at Jake.

"Keep going," Jake said.

The very next page had a color picture of Jake lounging on a beach.

"That's me!" Jake shouted.

"That's you!" Brady exclaimed.

"Holy cow!" Jake cried. "I remember that day. That's...Santa Cruz, I think?"

"Wait. Your ghost is Jake Madison?" Clint asked. "The ghost of Jake Madison is in my store?"

"Who?" Brady asked.

"That's...that's my name," Jake said, realization washing over him. "I'm Jake Madison."

"Madison was this overnight success," Clint explained, not hearing Jake. "Like, went from supporting actor to leading man in no time. He was going to be big time. Then, well, he got drunk the night before some huge audition and drove off Mulholland. *Total* cautionary tale."

Brady paled. Jake stared at Clint in disbelief. "I what?"

"Are you sure?" Brady asked.

"Totally. I'll bet *Heartbreaker* covered the hell out of it, too," Clint said, digging around until he found one with Jake's photo on the cover. "Here we go. 'Jake Madison, 1954-1976.'"

Jake's mouth fell open. He was dumbstruck.

"You *sure* your ghost is Jake Madison?" Clint asked.

Brady tapped the watch on the cover model's wrist. "He's wearing this watch right now. How much for the issue?"

"Are you kidding?" Clint asked. "Take it. Probably the most useful thing we'll sell all week."

Brady picked it up and turned to Jake, but the ghost was already out the door. When he got behind the wheel, Jake wouldn't even look at him.

"Where did it happen?" Jake asked quietly.

Brady flipped through the magazine until he found the right information. Jake's car had gone off a tight curve near Skyline Drive overlooking Fryman Canyon.

"Can we go there?" Jake asked.

"Of course."

They snaked up the narrow canyon roads to Mulholland,

the street that wound along the high ridgeline of the Hollywood Hills and marked the divide between the Los Angeles basin and the San Fernando Valley. There were no other cars on the road this time of night and few streetlights, the only outside illumination coming from the moon above.

When they neared Skyline Drive, a coyote appeared in their headlights. A dead gopher hung limply in its mouth. It disappeared into the shadows.

And then they were there.

Brady pulled onto the dusty shoulder and turned off the car. He jogged to the cliff's edge only to find Jake already there. The ghost stared into the thick underbrush growing on the hill, a copse of young oaks at the bottom.

"What a joke, right?" Jake said. "Here I thought I'd been murdered, and we were hot on the trail of my killer when really I'm one more Hollywood cliché."

"No, Jake. It's not—"

"You saw those pictures," Jake continued. "I had the whole world at my feet. I was a star. And I blew it. Drunk driving? What a joke. It's like *A Christmas Carol* without the redemption. 'Yeah, we're here to resurrect you a few years after your death to show you that your best friend is running a studio, some old rival of yours is a big movie star, but you? No, you blew it and got yourself killed.'"

"That's not why you're here," Brady said. "You heard what that psychic said. You have unfinished business."

"Yeah?" Jake said, nodding to the cliff. "What if this was it? Find out how you wasted it all? You think that's worth me coming back to drain your life away, Brady? Because you happened to find me with a chunk of engine stabbed through my chest or something?"

"No, that's why I don't think that's it," Brady said. "She said you were created through trauma. If you were the author of that, your quarrel would be with yourself. But here you are. And yeah, if there's been some mortal injustice, some right that needs to be wronged, you're damn right that's worth me sacrificing my health for a couple of days."

"What about your life?" Jake asked.

"Guess we'll see," Brady said.

The two stood there for a moment, recognizing there was as much strength in their bond as potential weaknesses.

"Thanks, Brady," Jake said. "I'm lucky I found you."

"No problemo, Jake," Brady said. "Let's go get your body."

It was past midnight by the time they returned to the studio lot. Brady opened the footlocker one more time to look for the piece of metal, sifting through the mud and muck of the day's shoot, but still came up empty.

He closed up the footlocker and carried it to his car.

"Going to wash my hands," he said to Jake, heading to the nearest restroom.

"Will you leave me the magazine?" Jake asked.

Brady nodded and opened the issue of *Heartbreaker* to the story of Jake's death before walking away. He thought the restroom would be empty this time of night so was surprised to find someone inside.

"Hey, man!" Paul Staggs said, standing over the sink washing his hands. "No drugs or girls this time!"

"A good thing," Brady agreed.

"Guess we're both night owls, huh?" Paul said. "It's the one time of day you can get stuff done, right? No one's knocking on your door. No phones ringing."

"Sure," Brady said.

"By the way, I'm still beyond sorry for burning down a chunk of your workshop," Paul continued. "I'm having a party this weekend in Malibu for senior Reliance-Majestic execs and talent. How about you come out? You can mix and mingle, maybe increase the size of your network? Bring your wife, girlfriend, or other significant other."

As Paul wrote the address out on a piece of paper, Brady wondered if this was the kind of thing Esmeralda might like. He scoffed to himself. Of course, it wasn't.

"Thanks," Brady said when Paul handed him the address.

"See you there!" Paul said.

Brady shoved the slip into his pocket and headed back to his car. Jake was staring intently at the magazine.

"You found my body in an unmarked grave in a potter's field, right?" Jake asked.

Brady nodded.

"Then who's in there?" Jake asked.

He pointed to the open issue of *Heartbreaker*. There was a photo from Jake's funeral, a dark casket surrounded by mourners and flowers.

"This says you were buried at Forest Lawn in Burbank," Brady said.

"Exactly! So, why was my body all the way across town?" Jake asked.

"And who the hell is in that coffin?" Brady asked, tapping the picture.

"Sounds like unfinished business to me," Jake said. "Whatever's in that grave will tell us the truth."

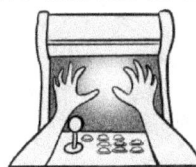

The plan for the next day was simple. Drive to the lot, clock in, then head over to Forest Lawn to investigate the "real" grave of Jake Madison as soon as it opened. Brady knew they couldn't open the grave then, however. Not in the middle of the day. Forest Lawn was where stars like Clark Gable, Carole Lombard, and Humphrey Bogart were buried. There was constant foot traffic and security.

The best they could hope for was to scout the location, determine what tools they'd need, and map out the best way to sneak in later that night. Even then, given the number of souvenir hunters, there'd be cameras, guard dogs, and security patrols.

It wouldn't be easy.

To make things worse, when Brady awoke, he felt sick all over again. Weak. The words of the psychic rang in his ears.

I don't know how much time you have. But I'd hurry if I were you.

"You...don't look great," Jake said when Brady entered

101

the living room.

Jake, it turned out, didn't need sleep. Brady had popped in a VHS tape of old horror movies he'd taped off the TV. *The Seventh Victim* was finishing.

"I'm fine," Brady said. "But we get moving."

They arrived at the lot well before seven. Brady thought they'd have the place to themselves only to discover a line of vehicles parked near the prop shop. What looked like a ragtag film crew were jogging from building to building grabbing supplies—drinks and snacks from the commissary, costumes from wardrobe, and even lenses from the camera department.

In the midst of this was Shelley Jensch chatting with another woman.

"Brady Harrington!" Jensch yelled when she spied him. "Just the person I was hoping to abuse the good will of."

Brady laughed.

Jensch nodded to the woman. "Have you met Lilian Urrea? She's producing this zero-budget horror movie for Concorde-New Horizons out in Santa Clarita today. This first-timer, Marcel Cassara, is directing."

Brady didn't know Cassara, but he'd seen the last movie Urrea had produced. It was about a killer man-fish stalking a surfer gang. He'd loved it.

"Anyway, they've got no money for effects, which is why I snuck them on the lot to grab supplies," Jensch continued. "I also told them about your great monster prosthetic. Can they rent it for the day? Also, you? If anyone asks, I'll say you're directing my second unit."

"We can't pay much, but at least we can promise the shoot will be hot and miserable," Lilian added.

Brady was torn. Getting in good with Lilian Urrea could lead to more work. But he had Jake to think about.

"Any other day—seriously *any* other day—and I'd love to help, but—"

Brady was cut off by an icy feeling on his arm. It was Jake.

"I know that guy," Jake said, pointing to someone on the catering crew.

The fellow was in his mid-thirties, gaunt to the point of

emaciation, and so deeply tanned Brady figured he lived in the desert.

"My last memories, ones that run up right to right before I died—they're of him," Jake said.

A chill ran through Brady's body. "What about Forest Lawn?" he whispered, ducking away from Jensch and Urrea.

"Later," Jake said. "I have a feeling about this. I think it's important."

Brady heard the urgent tone in Jake's voice and turned back to Urrea. "Anything to get away from the lot for a day, right?"

The caravan of filmmakers hit the freeway for Santa Clarita. The desert rat rode in a catering truck that stayed a couple cars ahead of Brady. Jake didn't take his eyes off of it.

"He sparked a memory?" Brady asked. "Like when you saw Julia?"

"It's a trickle. A few images, a few feelings," Jake explained. "It's harder to make them connect. I remember a bar. Country music."

"In LA?"

"I don't know yet. All I know is I knew that guy and he knew me."

"We'll talk to him."

As promised, the day's shoot was hot and miserable. But for Brady, it was also what he loved doing more than anything else. The day's shot had a monster, played by Jake's body, rising out of the bed of a speeding pickup truck to attack a group of teenagers racing alongside it in a dune buggy. It was filmed on a long stretch of desert with a camera tucked into the backseat of the buggy and two more following on camera trucks. The Cassara directed the action while lying on the buggy's rear floorboards.

It was fast and loose. Well, not *too* fast as the cars barely went above twenty-five miles per hour. To Brady, working the "prosthetic" in the back of the pickup, the dust and wind made it feel like they were doing fifty. At least.

Whenever he looked at Jake, the ghost was staring toward the catering trucks as if willing the truth to emerge from this mysterious stranger. The secrets of his life agonizingly close but just out of reach.

As they neared lunch break, the director still hadn't gotten the shot he wanted. Brady leaned over to Jake.

"Why don't you hop in this take?" Brady said, remembering how it lifted Jake's spirits before. "Give it a little juice?"

"Aren't you worried about what it'll do to you?" Jake asked.

"Maybe if I'm ready for it, it won't be so bad," Brady said. "Besides, it'll get us over there faster, right?"

"Okay," Jake agreed. "If you think it'll be okay."

The cars rolled back to their starting places. The cameras rolled. Brady knelt behind Jake's body.

"Action!" called Cassara.

As the buggy and the pickup ambled forward through the desert, Jake disappeared. Brady felt the prosthetic come alive. Immediately, his stomach tightened. His nausea returned. Jake, as the monster, lunged over to the dune buggy, grabbing at the teen actors. Though they weren't scared like the ones on the soundstage, the ferocity of Jake's performance pumped up their own reactions. They flailed and screamed and ducked away.

"Cut!" Cassara yelled after a long take. "Good stuff, everyone."

"That's lunch," the 1st AD called over the radio.

The vehicles slowed and turned back for base camp even as Brady gasped for breath. Jake appeared next to him, seemingly oblivious to his condition.

"How was that?" Jake asked.

"You were great," Brady said, trying not to look as ill as he felt.

Base camp consisted of a few transportation vans, makeup, prop, and camera trucks, honey wagons (read: bathrooms), and the catering trailers. Lunch tables were set up under canopies with a buffet line beside them. One of the people ladling food onto crew trays was the desert rat.

Jake started to head over. Brady shook his head.

"Let's wait until the line's down," Brady suggested.

Jake agreed. When everyone else had been served, Brady took a plate, grabbed a roll, and moved in front of the desert rat.

"Green beans or corn?" the man asked.

Brady noticed a number of scars running down the man's arms. Needle tracks. When the desert rat caught him looking, he lowered his sleeves.

"Eric," Jake said softly.

"Eric?" Brady asked, surprised.

"We know each other?" the desert rat asked.

Jake moved to the man's side and ran his fingers over the scars. "Eric. Oh, no. Eric."

Eric flinched, feeling the cold touch. "Are you doing that?" he asked, startled.

"Did you know Jake Madison?" Brady asked.

"What? Who are you? If you're a reporter, I don't talk to press!"

A few members of the crew looked up from their plates. Brady raised his hands.

"I'm sorry," he said. "I'm not looking for trouble. I—"

"You should get going!" Eric demanded. "*Bye.*"

Brady was about to press on when Jake raised a silencing hand. The ghost touched the tip of his finger to a warming tray's lid. The cold of his hand drew a line through the condensation.

Hey, Tex, he wrote.

"Wha...what?" Eric exclaimed as the letters formed. "How're you doing that?"

Jake continued writing. *I'm just passing through. This is my friend, Brady. Didn't mean to scare you. Miss you.*

Eric stared at the words then looked up at Brady.

"What's going on here?" he asked, voice barely a whisper.

"Maybe we can find somewhere to talk?" Brady asked.

Eric nodded quickly and conferred with one of the other caterers then led Brady behind the trucks.

"Only one person ever called me, Tex," he said. "Is he really...*here?*"

"Tell him I'm right beside him," Jake said. "Tell him my memory is patchy, so I didn't recognize him at first."

Brady related this.

"Why can't I see him?" Eric asked.

"He's tied to me somehow," Brady said. "We're still trying to figure that out."

"Can you ask him how we met?" Jake asked. "I can't remember. But I really want to."

"How'd you meet?" Brady asked.

"At the beach," Eric said. "He loved the beach."

Jake smiled. "That's it. We met on Seal Beach."

"Seal Beach?" Brady asked.

"That's right!" Eric said. "It's like you're reading my mind."

Jake touched Eric's scars. Eric's fingers followed Jake's.

"That's him?" Eric asked.

Brady nodded.

"Hate to admit it, but after he passed, I went to a pretty dark place," Eric said. "I wanted to forget it all so bad. I regret those lost memories now."

"Ask if he remembers when we drove out to Bakersfield to see Waylon Jennings," Jake said. "And if he remembers what song we slow danced to."

Brady did. Eric grinned and hummed a few bars of a country song. "*She's Looking Good* was the song. I'd forgotten all about that. Everybody was shooting us mean looks, but we didn't care. How is it…that he's here?"

"Somebody told us it was about unfinished business," Brady said. "Could that be about you?"

"Don't know," Eric said. "I wasn't okay, but I am now."

"What about his death? Anything suspicious?"

"Other than everything?" Eric said, scoffing. "This is a guy who drank, didn't have any business up on Mulholland, and had this big audition the next morning—a third callback for that movie, *Bullseye*. He never, ever went out the night before an audition. When we talked the afternoon before, he told me he was going to bed early and planned to sleep in. The next I heard was when Julia called to say he'd been killed."

106

"You knew Julia?" Brady asked.

"Little bit. She's the one they called to identify the body. She could barely stop crying to tell me what happened. He'd been burned beyond recognition."

"Jesus," Brady said.

"The car went over the edge then pretty much exploded," Eric said, voice trailing off as tears filled his eyes. "He didn't have any kind of dental records, but it was his car, they found his wallet, and he was still wearing the watch he got from Julia."

Brady looked at the watch on Jake's wrist. While the body at Evergreen Cemetery had been wearing the same shirt, shorts, and shoes, the watch hadn't been there. This rang all kinds of alarm bells in Brady's head. He was about to ask about it when Jake touched his shoulder.

"That's enough for now," Jake said. "I don't think it's that easy for him to relive it."

Brady held back.

"I don't know how any of this ghost stuff works," Eric said. "But do you think we could have a second? I know he can't talk to me, but there are a few things I'd like to say to him."

"Absolutely," Brady agreed and headed away.

He worked with the effects team for the rest of the afternoon, making sure to stick close to the catering trucks. When he didn't see Jake for a while, he wondered if speaking with Eric might really be the ghost's unfinished business he had to clear up and that he wouldn't see him again. It wasn't until the crew broke for the day that Jake reappeared alongside him.

"Thank you," Jake said quietly.

"No problemo," Brady replied.

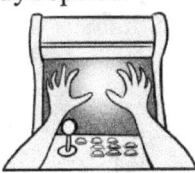

When they got back to the lot, Brady went straight to Julia's office hoping to run into her. But it was a Friday in the summer and the studio had emptied out.

"Just missed her," Julia's assistant confirmed. "Oh, and if you need her in the short term, you should leave me a message as she's heading out of town."

"Where's she going?"

"Off to visit location shoots in Malta and even Czechoslovakia if you can believe that," the assistant said. "You have to bring in everything when you shoot Prague. They don't even have pencils! Should be back after that."

Brady didn't think they could wait that long. Then he remembered something.

"You think she'll be at Paul Staggs's party tomorrow night?" he asked.

"She'll probably drop by for five minutes to say she did then skedaddle," the assistant said. "She's not a big party person."

"Thanks," Brady said, then led Jake back down the movie poster-lined hall. "Guess I know where we'll be tomorrow."

"What about your date with Esmeralda?" Jake said.

Brady had forgotten about that. "Well, what's better than a fancy party in Malibu?" Brady mused. "If you haven't drained all my 'lifeforce' by then, of course."

"Of course."

Brady's eyes fell on one of the old Reliance-Majestic movie posters. In the foreground was a young policewoman holding up a gun as gangs emerged from a nightmarish cityscape behind her. The movie's title was *Bullseye*.

"Eric mentioned this movie," Brady said. "It was the one you were auditioning for when you died."

"Looks terrible," Jake admitted. "Ever seen it?"

"Nope. What part were you up for?"

"One of those gang members, I think," Jake said.

Brady's eyes traveled across the credit block, stopping cold on the last name.

"Was the character's name Richie?"

"Yeah! Richie Verona. Why?"

Brady tapped the poster. The last credit in the block read,

and Lance Caruso as Richie.

"Wait. No," Jake said, the same thought seeming to occur to him at the same time as Brady.

"Could he have known you were up for *Bullseye?*" Brady asked.

"Maybe?" Jake said. "I barely knew him back then. Neither of us had been in that much. Are you really thinking Lance Caruso is somehow behind me getting killed? Over a *part?*"

"You heard what that guy in the store said. He was a big backstabber."

"He didn't mean it literally!" Jake said. "Everybody was back then. Doesn't mean he's a murderer! I read with at least three different actresses who were up for the lead. They didn't kill each other to get on the poster. Besides, how could he have known it would lead to some huge career?"

"I don't know," Brady said. "Somebody dumped your body at Evergreen Cemetery and had Julia identify a burned-up corpse that was interred at Forest Lawn."

"I still don't see it," Jake said. "But if he's a big Reliance-Majestic star, he'll be at Paul's party, too, right?"

"Probably," Brady said. "But doubt he's the kind of guy who'll tell his deep dark secrets over a cocktail."

"Yeah, but the longer I'm around somebody, the more my memories about them resurface," Jake said. "Get me in a room with him. I'll do the rest."

It was dark. Brady smelled grass and earth. He was on his back staring at the stars but also in motion. Being dragged.

He tried to sit up but couldn't. Then he was weightless. Airborne. He landed hard, surrounded by high earthen walls.

"Wha...?" he said, gasping for air.

Something soft rained down over his face.

Dirt.

"Hey!" he yelled. "What's going on?"

More dirt landed on his face.

"HEY!" Brady shouted.

He tried to move but was paralyzed. The dirt landed in his nose, mouth, and eyes. He spit it out only to get a second dose directly down his throat.

"Hey! Stop!" he roared. "What're you doing?"

That's when he saw Jake at the rim of what looked like a grave shoveling earth over him. The ghost looked unperturbed.

"Jake, what're you doing?"

He thought the ghost didn't hear him. Then Jake made eye contact with Brady. The ghost exhaled, nodding grimly. Then raised the shovel and continued to bury him.

"JAKE!" Brady screamed.

"Are you okay?" Jake asked.

Brady opened his eyes. He was in his apartment. A concerned-looking Jake was sitting beside him.

"What was that?" Brady asked.

"Sounded like a nightmare," Jake said, then nodded to Brady's soaked pillowcase. "You've been tossing and turning all night."

Brady felt his forehead. He was burning with fever.

"I need rest," Brady said. "Enough to get to the party tonight."

"You're sure about that?" Jake asked.

"No, but you'll be there to help, right?"

"Of course."

Brady nodded, drifting off to either sleep, delirium, or somewhere in between.

Brady slept in the next day, waking in the mid-afternoon feeling only slightly better. He still had a fever, but it was mild enough that he could get up and move around.

"You sure you want to do this?" Jake asked.

"Given the alternative, I'm not sure we have much of a choice," Brady admitted.

He took it easy until it was time to get ready to pick up Esmeralda. He felt shaky as he headed for the door but resolute.

Esmeralda's shoot was at Fairfax High on the other side of the hills from Sherman Oaks. Brady took the long way, going up Laurel Canyon, cruising down Hollywood Boulevard, and winding his way down Melrose to give Jake a look at the Los Angeles of the future.

"Biggest takeaway?" Jake said. "Like, twice as much pollution?"

Brady laughed. "True."

"Also, what's *Top Gun*?" he asked, having seen it on the marquee of the Cinerama Dome.

"It would blow your mind," Brady assured him.

Esmeralda was waiting by the high school's basketball courts when Brady pulled up to the curb. Brady helped load her makeup bags into the backseat, remembering that Jake's body was still in the trunk. He didn't want to explain why he was hauling around an alleged monster prosthetic.

"I am *so* ready to get away from all this," Esmeralda said, piling into the passenger seat as Jake slipped behind her to avoid being sat on/through. "What should we do? Hit the Strip and see a show? Grab a slice and go mini golfing? Skinny dip in the Silver Lake Reservoir? I'm up for anything as long it doesn't involve movies."

Brady would've preferred to do *any* of these things but knew what he had to do.

"*Well*, Paul Staggs did invite me to this fancy Reliance-Majestic exec party out at his house in Malibu for execs and higher-ups."

"Ha-ha, yeah right," Esmeralda said, then saw Brady was serious. "Oh, come on! The last thing I want to do is hang out with a bunch of people who think cocaine and acquisitions is a personality."

"We don't have to stay long," Brady insisted. "We'll say

'hi' then be out the door for a late show."

"What late show?" she asked, still sulking. "Don't say *Top Gun.*"

"*Rocky Horror* at the Nuart?" Brady asked. "They've been showing *Stop Making Sense* since February but now *Rocky's* back."

She raised an eyebrow. "I haven't gone to a midnight *Rocky* since high school."

"We'll trade insufferable people on drugs in Malibu for awesome people on drugs in Santa Monica. Cool?"

"I can dig it," Esmeralda agreed.

Paul Stagg's house turned out to be at the end of a long, winding road high in the hills overlooking the Pacific. It wasn't the usual faux Mediterranean mansion like others on the same bluff but a hyper-modern, glass, steel, and concrete pile full of jagged edges and soaring balconies that seemed to defy gravity.

"Guess Paul wants people to know he's rich," Esmeralda said as a valet in a red vest took Brady's car keys. "Oh, wait. You can smell the ocean all the way up here. Now I wish I were rich, too."

Brady looked over the cliff's edge, able to see all the way to Point Dume off one side, the lights of the Santa Monica Pier's Ferris wheel to the other. Jake, who'd stayed mostly silent on the drive, was already scanning the party. The house was packed with so many people they spilled out onto the grounds and balconies.

"You see Lance?" Brady whispered, letting Esmeralda get a few steps ahead of him.

"Not yet," Jake said. "I'm going to look for him."

"Don't get lost," Brady said.

Jake scoffed. "All these houses look the same."

Jake headed away as Brady and Esmeralda neared the front walk. Paul appeared in the doorway, arms outstretched.

"You made it!" he exclaimed before turning to Esmeralda. "I know you. Hair and makeup? Estefanía?"

"Esmeralda," she corrected.

"Right," he said, nodding to the ocean. "Nice view, huh?"

"Can almost see Hawaii," Esmeralda suggested, in a voice that told Brady she was tolerating Paul more than enjoying speaking with him.

"You ever been to Hawaii?" Paul asked.

"Nope," she said. "Going to assume you have?"

"In my TV-movie days. Network put us up in this great hotel. You walked out the front door and were right on the beach. It was amazing."

Brady pictured going to Hawaii with Esmeralda one day. That would be a fun date.

"Anyway, good to see you," Paul said, as if he'd topped off his quota of small talk. "Bar upstairs, buffet down. Mingle. Make friends."

Paul disappeared back into the throng of guests. Brady nodded to the second floor. "Get you a drink?"

"Could definitely use one!" Esmeralda said. "Then we'll take ourselves on a tour and see if there's anything I can steal for an impromptu Magenta costume."

Brady climbed the outdoor staircase to the second-floor bar, looking for Jake. He knew he couldn't be far, but it worried him that he'd lost track of the ghost. He got in line at the bar and was scanning the faces of the well-dressed friends of Paul Staggs when a hand clapped down on his shoulder.

"Just the guy I'm looking for," said Lance Caruso.

"Oh. Hey, man," Brady said, glancing around for Jake. "How's it going?"

"Good, good," Lance said, breath heavy with the scent of bourbon. "I wanted to tell you how sorry I am about the other day. I couldn't say anything then, but the studio has me on all these crazy pills to keep my weight down. They scramble my brain and make me all edgy and nuts."

"That sounds awful."

"That's Hollywood, right?" Lance said.

The actor swayed drunkenly to the left as if on a ship at sea. That's when Brady saw Jake standing directly behind Lance, absorbing his every word and gesture.

"Still, must be nice being a star, right?" Brady asked.

"Sort of?" Lance queried thoughtfully. "But once you've

been at the very top, everyone in this town at your beck and call, it does a number on you when you have a flop and they jump to the next guy. It's not you they care about but whoever's in the throne that week."

"Huh," Brady said. "Speaking of stars, do you remember an actor named Jake Madison?"

"Doesn't ring a bell," Lance said.

"From the mid-seventies. You were up against him for roles. Like *Bullseye.*"

Brady carefully watched for Lance's reaction. He looked for guilt. For fear. For a flash of anger.

He got distant recognition and a slow nod.

"Oh, yeah! He's the guy who died, right?" Lance exclaimed. "Not really a star, though, right?"

"Did you know him?" Brady pressed. "Kind of a rival of yours, right?"

"Nah," Lance said. "And no, I didn't know him."

"You sure?"

"Totally. Like, I remember when they told us on set. Half the cast broke down in tears and started booking flights back for the funeral. I had to ask like three people what I might've seen him in."

"Flights back?" Brady asked.

"I was in Georgia filming this comedy. Did you know him or something? People. Said he was a great guy."

"What about *Bullseye*?" Brady asked.

Lance looked surprised. "What about it?"

"He was up for the part you got," Brady said. "There were final callbacks the week he died. Wouldn't you have been in LA auditioning?"

"Nah, that didn't come along until—wait," Lance said as Jake leaned forward. "That's why I knew the name. He was going to be Richie and they had to delay it. I kept hearing the name because one of the producers spent the shoot telling me how much better Jake would've done in the part. When I called him on it later, he said he was trying to motivate me. Again. *Hollywood.*"

Brady glanced to Jake. The ghost's face fell.

"Another dead end," Jake said, moving away.

"Ja—"

"Dammit!" Jake roared, punching the bar.

Though his hand went right through, Brady felt the ghost's rage ripple through his own body with such tremendous force he vomited.

All over Lance.

Everybody in their vicinity gasped. Others laughed. Still more waited for Lance to punch Brady in the face again.

The actor simply shook his head. "Two times in one week! Jesus, man."

"I'm so sorry, Lance," Brady said.

"It's fine," Lance said. "Guess I had it coming. I'm going to go get cleaned up. Maybe be somewhere else when I get back?"

"I can do that."

Lance headed away. Brady looked around for Jake only to see Esmeralda at the top of the stairs. She looked from Lance to the floor to Brady.

"Are you okay?" Esmeralda said, confused. "Did he hit you again?"

"Gotta find a bathroom," Brady said. "Then we'll go to *Rocky*?"

"Sure thing, Brady."

He hurried away, feeling embarrassed and dazed as he pushed past other party goers. He waited for the dizziness to subside, but it only grew stronger. He felt feverish all over again, a cold sweat rising on his face and arms.

He barely made it to the bathroom before collapsing onto the tiles.

"*Jake*," he whispered.

There was no response.

He sat there trying to compose himself, trying to come up with a new plan. His breathing was ragged. He could barely sit up straight. The pain was beginning to ebb, but in a way that told him it could return at any time. He felt betrayed by his own body.

He finally rose, splashed some water on his face, and

headed out the door to find Esmeralda.

Only, instead of exiting into the hall, he somehow went out a second door and found himself in a study with leather chairs and a sofa, a fireplace with an antique wrought iron grate in front of it, and a large balcony, its doors already open. The walls were covered with dozens of framed movie posters so close together a pin wouldn't fit between them.

Some were decades old, featuring the stars of yesteryear. Some more recent. Brady was trying to remember if he'd seen any of them when Paul strode into the room.

"You found my Hall of Shame!" Paul announced.

"I did," Brady admitted.

"Heard you got sick and came to find you," Paul said. "Are you okay?"

"Yeah, I think I ruined your carpet."

"Nah, all you ruined was a movie star's shirt and a mat put down by the catering company. Don't sweat it."

Brady was relieved. "These are your movies?" he asked, eager to change the subject.

"Yeah," Paul said idly. "I mean, for some of them I was the assistant to the assistant to the assistant on, but the more recent ones are from my time at Reliance-Majestic."

Paul nodded to a French one-sheet for a Gregory Peck-starring postwar spy thriller. "Had my first speaking role in that. I asked Peck, in my best German accent, if he wanted to buy an apple. I was *four*. Think I made $50."

"I didn't know you'd been an actor," Brady said, only now realizing some of the posters were way too old for Paul to have been involved with as a studio executive.

"I didn't stick with it," Paul admitted wistfully. "I got close to a few big, life-changing roles—*agonizingly* close—but they'd always go to the flavor of the month, not the child actor with actual experience. So, I became a suit."

Brady nodded idly, his gaze traveling to the fireplace. There was something familiar about the wrought iron grate in front of it. It had four decorative andirons rising from the front topped in brass.

Only, one of them was missing its top.

"Even lost a part to Jake Madison," Paul said. "*Bullseye.*"

Brady suddenly realized where he'd seen the andiron design before. The missing part matched the chunk of metal that had been driven into Jake's corpse's chest.

That same piece was now in Paul's hand.

"Paul," Brady said. "What's—"

"So, it really wasn't Whit who stumbled upon Jake's body," Paul said. "Guess I iced the wrong effects guy."

"Whit?" Brady asked. "I thought he had a heart attack."

"Oh, he did," Paul said. "I'd gone to the props warehouse to make sure you weren't gonna rat me out for the fire and found Whit there holding the andiron while standing over Jake's body. Did *not* expect to see that ever again! Wow!"

Paul chuckled and closed the door behind him.

"Have to admit, I kind of panicked," Paul continued. "Luckily, I knew Whit was a casual coke guy, so I offered him a bump. Only, I'm a casual heroin guy, so what he snorted up went straight to that cholesterol encrusted heart of his. He didn't have a chance."

Brady flushed with anger. "You didn't have to kill Whit."

"Yeah, found that out once I started following your extracurricular activities," Paul said. "When I heard you ask Lance about Jake a second ago, I began to wonder."

"Thought Jake Madison died in a drunk driving accident," Brady said.

"Nope!" Paul said.

"He's right," Jake said, appearing beside Brady. "I knew I recognized this house. I was killed right in this room. Maybe a foot to the left of where you're standing now."

"You killed him here," Brady said. "Right here."

Paul cocked his head at Brady. "Huh. Good guess. How'd y—"

"Why?" Brady asked. "Why'd you kill him?"

"*Bullseye* was my last shot to make something happen with my acting career," Paul said with a shrug. "When I found out they were making the offer to Jake, that I was runner-up *again*, I lured him up here the night before with some story about this buddy-comedy I'd set up as a producer with a cash

117

offer ready for him to be one of the leads."

"I was so naïve," Jake said, shaking his head.

"Told him it was contingent on an in-person meeting and the clock was ticking. Like an idiot, he drove right over. Never suspected a thing. Irony is it was all bull. I wasn't the runner-up at all. They gave it to friggin' Lance Caruso!"

"What about the body?" Brady asked. "Who's in Forest Lawn?"

"You can't kill somebody like Jake Madison without also making him disappear," Paul admitted. "Lucky for me, it only cost a couple of bucks to switch out his body for a vagrant's corpse waiting to be buried at…where was it? Evergreen Cemetery. A little harder to send the body over a cliff in Jake's car, but I got that done, too. A watch, a wallet, his own car. No one suspected a thing."

Paul stepped closer to Brady. Brady tensed, ready to fight. Only, he had no strength.

"I don't know how you tracked all this back to me, but I guess it doesn't matter," Paul continued. "Everybody out at the party already saw you get sick. Who'll question it when I run back out there and say you fell over the balcony?"

"Paul—"

The exec lunged at Brady, shoving him with all his strength toward the balcony's open doors. Brady flew backwards, saved only when he tripped a foot short of the balustrade and landed on the railing.

"Got to do better than that," Brady said, fighting to regain his balance.

"Okay," Paul said, racing toward the balcony.

Before Brady could react, Paul ducked low and grabbed Brady around the ankles, hefting him over the railing.

"Tell Jake I said, 'Hi!'" Paul hissed.

Brady fell into darkness. He crashed onto the ground two stories down, breaking his left arm and dislocating his right shoulder.

Then he began to roll.

As the screams of party guests echoed in his ears, he flew down the hill. He struck a rock, opening up a cut on his forehead. He tried to slow his progress, but gravity won out. He rolled faster and faster, picking up speed until he thought he'd sail right off the cliff and into the ocean.

Instead, his head struck a car tire and spun his body around an almost full 360 degrees, stopping him cold.

"*Unh*," he grunted.

He looked up only for blood to seep into his eyes. As best he could tell, he'd rolled into a cul-de-sac on the inland side of Paul's mansion surrounded by expensive cars.

"*Jake*," he whispered.

"I'm here," the ghost said, beside him. "You've…looked better."

Brady scoffed. "Can you see my car? I think this is where the valets park everything."

Jake stood up. "It's two cars over. Why?"

Brady heard a sound from above. Party guests stared and pointed. Paul hurried down the cliff as best he could, kicking up dirt and rocks, as if coming to help.

But there was no mistaking the fury on his face, even from that distance.

Brady fought against the pain and rose to his knees.

"Do you see the keys?" Brady asked, crawling in the direction of his car.

"On the windshield," Jake said. "What's your plan? You're too weak to fight this guy, Brady."

"Yeah, but you're not," Brady said. "Your body's in the trunk. You can do it."

"That would kill you!" Jake protested. "You're half-dead already!"

"What do you think Paul's coming down here to do?" Brady asked. "If you don't stop him, it's the end for both of us. All this will be for nothing."

Brady reached the car and grabbed for his keys with his busted right arm before crawling for the trunk. His hand shook as he inserted them into the lock.

"Brady, look out!" Jake yelled.

It was Paul. He stood over Brady, fist clenched.

Everything went black.

119

Brady's eyes blinked open a moment later. His head thudded against asphalt. Paul was giving him the beating of a lifetime. Beside him, however, the trunk was open. Paul turned, as if having heard something.

Brady's eyes blinked open a second time.

Jake's corpse was now half-in, half-out of the trunk, its skeletal hands wrapped tightly around Paul's neck. The studio exec clawed at the hands, eyes bulging in terror.

"*Tell Jake I said, 'Hi!'*" roared the most unholy voice Brady had ever heard.

This time, everything went white.

When Brady opened his eyes the next time, his body felt different. Numb pains, not sharp ones. He wasn't outdoors anymore. Jake was above him, smiling and holding his hand.

"I owe you a lifetime, pal," Jake said simply. "Thanks for all of it, Brady."

"No problemo," Brady said.

The ghost tightened his grip on Brady's hand and kissed him on the cheek.

Brady blinked.

When his eyes opened back up, it was Esmeralda who'd kissed him. They were in a hospital room.

"Hey," Brady said.

"Hey. How are you feeling?" Esmeralda asked.

"Not sure yet. What happened?"

"Well, that's what a lot of people want to ask you," she said. "Best anyone can tell, Paul went crazy—he had enough drugs in his system to kill a herd of elephants—and attacked you. You fought back and managed to survive. He didn't."

Brady nodded, taking this in. "I'm really sorry about our date."

"Yeah, I had to find my own ride home and everything," Esmeralda said.

Brady laughed. Everything hurt when he did. Esmeralda smiled and kissed him a second time.

"You owe me a trip to *Rocky Horror*."

"I do," Brady agreed before slipping under again.

Brady didn't see Jake again. Not at the hospital nor his apartment after he was discharged. Not in his car. Not on the studio lot. Nor anywhere else.

The unfinished business was Paul, Brady decided. Jake, wherever he was, could finally rest. Brady missed him all the same.

After a few weeks of recovery, he slipped back to Evergreen to rebury Jake's body. When he arrived, the cemetery felt so empty. So barren. How could he leave behind the remains of someone he'd gotten to know so well?

He went home and wrote two letters, admitting everything and going into detail about all that had happened from beginning to end. He hesitated before mailing them then did anyway.

Two Sundays later, he drove back to the cemetery before midday and waited at Jake's grave. Around noon, two figures approached from the parking lot.

Julia and Eric.

"Thank you for coming," Brady said. "Also, for not calling the police."

"I thought you were insane," Julia admitted. "But then I reached out to Eric. He told me what happened in Santa Clarita."

"I only knew him for a couple of days, but he seemed like a great person," Brady said. "He cared about the two of you very much."

"He was a wonderful human being," Julia said. "I miss him all the time."

"Yeah, it's actually nice adding someone to that small, select group still carrying around his memory," Eric added. "I'm glad you got to know him a bit."

They sat there, six feet above Jake's mortal remains, Julia passing out beer and Eric slices of pizza, both asking Brady to retell the story of Jake's haunting, minute by minute. She and Eric then told stories of their own. They stayed there, laughing, drinking and reminiscing well past sunset.

And on into the night.

This Place Has Got Everything

CHRISTINE MAKEPEACE

"Just take out those trash bags while I count the drawer. Then we can get outta here."

"Sure, Karen." Jenn blew her bangs out of her eyes, a bulging black garbage bag in each hand. She toddled down the center aisle, eyes absently scanning the blur of VHS tapes as she passed.

"Wait!" Karen yelped, hurrying around the counter and bounding after her. "Do you know how to get to the dumpster?"

"Yeah, Dallas showed me last night."

"Okay. But do you *remember*?" She stretched out the words like they were made of something sticky and unfamiliar. Like she was worried Jenn had never heard them before.

"Sure. It's just around back."

"Uh huh. But you know how to get back there, right?"

"Um... I mean, just follow the hallway?" Jenn shifted, the bags getting heavier the longer she stood. She looked past Karen at a VHS cover with a cartoon woman holding a sword above her head—a skeleton man loomed behind her. Jenn fought the urge to glance over her shoulder.

"There's, like, a very specific way to get back there. Dallas showed you that?"

Jenn nodded.

"And when Dallas showed you, you found it okay? Everything was cool? You just walked down the corridor and then walked outside and, bam! Dumpster?"

"Yes?" Jenn answered hesitantly.

"Awesome," Karen mumbled, her previous intensity melting away. "Rad..."The two women stood awkwardly, the neon pink lights that trimmed the wall reflecting off Karen's big, round glasses.

"So..." Jenn began, inching backwards.

"So, are you liking it so far? I mean, it's kinda lame, but, like, not totally heinous. Right?"

"Right," Jenn agreed.

"Yeah, I like it. We get a lot of dweebs. But some cool people, too. So, it balances out." Karen tapped a bright yellow fingernail against her front teeth.

"I should get this trash outside..."

"What do you do for fun?" They spoke at the same time, words careening into each other as Jenn grimaced.

"Yeah, bring the bags out," Karen ordered with a distracted wave. "I have to motor anyway. Meeting my boyfriend." She smiled wide, eyes sparkling. "I just wanted you to know that even though I am third keyholder here, you don't have to be so majorly formal. Like, chill and stuff."

"Uh, all right. Thanks, I guess."

"No problemo." Karen shrugged, hustling back over to the cash register. "Be careful!" she called after Jenn.

"Got it."

"And remember to prop the back door open!"

"Uh huh," Jenn grunted, shouldering open the door to the backroom.

"If you don't prop it open you might not find your way back!" Karen called just as the door swung shut.

"Thanks!" Jenn shouted at the empty room. She dropped the garbage bags and they landed with a hollow thump. "I *have* worked in a mall before," she mumbled, picking her way across the cramped backroom. Boxes were stacked high— cardboard fingers reaching towards the sky—and Jenn slinked past them to the back door. She pushed it open, poking her head out.

She looked left, then right, ponytail flopping dramatically against her head. The corridor was empty and gray and seemed to stretch on forever in either direction. Dallas had explained that all the gray—the concrete floors, the drab walls, the metallic ceiling—created an optical illusion. That the hallways running throughout the mall, behind every store, weren't eerie and never-ending. It was just a trick of the eye.

Still, she stared down its length for a little longer than necessary, just listening. Waiting. There was a stiff sensation in her joints, like she'd just woken up. She felt uneasy and wasn't sure why. It was just a hallway—just a dumpster. And granted, people seemed *really* intense about the dumpster, but Jenn figured it had to do with how grody it was back there. She'd leapt over vile puddles of anonymous liquid when she and Dallas had gone out the previous night. It stunk of sulfur and rotten meat.

Jenn let the door close with a quiet click, shuffling over to the hulking trash bags. She hoisted them up and maneuvered carefully back to the exit. She kicked the scuffed door open, barreling out before it could swing back and close on her. Safely out of the way, she stuck her foot out, hoping to catch the heavy metal with her toe before it could slam shut.

But the corner swept past her dirty white sneaker and Jenn watched, hands full, as the store's back door closed with a muffled slam. She blinked at it, tall and unremarkable and gray. Just like the rest of the corridor. There was no handle or sign or doorbell.

A hazy panic gripped her, and she dropped the bags, inching her fingertips into the small gap at the frame, getting no traction as she tugged uselessly. She pounded her fist against the cool metal, but the sound it produced was soft and muted.

"She's not going to hear that," Jenn muttered, looking around helplessly.

She'll have to come look for me eventually, she thought as she weighed her options. *Might as well get rid of the trash now so we can get outta here sooner.*

Jenn grabbed the black plastic bags again and dragged them behind her. She went right, just like Dallas had done the night before, shoes squeaking on the polished concrete.

"Huh, no sign on this one either," she whispered as she passed the next door. *How does anyone get deliveries in this place?*. She tried to remember what store was next to hers, vaguely recalling sausage and cheese, but not feeling particularly confident. She paused in front of it, lip caught between her teeth—thick, sweet gloss coating her tongue—and she wondered if she should knock. Maybe they'd hear her, let her out their front gate so she could sheepishly explain to Karen her silly mistake.

But she didn't. She kept going.

Slate gray door after slate gray door passed, and she began to lose track of how many she'd gone by. That's when it hit her. "Ugh, you goober!" she exclaimed. "How are you going to know which one's the video store?"

Jenn turned around started back towards where she'd come from, trying to guess how far she'd gone—how many doors she'd seen. She looked for landmarks—anything remarkable—and found there was nothing. So, she guessed, stopping in front of a door that could've been hers, or anyone's, and she knocked. After three loud raps that left her knuckles raw, the door began to shudder.

Jenn stepped back, breath trapped in her body, as it swung open.

"Oh, hey." A boy popped his head out, thick brown hair curling around his ears. "Who are you?" he asked a dumbfounded Jenn.

"I'm—I'm Jennifer."

"Uh, okay. What do you want?" He straightened up, placing more of his body in front of the sliver of open air. Jenn could *almost* see past him into the backroom.

"Yeah, sorry. I'm lost, I think," she said self-consciously, glancing down at the tag pinned to his shirt. It was shaped like a cassette tape and read *Danny*. "Is this the record store?"

"This?" he hooked his thumb behind him. "Yeah, but it's not just any record store. It's the most wicked store in town. Totally radical. You should come in."

Jenn took a step back, unable to stop herself from recoiling. There was something in his eyes, in the tone of his

126

words, that made her feel uneasy. *But*, she reasoned, *this is exactly what you want. You want to get to back into the mall.*

"Do you know where the video store is?" she asked instead, clumsy tongue tripping over the words.

"The video store? Yeah, that's waaay down that way," he said, pointing down the hall.

"No way," Jenn barked.

"Uh, yes way. I'm not the one who's lost. How long have you worked here?" he asked, looking her up and down, a sly smile playing at his mouth. He stroked his chin and she pulled her bulky sweater tight around her body.

"Come in," he repeated, inching further out of the storeroom. "Come listen to this killer new Billy Idol tape we got in. You'll love it."

Jenn saw something move over Danny's shoulder and she couldn't help but shift her gaze to it. He watched her eyes move, turning his head slowly to look in the same direction. The new angle provided Jenn with a much better view of the room, and what she saw made the world tilt on its axis.

"Is that...is that The Devil?" she asked, pointing at the abnormally large figure curled over a cluttered desk. Its skin was a cracked red, like magma or a burnt pie. She could see a little tail peeking out from around one of its massive haunches. She struggled to breathe.

"No! That's not *The* Devil," Danny said around a laugh. "But it is *a* devil."

Jenn knew it shouldn't, but it made sense, and as she let herself drink in the thing's unnatural form, she knew Danny was telling the truth. There was a demon standing in middle of Tape Town's backroom.

"How?" she asked, voice small and shaky.

"How what? Do we afford him? I know, right? Pays for himself though. And he's so bitchin'! Like something off a *Heavy Metal* cover."

"No. I mean, why?"

"Whaddya mean 'why'? So, he can record subliminal messages. Duh."

Jenn stared, mouth open and eyes as wide tennis balls.

"What?" she whispered, ready to run but not sure how to start.

"Ya know, to play behind the music. Ya know?" He watched her carefully, reaching out one thin-fingered hand. "Hey, why don't you come in?" he asked again. "Then we can talk all about it. I'll take you back to the video store and everything. Just come in and meet him." Danny's smile was too wide—his skin too smooth and voice too close. Every inch of her was *screaming* to get away, but it was all so appealing, made so much sense and felt so easy.

Jenn's hand seemed to move on its own accord, reaching to meet Danny's in stuttered slow motion. She looked from the boy's eyes to the devil's, and saw they held the same glassy hunger.

"I have to go," Jenn announced suddenly. With her arm still outstretched, she turned and ran in the direction she thought she'd come from.

"Where ya going, lost girl? Movie store ain't that way," Danny called after her. His laugh chased her down the hall until she heard the door slam shut. But she didn't stop running.

Like an avalanche, images of the *thing* she'd just seen crashed down on her, pelted her like hail, and she wanted to get far away from it. She stopped when she realized she'd left the trash bags. It was an involuntary reaction, skidding to a halt because she'd forgotten literal garbage. But she did, and when she whipped around to look for it, she saw nothing.

Two massive black bags should've sat blocking the endless corridor, but there was nothing as far as she could see. And she could see for miles.

"What the fuck is happening?" she panted, doubled over with her hands on her knees. She swallowed massive gulps of air, hair-sprayed bangs sticking to the sweat on her forehead. "I need to get outta here."

Jenn scanned the walls. One side was lined with doors, the other was a dirty matte gray. *Welcome home* was scratched into the plaster and she read the words over and over like an incantation.

"You're wiggin' out," she assured herself. "Just move."

Jenn pulled the thick, cable knit sweater over her head and tied it around her waist. She was left in a too-small, fluorescent pink t-shirt that she never dared wear alone. But her exposed midriff was the least of her worries as she began a slow jog down the hallway.

"Gotta be an exit into the mall somewhere," she mumbled under her breath. Every few doors she paused and tried to open one—pressed her ear to the tacky painted metal to see if she could hear anything.

As she pressed her flushed cheek to the door in front of her, she felt it tremble. She flinched, but didn't move away, mesmerized by the sound on the other side. It was soft and sweet, like singing, except there were no recognizable words or melodies. But it was beautiful. Calming. Hypnotizing. She felt around for any way to open it, but like all the others, the door was sealed.

The song continued, unwavering, the sickly music leaking out, pouring from the cracks and hinges, and Jenn could almost taste it, rich on her tongue. Without thinking, she dropped to the floor on her belly, the cold concrete instantly biting into her flesh. She tried to see underneath the door, but the angle was wrong—the crack not nearly wide enough. She jammed her fingers under, groping around, trying to pull the lovely sounds to her. She wanted to shove them down her throat and choke on it. She wanted to drown.

Something warm and fuzzy brushed against the fingertips wedged under the door and she gasped. The singing stopped abruptly, and she felt a searing wetness slither across the fingers she now realized were trapped. She pulled back—hard—knuckles caught and refusing to budge. What she assumed was a tongue continued to lap at her skin as she yanked away violently, her hand only coming loose when blood began pouring from her self-inflicted wounds.

Delicate droplets pattered against the floor—stained the lip of the door—and as she stood, cradling her wounded hand to her chest, the melodious humming resumed. Jenn moved away as fast as she could, still disoriented, still entranced by the rising trill emanating from the storeroom. Jen shrieked when a tiny hand reached out from underneath the door, thick and furry like a paw, but with four distinct, humanoid fingers. She watched as it painted a messy picture with her blood, singing a merry tune as it went.

She turned and ran into the endless nothingness.

Jenn stopped when her breath was too labored to continue, perspiration mixing with the sweet strawberry scent of her shampoo. It smelled too much like candy and it made her stomach lurch. She leaned against the bare wall, chest heaving, staring at yet another unremarkable door.

"Wonder what bullshit is behind that one," she sighed, waning adrenaline leaving her dull and heavy. She heard it then, a small—almost imperceptible—squeak. Like a door swinging open on unoiled hinges. But she didn't know where the noise had come from, the corridor simultaneously muting and amplifying sound. So, Jenn walked, because that's all she could do.

Jenn walked until she saw something remarkable appear in the sea of repetition: one of the doors was propped open by a piece of wood. She rushed to it, only slowing when she remembered what she'd found behind the other doors. *There could be a Yeti behind this one,* she thought. A vampire... Another dimension.

She approached cautiously, eyes narrowed, attempting to see through the slit in the door. Three heads of thick, wavy, auburn hair bounced into her field of vision and she gasped. The three heads turned towards her and the door was thrust open.

Jenn staggered backwards as she tried to make sense of the three young women who stood in front of her.

"Hi!" the first greeted with a big, toothy grin.

"Hello," the second waved.

"Hey. I'm Gigi. And this is BeBe and Chi Chi," the third offered, pointing to the other two. "Who are you?"

Jenn stood, mouth agape, taking the strangers in. Each wore denim shorts, hiking boots, and a striped shirt. BeBe's was red, Chi Chi's yellow, and Gigi's a light purple. They smiled at her warmly, three sisters who looked nothing alike.

Three versions of the same pretty girl.

"I'm Jenn," she offered, feeling rude for not responding faster, for being so freaked out. She immediately felt stupid for feeling so rude. *The Devil tried to brainwash me! And some animal drank my blood,* she argued with herself as she tried to assess the girls' threat level.

"Hi, Jenn!" the three called in unison.

"Uh, yeah, thanks. Hi," Jenn mumbled.

"But you shouldn't be out there in that grody old hallway. You should come in here and party with us!" Gigi announced, the other girls shrieking their agreement.

"Uh..." Jenn hesitated, peering around their heads into the backroom. "I'm not sure I should."

"Ugh! Don't be lame, Jenny! Come in and chill with us! We'll have a totally bitchin' time!"

"Shouldn't you be working..." Jenn protested as the three grabbed her and yanked her out of the hall and into the room.

"We are working!" BeBe exclaimed, jumping up and down.

"Yeah, take a chill pill and party with us," Chi Chi agreed, producing a six pack of beer out of nowhere.

"Oh, I don't drink," Jenn offered reflexively, pulling away from their grabby hands, trying to reorganize her thoughts.

"Lame!" all three yelled simultaneously.

"Are you a dweeb, Jenny? Or are you bodacious babe like us?" Gigi slurred, suddenly sounding drunk.

"Are you a dweeb, Jenny!" Chi Chi yelled, taunting.

"I think I'm just going to go," Jenny said too softly, trying to push past the tight circle of women. "Can I go out through the front?"

The three gasped in perfect harmony, cupping their hands over their glossed lips. "You can't go out that way," Chi Chi whispered.

"No. No way. No can do." BeBe shook her head adamantly.

"Well, why not? I'm stuck in this hallway," Jenn gestured behind her, "and if I could just, like, get back into the mall, I know I could find the way back to my store."

"Oh, where do you work?" Gigi asked.

"The video store."

Gigi giggled. "That's harsh."

"Why?"

"That's like, on a different level," Gigi replied, still chuckling to herself.

"What do you mean?" Jenn was getting impatient—wanted clear answers—but the gaggle of girls seemed incapable of providing them.

"That's on level 1," BeBe interjected. "We're on level 3."

"That's impossible!" Jenn exclaimed. "That's... that's not possible."

"Totally possible and totally true," Chi Chi agreed.

"And, totally tubular!" Gigi shouted, still laughing at nothing.

"Please just let me out the front and I'll figure it out on my own," she begged.

Gigi straightened up, manic giggles finally subsiding. "We told you. You can't go out there." She dropped her voice, adding in a whispered rush, "*He's* out there."

"Who?"

"Him!" the three cried at once.

"Who!" Jenn shouted only to be immediately shushed by the chorus of bubbly voices. "What kind of store is this?" she asked with growing dread.

"Camping store," came the three simultaneous answers.

"And what happens if we go out there?"

"He'll hack us to pieces and throw them in a bonfire," Gigi replied matter-of-factly.

"Who!"

"Gary," they whispered.

"Gary?"

"Yes," Chi Chi hissed. "Some counselors let him play with matches and he lit himself on fire. So, as revenge, he murdered them."

"What?"

"Yeah," BeBe continued. "And now every night, Gary is conjured from the fire and takes corporal form to continue his killing spree."

"What?"

"And if we go out there," Gigi interjected, "he'll kill us immediately. But, if we stay in the stockroom for a while, it takes him longer."

"Huh?" Jenn's heart was thumping so hard she could taste the vibrations.

"What part aren't you getting?" Gigi snapped.

"All of it?" Jenn replied meekly.

"Do you have any idea where you work?" Chi Chi asked, hair bouncing as she lifted her nose to the air.

"The video store?"

"No, you dip. This is, like, a haunted mall," groused Chi Chi.

"It's more of an occult mall," Gigi interjected.

"Same thing!" Chi Chi huffed.

"Actually—"

"I don't care!" Jenn interrupted, voice shrill and wobbly. "I'm going out the front. Please unlock the gate for me."

"As if!" they cried out.

"Fine. Let's do it your way. Let's go meet Gary." Jenn pushed past the girls, running onto the sales floor. But when she crossed the threshold, she wasn't in the camping store anymore; she was in the woods.

At least that's how it looked.

A campsite was meticulously set up, chairs and tents placed lovingly around glowing embers. A row of colorful sleeping bags lay at the ready. Her steps slipped—felt unstable, and when she looked down, the floor was covered in a layer of fine, brown pine needles.

When she looked up, she saw only darkness.

"What the fuck..." Jenn murmured.

"See?" Gigi came up behind her, and Jenn screamed, hands rushing to clutch her chest. The cuts on her fingers began to bleed again, and she wrapped the dangling arm of her sweater around them.

"What is this place?"

"Camping store," BeBe replied.

133

"Like we said," Chi Chi chimed in.

"Oh good, you're all here," Jenn muttered before turning to face the squad. "Will you let me out?"

"Yes," they replied.

"Really?"

"Uh huh," Gigi continued. "BeBe made an awesome point."

"I did?"

"Yeah you did, wastoid!"

"Oh yeah!" BeBe preened. "What was it again?"

Gigi huffed, unhooking a ring of keys from her belt loop. "Maybe if we help you, it'll help us. Maybe it'll make Gary stop."

Jenn gazed into the young woman's eyes and it felt like falling down a well. It felt like being pulled into the undertow. Like being trapped. It was despair and fatigue and hopelessness incarnate. "You're stuck here," she said, the realization rolling off her tongue like lead. "He kills you every night."

The three nodded, heads heavy.

"I'm so sorry," Jenn whispered, barely audible, looking each woman in the eyes. She could see the weariness—the violation—unsure how she missed it before.

Gigi handed her the keys. "If you keep running straight through, you'll see the gate." Jenn glanced over her shoulder warily. "I promise," the woman assured with surprising tenderness.

"We'll distract him," BeBe added, a sad little smile tugging at her lips.

"I can't ask you to..."

"You don't have to ask. We're doing it," Gigi shrugged.

"It's our job," BeBe echoed.

"He's going to kill us anyway," they said.

Jenn grabbed the keys, turning and running without looking back. Tears streamed down her face and she told herself it was because she was scared. Not because she was running away from three people who were about to be slaughtered. Three people who had helped her. Three people who were trapped, just like she was.

"Lock the gate behind you!" someone yelled. "So he can't get out," another added. And just as Jenn was about to turn back—to accomplish what, she didn't know—the gate materialized where a tent had once been. She scurried over to it, slotting the key, and raising it just enough to shimmy under.

Popping up on the other side, Jenn panicked as she groped for the outer lock. She slid the key in and turned it roughly, the motor engaging as it shuddered towards the bright-white tiled floor. Jenn heard a series of ragged screams—saw a flash of purple fabric dart from behind an impossible tree trunk. She stood, face pressed to the metal gate, staring into the darkened forest, wondering how any of it was real. *If* any of it was real.

The screams faded into the starless night, and Jenn was left with the sound of her own labored exhalations. She closed her lips tight, held her breath and counted to 10, but she could still hear the harsh gasps. Out of the corner of her eye, by the edge of the gate, she saw a moon-white face—two black orbs for eyes. It peered out of the darkened store, a deep hunger radiating from its stony expression.

"Gary," Jenn mouthed the name like a secret she didn't want to keep. She waited for him to strike out, rip the gate off its tracks. But he didn't. His leering, skeletal face just stared with an ugly abandon. And she stared back.

"I'm sorry," she said as she turned to run away. "I'm sorry he does this to you." There was no one to hear her, but she needed to say it or else it would devour her whole. Like Gary wanted to. Without looking back, Jenn darted to the middle of the mall and found that the girls had been correct—even though she'd never left the first floor corridor. She was somehow on the third floor.

Her sneakers squeaked on the polished tile. She was near the food court, orange neon lights broadcasting its location throughout the mall. It cast a sickly glow across the slick floor—across her shoes. Her skin. *Just have to get downstairs,* she thought, wondering if any of the exit doors were unlocked. Wondering, for the first time in what felt like hours if Karen was around. If she was okay.

She felt the urge to sprint but thought better of it. She didn't want to attract attention, so she hustled to the side and hugged the wall, peering through every door and gate as she passed.

The toy store sign was big and red, and it made the white floor look like it was doused in blood. Jenn backed away from it, the escalator just a few yards further. As she passed, even from a distance, she could hear grunted exclamations. She tried not to look, but couldn't help herself, the large windows inviting her to gaze unabashed.

A small army of dolls, each about two feet tall, were gathered around the glass door. They stood, silent and still, like they were waiting. Their glassy eyes followed Jenn as she passed, and just as she reached the escalator, she saw a body flop into view. A man, bound with cord, struggled to free himself. The dolls turned and descended upon him like a hoard of ravenous rats.

Jenn didn't stay to watch, taking the escalator steps two at a time, racing down to the second level and away from whatever nightmare she'd just happened upon. She strained to listen for any indication of what she was running towards but felt only a light breeze against her hot skin.

As she bounded down the steps, the breeze picked up; the soft, comforting draft developing into relentless gusts. Jenn's hair whipped around her face and she braced herself against the escalator's railing. She looked up, finding a great cloth banner had blown across the mall's massive open ceiling.

The banner trembled and undulated.

It curved majestically, catching the wind and coasting effortlessly. Jenn watched it dance and sway. It took her too long to realize it wasn't a banner. Or a sign. Or a tarp, or drop-cloth, or any of the other logical things her brain wanted to make it.

It was a wing.

It was a mammoth, behemoth, inexplicable wing cutting off the third floor from the rest of the mall.

Feeling too exposed, Jenn darted down the remaining steps, looking back to be sure the wing—and the wing's owner—hadn't advanced further. To her surprise, she found there was nothing there, the wind already a distant memory. *How could something so big be so fast,* she wondered. But her train of thought was derailed by level 2.

As soon as she'd bounced off the escalator, a thick fog rolled across the floor. It covered the pristine tile and violent slashes of red carpet. The wisps danced around Jenn's feet as she kicked at it, trying to clear a path. But it was no use. Moving only seemed to make it thicker and more difficult to traverse. She tiptoed slowly towards the next descending set of static silver stairs, an eerie feeling of being watched creeping over her like its own fog.

Something brushed against her calf.

She tripped, stumbling forward.

She felt a tug at the sweater still dangling from her waist.

Jenn screamed once in surprise, then again as she watched hands reach up from beneath the layer of fog. They stretched towards the glass roof that soared above them, skin damp and glowing a pale green. The stench of decay overwhelmed her.

She ran, knees kicking high like she was sprinting across tires in gym class. Jenn threw herself at the escalator, which now seemed more an oasis than an actual means of escape. She didn't know if she *could* escape. And if she did, who would she be? She thought of the camping store and the three girls as her ankle twisted and she careened down the metal steps.

Jenn dug her tongue into the hole where her front tooth had been as she rose to stand at the bottom of the first floor escalator. She looked up at where she'd come from and saw no wing and no fog. Just the dark and quiet mall.

"Jenn?"

She spun around, fists raised and mouth bloody. "Karen?" she asked, red spit dripping from her lips.

"Where the fuck have you been? It's been, like, fifteen minutes."

"Fifteen minutes..." Jenn repeated incredulously.

"Yeah, I've been waiting forever. What happened to *you*?" she asked, as if only then noticing Jenn's general state of ruin. "Did you lock yourself out?"

"I uh—I did. I got stuck... and then I was in..." she trailed off and pointed weakly at the floors above them.

"Yikes. I told you to prop the door open and pay attention." Karen tilted her head nonchalantly, reaching into her denim purse to retrieve a tube of lipstick. She painted on a bright pink smile and then frowned. "You did find the dumpster though, right?"

"The dumpster?"

"Yeah, you know the place where you throw garbage? You found it, right?"

"No. No I...I got lost in the corridor...somehow. I got turned around. And I couldn't find the store. And then when I left the bags, they...I think they disappeared."

"Wait, you didn't put the bags in the dumpster?"

"No. They were gone, and I couldn't get out. And then this thing sang, and these girls! Oh, the girls! What is this fucking place?" she wailed.

"It's the mall, genius. And now we are fucked." Karen punctuated each word with a clap of her hands. "Those bags? Those bags are like our rent, ya know? That's how we pay to be here. Get it?"

"No?"

"Do you know the cost to operate in a mystical arcane bazaar?"

"What?"

"It's a lot. And the contents of those bags keep us up and running."

"I don't understand."

"Clearly," Karen barked. "I thought you said you'd worked in a mall before. Did Dallas not tell you anything?"

"He didn't tell me any of this!" Jenn snapped.

Karen shook her head. "Look, don't go ballistic, but I don't think this is gonna work out. You're fired."

"I'm fired! You're firing me? I quit! I quit! And I'm going to tell everyone what happens here."

Karen laughed, turning on her heel. "Everyone already knows. And no one cares. People *really* like malls. Come on, I'll walk you out."

Dumbfounded, Jenn trailed behind the woman, listening to the soft click of her heels against the immaculate tile. She felt so small as she traversed the sprawling space, the full moon winking down on her from the open roof.

"Okay, goodbye," Karen said in a rush as she unlocked a door at the main entrance.

Jenn stared in disbelief. "This is it?"

"You're fired. What else did you want?"

"What's in the bags?" Jenn asked without thinking.

"Fear."

"What?"

"Fear," Karen repeated dully. "And grief and joy and laughter. But they like fear most. In fact, most stores here harvest fear. It's big business."

Jenn's eyebrows knit together tightly, her lips pursed. Blood slid down her throat. "How do you get fear?"

"Well, at Video Valley, when you sign up for a membership, you sign away your rights to the emotions you experience while watching our rentals. When the VHS is returned, we collect said emotions and then toss them into the dumpster out back. I don't know *where* it goes from there. But it's on our rental agreement. Everyone signs them. We're not doing anything illegal."

"I don't believe it..."

"Yeah, isn't that the best part? No one believes it!" Karen tapped her foot, teased hair bouncing along. "Anyway, like I said, you're fired and I gotta motor. So good luck or whatever."

"Bite me," Jenn spat, elbowing her way past Karen.

"I think there's a place on level 2 for that," she laughed, pulling the door shut behind Jenn. "Chill out, kid. And let me give you some advice: All jobs are lame. Everyone's an asshole. And working in an evil mall is way more fun than a regular one."

Jenn watched Karen walk back into the mall, jaw clenched

and aching. She pulled at the door uselessly, letting her hand fall back against her side. "Gotta tell everyone," she grit out, remembering the grasping hands—thinking of the girls.

"Gotta tell them all..."

But by the time Jenn reached the bus stop, she'd forgotten what she was supposed to tell, and whom she was supposed to tell it too. Instead, she wondered where her tooth had gone, and why she was so tired. *Must've been a hard night at work,* she thought as she pulled on her sweater with a sigh.

Role With Disadvantage

KARA DENNISON

Amongst the Demons of Hell, there is one rule above all others: never screw up a job. Their side, after all, is not the one that believes in second chances.

Slugbile had centuries to meditate on this. Once he'd been assigned to the best and the brightest of humanity, tasked with carefully breaking down their morals and psyches like so many junk cars before letting them roll through the gates of hell under their own steam. 177,013 such souls had fallen under his careful ministrations; but it took just one getting away for the bottom to drop out. Failure was never an option. Not even once. Now, and ever since, he was doing grudge work for The Man Downstairs.

These days, he was mostly sent after higher-ranking demons—ones *he* would have outranked in his heyday—to enact *their* ideas. Most of the time this was nothing more than a low-tier bother. He did what was expected of him, walked away, and let it succeed or fail. What he hated were the jobs that he knew were good. The ones where he found himself thinking "Damn, I wish I'd thought of that," while knowing he was completely incapable of doing so. And the most recent one picked at him in just that way.

The human race had a peculiar penchant for outlining its own damnation—that is, coming up with *absolutely fantastic* ideas for it. And even crediting them to the Big Boss. None of these things was the work of the Lower Realms, of course. They were all human in origin—occasionally (funnily enough) with a sprinkle of Divine Inspiration, which was at least a small win where image was concerned.

But then the latest panic had sprung up in a flurry of 20-sided dice and fictional spells, and one foul baby of a go-getter had had an annoyingly brilliant revelation: just steal the panic and make it real. Actually *make* a tabletop game that issued straight from Hell, and pepper it with every little bad influence and mind-breaking subliminal suggestion. In essence, give them what they wanted.

And thus, *Wizard Knights* First Edition was born. Well, almost born. There was still the whole "creating it" and "selling it" and "making people like it" to get through.

"You've got the final proof in, then?" Toadpimple had his high-end shoes propped on the desk, filling a good portion of the communication portal between them. His senior's desk was irritatingly tidy, IN and OUT boxes smoldering only slightly with a few ever-burning missives.

Slugbile weighed his options. "Yes" was a lie; and lies were to be used only on clients. "No" was true, but not an acceptable answer unless he wanted to get popped even further down the unholy chain. He sucked in his breath, popping his grimy knuckles.

"Ah...*almost*, almost. It's just, y'know...things happen with the creative process. You can't rush this stuff. It's just a little longer—"

"Do. You have. The final. Draft?" Toadpimple flicked a sharp thumbnail on the pad of his index finger, lighting a cigar with the resulting flame. Slugbile cringed. Adolescent showoff stuff. *He* did it when he was starting out, sure. But all this did was serve to remind him just how far below the mean he'd fallen. "Yes or no. It's a simple answer."

"No."

"Why?"

Again—the real answer wouldn't sit well. But Slugbile wasn't in the mood for more scolding from a demon who used party tricks for intimidation. "I was told it would be a little longer. Just a few more kinks to work out. I wasn't given an ETA, but uh...it's soon. It'll be soon."

"Look." The feet came away from the desk and

Toadpimple leaned in, breathing acrid cigar smoke through the portal. "We aren't *told* what will happen. We *make* things happen. You do remember that, right?"

"Sure, sure."

The demonic overseer grinned. His teeth were disgustingly straight and white. "I know your situation, pal. Shoot, everyone does, let's not kid ourselves. But if things go well for Morningstar Games, that could be good for you, too."

"Yeah?"

"Yeah. Think of it." Toadpimple waved a hand in front of himself. A little moving image of "what if" sprang up between them—news flashes of weighty hardback books flying off the shelves, hands feverishly rolling many-sided dice. *"Wizard Knights,* the new game that's sweeping the globe. Fun, fantastic…irresistible. Wield magic weapons, travel to far-off lands, all with paper and pencil." The image snapped out of existence, leaving Toadpimple's million-dollar smile leering in its place. "With a few of our personal favorites sprinkled in among the spells. But you've read it, so you'll have seen them."

Slugbile had not, in fact, read it. He'd packed it along to its next port of call without even opening the envelope. But he wasn't about to admit that.

Slugbile scratched his head, flicking something squirmy and yellowing from his nail. It was nice talk, but Toadpimple would turn the project report in with anyone else's name tidily excised. No mention of the demoted demon who'd spent an ungodly amount of time on the phone with editors who always had one more excuse. The whole thing was sauntering vaguely toward Not Worth It.

"How about I just bring it back as is and we get on with things?"

Toadpimple pursed his lips disapprovingly. "Oh, no no no. We have to have a good *product.* We have to have something the people want to stick with. How do we stand up against the competition otherwise?"

There was no chance of getting this off his plate without some extreme movement. "Fine. I'll go in tonight and get it myself."

"Good fella." The big bright glittering smile was back, and Slugbile got the sense that seeing it directed at him was supposed to make him feel good. It didn't. "Use the thumbscrews. Psych 'em up. Do whatever you have to, but get me that manuscript."

"Oh, I know how to threaten their type. Don't you worry." Slugbile waved a hand to close the communication portal, but Toadpimple's own hand shot through it, holding it open.

"One last thing."

Slugbile sighed and gritted his teeth, allowing the portal to reopen just enough for his overseer's face to show through.

Toadpimple raised one finger. "One result. That's all we need. Prove our little game can win over *one* soul, and the job is done. Otherwise…"

"Otherwise?"

"Well, I wouldn't like to say." The overseer's arm slipped back through the portal, and the little hole in reality snapped shut.

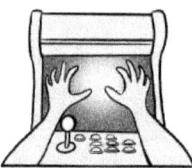

Elizabeth O'Brien scoured each page of the manuscript with a clinical eye, scowling and peering through her reading glasses. Debbie Olson watched her from the kitchen, pouring out coffee for the group that had gathered so far.

"She really is convinced she'll vanquish Satan and all the powers of Hell singlehanded tonight, isn't she?" Jeff laughed and kissed Debbie on top of her head as he squeezed past from the laundry room.

"Probably not a good time to tell her this might take a second night, then." Debbie took a sip from her own coffee as Jeff took two of the mugs out to their guests. "But it's why she's here, right? If it can survive her, it can survive anything."

"I've had my share of problem players," Jeff muttered,

"but she seems like she'll be an entirely new breed."

Jeff placed one of the two mugs of coffee next to Elizabeth. She failed to notice, too caught up in her perusal of the potentially demonic manuscript before her. The other mug went to Eric: Debbie's brother and the third of the night's four party members. Contrary to Elizabeth, he was aware of, and awaiting, the caffeine boost. "Thanks. We'll be needing this, I'm sure."

"What's this?" Elizabeth tapped her index finger irritably on the paper in front of her. "Hellish Agony. *Really?* That's the sort of thing you're encouraging literal children to engage in?"

Jeff smiled patiently. After three solid months of testing and editing and re-testing *Wizard Knights* with Debbie, he didn't need to look at the sheet. Level 10 Dark Scholar spell, 3+ successes to hit unless routed by a successful defense roll or the spending of a Luck Point.

Elizabeth O'Brien would not understand any of that.

"It's a spell to kill monsters," he said reassuringly. "You know. Fake monsters. It's not something I'm subjecting anyone to."

"You say 'fake' like I don't know that." Elizabeth took her glasses off and folded her hands primly atop the manuscript. She was in her early thirties, the same as everyone else in the house at the moment, but something about her puckered scowl and imperious tone reminded Jeff of his own grandmother. "It's not what you and I think. It's what *they* think."

"They?" Eric tested his coffee, found it still too hot, and put it aside.

"The *children,*" Elizabeth tutted. "Honestly, I would think you of all people would be most upset by this."

Eric stretched lazily, giving a little sigh of relief as the crick in his back was eased. "Your concern is commendable, but this *is* all a game, after all. And one my sister and brother-and-law have done an amazing job polishing up from a, er..." He weighed his words as he looked back at the pair, still lingering in the kitchen.

"A mess," Jeff offered.

145

"Diplomatic."

It was true. The Olsons were avid gamers—they'd met at a comic shop six years prior, Jeff running a weekend campaign, Debbie sitting in with a hastily-constructed wizard. So editing a tabletop sourcebook had sounded like a treat, especially compared to their usual work editing textbooks and instruction manuals. But the manuscript that arrived from Morningstar had been typo-ridden, full of plotholes throughout the game's patchy lore, and held up by a lopsided skeleton of poorly-calculated game mechanics. It had also been in a slightly on-fire manila envelope, but that was a much quicker issue to fix.

"It's all well and good to say it's 'just a game.'" Elizabeth turned her attention back to the manuscript, foregoing her reading glasses; apparently evil was just *that* visible. "But who plays these games? People who want to escape from the real world. Damaged, lonely, maladjusted people."

Eric grinned. "Thanks."

Elizabeth panicked. "P-Present company excepted, of course." The exception apparently didn't extend to Jeff and Debbie themselves. "But for the most part. Young people looking to detach from reality. They come to these games for that escape. And what happens when they find it? They forget who they are. They start thinking they're these…elves and ghosts and things. They lose their identity."

"No, they don't," Jeff muttered.

"You saw that documentary on the TV last Christmas. About the boy who tried to throw himself off the Empire State Building because he thought he was a knight or a warrior or something."

Debbie rubbed her forehead. "Twin Towers. And it *wasn't* a documentary."

"It was based on a true story, Deborah. Everyone knows that. And if you're going to insist on taking part in this disgusting hobby, someone has to keep you on the straight and narrow." She peered at the manuscript again. *"Mind Slave!?"*

The doorbell brought a momentary reprieve. Jeff cut

through to meet the final player for the evening's beta test. It would be Jason: a college student he'd run into at that same comic book store, an avid player of literally anything, and notorious for attempting all manner of rule-bending shenanigans. Besides being a welcome shot of humor for the party, he'd be a perfect stress test.

He was also not who was at the door.

Jason was in his early twenties, not whatever indeterminate "older" this person was. His hair was short and sandy, not sparse and greasy and ginger. He also didn't have an odd sickly-sweet smell about him, or rheumy eyes, or odd growths and rashes on nearly every visible part of his skin.

The man who was not Jason grinned—Jeff never knew a grin could *smell*—and stuck out a hand. "Olson, right? We've talked on the phone."

"Are you the guy who keeps trying to sell us a timeshare?"

The man pushed past Jeff into the house, his stained corduroy suit leaving a smudge on the doorjamb. Elizabeth was still engrossed in picking through the game book, but Eric raised his eyes and looked at the stranger curiously.

"This doesn't look like the kid you were describing," he called to Debbie, eyes still locked on the new arrival.

Debbie looked into the living room. "He's...not. In fact, I'm not entirely sure *who* he is."

"I told you," the stranger said again, still holding the grin. "We talked on the phone. About the book."

Jeff finally placed the voice. On the phone it had sounded like it was on the edge of a cold; in person, it was more like a gurgle through a rusty grate. "Oh, you're...what was your name?" He couldn't recall the contact from Morningstar ever actually giving a name. Just a grunt, a few questions about how much longer editing would take, and then he'd slam the phone down again.

"I didn't tell you?"

"No," Debbie said quietly, trying to find a spot on the new arrival's face where she could look without feeling like she was staring at...*something.*

The stranger seemed flustered. "Ah. Right, silly me. Uh.

Guy." He paused, as though riffling through the back corners of his brain. "Guy, uh. Normal. Man."

"Guy Normalman," Debbie echoed dubiously.

Eric smirked as he eyed the new arrival. "Think I might've gone to high school with your sister. Is her name Ima?"

Guy didn't answer, instead throwing himself casually down in the chair sitting open for Jason. "So, yeah. I heard you have a test game or whatever going on tonight. Figured I'd come help things along and then, uh…" He snapped his scraggly-nailed fingers. "Once things are all done here, I can just grab it and go."

"Guy?" Debbie's tone was strained and sweet at the same time. "Let's not talk shop in the living room." She nodded toward the back door. Jeff required no extra prompting, and plucked at Guy's greasy sleeve as he went by.

The saying goes that the greatest trick the Devil ever pulled was convincing the world he doesn't exist, and nothing could be further from the truth. You hear his name everywhere, see his likeness on everything, use his name in colloquialisms and expletives and cake recipes. You see him blamed for anything humanity doesn't like on this particular day, whether or not he had a hand in it.

Meanwhile, his subordinates work away on insignificant corners of life. Evening plans. Traffic jams. Minor disagreements. Moments that seem tiny and pointless in the face of war and crime and this week's violent video game release. Moments so personal that you'd feel foolish to admit to anyone else that you felt his presence there. And that's because, like any other skilled magician, the greatest trick the Devil ever pulled was simple misdirection.

If it hadn't been for that fact, Jeff and Debbie Olson might never have taken the *Wizard Knights* job. There was something unsettling about the manuscript when it came in.

Something that crawled out of the words on the page, poking around in their brains for loose thoughts to latch onto. Neither of them remembered a moment when they'd actually discussed it. There was no point at which they had said, aloud, "This project issues straight from Hell itself, and we are all that stands between the ministrations of the Devil and an unsuspecting public."

But they both knew, and they knew the other knew, and they began working assiduously to clip those crawling, searching words from the text. To buffer it up with something that might hold at bay anything that had slipped through the cracks. And, just as importantly, to get a paycheck to fatten up their anemic bank account.

Two things had, at last, made them sure of their fears. One was a firm assertion from one of the people currently sitting at the game table; the other was the individual who had arrived at the door, smelling of sulfur and stress nightmares.

Guy Normalman (probably not his real name) remained casual as he followed the Olsons to the back porch and closed the door behind them. "Yeah, I get you. Don't wanna ruin the fun for the guests, right? No problem, we can clear this up out here and then get down to business."

Each Olson had at least three questions locked and loaded; it was just a matter of which bubbled to the surface first, and from whom.

It was Debbie: "Where's Jason?"

"Who's Jason?" Guy asked, directing his attention to something under one of his yellowing thumbnails.

"Our fourth player. He was supposed to be here by now. He's a good kid, never late. And he was excited about being here tonight. So, where *is* he?"

Guy shrugged. "Never heard of him. But hey, good luck, right? I can sit in for him."

Neither Jeff nor Debbie could shake the strange, chilling feeling that Jason's absence was deliberate, and they were sharing a cramped little concrete stoop with the person who arranged it. "I don't believe you," Jeff finally blurted out. It came out in a rush, not at all as confident or accusatory as he'd hope it would be.

"Hey, it's a free country." Guy lifted one lapel of his jacket and shoved his other hand underneath, searching an inner pocket for something. "Look, I know we talked on the phone, and I know I *said* I was giving you more time, but...you've had three months. Three months is a lot of time for a book to be in edits."

"It's really not," Debbie said quietly, feeling at least some relief in the knowledge that there must not be many editors where Guy came from.

"Regardless, my hand is being forced. I need that thing finished tonight." Guy continued to rummage.

Jeff burst out laughing. "Tonight!? Even if this game was enough to work out the last of the kinks, we'd actually have to integrate everything into the book. We're still testing out the new class."

"What new class?"

"Cleric. It's..." Jeff stopped short, realizing he couldn't afford to explain why they'd *really* shoehorned in a holy healer. "It's, uh, a matter of play style and party balance. Healing abilities are completely unbalanced across the other classes. There are no strictly defense types, and—"

Guy shook his head. "I don't understand what *any* of that means. If it's what's taking up your time tonight, then kill it."

"We're not," Debbie replied evenly, squaring up her shoulders. "We're not killing off things that will fix the game. If you want a good game, you'll have to wait."

Finally, Guy found what he was looking for. He began pulling out a large piece of paper...and it just kept going. Jeff wondered if it was some sort of prop he had loaded (though why, he couldn't figure out for the life of him). When the paper emerged in its entirety, the Olsons could see that it was a large prop check, about half the size of the sort handed off to charities and prize winners. An ink pen shot from Guy's shirt cuff into his free hand, and he began scribbling away on the business side of the check.

"I really oughta okay this with them first, but what the hell. Olson...Editorial...Services..." He stuck out his spotty tongue in concentration as he wrote. "And to put a rush on it, we'll say fifty...nah, *seventy* percent extra." A bit more scribbling, and Guy turned the check around proudly. The oversized check bore a line of scratchy calligraphy indicating, as promised, 170% of their original agreed-upon price.

"Look..." Debbie said hesitantly, unsure where to start. Work was drying up. Even the original sum would be a blessing—funnily enough.

Jeff cut in swiftly with diplomacy. "Mr., uh, Normalman. We really appreciate the offer. Honestly, I think we would like to take you up on it. But what you're asking is literally impossible. Unless you want to take it away now, as is— which, no offense, you shouldn't—we can't have it done tonight. There aren't enough hours. It's not possible."

Guy frowned, but it wasn't an angry expression. It was disappointed, but an expected disappointment. He'd wanted to be proved wrong, and he hadn't been. That was a shame but what had he expected? That's what the flat expression seemed to scream; and screaming it even louder were the two little gouts of flame that shot out of his palms, engulfing the check and reducing it to a tiny pile of ashes at his feet. The Olsons grabbed at each other's sleeves in shock, watching the check disintegrate.

"Okay, kids. I'll put it another way. Either I leave with this. Tonight. Ready to publish. Or you get zero dollars." He looked down at the little pile of ash and kicked it off the stoop with the side of one spotty shoe. "Good? Good. I'm gonna go get some coffee. See you in five."

The stranger excused himself into the house.

"That guy," Debbie muttered. "He's..."

"Literally the devil?" Jeff offered.

Debbie shook her head. "I wouldn't go that far. But I'm starting to think we invited the exact right people tonight."

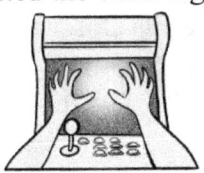

The south of Tantalia was a green and lush region of forests, rivers, and tight-knit little farming communities. At least, that's how it was after the Olsons got through with *Chapter 3: Setting and History*. When the *Wizard Knights* core book first came into their hands, the world of Beyondal was a few hastily-constructed countries comprised of one natural feature each. They'd joked early on that whoever had written this chapter had clearly never walked around on Earth for more than five minutes...a joke that was currently coming back to haunt both of them as they stared at the rep from Morningstar Games.

Debbie locked eyes with Jeff and shook her head, and he realized his mood must be getting a little too visible. *No, focus up.* This was his favorite part of the game: all the pieces had been assembled and were being held separate by five different people. The minute he opened his mouth, the fantastical chemicals would mix, and a story would be born that no one person could write alone. He loved that moment; and dammit, he'd liberate as much enjoyment from it as he could. Even if that meant playing dungeon master to a literal demon from the depths of hell.

He set the stage: a tavern, of course. All the best stories start at a tavern. It's where people who should never meet can meet, and the best parties are always made up of people who should never meet. That's the beauty of it—*a* beauty of it.

First, the halfling Spellgunner, Misha. Debbie's character from when they first met, retooled for the *Wizard Knights* system. An affable character mostly built for roleplay and attacking from a distance. If she played well, the game would fly for people who like less math in their evenings.

The human Truthspeaker, Eliza. Three guesses who was steering that one. "Truthspeaker" wasn't remotely what Elizabeth assumed as she exulted over seeing it on her pre-made character sheet: it was closer to a Bard, able to slay with words. But that wasn't the point of this exercise. The point was to keep her as appeased as possible without breaking the game...though all things considered, that might be easier said than done.

152

The elven Cleric, Arcturus Sunspinner. To be played by Eric, their resident expert (besides the Olsons themselves, of course). Having to create an entire class from scratch was already difficult, but seeing what he needed during gameplay would be a big assist—and, big flaming checks aside, Guy would just have to deal with that.

And finally, there was Demonicus the Death Warlock. Originally constructed to allow Jason to be his full ridiculous self and do his best to break the game (and Jeff), it now fell into the distressingly appropriate hands of one "Guy Normalman." Guy, however, did not seem especially impressed, turning the sheet this way and that and trying to make sense of all the numbers on it.

"You've all been to the Busted Cannon at least once before," Jeff continued after his basic setting of the scene. "Though never at the same time. Misha, you're a regular, of course. Eliza, you're here once a week, distributing pamphlets on the dangers of drink. You've saved, let's see..." A quick roll of the dice. "... three drunkards this past week." Elizabeth apparently liked this. "Arcturus, you normally go straight to the back room when you come here, in order to convey messages to the tavern keeper. You can do that now, if you want."

Eric heaved a thoughtful, fake sigh. "Ah, no. You know what? I never get to actually stop and enjoy myself. I'll take a table for a change."

"All right, you can sit wherever you want. And Demonicus, you—"

Guy slammed his hand on the table. "I burst through the doors and unleash unholy lightning on everyone in the tavern, killing them all!" Then he looked over expectantly at Jeff— or, rather, at the manuscript and pile of notes sitting in front of him. "Huh? How 'bout that?"

The rest of the table was silent. Elizabeth had gone somewhat pale, but the others just stared.

"What?"

Debbie pointed at her sheet. "Unholy Lightning is a Spellgunner ability, not a Death Warlock ability. I can do it,

153

but you can't."

"Uh…"

"Unless," Eric cut in brightly, "you have an ability that lets you trade out spells. I think I saw something like that for Warlocks?"

Jeff nodded. "Aura Shift. But that's only for Storm Warlocks."

Guy's face pinched up into a confused sneer. "What?!"

"Also," Eric cut in, "my Cleric is seated by the door and would have a Reaction move if he saw you start to cast something—"

"I told them to ditch the Cleric!" Guy shouted.

Elizabeth shuddered, and somehow the motion drew everyone's attention. It wasn't from cold or fright. It was just a hair below melodramatic—theatrical, but not ridiculous. She clutched her sweater more tightly around her with one hand and furrowed her brow. The meaning of the expression was clear to all: *This is extremely upsetting to me, and if I drop dead from shock you will live with that guilt for the rest of your lives.*

Even Guy was shamed into silence.

"We're not," Jeff said calmly, "dropping the Cleric. Moving on. "

Jeff looked at Guy, fuming silently in his—rather, Jason's—seat. Maybe it was his overly cinematic imagination, but for a moment Jeff thought he saw cartoonish steam issuing from under Guy's collar.

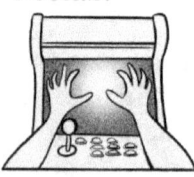

Considering the forces they were up against, the first half of the evening's gameplay had gone surprisingly smoothly. Well, perhaps "smoothly" wasn't the word. No one had put anyone else's head through a table, and nothing had exploded into flame. At the moment, those counted as positives.

Jeff got the party halfway through the evening's encounter

mostly on schedule. A bar fight brought the four characters together for their first real encounter, with the brawler transforming into a monstrous creature and doubling in size. Elizabeth nearly fainted at the mere suggestion. Eric, on the other hand, was flipping his sheet from front to back, carefully plotting at least three moves ahead; Guy was just flipping his sheet from front to back, trying to make sense of it.

"The spells you can do," Jeff offered, "are in that box in the bottom right."

Guy directed his attention to the little box. Jeff noticed the little flicker in Guy's eyes as he saw one of the spells...as though lighting on something he was familiar with. "Yeah. Thief of Time. This one. I'm doing that."

"Okay, tell me about Thief of Time."

Guy squinted at the paper. "Uh. Freezes enemy action for one round, and the next attack uses up the whole party's hit dice for the round...after which the spell ends. Whatever all that means."

"All right. Roll for it."

"Huh?"

Jeff pointed at the little selection of dice next to Guy's left hand. "The dice. You roll them to see if you can cast the spell."

"What do you mean if I *can?*" Guy scoffed. "Of *course* I can! I'm a Demon Lord."

"Death Warlock," Jeff corrected. "Your spell dice are 3d6...sorry, three of those normal dice. Just get two successes."

Guy rolled the trio of six-sided dice.

"Well? How many did you get?"

"That's a pretty loaded question."

"Come on."

The answer was one, and—much to Guy's chagrin—Jeff moved on to Debbie's turn as though nothing had happened. There was a little *pop*, then a *hiss*, and Jeff could see the corner of Guy's character sheet curling and browning, sending up a thin plume of gray smoke.

155

Elizabeth was so busy shuffling through her own sheet for things to disapprove of, she didn't even see it. Debbie, attempting to focus on her next move, couldn't help but be distracted by the irony: a literal spark of hellfire just two feet away from where she was looking.

Blessedly, Debbie and Eric carried the party through the majority of combat. After searching the body, Arcturus found items with labels from an apothecary two towns over. Cut to a span of clue-hunting and investigation to check some passive skills, which would lead to the next story beat a few towns over.

"I wanna read some minds," Guy said gruffly.

Both Olsons eyed him suspiciously. "Is it on your sheet?" Jeff asked tersely.

Guy snapped his sheet up and jabbed a finger at the box of spells. "Yeah? It's right *there!* Mind Scan!"

"Roll for it."

He did, barely squeezing past Jeff's (admittedly higher than usual) threshold. Well...this would be a test, then, wouldn't it? What would a literal demon do with a fake spell at his disposal? Eric seemed interested, too, reaching for the jacket slung over his chair and rummaging around in a pocket.

Jeff felt something brush past his mind—it was the only way he could think to describe it. A nudge, like a stray elbow in a crowded waiting room. Debbie threw Jeff a silent look. Had she felt it, too?

A sickening thought accompanied the nudge. If the spells in this game were made to mess with one's mind when "cast" by humans...what *was* their effect when wielded by a literal demon?

"Well?" Jeff asked—half challenging, half tense.

"I, uh..." Guy tapped one knobbly finger on the sheet. "I wanted to see if there's any gossip the locals aren't telling us about the apothecary."

Debbie looked to Jeff. Then to Guy. The mental nudge eased. "In the game, you mean?"

"No, the apothecary plying his humble wares up the street." Guy rolled his eyes. "Yeah, in the game! I can do that, right?"

He could. It was just something of a shock that he *would.*

After a few small battles along the way to test out shorter combat scenes, Debbie noted it was already after 9 P.M. Now the pair sat in the upstairs study as Eric made more coffee, Elizabeth borrowed the house phone to check in on the babysitter, and Guy did…whatever…in the bathroom. As Jeff sorted his notes, Debbie took the opportunity to make an overdue phone call.

"One bit of good news," she said after hanging up, looking much more at ease. "Jason is in his dorm, taking a nap. If Guy did anything to him, it wasn't serious." With that in mind, both of them were much more ready to talk shop.

"The Cleric build is actually holding up pretty well," Jeff noted, looking over his notes. "Eric didn't really have much to say so far. Maybe we actually *can*—"

"You're really going to work to Guy's impossible schedule?"

Jeff sighed. Put the notebook down. Wiped a hand over his face. "Actually? No. No, I'm sick of this. Our boss might be…" He paused, corrected. "Our boss *is* a literal demon. We can't have any part in that. Send them all home. Screw the money. We have some savings."

"Boot him out," Debbie offered.

"Call up Max von Sydow to give the place a once-over."

Debbie laughed. The laugh tapered off. "We don't have savings, do we?"

"We have five dollars to keep the account open, and then whatever is in checking."

"God." She grabbed Jeff's notes from him. "So we keep going. Elizabeth doesn't want players to be able to kill anything sentient, because she believes it will encourage young people to solve all their problems with violence."

"She is incorrect, so we will ignore her."

Fortunately, the rest of the suggestions were at least vaguely useful—even one from Elizabeth about the preponderance of Hell-themed naming conventions. (The fact that they understood why notwithstanding.) With their last ten

157

minutes of break, the Olsons put their heads down and began scribbling corrections across the manuscript and character sheets.

Meanwhile, in the bathroom, Guy ("Stay in character, man, deep cover") was perched on the tank of the toilet, using the closed seat as a footrest. The communication portal hovered in front of him, in line with the Olsons' sandy pink shower curtain sprinkled with seashell patterns. Toadpimple sat at his desk on the other side, shuffling useless papers back and forth and not looking Guy in the eye.

"You have it, then?"

"Yeah, absolutely." Guy glanced at the bathroom door. There wasn't much to speak of by way of a lock, and that bothered him. Not on the Olsons' behalf; if they wanted to get walked in on while they were doing their business, that was none of his concern. But he didn't feel at all certain that the rusty little switch under the handle would put sufficient distance between himself and the lady in the glasses. Her disapproval was distracting.

"Excellent!" Toadpimple directed his attention to the portal, reaching out a hand and flapping his fingers in a "gimmie" motion. "Hand it on over, then. Nice and quick. We'll get it to the typesetters in Circle Six and have the whole thing turned around by tomorrow morning."

"Uh..."

"Oh, it's going to be great, Sluggy. We've got a guy working on the artwork. Just line art for the internal pages, obviously. But the cover? So eyecatching. Can't look away. Like, literally. It imprints itself on your retinas. Heck of a trick."

"See..."

"Enough about that, though. I'm talking your ear off. Let's see this baby."

Guy grinned toothily and wearily. "It's gonna take a little longer to actually get it *from* them."

Toadpimple's cheerful expression dropped. It wasn't angry now—just cold disappointment. It reminded Guy of the lady with the glasses. "I thought you said you *have* it."

"Right, well. Obviously, for varying levels of 'have.' I'm in its presence, I've *seen* it. I just need to, you know. Leave with it."

"Did you threaten them?"

Guy chuckled. That, at least, he felt proud of. "Oh, you know it. You shoulda seen the looks on their faces. Showed them who was boss."

"And yet."

"Uh. Right."

Toadpimple waved a hand, and the portal began to shrink. "Next time I see your face, it had better have a completed book blocking it from my view." He paused, seeming to rethink his phrasing, but finally appeared to have committed himself to it. "Got it? Good. And remember—"

"Yeah, yeah, need to know it'll win one soul. Got it."

The last speck of open portal rolled inward on itself, cancelling itself out of reality, and leaving Guy Normalman sitting alone on a stranger's toilet.

Well, lies of omission technically weren't lies...but had they been, he would be guilty of a list of fibs as long as his own just slightly overlong arm. He hadn't mentioned the addition of a Cleric, and the fact that he had so far been unable to extract it from the book. He had omitted the bit where Toadpimple's carefully crafted Bad Influences fell swiftly in the wake of a bad roll of the dice... the ones that hadn't been completely edited out at least. But those were the least of the omissions. Two loomed over him still as he ran the water just long enough to make it sound like he'd done that human hand-washing thing.

Looming Thing 1: An agent of the Enemy was at the table, and knew what was going on.

Looming Thing 2: Guy was actually starting to enjoy himself.

"Why do I have to roll dice to look for something?" Elizabeth took up a handful of many-sided dice and shook them halfheartedly. "If I look around, I look around. If you wrote down in your notes that it's there, it's there."

"Yes," Jeff said patiently. "But if you go into a room looking for something you misplaced, do you automatically find it just because you looked around?"

Elizabeth had to admit that no, it never happened that way.

"Dice are the best way we have to simulate that chance," Debbie picked up. "Otherwise, well, everyone would just be able to do what they wanted all the time, and that's not a game." Then she smiled slightly. "That would just be...well...demonic tyranny. Wouldn't it?"

"Ugh." Elizabeth rolled the many-sided dice. "That's...no successes, I think."

Eric winced. "Ooh. My sympathies."

"You," Jeff said, "are still shaken up by your recent battle with the pixies, and thus end up not seeing much of anything. Misha—the sleeping dragon still has not noticed your party. You have some time to prepare. What are you up to?"

"Hey." Guy leaned in, addressing her in a low whisper as Jeff turned his attention to Debbie. "Hey, I get you. It sucks, doesn't it?"

Elizabeth eyed Guy suspiciously past her reading glasses. "It's a lot of complicated nonsense. I don't see how anyone can find this fun or edifying."

"Right?" Guy hunched down slightly lower as Eric excused himself for a coffee refill. "What does it say when you can't see because the dice said so? It's like..." He tried for a moment to put himself in Elizabeth's mindset—her terrified, overanalytical mindset. "It's like you're being told you're powerless. And what kind of message is that to give to kids, huh?"

He saw Elizabeth narrow her eyes a bit, thoughtfully. "It's true, you know. You're letting someone else control your actions and say what you can and can't do on a whim. It's almost as though you're being *trained* to be told what you can see and do."

"Yeah!" Guy pushed her on in an enthusiastic whisper. That was what was great about Elizabeth's type; they barely needed more than a prod to get themselves rolling. "Tell you what—they might not listen to you or me, but maybe together we can talk some sense into them. Take some of these stupid *checks* out. Give players more..." Oh, what was that phrase they loved so much? "...more free will."

Before Elizabeth could latch into the line of reasoning, Eric bumped by on his way back to the table. Something splashed over Guy's balding head. For a moment he thought it was just coffee...but coffee didn't bubble and burn with an acidic edge. He wiped his hands over his head...and his hands stung with the same acidic anguish.

Guy leapt from his seat and ran to the bathroom, knocking his chair and a few dice over along the way. The rest of the table watched, stunned—except for Eric, who sat down calmly with his cup of coffee. Out of the corner of her eye, Debbie could see her brother tuck a small metal flask, emblazoned with a simple cross, into his jacket pocket.

"He'll be fine," Eric said casually, sipping his coffee.

In the bathroom, Guy was not fine. He turned the shower on and stuck his head under the hot running water, waiting for the holy water's sting to wash away. As he rubbed his scant hair down with one of the Olsons' dusty rose guest towels, he saw a communication portal begin to emerge in front of him.

"Not *now.*" He swatted it out of the air like a slow-moving fly. Time was running short...and now, so was his temper. He heard the rest of the group trading notes in the living room as they waited for him to return. Instead of returning to the group, he pressed his ear to the door, listening intently.

"Anything else sketchy-looking?" Debbie asked Eric.

"Hmmm...I don't see anything else that worries me, but I also haven't looked at the conditional spells for every class. It's so rare you'd even get to use them."

"Sketchy-looking?" Elizabeth's voice wavered.

"Don't worry about it. Just fiddly editing stuff. I'll see if I can beg one more night off Guy so Eric can scour the appendix of conditional spells. We're almost done, anyway.

Just this last fight."

Not happening. Guy blasted his patchy wet hair with two gouts of hellish steam to dry them, straightened his suit jacket, and went back to finish things off.

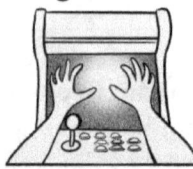

The "last fight" was already an hour long and counting. Jeff's finely painted miniature of a bronze dragon squatted in the center of his hastily drawn map, with pocket change scattered around it at intervals to stand in for party members. Miniatures had been the last thing on Jeff's mind as he rushed to get the book in working order, but it turned out they were needed.

Elizabeth was carefully picking her way through her spells on each turn. She used only one or two with any regularity; the rest, she had begun renaming, as the book names distressed her. "Hellish Reprimand" had become "Holy Reprimand," for a start...and no one had the energy to argue. Eric was back to flipping his sheet back and forth, keeping hit points (and spirits) high. Debbie was back in her element; she'd nearly forgotten about the literal demon seated diagonally from her, staring at the quarter that represented his Death Warlock.

Guy had asked to check the book for something, and Jeff obliged instinctively. He flipped through carefully, scouring the manuscript closer than he'd ever intended to, comparing it to his sheet, comparing it to his own knowledge. His eyes drifted to the digital clock sitting on top of the boxy television set a few feet away. It was approaching midnight. Time was running out.

Elizabeth slung another Holy Reprimand.

Time...

"Guy...Demonicus? You're up."

Guy put the book down. "All right. Sure. I'm gonna move here..." He shoved his quarter closer to the dragon miniature.

"…and try to cast Thief of Time again."

"Right. Freeze enemy action, divert the entire party's hit dice to your next attack. Roll for it. Two successes is all you need, a success is 4 or higher."

"Yeah, yeah, I know." Guy picked up the trio of six-sided dice and shook them around in his hand, hoping for a better role than the first time.

Wait.

He wanted to smack himself in the head with the fistful of dice. Honesty was only for coworkers. He was in the field right now. Lies were his number one weapon. Those dice were gonna land any damn way he pleased.

He threw the three dice down with confidence: a trio of sixes.

"I think that'll do it, yeah?"

Silence descended on the table…and, it seemed, on everything. Debbie got the same strange uneasy feeling on the edges of her mind as before, and judging by the look Jeff gave her, so did he. Elizabeth looked positively out of her element, suddenly faced with real fear. Eric had jammed his hand back into his jacket pocket, but his normally calm expression was furrowed in concentration.

"So…" Guy grinned. "You want me to tell you about Thief of Time again?"

Whether out of nervousness or just the sense that she ought to, Elizabeth looked over her shoulder. Through the living room window, she could see the outline of the dogwood tree in the Olsons' front yard in the darkness. Its leaves were rustling gently in the wind…or *would* have been, if the world outside hadn't stopped completely. Now the branches were skewed slightly sideways, frozen in place, as though a winter storm had plated it in ice while blowing it in one direction.

"See, you're right about one thing. There's a lot of screwy shit in that book. I really wish I'd bothered to look at it more before literally five minutes ago, because *oh, boy,* is it fun." Guy began pacing around the table, like an especially smelly lioness toying with her food. "There's all sorts of high-level stuff in there. You're not gonna see actual human beings shooting lightning bolts around Super-Duper Comics in a few weeks, nah. But there *is* stuff in there. And...ah, I owe you an apology. You guys *aren't* done. You did miss a few things, and it'll take a *lot* longer than tonight to tidy it up."

Father Eric Reid had shoved his character sheet aside, once again bringing out the little silver flask. Visually, his move was impressive, almost cinematic: he spun the cap open and swung his arm in Guy's direction. But instead of an arc of water and an acidic sizzle, the flask produced only a few stray drops—and all but one or two of those went astray. He was out.

Guy winced slightly, batting at the single drop that hit his face as though it were a bug bite, but looked otherwise unperturbed. Without hesitation, Eric dropped the flask and dug his crucifix out from under his polo shirt, eyes still locked on Guy *"Quicumque vult salvus esse..."*

At first, Guy looked shaken. He stared to shuffle backwards jerkily, as though pushed by something against his will. But he seemed to square up, dig his feet in, and regain his balance. There was some effort to it, but he was clearly intent on making it look as though that wasn't the case.

"Oh, that's a golden oldie, love it." Guy chuckled with more confidence than was likely warranted, Eric's prayer continuing under his speech. "Where was I? Oh, right. Your little cleaning job. That would take weeks, months, years...if you hadn't edited most of it out and stuck in a Cleric to counteract everything, of course...but for me? Right now? *Bam.*" He snapped. "And that, as they say, is how they get ya."

He turned his attention to Elizabeth. "You're terrified of your kids getting sucked into one of these, aren't ya? Losing all their time, not coming to the dinner table, not going to church or doing their homework. Yeah, don't need a Mind Scan to see that. That's Thief of Time, see. For *you* guys, I mean. Throw it down enough, and that's what you'll start seeing. For *me,* on the other hand...well. I control the party, right?"

Jeff felt a shudder of panic. He looked down at his hands,

164

as if expecting to see them move without his approval.

"Oh, calm down," Guy grumbled. "Your precious free will isn't going anywhere. But I'll tell ya what is." He gestured to the outside world. "Everything else out there. The world has stopped for us. And it's *gonna* stay stopped until I get the book."

Debbie pointed at the book, her hand shaking. "Look. It's there, okay? Take it. You can have it. We don't even want the rush fee."

Guy wagged a finger. "No no no no." He sat back down at his seat, drumming his knobbly fingers on the manuscript. "I don't want *this*. I want it the way it's supposed to be. No clerics. No sneaky editing out of the stuff that's *supposed* to be in there." He side-eyed Elizabeth. "No wimpy name changes."

Elizabeth glared imperiously. "You think this is any way to behave? To punish people who were trying to do *good* for the world?"

"Little late in the day to see that," Debbie muttered, "but I'll take it."

"Lady." Guy fixed Elizabeth with a glare of his own, a tired one. "I'm a literal demon. You know. The kind you keep thinking you see everywhere. I don't know what you were expecting."

Eric's Latin drone had ended. Nothing had budged, but he still held the crucifix in front of him. Guy relaxed slightly—the attempt had rattled him, and might have worked on some other night. Tonight, though, it was less an exorcism and more an inconvenience.

"We're not doing that," Jeff said, more calmly than he felt.

"Then I guess we're just gonna stay here in this little split second of time forever." Guy examined his nails. "I can make it go on as long as I want, you know. Decades. Centuries. My record is 594 years—wanna see if I can break it?"

Jeff lowered his eyes and reached across the table for the manuscript. Elizabeth shielded it from him. "Jeff, *no.*"

"What's your plan, then? Leave us all here to be tormented? Literal hell on earth? I thought you were against

165

that kind of thing."

Guy picked up the manuscript and handed it to Jeff over Elizabeth's shielding arm. "Good man."

"Wait..."

Debbie's voice was small. She wasn't looking at Guy, or anyone else. She was looking at the hastily sketched map.

"Not now, lady. You two have work to do."

"You still haven't used your attack."

Guy snorted. "My what?"

"Yeah, remember? The one where you use the party's hit dice. You still need to do that."

Jeff looked down at his notes, still shaking a bit, but seeming to gain confidence. "I mean...it's true. It would be a good chance to test out Unholy Twin, too. That's one we haven't seen anyone use yet, and it'll do a lot of damage even with one person's dice."

Guy glared at the miniature on the table. "That's not the..." His eyes traveled down to his notes.

"Unholy Twin," Debbie pressed on, "turns your main weapon into two shadow versions of itself. Each of those gets a huge bonus to hit. You could slice that thing up like a Christmas ham with a good enough roll."

"Which he would get, right?" Elizabeth's voice was uncertain. "He would get to use all our dice because of the...spell thing."

Eric raised his eyebrows thoughtfully. "It *would* be cool."

Guy found himself reaching for his dice without thinking. "...It *sounds* cool."

"You need three successes," Jeff added.

Guy didn't even think to fudge them—so as the dice dropped from his hand, he held his breath in anticipation.

A four. A five. A one. Guy actually felt his stomach drop. Why? *Why?*

Elizabeth slammed a hand on the table. "I, um..." She scoured her sheet. "I use one of my Ascension Points! That gives him another success, right?"

Jeff nodded. "Mark it off on your sheet."

Everyone rolled all their dice. Jeff rushed to total them up on his little scratch pad. Guy stared expectantly.

Slowly, Jeff reached over and turned the dragon miniature gently on its side. "Tell me how it goes, Demonicus."

Guy was excited. He didn't know why. All he knew was he was about to slay a dragon with two shadowy maces twice as tall as himself, and maybe that wasn't happening for *real,* but damn, he sure could see it in his head, and *damn, it sure was cool.*

As he described the scene in grisly detail—from the threads of inky darkness stretching between his mace and its new copy, to the one-two punch at the weakened dragon's underbelly—the world outside began to move again. The dogwood kicked back into gentle motion, like a film projector slowly getting up to speed.

And then—and then—the digital clock on top of the television set flashed over to 12 A.M. The game was over. It was tomorrow. And Guy lowered his arms, which absolutely did not have shadow maces in them, and he said:

"God damn it."

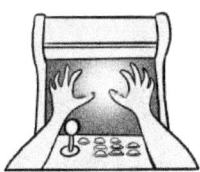

Slugbile had never actually been in Toadpimple's office in person. He'd seen snatches of it through the communication portal, decorated here and there with postmodern art prints that were almost certainly more closely connected to money laundering than to art. The rest of the office was oddly bare; it seemed as though his superior had only bothered to spice up the bits that would be seen through the portal, and left the rest to crack and rot.

"And there it is," Toadpimple said with a grin. "Bad luck about the…what did you say it was?"

"Attempted exorcism," Slugbile volunteered, handing the finished manuscript forward. "Was laid up for a day, not my fault, but I just got a few burns. No big deal." He patted his slightly singed, slightly bald pate. *A half-lie. It was fine, surely.*

"Excellent, excellent. We'll send that down to get formatted and printed." A portal of inky blackness opened at Toadpimple's left elbow, shaped like a mail slot. Anguished cries echoed through it, underscored by the boys on tormenting duty chiming in with things like "Could you do a few different versions?" and "Just one more little change, I promise!" and "Here, I'll just sit over your shoulder and direct you." He slid the manuscript through the portal.

"When do you need this by?" a voice called up weakly.

Toadpimple chuckled. "Oh, yesterday, if you could!"

The portal closed, cutting off a chorus of agonized groans as he directed his attention back to Slugbile. "So, of course. The other matter."

"Other matter?"

"The quality. Is it actually going to *work.*"

"Oh! Right, right, right."

Toadpimple propped his feet on the desk. Slugbile focused on his office chair, willing it to tip backwards. It didn't work. "So tell me: does *Wizard Knights* have the capacity to win over a soul?"

"Absolutely." Slugbile nodded slowly. "In fact, I think it already did."

Toadpimple rubbed his hands together, grinned, said something about upward momentum and synergy, and kicked Slugbile unceremoniously out of his office.

No matter. Slugbile returned to his own cramped corner room. He turned on his desk lamp, waking up the desiccated moths who spent their afterlives flittering in its dim light. He took out his photocopied manuscript of *Wizard Knights* and Father Reid's notes and spread them out on his already cluttered desk. And then, licking the tip of his favorite, slightly singed pencil, Slugbile started making his first Cleric.

Cheyne Walk, 1985

JOSH REYNOLDS

Enyo Andraste sat in the back of a white van, wondering how and when it had all gone wrong. So very wrong, so very quickly. One moment, she'd been sipping coffee, passing along the messages of the dearly departed to their loved ones, and the next she was being tossed into the back of a van, bag over her head and restraints on her wrists.

She'd been arrested before, though never in such an abrupt fashion. It didn't matter that she truly could talk to the dead. No one believed her, not even the people who were paying her to speak to their dead grannies. Habitual offender, they said. Fraudster.

It was easier to sick the ombudsman on her than to pay her fee. Only it wasn't the Old Bill who'd come for her this time. Her captors were dressed in suits and spoke little. They looked like barristers or accountants, not plods. They were armed, as well; discrete bulges that threw off the line of their jackets.

Enyo leaned back against the side of the van. The vibrations gave her a headache. She wasn't sure where they were going. She suspected she wouldn't like the answer. At least they'd taken the sack off her head, though they'd left the restraints on. Maybe they thought she was dangerous. The thought almost made her smile.

"Bastards," Fitchwell muttered. He sat across from her, on the opposite wheel-well, reading today's copy of *The Telegraph*. The paper rustled as he shook it. The sound of it grated on Enyo's nerves. Fitchwell had been reading the same paper since they'd taken the bag off her head, growing more irritable with every article.

"And which bastards might those be, Mr. Fitchwell?" Morris asked, from the front of the transit van. She was a tall woman, with cheekbones that could cut glass and eyes like faded jade. Of Enyo's captors, Morris frightened her the most. It might have been because she was the only woman. Or maybe it was because she was clearly in charge. "Foreign or domestic?"

"Oxford."

"Ah. Domestic. And what have they done to upset you so?"

"They refused to give Maggie Thatcher a degree is what," Fitchwell said. "Commie poofs, the lot of them. That's what I say."

"And so it must be true," Morris said. Fitchwell peered at her, but wisely refrained from commenting. Instead, he went back to his paper, looking for something else to get angry about. Fitchwell was always on the cusp of blowing his top. He simmered with an omnipresent hatred of...well, everything.

Fitchwell hated foreigners, radicals, Labour party members, moderate conservatives, miners, farmers, women and minorities, several of which applied to her. Enyo could feel his hate, and it made her more than a little nauseous, thanks to her talents. She wondered if that was why Morris had set Fitchwell in the back of the van with her.

Still, better Fitchwell than Keats. Keats sat in the driver's seat, tapping the wheel. He *vibrated.* That was the only way Enyo could describe it. He resonated with the need for violence. Not because he hated something, but because there was an emptiness in him that could only be filled with the pain of others.

Occasionally, he'd glance back at her, and she'd feel it radiating from him. A black, groping emptiness that did not show on his face, or in his bland gaze. If Fitchwell was a fire waiting to flare up, Keats was a hunger, ravenous and insatiable.

Enyo had always been able to tell what other people were thinking. It went along with being able to see the dead, though she wasn't sure how or why. The living were open books to her. She couldn't read minds as such, but she could feel them...feel what they were feeling. Educated guesses often did the rest. When she looked at Fitchwell and Keats, she knew them inside and out, whether she wanted to or not.

But Morris—it was as if there was nothing to her. Her mind, her emotions, they were like polished glass. Enyo only saw herself when she looked at the other woman.

"You look worried, Ms. Andraste," Morris said, smiling at her.

Enyo realized she'd been staring and hastily turned away. "What do I have to be worried about?" she said. "I've only been kidnapped by three strangers, tossed into an unmarked van and driven God knows where..."

"Cheyne Walk."

"What?"

"We're here," Keats said. He brought the van to a stop. Fitchwell hauled her out of the van, nearly dropping her on her ass. Keats removed her restraints. Morris ignored all three of them. She only had eyes for the house. At first glance, Enyo didn't see what was so special about it. It was a house like any other on the Embankment. Older than some, perhaps, and strangely neglected despite the eternal popularity of the area.

A wrought iron fence rose from stone foundations, encompassing an overgrown front garden. Two storeys and a ground floor. The windows dark—not boarded over, but they might as well have been. The door was closed. No lights were on.

The longer Enyo looked at it, the more uneasy she became. A feeling grew in her. As if someone were standing inside, looking out at them. Watching them. Waiting...for what? She didn't know. She didn't want to know. She wanted to leave. To run.

Was running, until strong hands caught her and held her. "Excellently done, Mr. Keats," Morris said, as she turned around. "And a sure sign we're on the right track with this one. A strong reaction. As I hoped."

Enyo turned away, looking out towards the Thames. The river was a dull stretch of muddy browns and grays beneath an overcast sky. The air smelled like rain.

"What do you feel, Ms. Andraste?" Morris asked.

"I want to leave."

Fitchwell sniggered. Keats forced her to turn around, to face Morris. "And so we shall, after we accomplish one minor task." She caught Enyo's chin. Her grip was light, but unyielding. "Do you understand the situation you have found yourself in?"

"You mean you kidnapping me?"

Morris smiled. "You see dead people don't you, Ms. Andraste? You receive communiques from across the Styx, so to speak?"

Enyo opened her mouth. Closed it. Morris' smile widened into something fierce. "Yes, we have quite the dossier on you. We've been compiling it for months—years. Your family has always been of interest to the Ministry of Esoteric Observation and Defense."

The name meant nothing to Enyo and she shook her head. "I don't understand."

"Oh, but I think you do. Your grandmother was the first to come to our attention. Like you, she was a medium of no small ability. Your whole family, in fact. All gifted with extrasensory abilities far greater than any the Ministry has at its current disposal."

Enyo tried to pull away, but failed. Morris' grip tightened painfully. "Pay attention, Ms. Andraste. Your life may well depend on it." She turned Enyo's face towards the house. "There...do you see it?"

"The house?"

"Yes. Good. You've passed the first test."

Enyo frowned. "What test?"

"Most people can't see it," Keats said, lighting a cigarette. "They know it's there, well enough, but their eyes sort of...slide past it. It's there, but it doesn't register."

"But you see it," Enyo said.

"Because we know what to look for," Fitchwell said. He studied the house warily, as if afraid it might suddenly leap off its foundations and come prowling after them. "Even then, sometimes we forget exactly where it is."

"You might," Morris said. "I always know where it is. It's like an ache I can't soothe." She released Enyo and stepped back. "Until today. Today, we deal with it once and for all. And that's where you come in, Ms. Andraste."

"I don't understand…"

"She means you're a freak," Fitchwell said. "That's a freak house. Only freaks allowed in." He shivered and pulled up his collar. "Hate it here. Too much wind."

Enyo didn't feel any wind at all, but chose not to say anything. Fitchwell looked as if someone had stepped over his grave. Of the four of them, he was the most normal, for a given value of normal. Just a thug with a pension. Keats didn't seem to feel anything at all, and Morris—Morris radiated anticipation.

"That doesn't explain anything," Enyo said, softly. "You kidnapped me—banged me up—for what? So you could send me into an empty house?"

Morris smiled. "Oh, it's not empty. That's why you're going in." She started towards the house. "Bring her."

The front gate wasn't locked. The hinges did not squeal. Even so, a shiver ran along Enyo's spine as Fitchwell shoved the gate open. The overgrown grasses rustled, though there was no breeze. Fitchwell looked nervous, like he'd been here before and hadn't enjoyed it. "Rats," he muttered.

"Not rats," Keats said. He didn't seem afraid. But his hand was near the bulge under his coat. He shoved Enyo along, propelling her up the walk towards the door. Morris led the way. If she noticed the rustling, she gave no sign.

When they reached the door, Morris caught the handle, gave it a tug, but it didn't budge. She didn't seem surprised. "Stubborn to the end," she murmured. "Your turn, Ms. Andraste. Open the door, there's a good girl."

Enyo held up her hands. "It would be easier if you took

173

these off."

"Bugger that," Fitchwell began.

"Do as she says," Morris interjected. Fitchwell looked at her in astonishments.

"And if she scarpers?"

"Then Keats will shoot her and we'll figure something else out."

Fitchwell grumbled, but did as she ordered. Enyo rubbed her wrists and looked at Morris. "You know you didn't have to kidnap me. I charge very reasonable rates."

"The door," Morris said.

Enyo frowned, but did as Morris directed. She expected resistance, but the door clicked open at her touch. Her eyes widened. "What?"

Morris sighed in satisfaction. "There we go. There's an…enchantment of sorts on this place. Just like in your better class of fairy story. Only family, so to speak, allowed inside."

Enyo looked at the other woman. "What do you mean?" She had no trouble believing the other woman. If ghosts were real, it followed that magic—or some form of it—was also a possibility. That she'd never experienced it herself did not mean that it did not exist.

"Keats," Morris said. Keats nodded, turned and moved towards the open door. It slammed shut in his face. The house…*creaked.* It reminded Enyo of the growl of an animal, and she felt a chill run through her. Every window was an eye, fixed on them.

"What is this place?" Enyo asked. She thought she'd known every haunted house in London. But she couldn't recall hearing any mention of this one.

"It once belonged to the Royal Occultist."

"The who?"

"A traditional posting, now mostly forgotten. A holdover from less enlightened times." Morris sounded as if she disapproved. "The less said of them, the better." She knocked on the door. "The last person to hold the post was a spiteful sort, and arranged matters so that we could not…take possession of the property."

"They locked you out, you mean."

Morris grimaced. "We've never gotten past the threshold. Not once in almost thirty years. The last time was 1953 or thereabouts. Mistakes were made, lines crossed. All water under the bridge nowadays, of course."

"But you still can't get in."

"No. But you can." She looked at Enyo. "Your grandmother was allowed in. That means you are as well. It took us forever to trace the bloodlines—to figure out the connections. Besides you, the only person able to get in is a rather obstreperous European gentleman."

"So why not kidnap him?" Enyo asked, already knowing the answer.

"Because he lives in Venice, and you live on an East London council estate," Keats said, studying the river. "Handy, that."

"Not for me."

"From time to time, even the humblest of her subjects is called upon to serve Her Majesty. It is a duty and a privilege, Ms. Andraste. And, well, either you do this, or we bang you up in Pentonville on charges of conspiracy to defraud. Your choice."

Enyo looked back at the door. The grotesque knocker seemed to be leering at her. She felt a tremor run through her, and she wanted nothing more than to flee this place, the city—maybe even England itself. But that was no longer an option. "What do you want me to do?"

"I want you to find something. An object...this." Morris retrieved a folded sheet of paper from her coat pocket and extended it. After a moment's hesitation, Enyo took it. The paper was old, yellowing. It looked as if it had been cut from a book at some point. There was a drawing on it—something like an Egyptian ankh, but with more bits.

"What is it?"

"The Monas Glyph." Morris tapped the picture. "Or Hieroglyphic Monad, if you prefer more technical terminology. Created by Doctor John Dee, during the reign of Good Queen Bess. It is an artefact of some potency and not a little historical curiosity."

"What does it do?"

"You don't need to know what it does. Just find it." Morris put the picture away. "There's a study on the second floor. The last person we sent in managed to make it that far. That is where I would check first, were I you."

"And if I find it, you'll let me go?"

"Free and clear." Morris smiled again, quick and sharp as a knife thrust. "You will never see us again, that I promise."

Enyo took a deep breath. She reached for the door. It swung open, as if in invitation. With a last look back at her captors, she stepped inside. The door shut behind her—it didn't slam, or creak. It merely clicked shut. That was almost worse.

The first thing she noticed was the silence. Pervasive and stifling, it lay over everything like a shroud. Cobwebs blanketed the corners, and there was dust in the air. Coughing slightly, she moved forward. There was some light coming through the cracks in the curtains, but not much. The carpet under her feet squelched and she bit back a grunt of disgust. There was a smell of rising damp.

Ahead of her, a short corridor led to the kitchen, and what appeared to be a door to what had likely once been a garden. To her left, a set of stairs rose to the upper storeys. To her right, what could only be the sitting room. She hesitated, and then went right. Morris could wait outside for all Enyo cared. Besides, there was something up there—she could feel it— and she wasn't all that eager to find out what it might be. Not until she had to.

The sitting room was occupied by canvas draped furniture, including an old fashioned television and floor to ceiling bookshelves that were mostly empty. A few books were scattered here and there, their covers obscured by shadow. There were other odds and ends stacked atop the mantle of the large Restoration-era fireplace that dominated one wall. Canopic jars and other oddities she had only ever seen in books. Even a skull.

She approached the fireplace and looked at the skull. It

was old. Brown and cracked, with teeth missing from its jaw, and a puckered hole in the centre of its cranium—a bullet hole, perhaps. At some point, someone had scratched various nonsensical alchemical symbols into the flaking bone, probably to make it more impressive looking.

She leaned closer. There was something—

Enyo leapt back with a yelp, nearly falling over a mildew stained ottoman. For a moment, she thought she'd seen something very much like an eye glaring at her from within the bullet hole. And she could hear—what? Something like...fingers rubbing against bone. The sound sent a chill through her and she turned away.

To her left, something low and lean scuttled out of sight. She froze, recalling the rustling in the grass. She could hear the tic-tic-tic of claws on the floorboards. The silence seemed to enfold her in anticipatory fashion, as if the house were holding its breath.

From outside, she heard the murmur of voices. Or was it from inside the house? It was hard to tell. The tic-tic-tic drew closer. Whatever it was, it was circling the room. Enyo turned, following the noise. The curtains swished, as if something had darted behind them. A soft sound followed, like the noise a child might make.

On the fireplace mantle, the skull clattered. Rolling one way and then the next. She heard a sound like windblown leaves—or perhaps harsh whispers. Unable to stand it, Enyo made a break for the stairs. The sound pursued her, growing louder until it seemed as if it were right on her heels. Something pushed against the small of her back and she stumbled—fell against the steps, rolled onto her back, hands raised to defend herself...

Nothing.

Nothing but shadows and dust. Nothing but the silence. Heart hammering, she pulled herself up and, after a moment's hesitation, continued up the stairs. They creaked and bent beneath her weight in the way of all old houses, but her unease only grew the closer she got to the landing. It was as if there were a fire, just out of sight, but she could feel the heat.

177

Worse, the whispers had returned—and redoubled themselves.

Enyo was used to the murmurs of the dead. It had been the background noise of much of her life, and normally amounted to little more than the static-y mumble of a radio left on in another room. This time it was different. Louder and harder to ignore. The dead were demanding her attention now, plucking at her perceptions with cold fingers.

By the time she reached the second storey landing, it was all but impossible to ignore. Her breath frosted the air. It was colder in the house than outside. Then, that was to be expected. She forced herself to stop. To calm down. To think.

"This isn't the first haunted house I've been in," she said, out loud. "You won't scare me with shadows and sounds. I don't want to be here any more than you want me here. Let me do what I came to do, and I'll go away." It wasn't likely to work, but there was a first time for everything.

She paused, waiting. Listening. Whatever had been prowling about the sitting room seemed to have retreated, as had the unseen whisperers. As if someone or something had called them off. But even as she allowed herself to relax, she heard the rustle of cloth and turned. Something—someone—stood at the end of the corridor.

A heavily bearded man, hunched with age, wearing heavy robes and a skullcap, like something out of a BBC costume drama. His eyes were sorrowful, and his expression one of regret. She took a step towards him, and he was gone. Perhaps he had never been there at all. Enyo paused, as a chill thrust through her.

"Okay," she murmured. "Okay. If you want to speak to me, I'm listening."

Behind her, she heard the clump of someone ascending the stairs. She turned slowly, and saw a shadowy shape, broadly built, wearing a curious wide-brimmed hat and a long cloak, rising towards her. She caught a glimpse of his face beneath the brim of the hat, pitted with scars. He was dressed like a reenactor, puffy sleeves, leather jerkin—Restoration, she thought, where the other had been Elizabethan.

The sight did not startle her, but she was wary nonetheless. Almost every home in England had its share of ghosts, unless it was a new build. She had grown up seeing them, hearing them. Most had no more agency than a film reel—performing their final moments on a loop, over and over again. Others had some dim understanding of their situation. Those were the worst, for they often acted out their frustrations on the living.

The newcomer studied her mournfully, and then swelled and stretched, his dark form becoming one with the shadows. But she could still hear the thud of his boots, drawing ever nearer. She backed towards what she hoped was the door to the study. As she stepped through, the footsteps stopped. Receded. Faded into silence.

Enyo emitted a soft breath and turned. The study was a cramped space overlooking the Embankment. Heavy oaken bookshelves, like smaller versions of those downstairs, filled the walls, and glass-faced cabinets, long empty, crouched beneath the windows. Most of the floor space was taken up by a wide, claw-foot desk. On the wall above it was hung a crude, wooden mask, carved to resemble a snarling bear.

She stared at the mask. In the gloom it seemed to leer at her. She did her best to ignore it. She started with the desk, opening drawers at random. She found nothing save a few old letters, addressed to persons with names like Jobson and Smyth, and a few telegrams that were yellowed and crumbling with age.

One of these, sent by someone named P.V. from Thunder Bay, Ontario, said, simply, 'We burned it in the end, as you advised.' She wondered who P.V. was, and what they had burned. Tossing the telegram onto the desk, she turned to the nearest shelf. As with downstairs, there were few books, and some odds and ends. The whole house gave off the sense of having been deliberately emptied of all save a few items left behind out of negligence, or perhaps as...bait?

The thought made her pause, and her unease returned full force. Morris had said they'd been trying to get in for thirty years. That the last person they'd sent in had managed to make it to the study.

Enyo whipped around as something flashed across the edge of her vision. It was fast, and moving low. Larger than whatever had been creeping about downstairs. She reached for a letter opener, left on the desk. It wasn't sharp, but it was something. She wondered if she should call for help, but knew it wouldn't do any good. Even if Morris and the others had been willing, the house wouldn't let them.

Letter opener in hand, she warily circled the desk. Whatever it was, it was keeping just out of sight. She could hear sharp things gouging the wooden floor—not claws, she thought. Something metal. There was another sound as well, a soft sandpapery rasp. Not breathing, but the sound of wood rubbing against wood.

She moved to the far shelves, hoping that whatever it was, it would retreat as the ghosts had. Instead, it drew closer, stalking her. When she heard it just behind her, she whirled, letter opener raised.

It was the size of a large child, its head barely reaching her chest. Thin, stick-limbs jutted from a narrow body. Its head was elongated and solid, perched on the stub of a neck. Carved features glared at her. Even in the gloom, she could tell it was not a thing of flesh and blood, but rather composed of some dark wood. Nail had been hammered into every inch of its form, and their rusty points jutted in all directions.

It sprang at her with simian grace, and she narrowly ducked aside, a yelp escaping her as she hit the floor. Even as she scrambled to her feet, the creature—the thing—clambered across the shelves, readying itself to leap again. Suddenly, the letter opener wasn't the comfort it had been earlier.

She retreated, and it pursued. It sprang from the shelves, onto the desk, cutting her off from the door. She stumbled as it crept towards her, and lashed out with the letter opener. The thing swatted the blade from her hand, and she fell onto her rear.

Rather a sticky wicket, what?

"What?" Enyo looked around, trying to find where the voice was coming from. The thing had ceased moving, its nails gleaming in the light that now swelled from the

180

doorway. It scuttled away, nails clicking against the hardwood floors.

Not an ideal situation at all. Then, I gather it's not really your fault, is it?

Enyo rose slowly to her feet. Curiously, the fear she'd felt only moments earlier was gone; if not completely, then almost. The light swelled. It wasn't a torch as she'd first thought. It was something else—a pale, flickering radiance that put her in mind of moonlight dancing across the Thames. As it grew, the temperature dropped.

As the speaker stepped into the room, she backed into the desk, heart thudding, skin prickling.

"Please—please stay back," she said, softly.

Am I so frightening then?

The way it—he—said it almost made her laugh. As if he were disappointed. He—the ghost—was of medium height, and dressed like a model off of a Leyendecker print. He was, or had been, handsome, with dark hair and sharp features. He fiddled with his cufflinks as he stepped into the room, and looked around.

It was always so blasted hard to keep this room tidy. Not a one of us ever managed

"This—this was yours?"

For a time. Might I ask why you're here?

"You're very polite for a ghost." She paused. "You do know you're a ghost?"

I should hope so. Had quite a few years to get used to the idea. He looked around again and then, in the blink of an eye, was at the window. The curtain twitched aside, though she had not seen him touch it. *It's the house, you see. It gets rather lonely, the old pile. And sentimental as well. Can't abide it myself, but, well, one doesn't have much choice in these matters, does one?*

"I—I don't understand," Enyo said. "The house, it's...keeping you here?"

In a sense. Duty demands, what? He did not look at her, for which she was grateful. His eyes were empty holes, black and deep. His gaze threatened to pull her in and swallow her

181

up. *Not a bad sort of afterlife, really. Better than what I expected, if we're being honest. What's your name, by the by?*

"E-Enyo...Enyo Andraste."

Suddenly, he was before her, his eyes gaping wide—dragging her up out of herself. She tore her gaze away, and leaned over the desk, panting from the effort. Her lungs ached, as if she'd inhaled ice.

Andraste...

Enyo swallowed. Closed her eyes. "I've told you my name. It's only fair you tell me yours," she said quickly, before she could lose her nerve.

The chair creaked on its casters. She opened her eyes. He was sitting down, leaning back, legs crossed at the ankles. He was looking back at the window, mouth set in a thin line. "Well, who are you then?" she repeated. "Or rather who were you?"

You can call me Charles, if you like. Or Charley. Not Chaz, though. Never could stand that one. He paused. *That's a bad lot out there, on our doorstep.*

"You don't have to tell me."

No, I don't suppose I do, at that.

"They sent me in here. To get something." She licked her lips. "The Monas Glyph."

There was a creak from the shadows. She wondered where the statue had gotten to, but didn't dare look. She could feel something watching her, or many somethings. Charles turned and studied her with his empty gaze.

Yes, I rather suspected it was something like that. You're not the first, you know.

She didn't care to think about the implications of that. Instead, she asked, "Why are you talking to me, when the others didn't?"

Ah, you saw poor Cadmus, then.

"Is he the old man, or the other one?"

And Dee as well. You must be quite the sensitive. Dee hasn't shown himself in years.

"Dee?" The name sounded faintly familiar. "John Dee?"

Got it in one. As to why they didn't speak, well...as the new boy, so to speak, I'm the designated representative. Charles smiled, but it was an unpleasant thing—like a crack in bone. *I am the last to be bound here. The last volunteer, at least.*

Enyo shivered. "You're—you were—the Royal Occultist?"

I was. We all were. Thankfully, I was not the last. Just the last chosen for this particular duty. I'm pleased to see someone remembers us, though.

"I didn't know about you at all, until I was told."

Oh. Ah well. For the best, perhaps. He looked at her. *Were you—are you an investigator, then?*

"A medium." Enyo picked up a statuette from a shelf and set it back down. "This isn't the first haunted house I've been in. But you are the first ghost I've spoken to for longer than a few moments. Mostly, your lot aren't very...lucid."

I should say not. Being dead is a rather confusing experience at the best of times.

Enyo decided to change the subject. "You wouldn't happen to know where the Monas Glyph is, would you?"

I would.

"Will you tell me?"

If you like.

She waited. A few moments later, she said, "Well?"

Oh! Under the floorboard, there. Mind the nail.

Enyo crouched and carefully pried up the loose floorboard Charles had indicated. A box sat nestled below. It was a plain, steel thing—like a safety deposit box.

"I was expecting something fancier," she murmured.

It used to be. But the first box was hidden elsewhere—bit of the old snipe hunt, eh?

"Why do they want it so badly?"

Because they know it is the key to breaking the enchantment my successor placed on this house. The Ministry has been lurking on this particular threshold for years. They'll stop at nothing to plunder its secrets, all in the name of King and country...

"Queen."

Eh?

183

"We have a queen now. Have for awhile."

How times change.

"The Prime Minister is a woman as well."

My word. Labour, I should hope.

"No."

Ah. My condolences. He paused. *You know that if you try to leave without it, they will kill you.*

"And what if I bring it to them?"

They will still kill you.

Enyo sat back on her heels. "I figured as much. Any advice?"

One thing springs to mind, but—I hesitate to suggest it.

"Tell me."

You could invite them in.

Enyo looked at him. "What do you mean?"

You are here. The house acknowledges your blood-right. If you ask, it will allow.

"And then what?"

The ghost was silent. Enyo stood. "You said I wasn't the first. How many others?"

Charles circled the desk, tracing the objects on it with insubstantial fingers. *A handful, over the years. Most were like you, forced into it. Some couldn't get in. One or two managed but...well. The house is protective of its secrets.* He looked at her, and again his face was no face at all, but a grinning skull. *It has held a darkness within itself since its foundations were first laid, and it will not loose its hold on any of us now.*

Enyo's skin crawled as he spoke. "What—what do I have to do?"

Simply open the door.

And then he was gone, as if he had never been there at all. She looked down at the box. She hadn't yet looked inside. She didn't want to. She could feel its power—dormant now, slumbering as it had for years. She had a feeling that if she disturbed its rest, she might not easily be able to put it back to sleep.

Instead, she put the board back into place and turned to the shelves. There were a number of dusty boxes that were around the correct size. She selected one, wiped it down and retrieved the letter opener from the floor. She slid the blade into the box and carried it downstairs. She deposited the box onto the mantle, beside the skull, and went to the door. Carefully, warily, she opened it.

"Hello?" she called out.

Morris was at the gate an instant later. "Ms. Andraste— I'm impressed. You're still alive. Have you found it?"

"I have."

"Well, bring it out then."

Enyo paused, took a breath, and said, "No."

"No?"

"But you can come in." She threw the door open, and stood in the doorway, exposed. "It's safe, for the moment. I've put what you're looking for in the sitting room. I'm going out the back, now."

"And why would you do that?" Morris asked, moving up the walk. Keats and Fitchwell followed her. Enyo backed away. "Why not simply bring it out?"

"You wanted inside the house? Here you go. I'm inviting you in." Enyo glanced back as a shadow passed across the edge of her vision. Something crouched at the top of the stairs. She risked a look at the kitchen. The door to the garden was open—inviting her to depart. She turned and sprinted for it. Behind her, she heard Morris shout, and a pounding that she knew was Keats or Fitchwell, in pursuit. She reached the kitchen and closed the door.

The garden door was still open. Beyond it, she could see overgrown bushes, and rustling grasses and past them, a brick wall. Over the wall was freedom. All she had to do was take it. Instead, she turned back.

The sounds of pursuit had stopped. Floorboards creaked. Unable to help herself, she cracked the door and peered down the corridor. Morris and the others stood in the foyer, looking around, visibly surprised that they were inside at all.

"Ms. Andraste?" Morris called out. She looked around, expression tense. Eager.

185

"She's gone," Keats said. He stepped into the sitting room. "Box on the mantle."

Morris smiled. "That must be it. Clever witch. Bring it to me."

"I hear something," Fitchwell muttered. He glared up the stairs, one hand in his coat. "Definitely not any bloody rats, though."

"Whatever it is, its days are numbered." Morris sighed softly as Keats brought her the box. She ran her hands over it almost lovingly. "Finally." Her face fell as she opened it. She let the box fall to the floor with a thump. "Is this supposed to be funny?" she called out.

I found it rather amusing, what?

The front door swung shut with a click. Fitchwell turned and cursed, scrabbling at the handle. "Locked. We're bloody locked in!"

I'm afraid you are.

Charles sat in a chair visible from the kitchen door. He did not look in her direction, but Enyo knew that he was aware of her. Morris and the others turned. "A focused ectoplasmic manifestation," she said, in a tone of wonder. "A Class 4 on the Spengler-Stantz CDI, unless I am mistaken." She cleared her throat. "What is your name, oh spirit?"

Charles. And you are?

"Morris."

I've known a few by that name. Most of them came to bad ends.

"I'll keep that in mind." She reached slowly into her coat and produced a thin lump of wax and a lighter. "In the meantime, I think we need a bit of light." As she lit the candle, Enyo saw that it resembled—no, *was* a human finger, dipped in wax.

An ugly, pallid light sprang from the finger, driving back the shadows. Charles flinched, shading his eyes. Enyo felt a creeping sensation in her gut. The finger-candle radiated malignity.

Is that one of the fingers of Abbot Thomas, by chance? Foul thing.

"Yes, but useful. Especially in situations such as this." Morris raised the candle. "The light holds your sort at bay, doesn't it?"

At bay, yes. Charles paused. *You want the Monas Glyph.*

"We do. Where is it?"

Somewhere safe. Why do you want it? Why go to all this effort?

"There's a Cold War on, or hadn't you heard?"

Oh, I know. The Russian Bear has been at the gate for more than a century. The names change, but the story stays the same. Charles reclined in the chair, if a ghost could be said to recline. *I won't let you have it.*

"Keats," Morris said. Keats drew something from his coat. A knife, but unlike any knife Enyo had ever seen. It was a heavy thing, with a wedge shaped blade etched with strange sigils, and devilish faces with wicked tusks and protruding tongues, had been carved upon the crosspiece. "I assume you recognize this, as well?"

Ah. I wondered where that had gotten to.

Morris smiled. "Over the years we've managed to acquire a good many pieces from your collection. Including this ugly little thing—the ghost-knife of John Subtle."

Charles crossed his legs and steepled his fingers. *Wherever did you find it? I thought it lost forever, after that bad business in Berkeley Square in '41.*

"Car boot sale," Keats said. "If you can believe it."

I hope you paid a fair price for it.

Keats' smile was ugly. "He won't be complaining."

Still crouched by the kitchen door, Enyo felt the temperature dip. The mood of the house was turning nasty. And there was something else—other spirits, gathering in the shadows. She could feel their discontent, their anger...and their pain. The light from the candle kept them back—but for how long?

"So much as twitch, Charles and we will sever you fully from this mortal coil, and send you to whatever reward awaits a soul like yours."

Threats and bullying. The more things change...

187

"Why are we still talking to this fucker?" Fitchwell barked. "Slice him, and let's find the damn sigil."

Morris waved him to silence. "Where is the girl?"

Gone.

"Dead?"

Gone, Charles repeated. *You are not welcome here. You should go.*

Morris turned. "Keats, stay here. Watch him—it. Fitchwell, come with me."

"Upstairs?" Fitchwell asked, nervously.

"Unless you'd prefer to go look for Andraste?"

Fitchwell licked his lips. "No. No, I'll help."

That would be a mistake, Charles said.

Morris paused and glanced at him, her eyes narrowed. Then she smiled. "You sound nervous, Charles. You never expected us to get this far, did you?"

I long ago gave up trying to predict human behavior.

Enyo carefully closed the door and turned, as they started up the stairs. If she was going to leave, now was the time. But something held her rooted to the spot. She looked back, wondering if there was a way to get that blade from Keats.

Something rapped against the wall, startling her. She turned. The old man in his robes and skullcap stood behind her, a look of quiet sadness on his face. The old man—Dee—pointed a crooked finger at the cabinet, a slight smile on his weathered features.

Frowning, Enyo opened the cabinet and saw a selection of rusty, dusty tins. Pre-war beans and sprouts. She selected one, and turned. Dee was gone. But he'd left her with a plan. Not a good plan, but it was the best she had. She went back to the door and counted to three. Then she rolled the tin into the corridor.

Through the crack in the door, she saw Keats turn, eyes narrowed. He didn't bother to ask who was there. Knife in hand, he prowled towards the kitchen. She backed away, snatching up a cast iron pan as she did so. She didn't rate her chances against Keats, but she knew she had to do something. Clutching the pan, she waited.

Keats entered the kitchen, and a lump of ice settled in her gut. The knife in his hand glowed with a sickly radiance. She didn't doubt it would cut flesh as easily as ectoplasm. Keats turned, almost sniffing.

In the far corner of the kitchen, the shadows thickened. Keats turned, lips peeling back from white teeth as a man stepped into the glow of the knife's radiance. She recognized the Restoration-era soldier from earlier. Cadmus drew a rapier and saluted. Keats snorted softly and took a step towards the phantom.

When she was sure his back was turned, Enyo hit him with the pan. The sound it made was softer—and wetter—than cartoons had led her to believe. Keats didn't stagger so much as fold up like a marionette with its strings cut. The knife slipped from his hand as he sank down. He didn't utter a sound. Panting, she waited for him to rise, to curse, something. When he didn't move, she set the pan down and checked his pulse.

She closed her eyes. Dead. Thankfully, he didn't appear to be sticking around. Keats alive had been bad enough. She didn't want to think about him as a ghost. Cadmus was gone as well. Carefully, she picked up the knife and weighed it on her palm. Then she rose and turned towards the sitting room. One down. Two to go.

She stepped into the corridor—and came face-to-face with Charles. *Well done*, he said. She looked away.

"There's still two of them left."

Yes.

"You don't seem worried."

I'm sure we'll think of something.

From upstairs, a gunshot. Then another, and another. Enyo heard the sound of something clattering across the floor above. Something studded with nails. Fitchwell was cursing now, loudly. Morris was shouting as well. Another gunshot. Charles shook his head. *I warned them. He's quite playful, in his fashion.*

"Will it—he…?"

Oh no, I shouldn't think so. The Ministry are well-versed

in dealing with such minor grotesques as that. But he'll preoccupy them for a few moments yet. And there are worse things waiting. He looked back towards the sitting room, and suddenly she recalled the skull.

"On the mantle—that thing…what is it?"

A worse thing.

She glanced at the knife. "Will the blade protect me?"

Charles turned away. *That is certainly a possibility, yes.*

"You're not filling me with confidence," she said.

You sound like someone I used to know, he said, without turning around. *And like her, you more than make up for my deficiencies.*

She could hear the sadness in his voice. She wanted to ask—but decided against it. There were more important things to worry about. "The skull," she said. "How do I…?"

Break it.

"Of course." She swallowed and hurried after him. She could hear Morris and Fitchwell thumping around upstairs. As she reached for the skull, another shot echoed, followed by a sound like splintering wood. She flinched and picked up the skull. Something sloshed inside it, and the eye reappeared in its hole, glaring at her. She lifted it.

"Put that down, damn you."

Morris stood in the doorway, candle in one hand, pistol in the other. Enyo froze. "Keats," Morris called out. "Where are you?"

He's not going to answer you, I'm afraid. Charles spread his hands. *Gone on to his just reward, poor fellow.*

Morris grimaced. Before she could speak, Fitchwell called down from upstairs. "Is everything all right?"

"Tip-top, Mr. Fitchwell. Continue the search. I have the matter safely in hand." Morris swung her pistol towards Enyo. "You should have left when you had the chance, Ms. Andraste."

"That makes two of us," Enyo said. She flung the skull at Morris. Morris fired, shattering it. Something erupted from the tumbling shards of bone—it was like mud, or smoke, only colourless. Feathery fronds stretched in all directions, and

Enyo instinctively slashed out at those that came near her. As she did so, there came a shrill roar and something that might have been a face formed in the spooling, smoky mass—a face as imagined by a child or a lunatic. It shrieked again, and Enyo cried out in fear.

It lunged for her, and then fell away as she brandished the knife. It swirled about, turning towards Morris, who stared at it in shock. "A Saiitii manifestation," she breathed. "Amazing..."

The thing undulated towards her, gibbering. She fell back, dropping her pistol in her haste. Desperately, she thrust the candle out, and the entity jerked back as if burned. "Stay back," she snarled. "Back—or I'll send you howling into the Outer Dark!"

Still shrieking, it flowed up the stairs in a billowing, writhing cloud. A moment later, from somewhere above, Fitchwell screamed. Just once. A sharp, piercing sound that ended abruptly. Enyo flinched from it, trying not to think about what she might have instigated.

I warned you, Charles said, his voice like the hiss of Autumn leaves. *Will you run for the door, or press on?*

Morris thrust the candle towards him. "You can't harm me. Not while this candle is lit." Her grin was savage. "But I can hurt you—the knife wasn't the only weapon capable of harming your kind." She reached into her coat, but never managed to reveal what secret she held, for something pale and unpleasant leaned over her and clamped bony hands over her arm and wrist. Morris froze, eyes rolling up.

Well timed, my lord. Charles gestured. *Ms. Morris, might I introduce you to Rupert, Duke of Cumberland?*

Something that might have been an exhalation emerged from the skeletal jaws. The candle went out. The woman from the Ministry had time for a single, enraged cry—and then, she was gone. As if she had never been at all.

Thank you, my lord, Charles said, solemnly. He turned towards Enyo, his hands clasped behind his back. *And then there were none.*

"Except me," she said. She glanced down at the knife, and

pulled it close. If he noticed, he gave no sign. "What—what happens now?"

The door is there. It is not locked for you. You may leave at any time.

"What about that creature, from the skull? We can't just leave it to roam about." She tightened her grip on the knife. "And what about them? Morris and…and Fitchwell?" She resisted the urge to glance towards the kitchen, and Keats' cooling body. "What'll happen to them?"

It has already happened. The outcome was never in doubt. Charles drifted closer. *As for the other, well…what's one more ghost in this house, eh?* As he drew near, she instinctively raised the knife. He stopped, and what might have been a look of sadness passed across his features. *Keep the knife. You may well need such a tool one day, if you persist in entering haunted houses.*

Still, she hesitated. "Is that…is that it, then?"

For now, yes. Go.

Enyo sidled past him. He did not follow. As she reached the door, she turned. "Will you be all right then?" she asked.

Oh, I expect so. He smiled. *Though if you should ever wish to pay us a visit…the door is always open.* His smile flickered, and again the skull poked through the mask of flesh.

But for now…out you go.

She shuddered and turned away, closing the door behind her.

Outside, she left the van where it was. She had no doubt that someone would come for it eventually. She took a deep breath. The knife was a comforting weight, in her coat pocket.

But as she stepped through the gate, she could not help but look back. Something that might have been a face—a woman's face—was pressed to a window, mouth moving, eyes wide. A moment later it was gone. As if it had been yanked back, out of sight.

Shivering, Enyo Andraste started for home.

192

Pioneer House

JON BLACK

I believe from the day he was born, coincidence doomed Gavin Sadler.

Gavin was an extraordinary person in an ordinary world. I think he felt connected to Pioneer House, with all its mystery, wonder, and terror. It was a window to something beyond the banality surrounding him. His nature wouldn't let him choose otherwise. I doubt he even wanted to.

Our fifth grade teacher, Ms. Ehrlich, sealed his fate. Not intentionally, of course. A field trip to the public library seemed harmless enough. To teach us how to use the microfilm readers, Ms. Ehrlich assigned us to look up the edition of the county paper, the *Koenigsburg Times,* from the day we were born and write down the headlines.

Dutifully, I wrote "Details on Attempted Ford Assassin Released," "West German Surgery May Help Heart Patients," and "Former Dallas Mayor Earle Cabell Dies" on a sheet of blank notebook paper. Afterward, I wandered over to Gavin. He was engrossed in a story which, unlike any of mine, was local. I read over his shoulder.

Mystery Lights Sighted on Brockenberg

Multiple county residents reported strange lights around historic Pioneer House on Brockenberg's south face Monday night. "There were about a dozen of them up there," says rancher Jerry Blucher, "They looked like colored fireflies, bobbing up and down around that old house."

Sheriff Travis Shelton says his department investigated the sightings in accordance with standard procedure, "Deputies and county fire services checked Brockenberg for wildfire or signs of criminal trespass at the county park up there. Indications were negative." A spokesperson for the National Weather Service suggested Monday's lights were atmospheric static electricity related to the recent unseasonably hot, dry weather.

Measuring 1,083 feet from base to summit, Brockenberg is Junzt County's highest point. Sightings of the Mystery Lights date back to the county's earliest settlers and feature in Native American folklore. "People typically report a single light, maybe two," says William Mueller, professor of folklore at Goethe College. "This is the first time I am aware of a dozen or more being seen."

According to Mueller, the Mystery Lights often appear near Pioneer House, "Settlers claimed it was the original owner's ghost checking on his property." The house is one of our county's greatest mysteries. The elaborate and remote structure on Brockenberg appears to predate documented non-native settlement in the area. "No satisfactory explanation has ever been advanced," Mueller comments.

Calls to the Tasiwóo tribal historian for comment on this story were not returned.

Ignoring the rest of the front page our teacher had assigned him to copy, Gavin sought out more stories about Pioneer House and the Mystery Lights. When time came for our class to go, he didn't want to leave. Ms. Ehrlich had to physically drag him out of the library. From that day, Gavin was obsessed. As always, I came along for the ride.

We had been inseparable from the first day of first grade. It all started with me beating on him. He had called me by my given name, Esther. It's been "Essie" since I was old enough to talk. Only two people got away with calling me Esther. Mom, on the rare occasions when she *was* in a bad mood.

And Dad, on the rare occasions when he wasn't on the road driving his rig and *wasn't* in a bad mood.

For some reason, Gavin thought me beating him up made us friends. I guess all the years that followed proved him right.

One late April day when I was eleven and Gavin twelve, his parents drove us up to the county park on Brockenberg. Junzt County sits in the middle of the Hill Country, a region stretching westward from Austin. With rolling hills and woods that are green most of the year, it's not what people picture when they think "Texas." Native Americans were here first, of course. Czech and German immigrants came in the decades before the Civil War, only later joined by settlers from elsewhere in America.

It was the perfect day for a road trip. The sun was warm but not yet hot. Wildflowers carpeted everything beneath the blue sky. Heading east out of Goslar, by the time we hit State Highway 86 north of Koenigsburg, Brockenberg was already visible in the distance. Even as a child, I found something unsettling about the too perfect curves of that vast gray-pink dome, like the petrified eye of a sleeping giant.

North on 86, we drove through wild, forlorn country. The few lonely houses and farms didn't so much push back the wilderness as hold it at bay. There were hills here, it's called the Hill Country for a reason, but the woods were what I really noticed. Not tall, but thick and deep. These trees keep their secrets. It's a fairytale woods. But not the kind of fairytale with cute animals, kindly strangers, and a "happily ever after." I'm talking about a proper German fairytale, like great-grandma Schaeffer told me when I was a young.

Where the main road curved east toward the village of Thale, a smaller one continued north. At Brockenberg's base, it began a slow switchback ascent to the county park near the summit. Built by the WPA during the 1930s, the park wasn't much to look at: a small parking lot, a scenic overlook, six picnic tables, and a rusted playground.

Exiting the car, Gavin and I rushed to the overlook. Low hills stretched to the horizon. Leaves glowed springtime green in the sunlight. A strong breeze blew from the clear sky, cut only by a few wispy clouds—except to the north, where gray-black thunderheads piled up in the distance. Far below us, wind caused the verdant canopies to ripple in waves, as if the trees whispered to each other.

We picnicked on sandwiches, potato chips, onion dip, and sodas. After we finished, while Gavin's parents packed up, he and I approached the only thing in the park not built by the WPA. The small interpretive displayed had faded badly and read like the afterthought it was. It identified points of interest visible from the overlook, listed local wildlife, and summarized Brockenberg's history and geology. Where his parents and I skimmed, Gavin read carefully, as if it held secrets. For him, maybe it did. "The Native Americans believed their dead spoke to them on top of Brockenberg," Betty Saddler read aloud what the rest of us had just read for ourselves. Wherever Gavin got his intelligence, it wasn't from Betty.

A gravel trail led away from the park, clinging tightly to Brockenberg's contours as it rose. I remember thinking one misstep is all it would take to plunge into nothingness. Still, Gavin and I rushed ahead with the reckless energy of youth. With his long stride, he led by a few paces. Black hair, already longer than mine, bounced as he ran. The Sadlers, seeming impossibly ancient but probably not yet 40, lumbered along behind and occasionally shouted at us not to run and to please be careful.

Farther ahead, the path forked. One branch continued toward Brockenberg's summit. The other deposited us at Pioneer House. Seeing it for the first time, in that moment, I shared Gavin's fascination.

This was no tiny cabin or rustic dugout. The sturdy and stately wooden house stood two and a half stories tall with a steeply sweeping roof extending over front and back. A raised porch wrapped around the front to both sides, while the house's rear pressed flush against Brockenberg. Grand windows, diamond-shaped and comprised of nine panes of leaded glass, looked out on the lowland below.

I intuitively grasped the mystery of Pioneer House. Even then, in 1985, building such a house there would have been impractical. In, or before, the county's earliest days, with no transportation, no place to buy tools or materials, and no skilled labor…"impossible" was the word I wanted.

As Gavin rushed through the front door, I stopped to admire the view.

Inside, I found Gavin talking to a grownup. These were days before "stranger danger," but there was something undeniably strange about the man. He was tall and thin, with a big mustache like the old German farmers. He spoke with an unfamiliar accent and wore old-fashioned clothes, including a diamond stick-pin and a black top hat adding to his considerable height. I assumed he was part of the exhibit, someone whose job was saying old-timey things and talking about pioneer life.

But what I remember most about the man is his smell. Not bad, just unusual. When I was six, a transformer blew out down the street from us. With it came an unfamiliar sharp, pungent smell. Dad, who was home that day, told me it was "ozone" and that electricity made it. The oddly-dressed grownup smelled like that.

Gavin was telling the stranger about being born the night when all the lights had buzzed Pioneer House. In response, the grownup made an unusual gesture with one hand. Afterward, he asked Gavin for his name. I had the impression the stranger would have preferred me not to be there. Surprisingly, I got the same feeling from Gavin. Not interested in being where I wasn't wanted, I wandered off.

A thousand times after the fact, I wish I had paid attention to their conversation. Perhaps I would have remembered something to make sense of what came later.

Pioneer House's sparse furnishings included a few

historical photos and paintings, though nothing original to the house. A large room on the ground floor, set aside for special events and the county's summertime nature classes, held a podium and maybe fifty chairs.

Gavin caught up with me as I stared out a second floor window. The landscape below was breathtaking. As was the speed with which storm clouds rushed toward the peak. "Who was that?" I inquired as we contemplated the approaching weather.

"Some old guy," Gavin replied with atypical nonchalance. More to form, he added "Says he's here a lot. He sure knows a lot about history. Maybe a professor at the college?"

At the time, his answer seemed like enough. "Yeah, I wondered if it was something like that," I replied.

We found another interpretive display inside. It said the house was in the Georgian style. Back then, I thought that meant the state of Georgia. Of course, I know better now. It explained such houses were common in the eastern United States but never seen in places like Texas. Even back then, I noticed the text's awkward undertone, as if the display's authors were embarrassed by how little they really knew about Pioneer House. The display also talked about the county's settlers. How they lived. How they died. How, when it was just Germans and Comanche, everyone got along pretty well, but then the Anglos came and messed it all up. There was even a tiny section on the Mystery Lights, saying they probably resulted from static electricity or something it called a "thermal inversion."

I felt almost as disappointed as Gavin at finding several parts of the house locked, including rooms at the back of the ground floor and the entire attic. Standing atop the high, narrow staircase as we tried the attic door in vain, the ozone smell returned. I wondered if the county had some kind of electrical equipment up there, which would be a perfectly good grownup reason for keeping it locked. Gavin, I think, would have tried to break into the attic had it not been for his parents' arrival.

After the Sadlers had poked around awhile, it was time to

go. Walking back, even his parents kept up a good pace. The wind had chilled and thunder rumbled constantly. The first fat, frigid droplets of water began falling as we reached the car. Before we got off Brockenberg, the skies opened. Late April is well into tornado season and it was a tense drive as Mike Sadler slowly picked his way through the rain and hail back to Goslar.

As Brockenberg receded in the distance, Gavin tugged on my sleeve. Following his eyes, I saw a globe of pale light floating around Pioneer House in the tempest.

Returning safely to the Sadlers' house, we all had cake and ice cream. Yellow cake with strawberry frosting. Though I've never met anyone else who found that combination particularly palatable, it was Gavin's favorite. The outing had been his birthday party. I was the only one who attended.

I wasn't the only friend Gavin had in elementary school. There was also Mr. Lynn, the janitor. Most students said the "Mister" part condescendingly. Stories circulated about him. That he had spent time at Koenigsburg State Hospital. That he had been a POW in Vietnam and come back not quite right. That he did time in prison after chopping up his wife and kids with an axe. Or some combination of the above.

Gavin and Mr. Lynn talking quietly as they ate lunch together in a corner of the cafeteria became a common sight. At first, I thought it was just the natural gravitation of one oddball to another. Though, where there was strength in Gavin's difference, not Mr. Lynn's. There was something undeniably damaged and delicate about the janitor. Children could sense that the way a shark scents blood.

"What's up with you and the janitor?" I finally asked Gavin while playing with our army men over at his house.

"He's interesting. You are, too. Some of the teachers are. The other kids aren't," he replied matter-of-factly. "He's another person I can talk to and not be bored. And he knows stuff. Including stuff about Brockenberg."

Students had tricked and ridiculed Mr. Lynn so many times. I don't think he completely trusted Gavin until just before Christmas the year we were in sixth grade. Gavin gave him a billfold. On the surface, it was a stupid gift: completely unremarkable in appearance and made of cheap tan pleather. But that simple, uninspired act finally convinced him that Gavin wasn't just one more kid out to get him.

When we returned from Christmas Break, Mr. Lynn had a present for Gavin. A tortoise shell that the janitor said he had found on top of Brockenberg when he was younger.

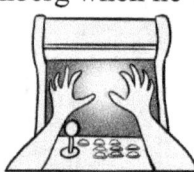

Our strange birthday outing and Mr. Lynn's gift fueled Gavin's fixation. In eighth grade, he and I were in the same Earth Science class. For his final project, Gavin did a report on Brockenberg. Its story, he said, began millions of years ago when a shallow sea covered the whole area. Pressure turned the thick layers of seafloor silt into sedimentary rock. At some point, a bubble of magma pushed up into the rock. When the sea receded and the land was exposed again, the softer rock eroded away leaving behind a dome of hard, igneous rock. Brockenberg.

He explained our county's landmark wasn't unique, similar features existed around the U.S. Mount Monadnock in Vermont. Stone Mountain in Georgia. Devil's Tower in Wyoming wasn't quite the same thing, but was related.

Gavin's presentation was full of terms like "igneous intrusion" and "batholith" which would strike most 14 year-olds as having way too many syllables. Nevertheless, the words rolled smoothly off his tongue.

Despite a brief and not especially scientific digression onto the topic of the Mystery Lights, Mrs. Fowler ate it all up. Not everyone present was so impressed. "Dork," Ward Randal said in a stage whisper as Gavin returned to his desk. Considering the source, had it not been in the classroom, his remark would probably have been something much nastier.

Sooner or later, Gavin was going to run afoul of Ward Randal. The worst thing you could have in Junzt County was the last name Randal. The family was trash. Gavin was everything Ward was not: graceful, beautiful, and cultured. Ward resented him for it, always trying to cut him down or intimidate him. My friend's obliviousness to it all only infuriated Ward even more.

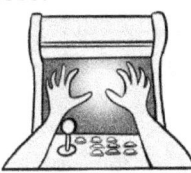

Gavin was an outsider, he had no choice. His dad came to Texas to be an accountant for a natural gas company. His mom got work as a typist with the county. Within the year, Gavin was born.

At school, the roughnecks' children were loud but kept to themselves. The Native kids, the ones who didn't go to reservation schools, were quiet and kept to themselves. We Germans were somewhere in between, and kept to ourselves. I hung with Gavin anyway. I knew I'd get out of Goslar someday. Until then, he was a shiny piece of that wider world, different and exciting, in my life.

My family has been here since the 1840s, part of the first group of European settlers in the area. On the cornerstone of Our Lady of Altotting Church you will find the name Matthias Parr, my great-great-great-great grandfather, listed among its founders. Growing up around the older Germans, I noticed certain things weren't talked about. I learned a lot by listening to what *wasn't* talked about. In time, I learned not to talk about those things either.

Lacking that example, Gavin talked loudly and often about Brockenberg and Pioneer House. I was younger then and happy to go along with it.

As teenagers, new possibilities and new complexities

entered our world. Older kids drove into Koenigsburg or even Austin. Younger kids, or those without rides, spent their time loitering and listening to the jukebox at the Dixy Freeze or playing video games at Main Street Pizza. I joined them.

And I discovered the woods, a rite of passage. Adults called it the Hexenwald or Hexenwood. Teenagers called it Witchwood and scared each other with tales of ghosts, vanished children, and Satanic cults. We would have been interested to know how little our stories differed from the whispers of our elders, whispers that went back to the very first settlers in the area. Of course, none of that kept us from disappearing into their concealing cover...to do what teenagers always did.

Indifferent to his peers' pastimes, Gavin wandered alone through downtown, read, or simply sat outside.

There never was anything between Gavin and me. Though, goodness knows, there was talk enough. He was tall and graceful with long black hair and blue eyes that gazed dreamily into the distance. But my attraction was not romantic. To me, he was equal parts mad prophet and lost puppy. As for Gavin, I'm not sure he ever thought of girls in that way. Nor boys either, if that's what you're thinking. Enigmas were his real love.

Things with Ward Randal came to blows on Gavin's sixteenth birthday. His parents gave him a white Ford Mustang as a present. Ward, who drove with a hardship license and a GMC so rickety it could barely be called a truck, couldn't hide his resentment. And didn't want to. Badly as Gavin was losing, I knew I shouldn't interfere. But when Ward said Gavin fought like a girl, I stepped in and showed Ward that was nothing to be ashamed of. I walked away with his tooth to prove it.

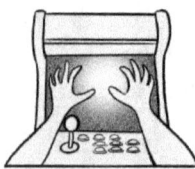

Our junior year, Gavin began frequenting the library at

Goethe College, the old college established by European settlers after they'd seen to the necessities of frontier life. Gavin used the library to ace his coursework. Driven by his obsession, he also consulted its holdings on Brockenberg and Pioneer House.

At first, he found ghost stories. Even for a region supposedly thick with hauntings, Brockenberg seemed to be a magnet for specters: lost settlers, Native Americans, Civil War soldiers, even a mysterious woman. But we could recognize that, despite a tweak here or a detail there, they were just variations on the same kinds of ghost stories found anywhere.

He was more interested to discover tales of the Brockenberg Fog. Though the thick, white mist often occurred in conjunction with the Mystery Lights, other times it appeared on its own. Something about the frequent descriptions of how the fog centered on Pioneer House, as if originating there before spilling out over the rock and down into the woods beyond, made me uneasy.

Digging deeper, Gavin uncovered bizarre lore surrounding the fog. Strange smells. Sulfur. Sea air. And...ozone. Weird electromagnetic effects interfering with radio and CB transmissions. The fog caused A.M. signals to bounce, pulling in broadcasts from Dallas and Houston or places even further away like Chicago, Los Angeles, or Mexico. One story even claimed it bounced a broadcast not across space but across the time. An old-timer caught in the fog swore his radio played part of a campaign speech by Lyndon Johnson, running for senate back in 1948.

And the fog held ghosts of its own, phantom vehicles reported again and again by those unfortunate enough to find themselves driving through the gloomy haze: a Model A truck, 1930s black slantback, blue '52 Caddy convertible, even a souped-up emerald green GTO sporting glasspack mufflers. That last one particularly interested Gavin because it came with a pedigree. "A car like that belonged to a guy named 'Smiley' Schreiber who was a bigshot in the Jericho Road racing crowd," he explained to me. Smiley and his custom ride both disappeared back in 1974.

But the most distinctive vehicle, "car" didn't fit, reported in the Brockenberg Fog was an antique coach-and-four. Not a stagecoach, like you might expect in this part of the country, but something older. Sightings dated back to 1844, first reported by an immigrant named Timmendorfer. I told Gavin that, even compared with everything else, it seemed a bit far-fetched. He agreed.

But, next time I saw him, Gavin felt differently. Hans "Hank" Timmendorfer had gone on to become a prosperous farmer and civic leader, his papers still preserved at the college library. "I checked his journals," Gavin related "and the account is in there. A coach pulled by four coal black horses. Even writing back then, he described its appearance as 'antique.'" There was more. Timmendorfer came from a North Sea fishing village and swore the fog surrounding the coach carried the same fishy-salty stink of a port town. Of the coachman, Hans recorded little, except the impression of a very tall gentleman dressed in simple yet elegant black and wearing a hat.

I shuddered, thinking of the strange man I had found Gavin talking to in Pioneer House on his twelfth birthday.

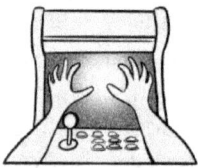

Eventually Gavin's enthusiasm soured for the ongoing parade of rather predictable and sensationalistic accounts of ghosts, strange atmosphere effects, and phantom vehicles he had uncovered. He wanted something that went deeper. Something for a thinker, not just a casual reader of local history. One day, obviously in a good mood, Gavin shared a discovery. He had overheard two graduate students talking about the library's restricted collection. That had driven Gavin to learn more. "The library's restricted collection might have materials that would be useful to me."

"That's great," I said. His view of the world, so unlike

anyone else I knew, was hypnotic. "What kind of materials?"

Gavin confessed he didn't know. To find out, and to access the collection's contents, he needed personal approval from the library director. He explained that the director, Doctor Ottmar, had for decades run the library like a tyrant ruling his private kingdom.

"Even most college students don't get access to the restricted collection," Gavin said anxiously, playing with his hands all the while. It was strange to see him, typically so confident that it never occurred to him to be otherwise, suddenly apprehensive and unsure of himself.

While Gavin's idiosyncrasies put most people off, Mr. Lynn and I were not the only ones who ever took a shine to him. The terrible Doctor Ottmar, too, must have seen something in him. Maybe it was his keen intellect or uncannily broad vision for his tender years. Maybe it was the passion marking a true scholar. Whatever it was, he granted Gavin access to the restricted collection.

A few weeks later, eating lunch together, Gavin reached into his backpack. He beamed while handing me a bundle of papers. "It's an unfinished monograph on the folklore surrounding Brockenberg written by two students back in the '60s," he explained.

I looked at the photocopied pages of a sloppily typewritten manuscript. Across the first page was stamped:

PROPERTY OF GOETHE COLLEGE
RESTRICTED COLLECTIONS
NOT TO BE REMOVED OR DUPLICATED

I raised an eyebrow. Gavin shrugged. "I sneaked the original out of the library and photocopied it. I put it back the same day. Nobody knows."

It didn't sound like the wisest decision in the world to me, but I figured Gavin knew his business. I started reading.

BROCKENBERG: HISTORY & FOLKLORE
[Third Draft]

By Lin Aschenbrenner and Donald Childs

After the title page, it skipped to Chapter Three. Apparently, Gavin hadn't needed whatever was in Chapters One and Two.

CHAPTER THREE:
PIONEER HOUSE AND "THE ALLY"

As detailed previously, the Tasiwóo community of Junzt Country displays notable linguistic and cultural differences from other communities self-identifying as Numinu or "Comanche" (Hoebel, 1933). Fitting this observation, much of Tasiwóo folklore appears unique to that Junzt County group.

This includes their foundational myth. As commonly told, their ancestors were led south by their shamans into what is now Junzt County. They found the land there already occupied by another people. As noted by Jameson (1960), Tasiwóo avoid direct references to this group, instead utilizing oblique euphemisms. Archeologists and historians refer to the Tasiwóo local predecessors as the Hoffmann People, after a key archeological site in southwest Junzt County (situated on property belonging to farmer Ambrose Hoffman).

The Tasiwóo considered the Hoffmann People repellent and dangerous. Folklore accuses them of engaging in "abhorrent rituals" and conflict erupted between the two groups. In their fight, the Tasiwóo were joined by an enigmatic individual known variously as "Dawn-Hide" or "The Ally." Folklore suggests fighting continued until the Hoffmann all fled or died.

Successive scholarship adds additional insight to this narrative.

Archeological and linguistic evidence date the arrival of the Tasiwóo and their struggle with the Hoffmann to the middle or late eighteenth century. That timeframe is consistent with the range of estimates for the construction of Pioneer House, 1720-1800. Though a link cannot be proven at this time, Occam's razor suggests the Ally and Pioneer House are related. Legends imply the Ally's difficulties with the Hoffmann predate Tasiwóo arrival but he had been unable to displace them on his own.

Analysis of terminology used in folklore supports the hypothesis that the Ally was neither Tasiwóo nor Hoffmann. Descriptions of the Ally as possessing abilities like those of a shaman, but not being a shaman as the Tasiwóo understood the term, further reinforce notions that the Ally was culturally distinct.

Multiple sources make the obvious (but not necessarily correct) connection between the other name referring to the Ally, "Dawn-Hide," and the pinkish tones of Caucasian skin. A dissenting voice, Wainwright (1949) suggests "Dawn-Hide" reflects an extreme northern manifestation of the Quetzalcoatl myth cycle, itself an embodiment of Frazer's "Great White God" archetype.

Later folklore indicates, after victory over the Hoffmann, the Ally disappeared by using shamanic powers to "travel among the spirits." Older Tasiwóo interviewed by the authors implicitly connect the Ally with Pioneer House, traditionally avoiding the latter. Folkloric proscriptions about Brockenberg as a place of power and safe only for shamans go doubly for Pioneer House. While not considered malevolent, the structure is seen as a focus for powerful energies dangerous to the uninitiated.

The earliest German and Czech settlers displayed similar aversion to the site. Whether they adopted these attitudes from the Tasiwóo or based them on independent experiences is, as yet, unknown and represents a promising avenue for future research.

I was interested. Gavin brought things into my world no one else did. But, having noted the "Third Draft" at the document's top, the issue which nagged me wasn't one related to the text itself. "Why didn't this thing ever get finished?"

"A question I had as well," Gavin said. "Lin

207

Aschenbrenner and Donald Childs started the paper their final semester at Goethe. After graduation, they took a hiatus so Childs could do a tour of duty in Vietnam. The plan was, afterward, for them both to enroll in grad school and finish it. But Childs took a bullet during the Tet Offensive. Aschenbrenner later disappeared under mysterious circumstances."

"Mysterious circumstances?"

"I've talked to people who knew Aschenbrenner. After Childs died, his partner became obsessed with the subject," Gavin answered, oblivious to the irony. "The night he disappeared, there was a major event on Brockenberg. Unlike anything seen for generations. Unexplained fog and a whole fleet of Mystery Lights. Guess what night that was?"

I had a sinking feeling, "The night you were born?"

He nodded. "I think he went up there to check things out for himself. And drove off a cliff, walked over the edge, or something like that. Or maybe whatever he saw up there affected him so much that he just walked away...from everything."

I sighed. Gavin and his interests fascinated me. But sometimes I wondered if he had invested too much of himself in Pioneer House and its strange surroundings. The paper from the restricted collection gave him a new focus. Ever since that first article back at the public library, Gavin had been aware that the Tasiwóo had their own stories about Brockenberg. Whenever he encountered them in Goslar, Gavin tried to learn more. But now that he understood the depth of that connection, it became his priority. He drove out to the Tasiwóo Reservation to ask questions. The younger people brushed his inquiries aside with a little good-natured mocking, seemingly little interested in the topic. Their elders humored Gavin, politely answering his questions while talking in vague circles. With benefit of hindsight, I imagine them wearing smiles that did not reach their eyes. Instead, reflected in those windows to the soul, I imagine anxiety. Perhaps even apprehension.

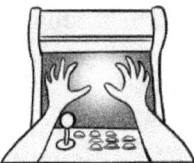

Gavin graduated salutatorian. His short speech at graduation basically told us all to expand our horizons beyond the mundane and prosaic. My class ranking was somewhere in the middle of the pack, neither honorable nor shameful. Although Ward Randal did not graduate with us, he found his own way to show off the education he had received. Most of the obscenities police caught him spray-painting on the school's exterior the night before graduation were at least spelled correctly.

Mike and Betty Sadler let Gavin take it easy that summer. Three last months of goofing off before going away to college. But I had started picking up shifts at the Dixy Freeze. So he and I weren't actually seeing much of each other.

I needed some work done on the hand-me-down Ford Ranger my cousin had given me. One morning I had Gavin follow me in his Mustang to Clay's Automotive in Koenigsburg. Though using a day-off to do that felt ridiculously adult, at least it allowed me to spend time with Gavin. After we dropped off my truck, I treated him to lunch at Moulton's. Though hardly fancy, it was a better restaurant than anything on offer in Goslar.

"So, what are we going to do today?" I asked afterward as we walked back to the Mustang.

The way Gavin smiled, I knew he already had a plan. "We're going to drive back to Goslar and see an old friend," he beamed.

"Old friend?" I wondered. "Other than me, who do you have that's an old friend?"

"I'm embarrassed that it took me this long to put the pieces together. You remember the tortoise shell that our old janitor gave me? I've been using it as a paperweight this whole time. The other day, I got to looking at it. And I started to wonder.

"I did some checking around. It turns out 'Mr. Lynn' is

actually 'Mr. Lin' as in Lin Aschenbrenner, the co-writer of that research paper I showed you who dropped out of sight after his cowriter's death.

Both of us knew he wasn't at the school anymore. Goslar is a small town and people talk. Fate had not grown kinder to the former janitor. He was living at St. Gregory House. The church operated that cheerless two-story redbrick and St. Rita's, its sister home for women, as a halfway house and residence of last resort for Goslar's marginal and vulnerable.

St. Gregory House didn't allow women beyond the common area. While the attendant fetched Lin Aschenbrenner we waited in a room sparsely furnished with a few black chairs, putty-gray couch, crusty coffeemaker, and a folding table. A crucifix hung from the wall behind the attendant's desk next to a portrait of the house's namesake, stern gaze suggesting he had little faith in those entrusted to his care.

The man we came to see shuffled into the room. If man was the right word. Though never an image of vitality, Lin Aschenbrenner had faded to a shadow of his former self. Thin and gaunt, he seemed like a scarecrow playing at being a person. Staring at us, blanked-faced, I doubted he recognized us.

Gavin, having the same thought, introduced us "I'm Gavin Sadler. This is Essie Parr. We were students at Goslar Elementary when you were the janitor."

"I remember," the man reached into the pocket of his threadbare pants and pulled out a brown lump. I took me a moment to recognize the wallet Gavin had given him all those years ago. The faux-leather's gloss had rubbed off to a dull matte color, the stitching was coming out, and Lin Aschenbrenner didn't seem to have much use for a wallet these days. That he'd kept the thing said a lot.

"It's nice to see a familiar face. Any face, really. But what do you want?" he asked, rather apprehensively I thought.

"You were Lin Aschenbrenner, weren't you?" Gavin asked.

"Still am. As far as I know."

"Is it true what they say? Did you really go to Brockenberg

210

the night all those lights showed up?"

A thousand-yard stare came into the man's eyes as he nodded.

"What did you see?"

Aschenbrenner flinched as if punched. "No. Not that. Anything else I know, I'll tell you. As long as you don't ask that. You ask again and we're done." He paused so long I started to wonder if he remembered we were there. "From the first time we talked about Brockenberg back at that school, I wondered if we'd have this talk one day. Talking to you was like looking into a mirror. I probably shouldn't have given you that tortoise shell. It probably just encouraged you."

They spoke back and forth for the next half-hour as Aschenbrenner answered the questions Gavin had always wanted to ask. I just listened, torn between fascination and a vague sense of discomfort that gnawed at the edges of dread.

"The Tasiwóo thought that Brockenberg was a place where creation's weave is weak," the onetime scholar and janitor put meat on the folklore his research paper had presented as bare bones. "I say 'thought' because I can't say 'think.' I haven't talked with any young ones to say what they think nowadays. Because of that weakness in creation, things from different times and places could pass through and muddle reality. Or get stuck in between, trapped forever someplace that was no place."

When Gavin said it seemed like the Natives had become less free with sharing their stories and legends over the years, Aschenbrenner nodded. "Why?" My friend wanted to know.

"Because they worried that some damn-fool outsider might go up there when the weave was especially weak," he replied, looking at the floor. "But it wasn't the weakness in the weaves of time and space that really worried them about Brockenberg."

"What then?" Gavin asked, a greedy expectancy in his eyes.

Aschenbrenner said that every culture had a term for it. But they all came down to a veil that separated our world from the other one. The Tasiwóo believed that veil was

211

dangerously thin atop Brockenberg. Sometimes so thin it might as well not exist.

He explained that was why only shamans were permitted on Brockenberg from dusk until the sun had risen a hand-span above the horizon, a period well after dawn. Only they could properly understand the voices of the ancestors when they spoke at the rock. "Other people might get confused."

Their greatest fear, Aschenbrenner explained, was what might come through that weak place. Or what already had. "You know about the Hoffmann People?" he asked us. As Gavin nodded, it took me a minute to recall the name which academics used for the group that had already been here when the first Tasiwóo arrived. The group they had fought with until the Hoffmann were destroyed or driven away. Aschenbrenner said that some of the oldest legends claimed the Hoffmann weren't people at all but something that had come through the veil to our world. Or people made inhuman through lengthy contact with an entity lurking on the other side.

When even Gavin's fountain of questions had run dry, the three of us sat staring at each other in awkward silence. Reaching into his pocket, Gavin handed the man a $20 bill. After a moment, I fished a second out from my purse. Lin Aschenbrenner took them both with a mixture of gratitude and resentment.

As we turned to walk out and Aschenbrenner returned to whatever sort of room he had, he called back to us. "Don't."

"Don't what?" Gavin responded.

"You know what I'm talking about. Just don't."

The September after graduation, Gavin went off to eastern Massachusetts for college. In addition to his excellent grades, a letter of recommendation from Doctor Ottmar was apparently instrumental in his admission. I started taking core courses at Hinn Community College in Koenigsburg, preparation for transferring out of state my last two years. To make ends meet, I started working as a carhop at Rock-It Burger full time. Carhopping wasn't bad work. Dale, the owner, could get awfully handsy with some of the girls but was smart enough not to try that crap on me.

The day Gavin returned for Christmas Break he visited me at work. I watched as he fell to his burger and fries with gusto, "You can't get a good greasy burger like this back East," he mumbled between bites.

After I was off the clock, Gavin told me about his classes and the school's library which he said was superior even to Goethe's. He thrilled me with tales of the strange, ancient town surrounding the college, sounding like another country if not another world. He also showed me his mobile phone, one of the first I had seen.

I caught him up on local gossip. Who was doing, or no longer doing, what with whom. The scandals of a small Texas town. Of special interest to Gavin was that his favorite resident, Ward Randal, was in the midst of a six-month vacation, courtesy of the Texas Department of Corrections, for assault. "If you bump into him again, be careful," I cautioned Gavin "he's not just a school bully anymore."

As we talked, I wondered if the semester away diminished his obsession. He soon let me know it hadn't.

"Have you ever heard of Charles Fort?" he asked.

My face must have said no.

"He was a New Yorker from around the turn of the century. Fort spent his life documenting weird and unexplained events and writing books about them. In one of them, *The Book of the Damned*, I found this," he pulled out a piece of paper and read.

In 1799, an entire house vanished overnight from Kingsport, Massachusetts. The building dated from the early Georgian period and had been abandoned for decades. It is unclear exactly what is meant by "vanished." The scant information available leaves one

with the impression that the house was literally there at
dusk and gone without a trace by dawn.

"You think it's Pioneer House, don't you?"

Gavin's eyes twinkled as he refolded the paper and crammed it back into his pocket. "I don't know. It's impossible, isn't it? On the other hand, a disappearing house and the existence of Pioneer House are both impossible. So, Essie, the question is: does an impossible answer to an impossible question become possible?"

He looked thoughtful, "Kingsport isn't far from where I go to school. Next semester, I'm going there for a few days to do my own research."

No, time away hadn't helped Gavin's obsession at all.

Spring Break rolled around. I had planned to go to South Padre Island with friends. But Dad tore a muscle in his leg and wasn't working much. So, I spent the week picking up extra shifts at Rock-It Burger instead. Gavin came to see me there one night. I knew he would, it was a special night.

"Happy Birthday," I told him, producing some longnecks swiped from our fridge as well as the cake I had baked him. He smiled, seeing the strawberry frosting and anticipating the moist yellow cake underneath.

After closing, we listened to the radio. Most people in Goslar our age listened to Top 40 or hard rock. Nirvana and their cohorts had just begun filtering through to the "hip" kids in town. Out in the deep Hill Country, Austin radio stations always came in fuzzy. That night, their signal was absolutely erratic, fading in and out. As I cleaned and mopped, when we could, Gavin and I were probably the only kids in town jamming to Wilco, Third Eye Blind, and the Donnas. Whenever Austin cut out, we made do with local radio. Between songs, a local DJ mentioned he was receiving calls from listeners in the north of the county. "The Mystery Lights are at it again tonight," the DJ said, "Sounds like quite a show up there."

Gavin's eyes lit up. "I went to Kingsport," he continued, as if we had never stopped talking about his favorite subject. "I hoped to find an engraving or a painting or something showing the vanished house. No luck." Gavin shook his head, "At the Historical Society, though, I found a 1796 tax record describing the place as having a side-gabled shingled roof, full-length nine-pane windows, and an elevated porch."

It did sound a lot like the house on Brockenberg. Of course, I wasn't the expert. "What do you make of it?"

"It's not enough to confirm it's Pioneer House," he concluded, "but there is absolutely nothing in that description ruling it out either."

As I bagged the last of the trash, two poor excuses for pickup trucks pulled into the parking lot and started doing donuts. "Crap, what now?" I went outside. Walking toward the vehicles, I waved them off. The trucks stopped. Ward Randal and a half-dozen of his low-life friends got out.

"What's up, sweet thing?" Ward asked with a nasty smile. The gap I put in his teeth years ago looked like a cavern.

"Get the hell out of here, the police are on their way," I lied.

Ward flashed a set of brass knuckles. As he and his buddies spread out to flank me, it occurred to me I might be in real trouble.

At my back, the universe exploded in a roar. Ward and his posse fell on their haunches, eyes wide as saucers as they stared behind me. Spinning around, I found Gavin holding the sawed-off double-barreled Marlin that Dale kept under the counter. Having discharged one barrel into the air to get their attention, he leveled the weapon at Ward and his friends.

"Get away from her and get away from this place."

Of course that bunch traveled armed. Their little minds were no doubt trying to work out whether they could reach their guns in time. But, a decade earlier, a bunch of Randals got shot up out on Lutherkirche Road. A meth deal gone bad, supposedly. Whatever it had been, it injected a rare note of caution into the family. Confronted with a shotgun, Ward and his buddies acted like dogs caught pissing on the rug: cowering, whimpering, and backing towards their trucks.

"Go on, get!" I shouted, "Or you'll lose more than a damn tooth this time. You leave us alone."

Halfway into his truck, Ward's spine returned. "You fucking weirdo," he shouted, presumably at Gavin. "You watch out. I'm going to get you. You, too, bitch."

On their way out, Ward and company tossed empty beer cans at us in a futile attempt to reclaim their masculinity. After laying rubber in the parking lot, the trucks roared onto Main Street and out of sight. I ran to Gavin. It was the only time in my life I remember hugging him.

The encounter with Ward, a rare taste of visceral life to a young man who lived almost entirely in his head, awakened something in Gavin. He shook with manic energy I had never seen in him before, a feverish light burning in his eyes.

"I'm going to do it, Essie," he said.

"What? What are you talking about?"

"I'm going up there. Tonight. Right now. I'm going to Pioneer House while the lights are there. Come with me."

"Gavin," I sighed. "It's late. It's dark. We've had a couple of beers. That's not a good idea." Those practical objections, all valid, substituted for a more ineffable feeling swelling in my gut.

"It will be fine. It's the perfect time. Just like the night I was born. Come with me, Essie."

"I'm not going," I said. "You shouldn't either. You're smarter than that."

He walked toward his car.

"Okay, I'll come with you," I lied.

Gavin got into the driver's side of his Mustang without another word as I buckled myself into the passenger's seat. Only once the car moved did I spring my plan on him. "We've got to make one stop first."

"What stop, Essie? What are you trying to do?"

"I've given you ten years of my life. The least you can do

is give me ten minutes."

I knew I couldn't talk him out of what my heart said was a terrible idea. But if anyone could, I knew who. The problem was finding him. People like to think homelessness is something that only happens in the cities. It's not. Lin Aschenbrenner had proved beyond even St. Gregory's help. I'd encountered him rooting through our dumpsters on more than a few occasions. Upon discovery, his eyes looked more like an animal's than a person's, leaving me even less certain he recognized me than I had been at St. Gregory's. On other occasions, driving home after closing, I had seen him wandering purposelessly around Goslar's small downtown. I hoped he was there.

Luck was with me. After failing to find him between or behind downtown's brick buildings, it occurred to me to check the small municipal park in the town square. Lin Aschenbrenner stood atop a large limestone rock, his body so rigid that at first I mistook him for a statue. I did not care for the way his maniacal gaze fixed northward. Though Brockenberg was miles out of sight, it was as if he somehow knew what was occurring there.

"Sadler," he said as if finally registering our presence, or at least Gavin's. "What are you two doing here?"

"I brought him," I shouted. "He's going up there. To Brockenberg. Tonight. Talk him out of it."

"Your friend is right," Aschenbrenner's soft, hollow tones contrasted with his feverish expression. "Boy, are you crazy?"

"No, I'm not crazy. I just want to know. How bad could it be? You went up and you're still alive."

"If you imagine that death is the worst thing that can happen to you, your view of the universe is extremely limited," he grew more lucid. "Last summer you wanted to know why only shamans could be on the rock from dawn to dusk, when the dead talk.

"If you had asked the people Donald and I talked to, they would warn you not every dead spirit that speaks is safe to listen to. Worse, not every voice you hear on the rock belongs to the dead. Sometimes things which have never lived try to pass themselves off as the dead, either out of pure malice or to use the unwary as a gateway to our world.

"So, after their battle with the Hoffmann, they set guards. On this side," Aschenbrenner continued, his tone one of personal conviction rather than scholarly curiosity. "But it wasn't enough. They needed a sentry. Someone on the other side. To watch for the Others. The Lights are the Others trying to break through."

"You sound like you believe those stories. About the Tasiwóo and the Ally. You certainly didn't when you were writing with Donald Childs."

"I was younger then. Now I'm too old not to believe," as he shook his head the fevered look returned. "I think they're right. But I think it's more than that. You want the truth? I don't remember what happened to me up there. But I know this, you can stay here and keep yourself. Or you can go up there and know. Though, if you do that, you can't be certain how much of yourself you're going to get back. Maybe none of if it."

For a moment, I thought he'd gotten through. Then I saw the steel resolve solidify in Gavin's eyes. "I've got to know," pulling keys from his pockets, he strode decisively toward the Mustang.

"Gavin, please don't go," I pled.

"Everything will be okay," he said, "I'll call you tomorrow and tell you what happened."

I watched Gavin drive into the night. I don't think I even said goodbye to Lin Aschenbrenner before beginning the five minute walk back to Rock-It Burger. When I got there, I tried eating the rest of Gavin's cake. Bitter tears did nothing to improve the flavor of yellow cake with strawberry frosting so I polished off the remaining longnecks instead.

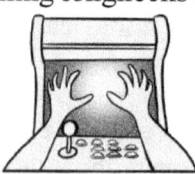

Killing the last beer, I returned to my final tasks before going home. The phone rang. "Rock-It Burger, we're way closed," I barked into the receiver, paying the call less than half a mind. A burst of static and prolonged hiss greeted me, clearly a mobile phone. I barely recognized Gavin's voice. I kept calling his name and telling him to speak up, but the connection never improved. As best I could tell, and as best I remember, this is what I heard:

"...beyond anything I ever imagined...electrical properties...old pickup truck...mystery lights...the portal in the air...more lights emerging...beautiful...some kind of intelligence behind it...shadowy figure...the ally?...can't understand him." With that, the line went dead.

I tried calling Gavin back, not caring that I'd catch hell from Dale for making long distance calls. After five or six tries went to voicemail, I gave up and went back to closing. As I was about to lock up, the phone rang again. I sprinted to the phone, "GAVIN?"

This connection was no better than the previous: a constant roar of static, or something else, against which Gavin sounded increasingly small and distant, "...so wrong about everything ...stranger...tried to warn me...many doorways...mystery lights...others...the laments of those banished outside...those who have never been inside...malevolent...scared...one chance...ally...the true portal...so sorry, Essie."

Although I'm fooling myself to pretend it would have done any good, I wish I had called the sheriff's department right then. Next day, when Gavin didn't turn up, I did call. They found his Mustang at the county park, door hanging open. But not Gavin. Search parties became helicopters and helicopters became cadaver dogs. Gavin Sadler was never found.

Over the following weeks, I spent a lot of time in the company of Sheriff Shelton. I don't think I was a suspect, exactly, but his department was at a loss and leaning hard on everyone in hopes of shaking loose a clue. Remembering Gavin's mention of a truck in his first phone call, I told the Sheriff about Gavin's history with Ward Randal. Ward claimed he spent the rest of that night in the old Odd Fellows cemetery outside Koenigsburg, drinking beer, smoking dope, and vandalizing tombstones. His friends backed him up.

Part of me wants that to be a lie, just so I can have some closure. Deep down, I know he's telling the truth.

These days, I look at the world from the wrong side of 40. Gavin wasn't the only one who couldn't escape his nature. I moved to Koenigsburg but never got farther. I've had a career, a marriage that wasn't worth saving, and two kids that are worth everything. Sometimes I don't recognize the face looking at me in the mirror, with her crow's feet and worry lines. I think about Gavin often but seldom speak of him. I can't tell anyone else his story, so sometimes I tell it to myself. But I'm not sure his name has passed my lips since my boys were born. They watch me and they notice there are things I don't talk about. In time, they will learn not to talk about those things, either.

Once in a Lifetime

CAYCE OSBORNE

If I have to use your grungy old hand-me-down softball glove I'm going to die. Like, literally, I will be dead. RIP. No more Nora. Adios."

I fixed her with my Mom Glare™. She wasn't fazed. Raising a teenager was a rollercoaster crash-course, but the inability to assert my (formerly tyrannical) parental authority is one of the most disconcerting parts.

"Kira has a gray Adidas one with her initials stitched on the outside. In pink! It's ah-*may*-zing. Seriously."

"Kira also has parents with more money than sense," I said around the last bite of my pot pie, cursing my loose lips, and rose to clear the dinner dishes. "Don't tell anyone I said that."

Nora rolled her eyes so hard I thought they'd gotten stuck to the inside of her skull. I remained firm on the glove, but she arranged her face into a pathetic mix of endearing neediness that has always made my ovaries liquify into gooey puddles.

"Okay, drama queen. I get it. Everything that has already belonged to another person is trash. Especially if that thing belonged to me, the least cool mother on the planet." I check my iWatch, wondering where my evening has gone. "It's getting late, we don't have much time before the stores close. I won't be able to go to Michael's to get a poster board for your science project *and* go to Dick's to get a new, non-tainted-by-your-mother softball glove. What's it gonna be? Sophie's Choice."

"Who's Sophie?"

It was my turn to roll my eyes. "Never mind."

My daughter wrestled between the social capital of a new glove and getting her school project done, knowing she'd make the right choice. She always did. But she wasn't above putting me through a bunch of teenage bullshit first.

"Ugh. Fine. I'll use your stupid old glove then."

"Now that you've called her stupid, I don't know if I should subject her to your abuse."

"Mother."

Uh-oh. My full name. I was in trouble.

"I call her Tawny Mittaen and she helped get me through my senior season. I want you to take good care of her, that's all."

"You are so weird."

"Yes, yes I am. You can make up for calling Tawny stupid by finishing the dishes. I'm going up to the attic to see if I can find her before I run to the store."

I didn't head up until she slouched to the sink to take up the sponge. Bracing myself for attacks from spiderwebs and nostalgia, I climbed up the steep stairs to our sauna-like third level. Six months ago, searching for a single item in the tangle of storage boxes and outdated clothing would've been a massive undertaking. Since Brian moved out, the formerly stuffed attic was mostly empty. He'd been the packrat, not me.

At the back, tucked into the shadowy, sweltering eave, were the few boxes I'd moved into this house directly from my parents' place. Childhood paraphernalia I had no use for during my college years but, as my mom had suggested, I might want once I had my own kid. As usual, she was right.

At what age will Nora start realizing that I'm usually right? Probably not until she had children of her own.

I pulled the cord on the bare overhead lightbulb and studied my Mom's careful Sharpie labelling, looking for the cardboard box marked: **Heather ~ Toys / Misc.** It was at the back, of course, just out of arm's reach. Tall-sided and sturdy, a safe place to store my childhood. As I shoved the other boxes out of the way and pulled it toward me, the lightbulb flickered. It was the only one in the house that Brian hadn't

224

replaced with compact fluorescents. The delicately coiled filament ended its stuttering, providing me with a steady glow as I reached once more for the box.

I crouched under the eave to unfold the top. Into the box I dug, past a Rainbow Brite sleeping bag, a pink plastic Barbie wardrobe carrying case, my Rock 'Em Sock 'Em Robots game (the red robot was missing his head, I remembered), and Catalina, my Cabbage Patch, before spying a finger of soft leather peeking out from behind the doll's yellow yarn hair.

Beads of sweat popped out on my forehead as I leaned over, cardboard digging into my stomach, into the gaping mouth of the box, reaching for the glove.

Ninety degrees in late September? A travesty.

"Fucking global warming," I grumbled aloud. As my breath stirred the dust atop the robot game, the contents of the storage box shifted, as if making way for my hand.

My middle fingernail brushed a leather tie on the outside of the softball glove. I leaned further, center of gravity tipping.

"Fucking Nora waiting until the last minute to tell me she needed this for tomorrow." Swearing felt good, illicit, like it had when I was a teenager and the words were new in my mouth, a foreign language I'd just discovered.

Blood pounded in my ears, but I still couldn't reach the damn glove. I leaned forward a little more; I was on tiptoe, the rigid cardboard wall of the box the only thing keeping me steady. The remains of the pot pie began to churn in my stomach. I could've stopped, pulled the box further from the eave or dumped its contents, but I was almost there. So...close. The glove seemed to reach out for me, fingers spreading, leather pockets inflating.

"I've almost got you, Tawny."

I took a steadying breath as fuzzy gray orbs danced across my vision. A wave of vertigo crashed against me. My ears filled with a high, tight whine. Like someone had taken the neck of an inflated balloon and stretched until the air began to leak from the narrow opening.

Sweat stung my eyes, so I closed them. I urged every

muscle in my body forward, elongating my limbs, reaching, until I felt something—buttery soft, smelling of damp leather and outfield grass—engulf my hand.

I didn't have time to pull back. Just the thought came: *Get your hand out of there!*

And then I was tumbling, something tugging me forward, face-first into the box, my eyes still squinched shut in fear. A topsy-turvy sensation of flipping head over feet, and I found myself standing, unharmed. The oppressive attic heat was gone; a soft breeze stirred my hair. I flexed the fingers of my left hand, feeling the familiar resistance of Tawny, my well-loved softball glove, around it.

Her reassuring presence gave me the courage to open my eyes.

I was in the parking lot of West Towne Shopping Mall. Familiar, yet somehow...wrong. My stomach roiled one last time before settling—the same queasy slosh as the morning sickness that plagued me before Nora was born—as I stared up at the Prange Way sign on the front of the building, looming over my head. The Prange Way that had closed in 1996 and was replaced by a Younker's, that was then replaced by a Boston Store, that was now a Macy's. My body was hollow, my fingers tingled. My scalp itched. I reached up to scratch and bonked myself in the eye with Tawny, still attached to my hand. I tugged at her with my right hand. She wouldn't come off.

Okay that's super weird don't think about it just try to figure out what's going on holy shit what's going on where am I and where's Macy's and what does this all mean?

The air smelled of french fry belches and hot asphalt. Black burnt-rubber swirls overlapped and made oblong shapes where I stood on the pavement—like the spirograph I'd had as a kid. Back in high school, this was the place everyone came to spin donuts in their cars, before the mall had put in better lighting and curbing and medians that broke up the lot and deterred shenanigans. I made a slow spin, taking in the area around me.

No curbs. No medians. A gull perched on the lone, rusted

light pole across the lot.

Judging by the emptiness of the parking lot and the brightness of the day, it was reaching mid-morning. Shouldn't the mall be open by now? I glanced down at my watch, but instead of the expensive iWatch that kept my life on track, a vintage Casio G-Shock wrapped around my wrist, just above Tawny. The one I owned in high school and had begged my mother to buy for my 16th birthday.

I raised Tawny, holding her in front of my face.

"What the shit is happening?" I used to talk to her this way, when I was stuck in center field and bored because I rarely saw any action. The West High Lady Regents did not face many teams with deep batting rosters.

The next batter's gonna smack it, right at us. I can feel it. C'mon, batter!

Back then she hadn't shown a single sign of life; no indication she registered my existence. I talked and she listened, that was our dynamic. But no more. I gaped as her leather ties unraveled themselves, twisted and bent to form a series of tiny hearts, and then re-tied into neat knots.

I sat down on the pavement. Perhaps not so much sat as crumpled to the ground after my legs gave out. That's when I noticed my fuchsia culottes and electric blue blouse with white squiggles. And—holy shit!—my teenage body. So much like Nora's it made my lungs clench until I could barely breathe.

I snapped to attention as the doors of the Prange Way opened and a woman in a boxy shift dress and black nylons unlocked the store. As if on cue, a station wagon turned into the lot and parked in front of the food court next door. I hoisted myself up and hurried to the sidewalk. I didn't know what the hell was going on, but I knew I didn't want to get run over. Especially not by a Clark Griswold wagon.

The french fry smell was stronger on the sidewalk. I debated what to do next, distracted by this slight body I was living in: the way my thighs didn't rub together anymore when I walked, and the swish of my side-pony against my shoulder. The bra straps that sat lightly on my shoulders instead of digging into my flesh.

Jangling me out of myself was a tug on my arm, strong enough to make me stumble forward. The elderly mall walker headed for the food court doors scowled at me, her tracksuit the exact color of a grape Razzle. I looked around for the yanker. There was no one else there.

Except Tawny Mittaen. She tugged again, stretching my arm toward the door.

It was clear: I was supposed to go into the mall.

Inside it was darker than I remembered, with inadequate fluorescent lighting set into the ceiling to look like skylights. Fake greenery spilled out of a center boulevard that split the wide hallways, casting wild shadows on the walkways.

Muzak piped through the ceiling speakers; a butchered Talking Heads melody was audible over the splashing fountains that greeted me as I emerged from the food court into the mall proper. Despite my still unsettled stomach, the smell of Hot Sam pretzels made my mouth water. The Auntie Anne's Nora and I treated ourselves to every year during back-to-school shopping just weren't the same. Junk food never tasted as good to adult taste buds as it did to my adventurous teenage tongue.

I wandered the hall, humming along with *Once in a Lifetime* even after the Muzak had moved on to Erasure, peeking into stores which, in my present time, were long closed. WaldenBooks, where my love of reading was born. Kay-Bee Toys, where I got my Cabbage Patch. I wished I'd thought to give her to Nora when she was little, but Catalina had remained cooped up in the box of toys, shoved to the back of the attic by Brian's boyhood treasures and unfinished rehab projects and the ski gear he never used. He spent a lot of time away from home after Nora was born, but he wasn't off skiing.

Even as I passed these childhood relics, drawing me back to the days of my youth, Nora was with me every step. I looked down at Tawny, happily dangling off the end of my arm, now more a part of me than the hand she engulfed.

"Walk a mile in Nora's shoes, is that the lesson here?" I

228

asked her. The glove clapped closed twice. "Okay, then."

I savored every second as my old self, walking the retro mall of memory, inside the same hormonal mix of fierce invincibility and devastating uncertainty that Nora lived with every day. Never knowing when I'd be whisked back home.

Back...to the Future! Doc Brown's voice whispered in my ear.

I looked through cassingles at Musicland, coveted the parachute pants at Chess King, giggled over dirty novelties at Spencer Gifts. I loved every moment of being young again, until I heard a familiar laugh echoing across the mall's central corridor. My stomach dropped as my face grew hot. I followed the laughter down the east hallway until I came to the sunken seating area outside the arcade, *Aladdin's Castle* in glowing letters over the entrance. The seating area's long, low couches were covered in burnt orange velveteen, on top of which sprawled a pack of teenage boys. One boy, their king, holding court at the center.

Once I saw him, everything—the mall, the Muzak, the other boys—blurred into the background. Brian, young again, like me.

I didn't really understand the meaning of the word charisma until I met him for the first time. At least that's what I'd told people when I agreed to marry him. Dark-haired, warm-eyed Brian. But charisma doesn't make someone kind. This was something I did not share with people, when they asked why our marriage didn't work out. Some things are too painful to say out loud.

When I was young, Brian's personality was enchanting, captivating. Around the time we first met, Madonna had a song called *Crazy for You*. It was on the radio constantly. That's exactly what I was: Crazy for Brian. When I was near him, he sucked the air out of the room while simultaneously producing the only oxygen I wanted to breathe.

Tawny nipping at my thigh, I stalked past Brian and his friends on wooden legs. They glanced up—the mall wasn't very busy yet, there weren't many people milling around—without a flicker of recognition.

Oh, so it's that day, then.

It came swirling back in a vortex of arcade plinks and the overripe stink of Hickory Farms cheese samples.

This is the day we met. For the first time. The day I lost my heart—which, if I'm honest, I still haven't retrieved, despite the divorce lawyers being very deliberate about whose possessions were whose.

But as of this moment, in this mall, we didn't know each other.

My memory of the day we met goes like this:

I'd taken the Metro bus to the mall, getting an Orange Julius and buying a keychain at Spencer's before playing video games at Aladdin's Castle for the rest of the day. I'd been kicking ass on Golden Axe, beating the hell out of Death Adder's henchmen, when Brian came up behind me to call next game, slapping a quarter down on the console to show dibs. I'd tossed him an annoyed glare, but when I took him in my inability to look away caused me to lose my rhythm. My virtual self died a swift death on screen, pixels dissolving.

"Oh, shit. Sorry."

He didn't look sorry. And I didn't care.

We'd taken turns playing after that, talking video games in between. His friends got bored and left. When we got hungry, we'd walked down to Hot Sam, discussing the odds of our parents buying us a Sega Genesis for Christmas. It started easy, our friendship. He was nearly done with high school; I had a couple years yet. Neither of us had siblings, and at first hanging out was like having a cool, slightly older brother to nerd out with. And nerd out we did:

D&D.

The reasons why Lucas should've set *Jedi* on an all-Wookie planet instead of on Endor. (We both despised Ewoks.)

Whether *Eat It* or *Like a Surgeon* was the best Weird Al song.

We covered it all.

That lasted a year. Soon he was in college and I was graduating from West High and things became less chaste.

230

Less friendly and more frenzied. My innocent adoration transitioned to full-on teenage lust. I worshipped him, and he liked being worshipped; this was always the core dynamic of our relationship. When we both ended up at the same college (yeah, yeah, Tawny, technically I followed him to the college he already attended) there was no reason to stay platonic. It seemed inevitable to me, and when he reciprocated my feelings it was all I'd ever wanted, or could want.

We had wonderful years together: wild sex, our shared nerdiness deepening. We got married, and it was still good for a while. But as we tip-toed toward true adulthood our responsibilities multiplied. (Less sex, fewer movie nights; increased stress, more work.) Nora was born and we were smitten. I was, at least. His ardor for both of us cooled when the frustration and exhaustion of parenthood overshadowed the baby giggles and warm milk smells and larger breast size. He stopped changing diapers, made excuses to stay late at the office, complained we never did anything fun anymore.

I wasn't fun anymore, he said. I didn't argue with his assessment, just leaned into parenthood, letting Nora fill the void Brian left in our partnership.

He and I both tried, for a long time. Until neither of us had the energy anymore. Even Weird Al, the patron saint of our marriage, couldn't save us.

Tawny, as if reading my mind—and who knows, maybe she could, being a softball mitt imbued by some sort of ghost-of-days-past spirit or whatever—hugged herself to my hip, the gesture oddly comforting.

The shared history between Brian and I spooled ahead of me like a VHS tape on fast-forward, as I watched his young self walk into the arcade. I took a step forward. My desire to go after him was physical. I needed to be there when he stepped up to Golden Axe. What if there was another girl playing it now, and he met her instead? I was desperate to re-experience our first magical day. To relive the meet cute I'd recited to Nora over and over, like a fairy tale.

I'd expended so much energy being hurt and angry at him over the last decade, I ached for a moment of joy. I wanted to remember what it felt like to be young and spellbound, dazzled by another human being for the first time.

But my feet wouldn't move any further. I didn't follow him into the arcade. A gust of air conditioning, tinged with the metallic scent of palm-warmed quarters, hit my face and I turned away, the hurt too great. Tawny tugged at my hip.

"I can't, I just can't," I sobbed, clutching her to my chest.

Forcing myself to walk away from the perfection of teenage Brian was harder than signing our divorce papers. But I couldn't recreate my innocence, couldn't un-know the husband he would become, couldn't pretend to be young me, no matter how much I looked like her. Those realizations were the only things that made it possible to leave.

If I'd gone after him, he would've seen our doomed future shining out of my eyes the moment he looked at me.

I left the mall—up the east hallway, down the corridor, through the food court and into the parking lot. To the spot where I'd arrived.

"Is *arrived* the right word?" I asked Tawny, a bit out of breath from speed-walking through the mall, earning a dirty look from the mall walker as I blazed past. One of Tawny's ties unraveled, seemed to shrug, and re-tied itself. "Materialized? Beamed?"

The lot had begun to fill with cars. I wound my way through, circling a red Trans Am to find the epicenter of the tire marks. I stood inside the empty oval in the center of the black whorls. I crouched, curling my body into a tight ball and cupping Tawny over my head. She flapped against my ears. It wasn't until a sharp headache began to form that I realized I was clenching my teeth, jaws grinding.

Or was it Tawny's fault, the way she squeezed my head like a vice, painfully tight?

At first, I thought the sound was a pain response, a manifestation of the headache. But no, it was real: the high whine of air escaping a balloon. The sound of my future rushing back. Of a way to Nora, my Nora, my person, my life.

I melted into the pavement, like the crayons I used to press into the space heater in my childhood basement. I was insubstantial as mist, I was a puddle, I was sinking into the earth.

When I opened my eyes, I was back in the attic. Sitting on the dusty floor next to the box of old toys. Tawny dangled off the end of my arm, but the dead weight of her told me she had returned to her previous state. An old piece of sports equipment, and nothing more.

I giggled crazily, trying to regain reality. My sanity.

The attic was still sweltering. Its little round window showed a slice of early evening sky. Here, for adult me, little time had passed. Maybe I hadn't traveled anywhere. Maybe I passed out from the heat, bumped my head on the low ceiling, had a stroke. Anything was more probable than...

I looked at Tawny, pulled her off my hand and turned her over. Every stitch of her was where it should be. I laughed at myself again, but I was back in control. Every bone in my 43-year-old body felt the aches and pains as I pulled myself to standing.

When I came down the attic stairs, ready to deliver Tawny into Nora's reluctant hands, the upstairs hallway was dim. The house felt sleepy, still. Lifeless.

"Nora? You done with the dishes?"

There was no sound, not the creak of a floorboard or the hum of our struggling air conditioner. I reached out for the stair post, to steady myself before heading down to the first floor. Blood pumped hard in my ears. A stroke was starting to feel like a real possibility.

The stair post wasn't there. My old, round newel—the one that felt like a wooden doorknob against my palm—was gone, replaced by a low railing, stainless steel cables that ran alongside the staircase.

Gone.

My familiar newel was gone. My stairway carpet was gone.

Gone, my old life was gone.

David Byrne's voice came back to me.

My God! What have I done?

I stumbled down the steps, into the living room. I

wandered to the kitchen in a daze.

Everything, everything about my house was wrong.

And with a rush of certainty-tinged dread, I knew why. This wasn't my house. Not anymore. Because I hadn't met Brian at the mall back then, which had been earlier today, which was impossible. All of this was terribly impossible.

If I'd never met Brian, we wouldn't have gotten married. Wouldn't have gotten pregnant with Nora. Wouldn't live in this three-bedroom house. That meant Nora wasn't...

Tawny fell from my limp fingers as I ran back upstairs to Nora's room. I didn't want to believe, wasn't ready, my mind incapable. I needed to see.

There wasn't even a bedroom there. Whoever lived in my house had knocked down a wall to make what should've been Nora's bedroom into a spa bathroom with a walk-in closet.

I didn't have a daughter. Because I'd failed my time-travel do-over, failed to see what Tawny was trying to show me. I wasn't an invisible observer in a *Scrooged*-style, revisit-and-learn from the past type movie. I was Marty McFly. Each little thing I did or didn't do had huge consequences for the future. My future. Nora's future, her whole existence.

I'd unmade her, in a matter of hours.

Urgent voices came from behind a closed door next to the walk-in. That's when I realized I'd not bothered to muffle my movements, had practically thrown open the door of the now-bathroom. And I was sucking in desperate breaths like I was running out of air.

I'd woken the homeowners. Dashing downstairs to scoop Tawny from where I'd dropped her, I ran for the attic before they could confront me. Pounding all over the house, I made a terrible racket.

I stumbled on my way up, foot slipping off the third stair so that I fell forward and banged my chin, my knees. I tasted blood.

"Shit!"

A woman's voice screeched in fear at my exclamation. I clenched my hands around Tawny in determination and kept going—*don't look back!*—to the rear of the attic, to the box. It was still there. I took a relieved breath, cheeks hollow with desperation.

I held Tawny up in front of my face. "Wake up, old girl. I need do-over number two."

I jammed her onto my hand and dove into the box like it was a swimming pool. Displacing toys, tearing cardboard.

I'd get my Nora back, or...or...there was no alternative. I had to. She deserved to exist.

I wanted all of her: the drama, the determination, the stubbornness, the struggle to grow up too fast. Every quality that made my life more difficult. I'd take them all a million times over, because they were part of her. And she was forever a part of me. The one part I couldn't bear to lose.

I squirmed my body toward the bottom of the box, squeezing my eyes shut, waiting for the swirling plunge. I prayed for the balloon screech to come, pulled Tawny against my face so she could feel my tears.

"Same as it ever was," I whispered against her leather, like a mantra. I inhaled her vintage 80s smell, touched her with the tip of my tongue. She was salty and soft.

I kept whispering until the screech came, filling me.

Same as it ever was.

When the box opened underneath me, I dove head-first into the past.

Battle for the Bugbots

JOSH WANISKO

THE BUGBOTS NEED YOUR HELP!

YOU WERE: Dalissa J, a little girl with a weird name and no friends, whose only refuge was in her Bugbots toys.

YOU WANTED TO BE: Brood Mother, the matriarch of HIVE, defending your children against the fearsome INSECTIVORES!

YOU ARE: You are D. Z. Jones, Executive Vice President of marketing at Comco toys. Comco has acquired the license for Bugbots and it is up to you to shepherd the property into the 21st century for a new generation of fans.

How far will you go to make it a success? Will it be a savvy update that keeps the charm of the original while updating it for the modern age? A shameless cash grab? Or something in between? And is there a truth to the sinister urban legends surrounding the mythology of the franchise?

Section 1

2020: You are Dalissa Zenobia Jones. Darcy Jones to the executive leadership team at Comco toys, DZ (or Dizzy) to your friends, and BroodMother72 on the Internet. You are excited, thrilled, terrified, exhausted all at once.

Your assistant Michelle looks up when you enter. "Is that it?"

You smile. "That's it. We got the last signature in that meeting. It's official. Comco toys has acquired the license for Bugbots."

"That's a big deal for you, right? You liked those toys back in the 60s?"

You can never tell when Michelle is kidding. She's young, but she's not that young. "In the 80s, yes. How old do you think I am? "

She makes a show of scrutinizing you. "50? 25? 70? 90?" She throws up her hands. "I have no idea."

"You make my travel arrangements, so I know for a fact that you've seen my driver's license and know exactly when I was born."

She shrugs. "Yeah, but like the talking doll says, math is hard." Then she adds, "I thought somebody else had it. I just saw the trailer for the movie."

You grit your teeth. You can't believe you're having this conversation in 2020. "Okay. You know how two similar things sometimes arise at the same time? Like those two Jungle Book movies being released within a couple months of each other. Two documentaries about the same previously obscure historical figure. Sometimes they rip each other off, but mostly it's because creative works don't spring forth from nothing. They're inspired by trends already present in the larger culture. Two people on opposite sides of the world might have the same eureka moment at the same time, leading to the convergent evolution of similar properties."

"Oh, yeah, I see. Like Antz and A Bugs life!"

"Right. But I didn't want to use those as examples because it seems too on-the-nose. Anyway, whatever forces were

238

present in the zeitgeist of 1982 gave rise to not one, but two transforming insect robot franchises. As far as anyone can tell, no one ripped off anyone else. They arose entirely independently. But Bugsbots premiered on September 15th and B.A.T.T.L.E.Bugs followed two weeks later. We have Bugbots, the Michael Bay bullshit you saw was for B.A.T.T.L.E.Bugs."

"So, was it a big rivalry?"

You sigh. "At first. But B.A.T.T.L.E.Bugs got traction in a way that Bugbots didn't. Probably because it appealed to the lowest common denominator." You pause. After decades of being a female geek of color, it's second nature to temper your enthusiasm. "How much detail do you want?"

"Just give me the Wikipedia version."

"Okay. B.A.T.T.L.E.Bugs was the VHS and we were the Betamax. Or, if you want to be less charitable, they were the Transformers and we were the Go-Bots."

"I don't know what that means."

"You should. You work at a toy company."

"Yeah, but I'm an executive assistant, not your archivist. I don't know every Depression era transforming insect toy."

"Freakin' kids. Get off my lawn." She grins and you answer it with your own. "Anyway, I think it turned off some of the boys that the leader of the Bugbots was a female. Brood Mother. I mean, it only makes sense. Every year, B.A.T.T.L.E.Bugs got bigger and Bugbots became more niche. The series was cancelled in 87 and the toy line lingered for a little longer. They produced some real gems near the end. Hard to find, though. Take the Mindworm limited edition..." A glance at Michelle's face advises you not to continue. "Or not. But that's when the real story starts. Freed from the constraints of having to write for a kid's property, the writers of the comic and the YA novels went bonkers. They each spun off into their own direction and they have their own totally irreconcilable canon, though that hasn't stopped people on the internet from trying to unify them. Then there were photocopied 'zines in the 'Wilderness Era' after the those ended, which became posts on BBS's and dedicated forums. You might know the Ovipositor creepypasta?" Michelle nods and shudders. "That's taken directly from some early fanfic."

You need to get this done.

If you want to remember your childhood and see if anything inspires you, go to Section 5

If you want to jump into work, go to Section 13

Section 2
Ratings and review for Bugbots Strike Force

Featured Review

Zero stars - Asssassinbug69

This game commits every cardinal sin of mobile gaming. Asks for too many permissions? Check. Exactly why do you need camera access and the names of all my contacts? Intrusive notifications? Check, but you can barely read them because of the pop-up ads. Microtransactions? Triple Check. I dropped a hundred bucks and I'm still seventeen shards shy of unlocking Brood Mother. The interface is awful, it crashes constantly, it has three, THREE!! unskippable sequences of flashing lights before the warning about them. The gameplay is surprisingly not terrible, probably because gameplay and assets were stolen from Gem Smasher Geo. Did you think we wouldn't notice, Comco?! On top of all of this, the biggest disappointment is that it has nothing to do with Bugbots. The still images (you think we're getting animated sprites? Dream on!) are overlaid on the Gem Smasher assets. It's your basic rip off mobile game. A shifty, sleazy cash grab that forever tarnishes the legacy of Bugbots. The fans deserve better.

Dalissa Jones ruined my childhood!!
THE END

Section 3
STING OF THE OVIPOSITOR

You can't get here through playing by the rules. No decision you can make will lead you to this segment. Turn back if you value your sanity.

Turn back, Section 7.

Push Forward, Section 14.

Section 4

"Honey, where you going?"

"I'm walking to Aunt Tabitha's house! I'm going to find Mommy and convince her to stay!"

"Oh, sweetie. That's thirty miles. She's already gone."

He's right.

She's already gone. You cannot change the past. Assassin Bug tried that in the prequel series.

The past is written and cannot be changed.

Return to Section 10 and make another choice.

Section 5

The year is 1983. You are Dalissa. You are ten years old. It's 7:30 on a Wednesday night. Your parents are fighting again. You can hear them even with the door shut.

Do you...

Turn on some music to drown them out? Turn to section 6

Play with your Bugbots and try to ignore them? Turn to section 9

Section 6

This is before compact discs and .mp3 players. Your friend Ali has a boom box, but your family is poor so you only own a thrift store record player and two records. Big Iron, by Marty Robbins and Another One Bites the Dust, by Queen. You listened to the B side of each record exactly once before return to your favorites. You couldn't even tell someone what songs are on the other side.

You remove the record from the sleeve and place it on the turntable. As much as you blast it, you can't drown out the sounds of your parents fighting.

Turn to Section 9.

241

Section 7

The Ovipositor is not mad. She's just disappointed. As any kid will tell you, that's even worse. Especially when she expresses that disappointment by paralyzing you and injecting you with eggs that will hatch within your body and devour you from the inside out.

The stinger slides into your lower back with no pain at all. The numbness that spreads is almost comforting. Your legs give out and you collapse in a heap in the basement. There is a pushing sensation from the stinger, which is technically the ovipositor of the killer's name, like blowing soda down through a straw instead of sucking it up.

You pass out. It's dark when you awaken. There is a stirring of malign life within you.

YOU HAVE DIED

Section 8

"Hello, Anderson residence."

Something tickles your ear. You pull the phone away and drop it, because maggots are swarming out of the receiver. Then each coil of the phone cord sprouts centipede legs, all twitching with desperate urgency.

What is going on?!

You flee into the foyer, where you see the Andersons entering.

Turn to Section 34.

Section 9

You take your favorites off the shelf. Brood Mother. Destroying Angel (you'd later learn that this is the name for a mushroom and not an insect, but you still don't care because it's such a cool name). Tarantula Hawk (you don't have the toy for him, so you use a stuffed animal in his place) and Dung Beetle.

Brood Mother goes on the pillows at the head of the bed. You run your fingers over the plastic of her face. The plastic is purple and the paint for her four sets of eyes is a shade of

242

neon green only found in the 80s and on old-fashioned radium watches. It's already flaking off, giving her a lopsided grin. You've just learned the word "sardonic" and decide it applies to her expression. You arrange the other toys in a semicircle as they seek audience with their leader.

"Brood Mother. The Insectivores have breached the outer walls of H.I.V.E." Tarantula Hawk says in the deep voice you use for him. He is calm even in a crisis. You've modelled his mannerisms after your dad's, though you won't realize that for years.

"That's it! I'm rolling out of here!" Dung Beetle snivels. He came with a scratch and sniff dung sticker, but now the smell has faded. Thankfully.

"No!" Brood Mother tells them. You turn the figure so she can regard each of her children. "This is our home. I am your mother. I will not leave you. If they fight us, we will kill them. If they eat us, we will choke them."

You move Destroying Angel's pincers into a cheer and vocalize his grunts of approval. Even the cowardly Dung Beetle is stirred.

You don't have any Insectivores toys, so you're looking around the room for something that can stand in for them when there is a knock at your door.

Continue to Section 10.

Section 10

Your dad knocks on the door and enters. Every kid thinks their parents are tall, but your daddy really is. He looms enormous in your memory. He's tall and bald and very, very dark.

He takes a seat on the corner of your bed, folds his huge hands in his lap. This makes you nervous. It's what he does when he's sad. You hate seeing him sad. It's why you try so hard to be a good kid and make him happy.

He takes a deep breath. His gaze moves over the Cindy Lauper poster on your wall and the pictures you drew of your own Bugbots that you hung next to it before settling on your face.

"Honey, I am afraid I have some bad news. Your mom, she's not coming back. It's over, honey."

Your lip quivers, like a little baby's. "What do you mean?"

"She's going to be staying with her sister until the end of the month and then she's moving away to California."

Do you...

Run to Aunt Tabitha's House and convince Mom to stay? Turn to section 4.

Cry? Turn to Section 11.

Stay quiet? Turn to Section 12.

Section 11

You wail. You cry so hard that you can't breathe. You shake and your daddy holds you and you worry that you're scaring him because you're shaking so hard that it must seem to him like you're being stabbed by an invisible knife over and over again. This is how people die of a broken heart. You weren't good enough and now mommy doesn't want to be your mom anymore.

When you've cried yourself dry, your daddy starts speaking again.

Continue to Section 12.

Section 12

Rejected. Unwanted. Unloved.

Daddy's talking, but you can't hear him. You think of BugBots and how insects can hear sounds that are too high-pitched for humans to perceive. Is that what's happening here? You could make sense of his words if you could hear at those frequencies. Is he somehow clicking out a secret message, and if you can figure it out then your mom will come home?

You know it's irrational, just make-believe, but it's better than facing the alternative. You deserve this. You drove them apart. You didn't do enough. They say these fights aren't about you, but they are. You don't pick up your socks, or you lose your legwarmers under the chair and Mommy gets mad and she's ready to fight when Daddy gets home. You deserve this. It's your fault.

"Dalissa," Daddy says, cupping a cheek in one of his huge, calloused hands. It's only then you realize that you've been crying. "It's not your fault."

He kisses you on the forehead. "We're going to get through this. You're your mother's daughter. You're tough. Like iron." He smiles. Daddy has the best smile. It's like the full moon. "No. Like Brood Mother. That Bugbot you like. Be like her."

Turn to Section 27.

Section 13

2020: It's now two days after all the paperwork has been signed. The company had a plan—you don't enter into this kind of thing without a plan—but it's completely null and void because of the B.A.T.T.L.E.Bugs movie.

The question around the office is "How did this happen? How were we not prepared?"

Todd Sheldon is President and CEO of Comco. He made a show of feeding the financial plan into the shredder. The gesture struck you as more than a little melodramatic and performative, but that's Todd. He's a bit of a jerk. He reminds you of a family you knew when you were younger, the Andersons. They couldn't keep a babysitter for more than a week.

"We bet everything on this, Darcy," he says to you. "How are you going to fix this?"

Todd's a jerk, but he's not wrong. You need to recoup your losses quickly.

If you want to fund development of a mobile game, turn to Section 2.

If you want to invest in a summer Blockbuster and beat B.A.T.T.L.E.Bugs to the theater, turn to Section 15.

If you want to delay the decision and instead think about what made Bugbots special to you, turn to Section 17.

Section 14

1989: You are Calliope Jones, babysitter.

"Thanks, mom!" you say as you slam the door to the station wagon. You're halfway up the path to the Anderson's front door by the time she notices you left.

"Call me if you need anything!" she calls. "I'll be here at a midnight to pick you up."

You respond with a half-hearted wave without turning around and jab at the doorbell, hoping the Andersons will answer quickly and rescue you from this encounter. Mom takes the hint and rolls up her window just as the front door opens.

Mr. and Mrs. Anderson are there, the very height of elegance. You know how adults appear gigantic to kids and it's only as you get older that they seem people-sized? The Andersons somehow reverse the effect. They're more impressive every time you see them. They pretend not to notice Mom's rustbucket backfiring as it pulls away from their mansion, a display of *noblesse oblige* for which you are almost embarrassingly grateful.

"Calliope!" Mr. Anderson declares in his stentorian boom. He's so effusive and so sincere, it's like he's a presenter welcoming U2 on stage, but there's something so reassuring in his easy confidence that makes you believe that you're worthy of this reception. "Come inside, won't you? You're right on time."

"Stop, darling. Can't you see you're embarrassing her?" Mrs. Anderson says as pulls on her opera gloves, light green and a perfect complement to Mr. Anderson's tuxedo. She's always reminded you of Kelly LeBrock, but if she had stayed as a model instead of selling out and doing Pantene commercials. You're pretty sure Mrs. Anderson was an actress in her youth, but you've never been able to work up the courage to ask her for the details. You thought your jean jacket made you look cool and sophisticated, but next to her you see how childish it is. You shift your knapsack to conceal

246

as much of it as you can.

Mr. Anderson takes you by the shoulder and looks you directly in the eyes. "The children have already had supper and they are now concluding their homework. They are being punished and they may not leave their rooms. You need not check on them. The telephone number for the theatre is posted on the refrigerator. I've left your payment on the kitchen table in case you want to order pizza. We trust you'll do us proud, Calliope. And we must be off if we're to arrive in time to be seated."

Mr. Anderson helps Mrs. Anderson into her fur coat, and they depart in their silver Mercedes. You settle in on the couch. It's leather and fancy. It's been quite a while since you've done any babysitting, but you still remember the basics. But you've got no boyfriend to call, Dalissa moved out to Chicago, and Jennifer is grounded, plus you're on a diet so there's no raiding the fridge, so you just settle in with your homework.

You're ten problems into your Trig homework when the phone rings.

Do you...

Answer it? Turn to Section 8.

Let the machine get it? Turn to Section 21.

Section 15
Bugbots renewed my faith in humanity in the 1980s
They destroyed it in the 2020s

1/10. submitted by SpiderDoc

I'm a Bugbots fan from way back, which gives you an idea of how old I am. Probably too old to be caring as much as I do about a forgotten franchise from 40 years ago. The Bugbots were never the cool choice. They were manufactured on the cheap and they looked like it. There used to be a joke on the playground. "How do you transform a Bugbot? You turn it over."

Yeah, they were made out of low-grade plastic and they had fewer points of articulation than B.A.T.T.L.E.Bugs, but they had character, darn it! B.A.T.T.L.E.Bugs always just seemed like a Bug-themed Transformers spin-off (and I have no idea how they released the Insecticons line without being sued back to Cybertron). Bugbots were great because of the lore, though we didn't call it that back then. The evolving tapestry, the unfolding text that got richer and grander, deeper and creepier and more bonkers with each release. Take a look at the wiki and tell me it's not great!

But the 80s ended and the Bugbots/B.A.T.T.L.E.Bugs rivalry went the way of the Berlin Wall, legwarmers, and New Coke. Until it flared up again, against all odds.

B.A.T.T.L.E.Bugs has its quarter billion dollar Michael Bay explosionfest blockbuster (did you know that fireflies explode like Pintos when you punch them?) I'm not going to get into the merits of the B.A.T.T.L.E.Bugs movie (B.A.T.T.L.E.Bugs: Bugs go Boom!!!!) other than to say that it's loud and dumb.

How is the Bugbots movie?

Sometimes it's helpful to describe things with metaphors. The Bugbots franchise was once a caterpillar. The particular type of caterpillar doesn't matter. Maybe it was one of those cute, furry woolly bears. Maybe it was the kind that grows into the monarch butterfly. Maybe it was even a very hungry caterpillar. Doesn't matter.

The next character in this story is the new leadership from Comco. We'll call her "The Ovipositor." (Remember her? Nightmare Fuel!) If you're not up on the lore, she was an ally to the Insectivores, basically the Slender Man version of that wasp that paralyzes caterpillars and lays eggs inside them. She will be played by Dalissa Jones.

While this caterpillar representing the Bugbots property was happily eating its pickle and slice of chocolate cake and all those apples, Jones sashayed up to it and stung it and implanted it with a bunch of eggs. These eggs are the movie and its associated toys. They hatched into the baby wasps who ate the caterpillar from the inside out.

At least the B.A.T.T.L.E.Bugs movie wants to *be*

something. Bugbots the movie wants to be B.A.T.T.L.E.Bugs and that's unforgivable. B.A.T.T.L.E.Bugs was already pandering to the lowest common denominator. Bugbots tried to do the same with half the time and a tenth of the budget. Frankly, it looks like a mockbuster version of the B.A.T.T.L.E.Bugs movie. It's cheap and shallow and dumb and mean. Looking on the internet, I see my review is more generous than most. This is going to kill the franchise for another 40 years.

See you in 2060.

THE END

Section 16

The kitchen is beautiful, like everything else in the house. Spacious, with gleaming brass cookware hanging over the island in the middle of the room. Your family isn't poor, but the Andersons are on the *upper* side of upper-middle class.

You're expecting wine and cheese and some fancy foods you can't pronounce inside their stainless-steel fridge. You're not expecting a blast of hot air and a stench like the reptile house in summer. You take a step back. The smell is so bad that you have to squeeze your eyes shut. You bury your nose in the crook of your elbow and gag at what you see.

Maggots swarm within a clear Tupperware container. It's filled to the brim. The squelching turns your stomach. Desiccated cats are curled up in the vegetable crisper as if sleeping in a display of blasphemy against the ancient Egyptian gods. You're not a doctor, but that cut of steak seems to have come to from a human arm.

You're about to slam the door when you spy an open can of Ecto-Cooler.

Do you...

Drink the Ecto-Cooler? Turn to Section 44.

Not drink the Ecto-Cooler? Turn to Section 20.

Section 17

1987: You are Dalissa Jones. Mom is very pale. Dad is very dark. You're what people in the twenty-first century call mixed-race, though the words the kids in junior high use to describe you are less kind. Your appearance is somewhere in between, with brown hair and green eyes and skin that looks tan even in the winter. People think you're white when they see you with Mom and they think you're black when they see you with Dad.

Four regional schools send students on to Three Rivers High School. Your middle school is the smallest of the sending districts. You have a chance to reinvent yourself. Do you...

Play it cool? Turn to section 19.

Play it too cool? turn to section 23.

Tell everyone you meet how much you love Bugbots as soon as you meet them? Turn to Section 35.

Section 18

You run. It's the only thing you can do.

You run down the hallway, past the framed family portraits. The kids are smiling there, but now you imagine that you see fear in their eyes. It is the nature of humanity to find meaning in madness. This is not the realm of reason, but still you seek it.

"Why are you doing this?" you demand as you flee.

The question may have saved your life, because the Ovipositor stops to answer. Her voice follows behind you. "Maybe I'm an avenging angel. Maybe I'm here to punish humanity for your crimes against the natural world. Maybe I'm from the ancient past or the distant future or the outer reaches of the galaxy. Maybe I just like playing with my food. Whichever it is, it pleases me more than I can say to see you die not knowing something that means that much to you."

You hear barking coming from the sunroom. The family dogs are there. The Ovipositor is such an affront to the natural order that they might take your side in this.

250

You could also slip into the basement. Its dark down there, but there are windows and storm doors leading to the outside.

Do you…

Head to the Sunroom? Turn to Section 26.

Head to the Basement? Turn to Section 50.

Section 19

You can do this. Bugbots are part of your life. Maybe they're the most important part of your life. But they're not the only part of your life. You accumulate acquaintances, but few genuine friends, in part because you're policing yourself.

Halfway through your sophomore year, you make the acquaintance of a girl named Calliope. You've seen her around, but never had the opportunity to chat. Once you do, you become fast friends. Soon, you're inseparable. You're naturally tan, she's fair and freckled, but you both have light green eyes and people often mistake you for sisters when you're together, which is all the time.

Turn to Section 29.

Section 20

You flee the kitchen. You're in full fight or flight mode, but you maintain enough presence of mind to remember that you need to protect the children. You're running to the staircase upstairs when you see the Andersons returning through the front door.

Turn to Section 34.

Section 21

The machine picks up after three rings. It's Mrs. Anderson's voice on the outgoing message. "You have reached the Anderson residence, home of Tom, Karen, Amanda and Michael. Please leave a message and we'll get back to you as soon as we can."

A man's voice speaks after the beep. "Hi Tom. It's David. I had a question about the Cooper account. I'll try you on your car phone."

Guess it was nothing. It's only 7 P.M.

Will you...

Raid the fridge? Turn to Section 16.

Eat the snacks you brought? Turn to Section 24.

Section 22

You fix your feet and lock your eyes on the top pair of her own. You're not going to be intimidated by this six-eyed freak.

Her lips curve into a smile that spreads all the way across her face, flowing across one set of eyes into the next. They're green, her eyes, not pale like yours, but vibrant and verdant, like bright blisters of some exotic poison.

Eyes are said to be windows into the soul, but this creature has no soul and her eyes are bottomless. You find yourself falling into that bottomless pit. You realize she's hypnotizing you somehow and squeeze your eyes shut, but you see them even still, six green candles, each luring the moth you have become to your doom.

Something behind your forehead snaps like a dry twig. You are fully dissociated from yourself. At her command, you kneel before her. You neither feel nor hear the crunch of your skull as she devours you.

YOU HAVE DIED

Section 23

The operative word in too cool is "too." Nobody likes a try-hard. School is school. You learn writing and writing, but nothing about yourself. You *eventually* become friends with a girl named Calliope Jones. You sat next to her for three years in homeroom, but you never talked about anything because you were hiding who you were. There's a lesson here, but you're sad it took you three years to learn it. She immediately becomes the best friend you ever had and the only bad part about your friendship is that you could have had an extra two years of it.

Turn to Section 29.

Section 24

You're trying to be good, so you unpack the snacks you brought with you and eat them at the kitchen table. Ants on a log and a Capri-Sun. Yay. You put the ants in a sandwich bag so the peanut butter wouldn't get smeared all over your books. It's fine. Nice that your braces have come off, because the celery always got stuck in there. The Capri-Sun straw goes through the pouch, just like it always does.

Do you want to…

Check on the kids? Turn to Section 32.

Do something else? Turn to Section 36.

Section 25

You sit down on the couch. It smells like leather and good taste. The remotes are lined up on a glass table. You've always liked that kind of table. It reminds you the scene in movies when the lead invites two close friends for a small party when his parents are out of town and they each invite two friends of their own who invite two friends of their own until there are a hundred people there. Cars are parked on the lawn, there are people swinging from the chandelier, but you know the party is completely out control when somebody smashes through the glass table.

You find the proper remote and turn on the TV. It's huge. At least 27 inches. This is where it gets confusing. One remote to control the television itself. Another for the cable box and a third for the VCR. Their laserdisc player is hooked up downstairs, which is a good thing, because a fourth remote would make things entirely too complicated.

While you're trying to find HBO, you notice the image on the screen. It's…this room. No sound with the video. The camera shows the couch from above. Okay, but a recording of this room, because you're not in the shot. Are the Anderson's recording you? You watch as Molly, a girl from your school walks into the frame with a bowl of popcorn. You're not friends, but you remember her name because she has red hair

253

like Molly Ringwald. She sits down on the couch, right where you're sitting now.

Now that you think about it, you haven't seen Molly lately. You already knew that she sits for the Andersons, but she had to cancel tonight. That's why you're filling in at the last minute.

She picks up the remote, the same one you're holding now. She flips through the channels, finds something she likes, sets it down. She laughs at what she sees.

You notice something behind her. It's in shadow and you lean forward trying to make it out. It's man-sized, but the silhouette is all wrong. Is he wearing a hood?

Molly hears something and turns. She screams and drops the bowl of popcorn. The shadow hits her once and...and tears off half her face. Your brothers rented Faces of Death and you walked through the room when they were watching it. During the scene with the biker. At the time, it was the most horrifying thing you had ever seen. You had nightmares for weeks. But this is happening to someone you know, right where you're sitting. And the Andersons have something to do with it.

You shoot to your feet, convinced that someone is sneaking up behind you. No one is, but the Andersons have entered through the front door.

Turn to Section 34.

Section 26

You flee into the sunroom. You like dogs and dogs like you. They yip at your approach. Holly and Ivy. You've always gotten on well with them. They're cairn terriers, like Toto in the Wizard of Oz. They have little bandanas around their necks instead of collars.

You hunker down and let them smell your hands. They slobber all over you in greeting and whack your chest with their tiny paws.

The Ovipositor enters to the door at your back, flanked by Mr. Anderson. The dogs growl at her, their ears flat and low, their teeth bared. They recognize her for the abomination she is.

"Sic her!" you shout, rising and pointing.

The dogs yowl, but do not charge.

"Do you know the difference between a locust and a grasshopper?" the Ovipositor asks suddenly.

The question is so unexpected that you blurt out, "Uh, what?"

A smile slithers across her beautiful, terrible face. "I didn't think so. There is no taxonomic distinction. They are the same species. Locusts are simply short-horned grasshoppers who undergo certain changes to their biology in response to environmental pressures. They become so savage that they have been known to cannibalize members of their own swarm in midair. Likewise, dogs are not far removed from wolves. A thin varnish of civilization painted over rotten wood. See how quickly they revert when subjected to the proper pheromones." She steps back and slides the door shut.

The dogs growl again. This time at you. The last things you see are their gnashing teeth as they leap for your throat.

YOU HAVE DIED

Section 27

That period of reflection was helpful. You have some ideas for the direction of the line.

If you want to fund development of a mobile game, turn to Section 2.

If you want to invest in a blockbuster franchise, turn to Section 15.

If you want to focus on a line of toys that will appeal to nostalgia, turn to Section 59.

If you want to think some more, turn to Section 17.

Section 28

1989. You look at the letter you have written and try to decide what to do with it.

Dear Calliope,

Hi. It's me. Sorry I've fallen behind with my writing. I've written a couple letters and I can't remember which ones I've sent, so I'll start from the top. My dad died in February. On the 12th. He had already ordered flowers for me for Valentine's Day. They arrived and it was like watching him die all over again. I put the flowers on his grave.

It was a brain aneurysm. Grammy found him dead at the kitchen table. The doctors said that they never would have found it even if they'd been scanning him regularly. I don't know what to do. Nothing makes sense.

I was numb through the funeral. I was grateful, because I couldn't deal with the pain. But now all the mourners are gone and people have stopped bringing their casseroles and asking how I was doing and I'm still numb and I don't know if I'll feel anything ever again. I don't know if something is broken inside me that I can't grieve my daddy. Was I always broken, but I could just pretend to be a real person until I faced a real challenge?

It sounds silly, but I used to take solace in my Bugbots toys and comics. They were reassuring, I guess. I could always come back to them and they'd be my bridge between now and the girl I used to be. I didn't feel the joy I felt when I was little, but I could remember it, you know? Now that's gone too, and the memories are so distant that I'm beginning to believe that I imagined them.

I'm still living with my Grammy, but my mom is here now. I'm going to be moving with her at the end of the school year. She's trying. I think she really is. She's trying to be a good mom. But she doesn't know who I am. How could she, when I don't know myself?

Okay, I didn't mean for this to turn into a Smiths song. I haven't made any friends out here, and I feel so alone. I miss you.

Your (best?) friend,
Dalissa

You look at it for a long time. It seems so plain. You used to doodle in the margins before...dad. The more you look at it, the more you realize what a bad idea it is. Calliope has her own problems. You'll just be burdening her by unloading yours on her. You're very conscious about the tone. You're just whining about how hard things are for you. You should just crumple it up and throw it away.

Do you?

Do the right thing and rip up the letter? Turn to Section 43.

Be selfish and send it? Turn to Section 38.

Section 29

April 1988. You're in Calliope's room. Her brothers are downstairs watching wrestling. Before you became close with Calliope, you would often wonder what her room looked like. The first thing a person noticed when talking to her is that she didn't seem to have any interests of her own but was instead captivated by whatever the person opposite her was discussing. That trait tended to turn off some people, it struck them as insincere, but the majority enjoyed being able to expound at length on their passions to a receptive audience.

The answer to the question of her room decor is...eclectic. She has a couple Bugbots posters above the bed (plus a B.A.T.T.L.E.Bugs poster, gag me with a spoon), Bon Jovi and Guns N' Roses next to them. A few Tiger Beats, a Rubik's Cube, a Pac-Man clock. It looks like it was decorated by someone's grandmother based solely what the evening news led her to believe was what kids these days were in to. You know she doesn't care about any of them. Calliope appreciates people, not things, but she displays these things because they're important to the people she treasures. (Though you're curious who her B.A.T.T.L.E.Bugs-loving friend is.)

Calliope told you that she didn't have many close friends and you believe it. Unless somebody is a total narcissist, they're not going to want to do all the talking in a

257

relationship. Calliope, the perfect mirror, had nothing to offer there, so she had many acquaintances but only one real friend.

And that number was going to drop soon.

The sheets on her bed depict the New Kids on the Block in bright primary colors. With anyone else your age, you'd assume that they were displaying those sheets ironically, but Calliope wasn't built that way. She flops on the bed and looks at you upside down from the edge. You turn the chair at the desk around to face her. You're suddenly self-conscious about the gesture. It seems like something people only do on sitcoms. Calliope grins her too wide grin. "So! What are we doing this summer?!"

"Um," you begin.

Do you

Tell her you're moving away? Turn to Section 41.

Wimp out? Turn to Section 33.

Section 30

People are hardwired to be reluctant to hurt each other. Even now, you can't bring yourself to kill Mr. Anderson. Instead, you go for his knees. The baseball bat connects with a grand slam crack as it knocks his right knee sideways. Dem Bones crazily flashes through your mind at that moment (The shin bone's connected to the knee bone…Well, not any more, fool!). He barely grunts as he topples over, but the leg is shattered so completely that he will never walk again. You grab the bat and scurry past his arms. You were always near the bottom of gym class, you'd typically chat with Dalissa in the outfield, pausing occasionally to watch a softball lazily bounce past you, but this sprint would earn you a gold medal and the Presidential Physical Fitness award all at once.

You shimmy through a window too small to permit Mr. Anderson. It leads to the area housing the enclosed swimming pool. Pools at night always struck as so peaceful, between the chlorine smell and the swish of the water, the hum of the filters and the reflected light dancing on the walls. Now you're reminded that cemeteries are peaceful too.

258

You hear Mrs. Anders-the Ovipositor skittering down the hallway. You can't see her yet, but even the sound of her movement is inhuman. You're completely exposed where you're standing. The only way to survive is to hide in the supply closet near the pool. You dive in and close the door behind yourself just as she enters.

She prowls around the pool. How do insects detect their prey? Dalissa would know. Is it smell? Movement? Sound? Can she hear your heart beating? They must be able to hear it on the moon. You can only see through the crack in the door. She moves out of your line of sight.

Now everything is silent, save for the humming, swishing sounds of the pool.

Do you take a peek through the gap? Turn to Section 55.

Continue to wait? Turn to Section 37.

Section 31
Review: Battle of the Bugbots (Netflix)

No one saw this coming. I'm not even sure if you can call the Bugbots a forgotten series, because that would imply that someone knew about them in the first place. It's certainly no lost masterpiece. The toys and the cartoon were bad, even by the standards of the day.

I don't know if there is a word for the opposite of nostalgia, but adults (and children who yearn to be adults) sometimes overcompensate in the other direction, and rather than mythologizing what they loved in their childhood, to have the tendency to dismiss the things they loved as mere kids stuff.

("...but when I became a man, I put away childish things.")

But everything is somebody's favorite. And a wise man once said, "There's no point in being grown up if you can't act a little childish sometimes." There was something real there. Those who love it wouldn't have fallen in love if there wasn't. It was buried under low budgets, broadcast standards, rush productions and executive interference, but it was there. Dalissa Jones must have seen it when she was a little girl.

She saw that nameless something and she was able to bring

259

her vision of the series, the platonic ideal of the Bugbots, and bring it to us as an animated series.

This is a labor of love from start to finish. But love isn't enough. Ask any tortured artist. Better yet, ask their spouse. The craftsmanship, the *care* that has gone into this series is unparalleled. It seamlessly blends 30 years of mythology into a coherent whole, while simultaneously being accessible to new viewers. It works for younger kids (though not too young, because the Ovipositor is scary!), it works for parents, it even works for teenagers, in large part due to the way the transformations of the insect characters (both in the sense of changing into robots and advancing through the stages of their life cycle) is treated as a metaphor for change.

Hats off to series creator Dalissa Jones. She tapped into something universal. She's been open with how the toys got her through some difficult times and you can see with a number of the story arcs, particularly "Manumission." I never thought a cartoon with the ridiculous name "Bugbots" (C'mon, we're all thinking it!) would make me cry, but here we are.

Bottom line, Bugbots reminded me of how I felt when I was a child, when the world was a place of wonder and potential and limitless possibilities and I will always be grateful for that.

THE END

Section 32

You make your way up the stairs. Your house is fine, but it feels stuck in the 70s, with all the wood paneling and shag carpeting that implies. Your parents just don't have the *class* that the Andersons do. Look at those drapes! That's sophistication. You could imagine them on the set of Dynasty.

The door to the bedrooms are slightly ajar. You push open the first. The kids are eight and ten and you expect to see a transparent phone. Maybe a TV, possibly hooked up to a Nintendo, because the Andersons are cool and love their kids and don't pay them an allowance so tiny that they're forced to supplement it with babysitting gigs.

You're not expecting two cocooned masses the size of the children hanging from the ceiling. They look like flies all wrapped up by a spider. The larger one (Amanda?) twitches feebly.

You have to get the police.

You rocket down the stairs in an adrenaline-fueled sprint. You're reaching for the phone when you see the Andersons return through the front door.

Turn to Section 34.

Section 33

You have to lower your eyes. You must look completely shifty, but Calliope doesn't seem to notice.

"I dunno. Wait for the new issue of the Bugbots comics. They keep hinting that Murder Hornet is a time-displaced Assassin Bug from when he got shunted thirty years into the future way back in the prequel miniseries." You shrug. "That's assuming that Claremont resolves it rather than weaving in another half dozen plot threads instead. Go to the mall. Play some Nintendo. Go to Action Park."

You continue to make plans with Calliope and talk about a future that you know will never come to pass. You finally tell her about the move the weekend before it's going to happen. She's hurt, of course and she skips your going away party. You send her several letters, but she never writes back.

Turn to Section 47.

Section 34

Your Great Nanny owns a cabin in the woods. Stuff belonging to old people always smells weird anyway, like a perfume of mothballs and hard candy and liniment oil, but there was something else on top of all those that you couldn't identify, some acrid ammonia smell. Your mom explained to you during the car ride back that you were smelling millipedes. They secret a chemical that releases that scent. (Later on, you made the mistake of mentioning this to Dalissa at school and she responded, "Oh yeah. I thought everyone knew that,"

261

which struck you as a little bit snotty at time.) Ever since then, whenever you smell ammonia you look around for creepy-crawlies, because you know they can't be far.

The millipede stink fills the room as Mrs. Anderson closes the front door. You're wearing your half of the Best Friends heart necklace and you unconsciously rub it for comfort. Mr. Anderson stands at attention, but he is not the warm patriarch you remember, but instead something…hollow.

Mrs. Anderson turns from the door, removing her opera gloves as she does, peeling them off in the manner of a surgeon disposing of used surgical gloves. "You've been a busy girl, Calliope. Snooping around. Picking your path through our humble abode. Did you find anything intriguing?"

Mr. Anderson stiffens. A choking sound issues from his throat, but you know it's not something he's doing, but rather the consequences of something being done to him.

You shudder. "What's—"

Mrs. Anderson smiles and closes her eyes. "What's wrong with him? Nothing. He's fulfilled his purpose and now he's nearing the end of his lifecycle as the host for a very specific strain of *Ophiocordyceps unilateralis*."

Dalissa told you about that once. It's the zombie ant fungus. She showed you a close-up picture of an ant with a stalk full of spores growing right through its head. You threw up as soon as you saw it, all over bed and the magazine full of creepy insect photos. Serves her right for making you look at that. And as horrifying as it was, seeing it in person to a human being that you like and respect is a thousand times worse.

"Mr. Anderson!"

"No," says Mrs. Anderson. "He has no name. He is food, a rotten log to be consumed so that he may midwife the spores within him."

"Mrs. Anderson!" you cry, looking for a way out.

"No. I am the *Te aitanga a Punga,* high priestess to my god, but you may call me the Ovipositor."

Mr. Anderson screams soundlessly and squeezes his eyes

262

shut. The eyelids bulge, then burst as the spore-stalks emerge from the empty sockets.

"He's dying!"

"Yes," says Mrs. Anderson, opening her eyes. A slit opens beneath her right eye and another eye opens there. Then on the left, and then again another set beneath those until she's staring at you through six emerald eyes. "But as they say in the software business, that's a feature, not a bug."

Do you...

Run away? Turn to Section 18.

Stare her down? Turn to Section 22.

Fight? Turn to Section 49.

Section 35

High school is a chance to reinvent yourself. Shed the past like a molting cicada. Except when you think of cicadas, you think of the twin Bugbots, Katydid and Katydidn't and pretty soon you're talking about how much you love playing with Bugbots and thinking about Bugbots and writing stories about Bugbots you designed and within a week you're once again known as the weird girl with the weird name who won't shut up about them.

Later on, you would tell people that this was a blessing in disguise. By being so totally yourself, you separated the wheat from the chaff. You're not pretending to be anything but the purest expression of yourself and the kids who stuck with you are the ones who like you for you. They're lifelong friends. True friends.

It's going to be great in the future. It just sucks right now. You eat lunch by yourself every day. You look at Dad's note, smile, crumple it up and toss it back in your lunch sack. You're doodling Bugbots in your Trapper Keeper when a girl flops herself down next to you.

"Hey! I hear you like B.A.T.T.L.E.Bugs!" she says.

You raise your eyes to this...intruder. Every stitch on her body is some shade of bright *Miami Vice* pastel. Dark blonde hair, pale green eyes, a million freckles. She's wearing entirely too many jelly bracelets. Teeth that would benefit from a retainer spread in a smile. You recognize her. She sits in front of you in homeroom because you have the same last name. She's Calliope Jones and it must be a relief for her to sit next to a Dalissa because it means she no longer has the strangest name in the school.

She's eyeing you expectantly.

"I like Bugbots. Not B.A.T.T.L.E.Bugs." Your stare is intended to be withering, but since she lacks your preconceptions about the merits of the franchise, she misses the meaning entirely.

"Oh. Whichever. Those are rip-off ones, right?" She tilts her head to get a look at your drawings.

"No! Bugbots came first! B.A.T.T.L.E.Bugs are the rip off."

"Okay, okay. Lighten up, Francis." She reaches for the Trapper Keeper and this time you let her have it. "What's this guy's deal?" she asks after flipping the page.

"Oh! That's Devil's Flower! I made him up. He's based on the insect of the same name. I tried to find real-life bugs that don't yet exist and make them as Bugbots. He camouflages himself as a flower and then strikes when his enemies come close."

"Radical! I like the way his legs combine when he turns into a flower." Pause. "Do you think of him as a bug who turns into a robot or a robot who disguises himself as a bug?"

You've been trying to tamp down on your impulse to include at least one piece of BugBots trivia in every sentence you speak, but it's so rare you have someone who actually wants to hear it. Dad listens to your stories, but he doesn't care about Bugbots; he cares about you. And now that you have a captive audience, everything explodes out of you at once like a volcano.

"Well...it depends! First generation the only source of lore was the data files on the package and the enclosed comics. It was confusing because they often contradicted each other, but the thrust of it was that they were robots disguised as insects.

264

Second generation, the TV show took the other stance. They were primal insects from an ancient civilization who were roused from their slumber when their ancestral enemies the Insectivores arrived to conquer the earth. Their combat forms happened to look like robots. They're dropping hints in the current season that there might be more to it than that and of course the comics are their own continuity." Seeing Calliope's dazed expression, you begin wrapping up. "For Devil's Flower, I drew on the look of the TV series for his appearance with a little bit of the flair from the comics. So, you can consider him a bug who turns into a robot!"

For the rest of the year, you two are inseparable. You have the same last name, so people think you're sisters and you let them think that because you wish it was true. In the summer between 9th and 10th grade, you go with her family on their vacation to the shore. Her brothers are pests, but they mostly leave you alone. You love your dad, but you need someone your own age and you have found her in Calliope.

Turn to Section 29.

Section 36

The kids will be fine. And trig can wait until tomorrow. When are you going to use this in real life?

So, TV or no TV? You know the Andersons get HBO. You think that's a laser disc player.

Do you want to

Watch some TV? Turn to Section 25.

Don't watch TV? Turn to Section 52.

Section 37

No way you're going out there emptyhanded. You're not sure what you can accomplish against such a monster, but you're not going to roll over and die. You tuck the Best Friends half-heart necklace in your shirt so it won't jingle or catch the light and give you away and you grab everything that could be a weapon or a distraction.

Were they always monsters? Mr. Anderson seems to be a

victim in all this. Is Mrs. Anderson too? Is the Ovipositor something that was *done* to her rather than something that she *is*? It doesn't matter. She's going to kill you if you can't escape.

And the kids. What about the kids? Are they in on this? Are they terrified victims? Or were they entirely ignorant of what their mother is until the events of tonight?

As if in answer, you hear the sound of soft footsteps. "Mom?" comes Amanda's voice. She looks like you remember, ten years old, straight brown hair down past her shoulders. The hair is matted down with the same clear slime that covers the rest of her body. She looks like some tiny animal that was just born into the world in a pair of footsie pajamas. She rubs sleep and slime out of her eyes. "Mom, what's going on?"

The thing that is her mother turns to face her. And you are reminded of the fact that many insects eat their young. You are faced with the most important decision of your life.

Do you

Defend Amanda? Turn to Section 45…

Make a run for it while the Ovipositor is distracted? Turn to Section 56…

Section 38

Against your better judgement, you send the letter to Calliope. The envelope seems naked, so you quickly sketch a cartoony Brood Mother on the back. You give her a speech balloon proclaiming, "Read Me!" Then you worry that the tone is too silly given the subject matter of the letter.

You walk it to the corner and drop it in the mailbox before you can change your mind. Then you walk around the neighborhood with no particular destination in mind. You see a little girl about five years old being pushed on the swing at the playground and you're suddenly furiously angry at her. Why does she deserve to have a daddy when you don't?

You take a deep breath. This isn't the first time you've felt this kind of resentment. You recognize it's irrational, you recognize that it's unfair to everyone involved. To you, the girl, her dad. Your dad. You diminish his memory with these thoughts. But you can't stop them.

Mom's trying to help. She is. You just don't have the kind of relationship that would allow her efforts to have meaning. Maybe you'll get there someday.

You spend a lot of time walking the local cemetery. It's quiet. Peaceful. A fine and private place. You're hardly a nature girl, but it's nice to be outside. It's hard to imagine a future where you're happy, but you come closest when you're in places like this.

You bring in the mail for Grammy when you get home. Mostly circulars. Some letters for Dad. Those still hurt. Oh, an offer for life insurance. "Andre Jones, it's not too late!" Uh, yeah it is.

And what's this? You heart freezes for a moment. A letter from Calliope. You take it to the table. You're afraid to open it. She's not mad at you. You don't send someone a letter just to let them know you're mad. You just don't respond. You find a butter knife and use it to open the letter. You take a long deep breath before opening it and reading it.

You smile. Calliope's letters are huge and blocky. They look like they were written by a child. Her penmanship has not improved in your absence.

HI DAL!

DID YOU KNOW THAT DAL IS A TYPE OF FOOD IN INDIA? AN INDIAN RESTAURANT OPENED NEARBY AND WE HAD INDIAN FOR THE FIRST TIME. IT WAS RAD! BUT VERY SPICY. I HAD AN INDIAN MILKSHAKE. I THINK IT'S CALLED A LASSIE. I THOUGHT THAT WAS A SCOTTISH WORD.

ANYWAY, I AM SO SORRY TO HEAR ABOUT YOUR DAD. HE SEEMED SO NICE ALL THE TIME. I KNOW HE LOVED YOU A LOT. I DON'T KNOW WHAT TO SAY, BUT I DON'T WANT TO BE THE

BAD FRIEND WHO AVOIDS YOU BECAUSE SHE DOESN'T KNOW WHAT TO SAY. I KNOW IT'S LONG DISTANCE, BUT I CAN CALL YOU IF YOU GIVE ME YOUR NUMBER THERE. MOM ALREADY SAID I COULD.

I'M SORRY THAT I'VE GOT TO CUT THIS SHORT. I'M BABY-SITTING FOR THE ANDERSONS TONIGHT (REMEMBER THEM?! WITH THE FANCY HOUSE ON HILLCREST?) AND I WANT TO GET THIS OUT BEFORE THE MAIL COMES.

YOU SOUNDED REALLY DOWN IN YOUR LETTER. PLEASE SEND ME YOUR NUMBER. OR CALL ME COLLECT, GIVE YOUR NUMBER AS YOUR NAME AND THEN I'LL CALL YOU BACK!

BEST FRIENDS FOREVER,

CALLIOPE

PS BUGBOTS RULE, BATTLEBOTS DROOL!

PPS I ATTACHED HALF A NECKLACE. I'M WEARING THE OTHER HALF. THINK OF ME WHEN YOU WEAR IT!

You feel around and find half a heart necklace. It's the right half and reads ST NDS, though you would have preferred the left half with BE FRIE. You sigh. That was nice. You needed to be reminded of what your friends see in you. You call her collect that night and she calls you right back. You talk for three hours and then you don't talk over the phone for a while because Calliope is grounded for the next month. But it doesn't matter because you've reconnected. Her letters give you something to look forward to and you slowly begin to remember what you like about yourself.

Turn to Section 54.

Section 39

The hardest thing you've done up this point was to hit Mr. Anderson. Now you've got to kill a thing that looks like Mrs. Anderson. You hold the sting of the Ovipositor ready to use.

It's heavier than you thought it would be. It's like holding a bone, still warm and slightly slick. You hold it but can't use it. Hitting Mr. Anderson was one thing. Adrenaline did the thinking. This is a cold-blooded murder of a helpless woman.

You don't know if she reads your mind through supernatural means or if simply interprets your hesitation by more conventional methods. "You can't do it."

She's right. You can't.

"I'm healing. In a moment, I'll tear you apart, drain you dry, hang your mummified corpse for all to see…"

"No," you say.

She pulls herself up to her elbows. "Yes. I'll summon a swarm to fill your living body. You'll suffocate on their filth. I'll feed you royal jelly and make you a queen, a deaf, dumb incubator for more monstrosities, with just enough mind left to recognize your torment."

"No!"

She reaches for your arm. You stab her in the belly with her own stinger with the other hand and bare your teeth. "Hey, Queen Bee: Buzz off!!!"

You drive it in as deep as it will go with the heel of your hand. She sags backwards, attempts to say something, shudders and dies.

And that is it. Your mom arrives at midnight to the lights of a dozen police cars. The evidence in the basement freezer is enough the prove the mundane aspects of the Anderson's crimes. You are safe. You're a hero.

This experience will shape the woman you'll become. There are many stories ahead for the adult Calliope, but for now, this is

THE END

Section 40

You haven't hit anyone in anger since you were a child. You wind up and club him with the baseball bat as hard as you can. Those creepy eyestalks explode in a cloud of spores. Your arm goes numb with the shock of the impact. He takes

269

too steps backwards to slump against the wall. He is silent, but you scream and scream and scream.

Until you stop. Quite involuntarily, your body stands up and walks up the basement stairs. The Ovipositor is there. She sits down on couch and you sit next to her.

"I know you're in there, Calliope. The *Ophiocordyceps* spores function differently than one might expect. They do not control the mind of the host, but rather they create their own superseding connections to the voluntary muscles. Your brain is in the driver's seat, but it's not steering. Now, you have killed my host, but you have replaced him. You will be patient zero for the new infection. I think I hear your mother now. Be a dear and get things started, won't you?" She closes her lower sets of eyes and smooths her dress to make herself presentable.

You scream in your mind, but no one can hear you. Your body rises and walks out the door. It walks down the path and opens the passenger side door and sits beside your mother.

"How was it, Calliope?" your mother asks.

"Great," you hear your voice say. "The Andersons gave me a present to give to you."

She puts the car in drive and pulls away. "That's so thoughtful of them. What is it?"

"Let me wait until we get home. I want to share it with the entire family."

THE END

Section 41

"This is hard to say," you begin.

"Is it antidisestablishmentarianism?" she asks, her grin impossibly growing even wider. "It took me forever to learn how to say it. Especially with braces. I'd tear up my mouth every time I tried."

"No. Listen. Please."

She turns herself right-side up and her smile vanishes. "What's wrong?"

"We're moving away."

"Oh." Gears whirr in her head as she thinks about what to ask. "When? Where to?"

Her Kirk Cameron poster is suddenly the most interesting thing in the world. You focus on that instead of looking at her. "At the end of school year. Dad's going to let me finish it out. He says it's not me, but it is. He needs help raising me. That's why we're moving back to be closer to his side of the family."

"Oh," she says again. "His family is from Chicago, right?"

"Yeah."

You're both silent for a while, then she says, "I guess we'd better get started planning your going away party!"

And that's just what she does. Calliope throws you the best party you've ever had in your entire life. Bugbots themed, of course. She buys you a tape player with a recorder so you can send cassette tapes back and forth through the mail. And you do, every week for the rest of the year. The tape player eventually breaks, which is what she gets for buying a Bugbots branded recorder.

Turn to Section 28.

Section 42

Isn't it fun reading through all the segments? It's like a box of chocolates! You never know what you're gonna get. There is a hidden story, but this isn't a part of it. It's just a Hitchhiker's Guide Easter Egg. But I like your style.

Section 43

What's the point? Calliope didn't write to you. She doesn't care anyway. You're on your own. Nobody knows how you feel.

You rip up the letter and throw it in the trash. You would set it on fire if you had a lighter. On some level you recognize that you're wrong. You do have friends and they do love you. You're just in a bad place and they don't know how to help. You'll eventually reach out.

It just won't be today.

Turn to Section 47.

Section 44

You know you shouldn't, but all that screaming builds up a powerful thirst. And it's *Ecto-Cooler!* Glug-glug-glug.

Ah! Refreshing. Your stomach gurgles. Your "ah!" of refreshment turns into an "ahhhh!!!" of pain.

It might have been in an Ecto-Cooler can, but whatever you drank was not Ecto-Cooler.

YOU HAVE DIED

Section 45

Oh boy. This is about to get extremely gnarly in about three seconds. You strap on whatever will serve as a weapon and you throw open the shed door. It scrapes and squeals to announce you. You take a deep breath and you shout as loud as you can, "Get away from her, you bitch!" Your last words might as well be good ones.

The Ovipositor turns. The world stands still. Her appearance has not changed significantly since her initial metamorphosis, but the aspect of wrongness surrounding her has multiplied and metastasized to the point that your brain refuses to process the input of your eyes.

Dalissa and your brothers were the science fiction fans, but you had a particular love for Transformers the Movie, in large part because of the soundtrack. Your favorite was "Dare," though sound quality being what it was on second generation copy-of-a-copy VHS tape, you thought that the song was saying, "Death! Better that all your dreams survive!" It was only that when you purchased the cassette and heard the words clearly that you realized that it was "Dare!" and not "Death!" You were so disappointed that you read the lyrics in the liner notes in the vain hope that it you were hearing it wrong.

The thing is, you liked your version more. The dreamer may die, but not the dream. It was the ideal accompaniment for a doomed last stand. And you can't stop hearing it now.

Death! Better that all your dreams survive!

The Ovipositor circles you slowly. Do insects play with their prey? You don't think so. That cruelty comes directly from the human part of her. She lashes out slicing the sleeve of your jean jacket but not so much as grazing the skin. You swipe at her with the machete you took from the shed, but she's already gone by the time you begin the motion.

Death! Better that all your dreams survive!

You're trying to keep Mrs. Anderson in your line of sight, but she moves so fluidly, like a sheen of oil on a puddle. You spare a glance at Amanda. She's wide-eyed, terrified, paralyzed with the horror. The Ovipositor slaps the machete out of your hand. You barely step back in time to avoid losing half your toes.

Death!

Something primordial awakens within you. You are not fighting for yourself alone or for Amanda or for the people of your small town who will be certain to die should this abomination be allowed to continue her rampage, but you fight for all of humanity and the ideals for which they strive.

Better that all your dreams survive!

You had grabbed the spray can of insecticide from the shed as a gesture of defiance and gallows humor. If you're going to die to an insecoid serial killer, you might as well go down with a can of Raid in your hand. You didn't think it would do anything. But when you depress the trigger, it is not a thin spray of insecticide that emerges but plume of cleansing fire that burns like the midday sun. The Ovipositor shrieks.

In your mind's eye, she is a woman superimposed upon a wasp with something darker looming behind them both. They are all burning. She stabs at you with her stinger held like a sword. She slows her movement enough that you can perceive what is happening and anticipate your death. She strikes you dead center in your chest, but the stinger does not meet flesh. It touches the Best Friends half necklace and the ensuing thunderbolt knocks you both senseless.

You think you're only out for a moment. The Ovipositor definitely got the worst of the exchange. Whatever power possessed you has fled, but it was enough. The stinger, which is certainly the ovipositor of her name, lies broken on the ground.

You have two options. She is wounded, but healing with preternatural speed and will kill you unless you act now.

Do you...

End the threat by stabbing her with her own ovipositor? Turn to Section 39.

Claim her power for your own? Turn to Section 53.

Section 46

Your eggs are shattered, and you may lay no more. Your brave children have been slain, save for those who now march against you. But the power still lives within you. The humans have no word for your radiance. It best translates into their language as "poison light." You summon its awful power, a power so great and so ancient it is said to be why Tithonus must wear a mask upon his face when manifesting to mortals.

Yes, you call your Radiance to you. You will boil their blood with it. Though you die here, in the empty halls of your hive, your ideals will live on.

THE END

Section 47

The time has come to make your final decision. You feel like you're almost there, but not quite. But you've run out of time. You have to make a call now.

If you want to fund development of a mobile game, turn to Section 2.

If you want to invest in a Blockbuster franchise, turn to Section 15.

If you want to bet everything on video game and hope it's a winner, turn to Section 48.

If you think nostalgia is the way to go, turn to Section 59.

Section 48
Review: Bugbots, Rise of the Bugbots

A disclaimer right up front. This review will focus primarily on gameplay elements. I can't speak to the lore elements of the game. I'm not a fan of Bugbots myself, but I have friends who are, and they say it's a faithful adaptation.

A camel, the old adage goes, is a horse designed by a committee. Before I started this review, I looked online to see if there was an insect with a camel in its name and there is! It's the camel spider.

And that's what this game is, a classification-defying genre-bending chimera of a beast that blends *Dark Souls*, *Red Dead Redemption*. and *Resident Evil* with a little bit of *Pokémon* and *Fallout*, mixes it with a heaping helping of nostalgia and blends it until smooth.

And smooth it is. Whether you're running, flying or slithering (I'm sure there's a more specific term for the locomotion of millipedes, but I've already spent enough time researching for this review) moving across the map is a particular joy. Combat is deep, with a wealth of options and it's punishing on higher difficulties without ever seeming unfair. It very much rewards player skill. The Nemesis system is particularly inspired, and the blend of scripted and emergent elements served to make the Ovipositor the most frightening video game villain I have *ever* encountered. There were points where I was afraid to continue.

A few bugs (heh heh) prevent it from being perfect, but once those are patched out, we are looking at a phenomenal start for what is surely only the first installment in a new video game dynasty.

9/10

THE END

Section 49

You're tough and scrappy and light on your feet. There's been some pushback against the stereotype of girls with older brothers knowing how to fight, but it's true in your situation. You know how to throw a punch and you know how to take

275

one.

Unfortunately, that wouldn't help against a normal adult twice your size and it certainly isn't going to help against two of them, even if they didn't have the proportional strength of an insect, which they do.

YOU HAVE DIED

Section 50

You open the door and hasten down the stairs as quickly as possible. The Andersons have a finished basement. You've always liked those, though you expect you may come away from this with a negative association depending on how this plays out.

A large standing freezer hums in the corner. You wonder if the remains of your predecessors are piled on top of each other inside. You're not going to end up that way. You look around for anything that could serve as a weapon. Pool cues hang over the full-sized billiard table. You're reaching for one when you spy something better, Mr. Anderson's autographed Louisville Slugger. He was always talking about the player who signed it, but you could never remember the name. They're all the same to you.

You pick it up. Its weight in your hand is comforting. The stairs creak and you turn your head as the fungus zombie Mr. Anderson descends them. He's between you and the exits. You're not getting out of this without a fight.

Do you...

Hit him in the knees as he's coming down the stairs? Turn to Section 30.

Wait until he's in the basement and hit him in the head? Turn to Section 40.

Section 51
This space left intentionally blank

Section 52

There's nothing on TV on a weeknight. Well, there probably

is, but you get three channels plus PBS at home and you have no idea where to find the good stuff. Besides, you're nervous about messing up their fancy cable setup somehow. They have three different remote controls and you don't know what belongs to what. Better to just leave it alone.

The Andersons return from their show at 11:45. They seem disappointed, somehow. It's so uncharacteristic that you have to ask, "What happened?"

Mrs. Anderson flashes a weary grin. "Nothing, Calliope. Things just didn't turn out like we planned."

"Oh, you can always try again next week," you say as a way of consolation. You hear your mom from outside, so you grab your coat and turn to leave.

She probably intends for it to seem enthusiastic, but her smile instead just seems ravenous. It's far too eager for her face. "Very true, Calliope. Very true. If you're available to help us again, we can try until we get it right."

THE END

Section 53

You take the Stinger of the Ovipositor in both hands and plunge it into your heart. It not a tool of matter, but of spirit, so it does not bite into your flesh, but deep into your being.

Life is change, but seldom so great as this. The spiritual venom from the shattered stinger explodes into you. It reaches every part of your being at once.

It was not wrong to kill Mrs. Anderson. She was too weak to be a proper vessel. You will continue the great work.

You hear Amanda screaming, so you take steps to stop the noise. Mr. Anderson emerges, dragging his shattered leg and pays you obeisance next to the corpse of his daughter.

Vistas unfold to you as you open your inner eye. And not just one. Six of them.

YOU WILL NEVER DIE

Section 54

This is it. The future of Bugbots is in your hands. You were a nerdy little kid who believed in an ordered universe. You believed, with all of your heart and soul, that all problems were solvable if you just made the right choice. The smart choice.

And you know what? You were right. What you decide here will be the legacy of Bugbots for the next generation.

So, what will it be, Dalissa Zenobia Jones? What does Bugbots mean to you?

Is it a cheap game on mobile phones? Turn to Section 2.

Will you chase B.A.T.T.L.E.Bugs and become a blockbuster franchise? Turn to Section 15.

Can you distill your childhood memories into an animated series? Turn to Section 31.

Is a video game the right route to take? Turn to Section 48.

Do you want to aim it at people your age and go for kitsch Appeal? Turn to Section 59.

Section 55

You were born in the early 1970s. Dalissa showed you *Aliens*, the 1986 sequel, but she could never get you to watch the 1979 original. If she had, you might have remembered the scene in the alien ship where Kane sees the egg start to open and he puts his face *reeeeaaalllly* close to it to check it out.

You haven't heard anything for a while outside the shed. She's probably gone. You inch a little closer to get a better look. You find yourself staring directly at the Ovipositor's stinger. The human eye blinks in one tenth of a second. She strikes so fast that you die with your eyes open.

YOU HAVE DIED

Section 56

You don't need Admiral Ackbar to tell you that this is a trap. The timing is far too convenient. Mrs. Anderson lunges for her daughter. The sound of Amanda's screams cover the noise of your escape. At least, the first four seconds of it. You climb the wall and escape to freedom.

The next two hours are even more terrifying than your time in the house. Ever shadow seems to hold the Ovipositor. You screw up your courage and walk the two miles to the nearest 7-11 and call your mom to pick you up. "The Andersons got home early and I wasn't feeling well, so I went to the store for some Tylenol." It's mostly true. She arrives in thirty minutes, just as the clerk is ready to kick you out.

You are silent on the ride home. Did you sacrifice an innocent girl to save yourself? No. She was in on it. That being true is the only way you can live with yourself.

You go directly to your room when you get home, not even stopping to wash your face. You escaped, but the Ovipositor is out there and she knows what you know and she knows where you live. You sit down on your bed. You want to cry, but you're still too numb. What are you going to do?

Tap.

The sound is coming from your window. On the second floor. You're afraid to turn around.

Tap. Tap.

Tap.Tap.Tap.

THE END

Section 57

The hourglass rune flares on Widow Witch's thorax and begins spinning clockwise. She has ensnared you in her web of time.

You fall...

Turn to Section 58.

Section 58

The hourglass rune flares on Widow Witch's thorax and begins spinning counter-clockwise. She has ensnared you in her web of time!

You fall...

Turn to Section 57.

Section 59
Retrieved from the Toycraft forums
Verdict: Fine, if that's your thing

You're never going to find someone who hates the Bugbots. There are contrarians out there who hate kittens or *Firefly* or *Hamilton* or football, but Bugbots never seems to give rise to any kind of dedicated animosity. With the exception of the stans you find in any fandom, those who remember it from their youth remember it with lukewarm goodwill.

That's what this toy series seems to want to exploit.

You're going to find these keychains or kawaii figures at a Hot Topic cash register. It's aimed squarely at those people who already like Bugbots. This seems like a confusing strategy to me. I doubt the fanbase is big enough to support this kind of push and this navel-gazing nostalgia trip isn't going to draw in any new fans. If you want to reduce it to a single word, that word would be "kitsch." And that just isn't enough.

THE END

Section 60
"I'll take transforming robot insect franchises of the 1980s for two thousand, Alex."

"The BATTLE in B.A.T.T.L.E.Bugs stands for this."

Beep!

"Dalissa!"

You take a long, deep breath.

"Dalissa?"

"Well, I mean, obviously it's Biomophic Autonomous Tactically Targeting Law Enforcement. Sorry, *what is* Biomophic Autonomous Tactically Targeting Law Enforcement? But Alex, how come all the questions in this category are about B.A.T.T.L.E.Bugs? We haven't had a single Bugbots question. What about the Bugbots, Alex?"

"I'm sorry, Dalissa, but our judges have determined that no one gives a crap about the Bugbots."

"What?" you say, putting down your signaling device.

Alex meets your gaze. "I think you heard me." He repeats what he said, enunciating each word. *No one.* Gives a *crap.* About the Bugbots."

You climb over your lectern. "Oh, them's fightin' words." It takes both contestants and half the Clue Crew to hold you back.

THE END

Authors

Suzanne Grieco Mattaboni's work has been published in *Seventeen, Newsday, The Huffington Post, Mysterious Ways, Guideposts.com, 50 Word Stories, Dark Dossier, Motherwell, Turtle, The Best of LA Parent*, and *SixWordMemoirs.com*. Her short fiction, essays, and poetry have appeared in anthologies including *Chicken Soup for the Soul – Miraculous Messages from Heaven, Little Demon Digest, Running Wild Anthology of Stories, What's a Nice Girl Like You Doing in a Relationship Like This?* and *2017 Stories Through the Ages*. She's the editor of the *Writes of Passage GLVWG 2021* anthology. Suzanne is a past winner of *Seventeen* magazine's Art and Fiction Contest and won honorable mention in the 2018 Writer's Digest Writing Competition. One of her short stories was nominated for a Pushcart Prize. Her debut novel, *Once In a Lifetime*, is scheduled for publication in 2022 by TouchPoint Press. She has two talented children, one hysterically fun husband, and two ever-ravenous cats.

Tina Marie DeLucia is desperately trying to put that creative writing degree to good use through the power of theme parks. If they had a nickel for everytime that's happened, they'd have two nickels. Which isn't a lot, but it's weird that it happened twice. Outside of omnimover ride tracks, they've last been seen contributing to *From a Story By: Volume 2* where they happily ripped apart *House of Dark Shadows* much like how vampire protagonist Barnabas Collins ripped apart his family.

They have also recently written for the Eleventh Doctor Who charity fanzine *A Pile of Good Things*, the short story collection about a theme park that never was in *Tales from OmniPark*, and the anthology collection *Defending Earth: The Adventures of Sarah Jane Smith*.

Natalie Potts has done everything from Air Traffic Control to Zoology, but writing has been a constant across all the years. Her short fiction for adults and young adults has been published in Australia, the US and the UK. She is currently trying to focus on her novels, but the occasional short story still demands to be written, especially where the 1980s are involved! To read more, please visit www.nataliejepotts.com.

Mark Wheaton has worked as a screenwriter (*Friday the 13th*, *Voice from the Stone*), novelist (the Fr. Chavez Trilogy, *Emily Eternal*), and comic book writer (Dark Horse's *The Cleaners*, *Sagas of the Northmen*) as well as a scripter for video games and reporter for magazines like *Total Film*, *SFX*, and *Fangoria*. His next sci-fi novel, *The Quake Cities*, arrives in 2021 from Severn House.

Christine Makepeace is a weird fiction writer and film essayist living in the Pacifc Northwest.

Kara Dennison is an author and journalist whose work ranges from anime hot takes to sci-fi literature and tie-in fiction. Over the years she has amassed bylines at *Mashable*, *Crunchyroll*, *Fanbyte*, *Otaku USA*, and more, and currently serves as *Sci-Fi Magazine*'s lead book reviewer.

Kara's past work includes *Vanishing Tales of the City* from the Obverse Books anniversary sextet, "Page Turners" in *Associates of Sherlock Holmes*, and the award-winning "Son of the Wolf" for *Sockhops & Seances* (currently being expanded into a book series). She is also the co-owner of Altrix Books with Paul Driscoll and co-creator of their *Chronosmith Chronicles* series, and co-creator of the *Owl's*

Flower light novel series with Ginger Hoesly.

Kara plays a lot of *Dungeons & Dragons* and usually rolls like a chump.

Josh Reynolds has been a professional author since 2007. He has over thirty novels to his name, as well as numerous short stories, novellas and audio scripts. Much of his work has been for Games Workshop's Black Library, as well as Asmodee's Aconyte Books. Born and raised in South Carolina, he now resides in Sheffield with his wife and daughter, as well as a highly excitable dog and something he hopes is a cat. A full list of his work, as well as his thoughts on monster movies, occult detectives and sundry other objects of interest can be found at his site, https://joshuamreynolds.co.uk/.

For more about the Royal Occultist, be sure to check out the Royal Occultist Facebook page at https://www.facebook.com/RoyalOccultist.

Writing from a 24-hour coffee house in Austin, Texas, **Jon Black** focuses on historical fiction with pulp, supernatural, or Mythos flavors. His award-winning *Bel Nemeton* series combines 6th century Arthurian historical fantasy with brainy 21st century pulp. Two of Black's short stories have won Critters Readers' Choice Awards. "Gabriel's Trumpet," a Jazz Age supernatural mystery, was named 2017's Best Misc. Short Story. "A Scandal in Hollywood," a tongue-in-cheek Sherlock Holmes homage set in Tinsel Town's golden era, won 2018's Best Mystery Short Story. He enjoys his vantage point close to the Texas Hill Country to write his Mythos-inspired Junzt County stories. Jon is also an internationally published music journalist, bringing his passion for music and music history to many of his works. His other writing activities include ghostwriting, speechwriting, and roleplaying games. Having first tried his hand at writing fiction at the age of 42, he wished he'd started a lot sooner.

Cayce Osborne is a writer and graphic designer from

Madison, WI. She works in science communication and public engagement at the University of Wisconsin—helping spread the word that "Science is Fun!" Her writing has been published in *Exposition Review*, *Typehouse Magazine*, *Toasted Cheese Literary Journal*, *Defenestration*, *Fudoki Magazine*, *Write Ahead the Future Looms*, *Meet Cute Press*, two story anthologies from Scribes Divided Publishing, and elsewhere. She has pieces forthcoming in the Spring 2021 edition of *Still Point Arts Quarterly*, and on Manawaker Studio's *Flash Fiction Podcast*. You can visit her online at cayceosborne.com. On Twitter she's @CayceOsborne; on Instagram, @CayceJOsborne.

Josh Wanisko: I live in rural New Jersey, USA with my wife and daughter and a whole bunch of cats. I have written for Big Finish Productions and Geek Speak and my work has appeared in *Time Shadows: Second Nature*, *Defending Earth*, *Sockhops & Seances*, *Master Switches*, *Unbound Imaginings*, and the *Lovecraft eZine*. Most recently, I worked with a number of talented authors for *The Eighth Day* audio story and if I can ever get past my lockdown malaise, I hope to complete an idiosyncratic time travel trilogy by the end of the year. And thanks for reading my bio! Here's a prize for you. There's a secret hidden side story in Bugbots! It starts in Section 3.

Preview

Bel Nemeton: Caledfwlch

Jon Black

As Camelot faded behind him into the misty morning, Myrddin rode hard toward the sea. He had an appointment to keep. And, if he didn't reach the grove before the other parties arrived, the possibility that murder might be done would be the least of his concerns.

On his way, he summoned memories. Myrddin had mastered the art of reliving the past, not merely recalling it. One more talent acquired during his long tutelage under Bleys. To prepare himself for the council which would soon occur, he needed to correctly remember every detail of what had come before.

The tourney, indecisive and leaving a king's broken sword in its wake, had been their second idea for rallying Britain's diverse and fractious kings, champions, and warriors around Arthur. The first, of course, was the coronation itself.

How long since Britain had witnessed such a spectacle? Decades? Centuries? Ever? Even the Kings of Dumnonia and Brittany envied the young king's crowning. Only a Roman Emperor could have found fault with its opulence and pageantry. Of course, that was only as it should have been. Myrddin and Bleys had spent two decades preparing for the event.

In that time, using their vast store of lost and forgotten lore, they had gathered Britain's treasures to serve the boy who would be its king. They uncovered hidden hordes of Roman coin, recklessly liberated fairy treasures from barrows and mounds across the land, and gathered ancient ivory from remote locations in Powys, Dumnonia, and elsewhere in southern Britain.

Sneaking deep into Saxon lands, Myrddin recovered a cache of Celt gold secreted during Boudicca's rebellion. Unwilling to be outdone by a former pupil, Bleys discovered an abandoned dragon horde less than a day's ride from Pendragon Castle. Perhaps the very wyrm which had given name to Arthur's line. Still, the final triumph belonged to Myrddin, wagering his life against the treasure of the giant, Gogmagoc, in a contest of riddles. Myrddin won but Gogmagoc enjoyed a giantish guffaw as he watched Myrddin attempt to spirit away the giant's proportionally-sized chest of garnet, jasper, and amethyst.

But before Arthur's coronation, his seat needed renaming. That had been Bleys' idea. True, the name of Pendragon was an old and honorable one. But the elder druid insisted that retaining the old name, already saddled with its own stories, triumphs, and tragedies, could hinder the Great Work. To serve as the seat of Britain's new dawn, the ancient castle required a new name.

Referring to the ritual as a "rechristening," Myrddin taunted his mentor with terminology borrowed from the new faith. Then, growing serious, he inquired what the new name should be. "Camelot," Bleys announced after reflection. For the uninitiated, the word was nonsensical. To understand its meaning, one had to delve deeply into the unwritten prophesies of Math, the great wizard and seer under whom

Bleys claimed to have studied. Something possible only if Bleys' claims of extraordinary age were true.

The coronation ceremony began with Arthur's procession into the throne room, filled with bright new banners, and flanked by his host in all their glory.

In the gathered crowd, aristocrats and warriors, Celt and Romano-Briton alike, stood shoulder to shoulder. As did druids and priests. Even a few Breton, Eiru, and Pict notables came to satisfy their curiosity, or apprehension, regarding the strange new king. The Isle's great merchants were welcomed with open arms. Camelot's master crafters and artisans were present. At Arthur's insistence, every remaining space was open to the common people of his lands. Only the Saxons remained aloof, as Myrddin had known they would. Just as well, he thought, as that would have been...complicated.

Standing before his guests, Arthur received spiritual blessings. As one wanting to be King of all Britons, Arthur would have to walk the line between those following the old faith and those who had embraced the God of Rome. Reflecting that delicate dualistic dance, representatives of both faiths anointed the new king.

Though one of Britain's most renowned druids, Myrddin could not perform the ritual. As Arthur's chief counselor, he had to at least pay lip service to impartiality. That, by extension, excluded Bleys as well. So, the celebrated Kian of Dubunnori blessed Arthur in the name of the great gods and of the land itself before encircling the king's neck with a golden torc.

Although Myrddin had a priest of the new faith he would have preferred, that cleric's presence at the coronation might reveal too much about the Great Work. Instead, St. Cadfan came from the Isle of Enlli to sprinkle Arthur with the cleansing water, administer the bread and wine which became flesh and blood, and bless him in the name of Rome's tripartite god.

From the great hall's rear, venerable Ector marched forward. Kneeling before Arthur, he presented him with a sword. Though Arthur had carried the blade for years, the ritual imbued it with additional meaning. It became the instrument of a king's strength, justice, and protection of his people.

Bleys and Myrddin had wanted Gawain to present the blade. Someone with a name, lands, and host of his own. But Arthur would hear of no one but Ector. For many years longer than Arthur had been alive, Ector captained Uther's guard. And, like Myrddin, he was as much a father figure to the young king as Uther. Witnessing the humility and affection with which Ector performed his appointed task, Myrddin acknowledged the old campaigner had been the correct choice. He considered whether to admit as much to Arthur. Realizing such prideful dithering reminded him too much of Bleys, Myrddin later complimented the new king on his instinct.

From Arthur's side, Ygreyn, the Dowager Queen, moved to face him. As he knelt, although she still dressed in mourning for the departed Uther, she was radiant. With both hands, she placed the golden crown upon Arthur's head. After she did so, her hand rested tenderly upon her son's shoulder for a moment. Tilting her head upward, she looked at the crowd. "Rise, Arthur. King of Camelot. Protector of Your

People." Ygreyn's normally demure voice resounded throughout the hall.

A tempest of cheers and applause drowned the echoes of the dowager's words. The most hide-bound and traditional of Celts still looked down on clapping, a custom brought by the Romans. The scene unfolding around them testified that they fought a losing battle. Myrddin said a quick prayer the same could not be said of Arthur.

The coronation complete, Arthur and his host processed from the throne room to greet the great throngs gathered beyond. The real work would begin the following morning.

Arthur hoped, as did Myrddin and Bleys, that Britain's great and good would rally to his banner. To this end, Myrddin and Arthur tried something else borrowed from the Romans. They invited the Celtic kings, war leaders, chieftains, and Romano-British *patriarchas* who came to see Arthur crowned to remain until the following morning. Then, Arthur would address them, setting forth his vision for Britain and asking for their support, perhaps even their allegiance.

Such a rhetorical flourish would have been common at the Roman Empire's heart. Among the kings and chieftains of Britain, however, no one had ever attempted such a thing. Myrddin hoped the gamble would pay off.

Wanting the king to begin with one powerful ally already in his corner, Myrddin arranged a private meeting previous to the speech. Of course, he had an ulterior motive as well. Myrddin's heart pounded as the woman entered the chamber. *The* woman because, from the moment he'd first seen Nimue, all others had henceforth been only *a* woman.

The Queen of Avalon, that magic-soaked isle west of Britain, Nimue's hair was the black of a moonless night in the dead of winter. But for the crow's feet which framed gray eyes resembling the ocean before a storm, she looked like one who had not yet seen thirty turnings of the year. "Falcon's feet, not crow's feet," Myrddin corrected himself upon seeing her again, for they imparted Nimue the look of a predator not a scavenger. The stout sword slung at her side reinforced that image, while her grace and muscular physique dispelled any notion the weapon might be purely ceremonial.

Morning light, streaming through Camelot's windows, sparkled upon the elegant bronze bracelet she had always favored.

In many ways, she and Arthur were kindred spirits. For generations, the Queens of Avalon had stood only as that island's "first among equals." Through force of personality and superior intellect, Nimue had all but succeeded in unifying the Isle of Apples' bickering clans behind her. Myrddin's fair-haired protégé sought to accomplish the same feat, on a grand scale, with Britain. That gave Myrddin high hopes for their private meeting.

Like Mark of Dumnonia, the Queen of Avalon would never swear fealty to an overking. Still, he hoped an alliance could be secured.

As she and Arthur parlayed, Myrddin became lost in Nimue's voice. It epitomized Avalon's distinctive speech, like that of the Welsh but even wilder and more musical. As the council continued, however, it became clear that more than water separated the Shield Maiden Queen and he who would be King of the Britons.

Arthur sought alliance with Avalon to access its magic, its

archers, and its warriors. Nimue, in turn, sought a mainland partner to help safeguard Avalon against the Scoti from Eiru. Already they threatened Pictland, holding its western shores and turning hungry eyes east. It seemed a vain hope that Avalon would escape their attention for long. While both regents wanted an ally, they had different fears: Arthur, the Saxons; Nimue, the Scoti. Each one dreaded being pulled into a war on two fronts. Nimue, in particular, worried that answering the call to support an untested British king would leave her island's defenses fatally thin. And so their private council came to naught.

Eschewing his throne, Arthur stood in front of the gathered nobles. "Spring is coming to Britain," he began, pausing to allow his words to echo through the throne room. "I ask your help in ensuring that spring turns to summer and that winter does not return before her season."

The king walked along the front row of his guests, "I am honored by your presence here. And by the many fine coronation gifts you have presented me. But I invite you to take them home with you, if you wish."

His statement drew surprised gasps, as he knew it would. Loudest of all, practically a cry of disbelief, came from King Mark, whose Byzantine-built racing chariot, covered with beaten gold and inlaid with semiprecious stones, had been less a gift than a warning: *whatever dreams you have, Camelot shall never be as powerful as Damnonia.* Close by, Ambrosius showed no response though his gift had been nearly as opulent, and backhanded, as Mark's. Presuming

Arthur, like most Celts, to be illiterate, the Romano-Briton's foremost *patriarchae* sought to mock the new king by gifting him a book. Even Myrddin had to admire how Ambrosius cleverly wrapped a second slight inside the first. The text bound between two silver and gem encrusted plates was none other than *Commentaries on the Gallic Wars* by Gaius Julius Caesar.

Arthur's offer breeched etiquette in manner both unheard of and bordering on offensive. Myrddin and his protégé had calculated the remark to grab their guests' attention and prepare them for anything which might follow. Raising his hand in a gesture of truce, the king allowed the expressions of surprise to die down. "Do not think me ungrateful for them. But there is a greater gift you can give, to me and to yourselves…"

For a moment, the king's features appeared to carry an extra two decades of hard earned wisdom. "Stop doing the Saxons' work for them."

If he had given them pause before, Arthur now shocked the nobles into silence. Though careful with his words, Arthur left an accusation of behavior just short of treason hanging in the air. Even Gawain, the king's prideful kinsman, bristled visibly. And, Myrddin thought, Drustan's hand had fluttered to his sword for just a moment.

"Too much?" the druid wondered. The next few minutes would tell. This time, his guests' reactions flustered Arthur, too.

The king sensed their anger as keenly as Myrddin did. Arthur's face grew blank, his lips mouthed silent words as he struggled to remember what came next.

The king continued, "My brothers and sister Celts, as long as we fight one another…" The line caused Myrddin to curse silently. Panicking, Arthur had omitted an entire section of his speech, chronicling the travails facing Britain. While this was, perhaps, a better response than standing there and stammering wordlessly, everything that Arthur would say afterward rested upon that foundation.

"So long as we steal each other's cattle, extort each other's merchants as they traverse our lands, and squeeze every bushel from our own peasants, make no mistake," Arthur proclaimed, finding his stride again. "We do the Saxons' work for them. And the work of the bandits, dragons, and giants who rob our people of their blood and hard-earned livelihoods." Myrddin carefully noted the crowd's reaction. As the Romano-Britons nodded, most of the Celts looked at the floor or away from Arthur, tacit acknowledgement of the truth in the king's words. A few, notably Cador of the Four Forts and Pelinyr, also nodded, openly acknowledging the problem, even if not that Arthur might be the solution.

Briefly, the king paused, seeking certain faces in the crowd and addressing his next words to them. "To those of you who hold to the ways of Rome, your many generations here, your blood and lines mingling with ours, have made you, too, part of Britain. This land has suckled and nurtured you as much as any Celt. But, secluded in your villas, you horde knowledge and arts the way a miser holds gold rather than using them to shape the future." This time, the Celts nodded knowingly, even as the Romano-Britons held their faces impassive while Arthur spoke on.

"I know some among you whisper 'Would life among the Saxons really be any different than among the Britons?' The Saxons are as much a plague upon Roman as Briton. Do you really believe that the Saxon chiefs will let you keep your fine villas and rich fields for yourselves rather than reapportioning them among their thanes? If you doubt me, ask your countrymen in Anglia, Mercia, and Sussex."

The king resumed pacing, this time along the throne room's center aisle which separated the gathered nobles into two halves, "So, too, do we let conflict between the old faith and the new tear us apart. I will not tell you such differences do not matter or that they can be casually set aside like children's toys. But I will tell you they should be wars of words not weapons. When the followers of Christ and Cernunnos kill one another, it is the Saxons who grow stronger." Returning to the room's fore, Arthur rested his right hand upon the Pendragon throne, "Here in Camelot, I will be king of Pagan and Christian alike."

Even Kian of Dubunnori and St. Cadfan, carefully chosen for their relative ecumenicalism, shifted uncomfortably as Arthur spoke on the topic. The Welshman Myrddin already had cause to know as Cei clutched the crucifix upon his chest while he found something very fascinating to consider outside the window.

Again, Arthur's voice rested. For a moment, Myrddin didn't know whether the young king had again lost his place or if he merely allowed his words to sink in. Then Arthur resumed, "So we come to the gift we can give one another and to our children and grandchildren. *When* Celts stop fighting one another. *When* Rome's great-grandchildren come out from their villas and back into the world. *When* Christian and Pagan, Celt and Romano-Briton, stop staring at each other with sullen suspicion, *then*, with Celtic strength and Roman knowledge we can stop the Saxons' slow digestion of our lands and our peoples. Perhaps, in unity, like the great sea-works built by giants ages ago, Britain shall even turn back the tide.

DID YOU ENJOY WHAT YOU JUST READ?

If you enjoyed this book,
please review it on Amazon and GoodReads!

It's the best way to support the author.

For fantastic fiction, in-depth articles by your favourite authors, open submissions, and more, please...

VISIT OUR WEBSITE
18thwall.com/

LIKE US ON FACEBOOK
facebook.com/18thwall/

FOLLOW US ON TWITTER
@18thWall

We'd love to hear from you! You help make these books possible.